THE DAY OF TRANSFORMATION

The first thrilling
Sanctifier Shenaria Calvert
chronicle

To Sonia ♪♪

Moderty is watching you!

Steven Popper

Enjoy!

authorHOUSE®

Stev Popper

AuthorHouse™ UK Ltd.
500 Avebury Boulevard
Central Milton Keynes, MK9 2BE
www.authorhouse.co.uk
Phone: 08001974150

First published by AuthorHouse 4/30/2010

ISBN: 978-1-4490-6749-6 (sc)
ISBN: 978-1-4490-6748-9 (hc)

The villains of this book are entirely imaginary and have no relation to any living person.

This book is printed on acid-free paper.

For beloved Sally, my wife and true love
In memory of gentle, devoted Trudy

Acknowledgements:

Many thanks to Sally Popper, Matthew Smith and Greg Jones for their careful reading and creative suggestions.

Grateful thanks to Rebecca Muirhead for her terrific front cover illustration.

And my special thanks to Sheena Calvert for the loan of her inimitable identity.

PROLOGUE

It had not been easy getting this far.

The sun was beginning to set now, casting an eerie blood-red glow over the snowy environment and the faces of his team as they waited for the signal to continue, still covering all approaches with their weapons as they did so. Christopheles looked up, seeing the splendid architecture of the main part of the building some way above. Its turrets, towers, massive gargoyles and leaded, arched windows made it look like an archetypal castle from a dark fairytale: an image which its exclusive mountain-top setting only enhanced. The Lazenby Club was reputed to be the ultimate retreat for the powerful and wealthy, and its architecture had been meticulously designed to evoke the romantic and mysterious narratives of childhood while simultaneously offering state-of-the-art comforts, services and leisure facilities. The lengthening shadows emphasised the building's other-worldliness and its seeming detachment from the daily decisions and realities of ordinary life. Normally the club could only be reached by a combination of private hover-speeder and funicular, but Christopheles and Popov had studied all available and classified maps of the locality carefully, and a combination of careful orienteering and hazardous, circuitous mountain-climbing had got them this close while still remaining undetected. They both knew that this would soon change.

The glare from the snow was so blinding that Christopheles paused for a moment, but not before checking that he and his hand-chosen retinue were all still in cover. Satisfied that the overhanging rocks and crags would conceal them from any nearby perimeter guards, he signalled Popov to halt his own weapons-team's advance. Then he gave himself a precious moment to consider their situation.

This was the cross-over point. It had been up to Christopheles to get them all this far without being discovered or killed. The rest of the advance would be led by Popov. Christopholes saw the older, more experienced man scrutinize the jagged territory carefully, in order to choose the right moment for their next move.

Above the little huddle of Sanctification agents were mighty reinforced steel girders and concrete supports which jutted out of the harsh mountainside and held up the lower maintenance platforms that encircled the immaculately designed mansion at the mountain's top. Christopheles and his companions were fifty feet directly below these exterior walkways, still hidden for the time being. Any guards looking over the platform's barriers would have only seen a sheer drop on the south side of the mountain, a ski-lift and ski-slopes on the west side, snow-capped peaks stretching out to the north, and a private access funicular waiting patiently on the east.

Christopheles, Popov and Popov's foot soldiers were scattered in various positions on the rock face on the south side. Climbing in the intense sunshine while wearing chameleon-clothing and carrying hefty backpacks had made them all hot and eager to be done with it, but all knew that such an attitude worked against proper caution, and, ultimately, survival.

Popov signalled and his group advanced once more. Christopheles had the impression of Popov's weapons-team seemingly disappearing into the rocks now that they had reached the first designated location. They were now close enough to detect the sounds of any boots moving on the surface of the platforms above them, even over the constant noise produced by the building's generators, pipes and the rest of its infrastructure. As Christopheles watched, Popov gave a hand-signal, and a dozen or so high-tensile grapple ropes were fired directly upwards, attaching themselves to the underside of the platforms above. As each team-member pressed a button on his rig he was instantly hauled up to collide into and grip the underside of the platforms as best he could. Popov checked his team were in place, then gestured as much to Christopheles, who fired his own grapple-gun and shot up through the air to join his comrades.

Once again Popov signalled, and three of his men, Brunnus, Drake and Thaddius, disappeared. A few moments later a would-be scream that quickly turned into a strangled gurgle was heard, then the silhouette of something falling over the edge of the platform was seen, shortly followed by another – this one clearly a body. They fell for a long time, but instead of watching them go, the rest of Popov's team launched themselves forward and helped their fellows dispatch the last of the unfortunate guards who had chosen the wrong time to patrol that particular part of the perimeter.

It had taken forty seconds between completing the ascent and finishing off the first wave of combat. As Popov's team sprinted towards their next objective, Christopheles was certain that the pace of events would only increase.

❦

Inside the premises the party was in full swing. The exclusive Lazenby Club catered only for the wealthy, the fashionable and the well-dressed, and tonight's festivities were marked by the presence of a large gathering there to be seen with a rising star of Antrobus II's movie industry. Their laughter and banter filled the air agreeably along with the music from the soft jazz quintet and the click of glasses.

Livilla, looking every inch the statuesque, haughty beauty so preferred by the world of cinema, adjusted her long, scarlet dress with her immaculately manicured fingers, shook her full-bodied golden hair, and glided towards the nearest table of delicacies, glass in hand. Admiring male and jealous female glances flickered towards her as she passed. Livilla breezed past and ignored them all, as if such looks were only to be expected, and effortlessly attached herself to three other similarly beautiful young women who accessoried a well-tailored, well-built man who exuded natural confidence and charisma. If the other three beauties felt any shock or surprise at Livilla's sudden appearance among them they were much too professional to show it publicly. Livilla expected them to glance at her with ill-concealed resentment at the very least, but the women seemed to smile at each other, as if sharing some private, malignant joke. For the first time that evening, Livilla felt disconcerted. Had the enemy seen through her performance already?

However, the charismatic, well-dressed man did not seem to notice her at all, and continued strolling towards a set of discreet double-

3

doors, engrossed in inconsequential conversation with another, rather more corpulent, man. Two well-trained servants opened the doors for the two dignitaries, and they passed through, together with the four glamorous women. A few moments later, just as the group strode towards a bend in the polished corridor, Livilla stopped to adjust her ankle bracelet. The rest of the gathering continued around the corner, paying her no heed. Livilla waited a few more moments until she was quite sure of being alone, then straightened up, her alert eyes scanning the opulent corridor in both directions. She heard the soft click of a door close from the direction that the little group had walked in. She waited a few more seconds, then, quiet as a panther, crept round the corner.

The hallway was empty. Only a closed door to the right could be seen. Livilla bent her head to the door, hearing a muffled collection of male and female voices from the ante-room beyond. Quickly she darted down the rest of the corridor and rounded another bend. Certain that her presence had not been missed, she raised her bracelet to her full, rounded lips.

'I'm in', Livilla sent to Christopheles.

'Be careful', came the reply.

Inside the ante-room that Livilla had just passed the well-dressed man and his companions smirked at each other and looked with cold eyes in the direction Livilla had gone.

'She's coming', the beautifully-tailored man sneered, his remark seemingly addressed to the very building itself.

❧

Christopheles, Popov and the weapons-team had moved on from the lower maintenance platforms, and were now reaching the walls just under the windows that looked out from the staff's residential quarters, which were themselves two storeys below the more ornate level where the funicular delivered the Lazenby Club's privileged guests. None of the party-goers were aware of their advancing presence, and, thanks to the recent quick and silent dispatching of another border patrol, nor were the staff. Christopheles began to feel hopeful about their mission when an unshaven man threw open the window immediately above his head, and leaned out, smoking a filthy cigarette. Incredibly, he didn't look down, but gazed directly ahead at the stunning evening view of the snow-covered mountain range, enjoying his moment of peace. Christopheles, Popov and the weapons-team all froze into position against the wall. The off-duty guard inhaled and exhaled deeply a couple of times, yawned loudly, stretched and returned into his room. Christopheles nodded for his companions to continue, but suddenly the man was back at the window, still with his cigarette, but this time with a vengeance-gun also, and shooting determinedly at the assaulting party. Thaddius choked and fell away from the wall before Christopheles managed to shoot the guard straight through his throat with his own silent pistol.

The assault team covered all the windows in sight, expecting the alarm to have been raised, but it seemed that luck – or the Saviour-King – was with them. Nothing stirred. Christopheles stretched up and, with some effort, pulled the dead guard's weighty body over the window sill and let it plummet below, before anyone could enter the room it had just inhabited and see the corpse slumping out of the window. Meanwhile, Popov studied the mansion above, comparing its details to the plan they had trained against. He used his True Light eye filters to search the walls for any infra-red or laser alarms. Satisfied that there were none near the team, he signalled them on, and the whole group began to move upwards, climbing over the hideous gargoyles and finding purchase on the edges of the immaculately even bricks.

As they continued to ascend, one of the gargoyles just used as a stepping-stone, like a massive stone harpy in shape, turned its scowling face upwards and looked at them. Its eyes filled with a fiery orange light, and a slow ripple of movement cascaded down its huge, scaly wings.

❦

Livilla adopted a suitably decorous pose as she perched on one of the gilded antique sofas along the north wall of the large crystal room. The long west wall or the room was taken up completely by a huge pane of glass and two sets of French windows that led to a balcony overlooking the ski-slopes below. Maids and man-servants brought

5

constant supplies of expensive refreshments from the two double-doors in the south wall to the assorted dignitaries and their entourages. A stage to the east of the room was currently populated by a torch song singer, a pianist and a double-bass player. Little round tables, chairs, sofas and chaise-lounges were scattered across the room, all at a discreet distance from one another. At one of the tables Livilla saw Aurelius, the governor of Imperial City, and a clutch of off-world diplomats, along with several spouses and bodyguards. A small group was gathered around a chaise-lounge on which sprawled several self-proclaimed artists and an elderly, bearded man, whom Livilla recognised from tele-vid as Rimbrant, the curator of the much-heralded *Divine Devotions* exhibition about to open at the City's Imperial Museum. He was clearly not a party animal, Livilla noted, and seemed ill at ease with the decadence of the surroundings. She guessed he was here out of protocol rather than desire.

One of the younger off-world diplomats excused himself from his party and came over towards her, two glasses in hand and predatory smile on his rather chinless face. Livilla smiled invitingly towards him and adjusted the position of her shapely legs visibly and seductively. She accepted and encouraged his very obvious attempts at worldly-wise conversation, laughing at the right times and consistently hinting that he might have some hope with her – not that he did. Livilla had found that nothing made a woman less likely to be perceived as a threat than seeming to be an accessory to someone with status and security clearance. Her camouflage now complete, her attention apparently on the chinless attaché, she continued to scan the room for her prey.

There. Coming out of a small stage door on the east wall was Enderby Clavicord, the owner and proprietor of the Lazenby Club. Balding, thick-set, dressed in a sharp suit and jewellery that was worth a small town, he angrily dismissed a down-cast, frumpily-dressed woman, whom Livilla correctly assumed was his wife, Calista, before turning his gaze and charm towards the assembled guests.

'My dear, dear friends', he boomed in a clear and fruity voice, 'welcome to the Lazenby Club!'

Everyone clapped, and Clavicord smiled modestly and gestured for them to stop.

'There's no need for ceremony here', he said, 'we are all at your service.' He clicked his fingers, and more maids and man-servants appeared with newly-filled trays. 'Eat, drink and be merry!'

'For tomorrow you die', Livilla finished off under her breath. 'Nothing', she said to the chinless man, before adding, 'Shall we?', and gesturing towards the new refreshments being brought in. The chinless man nodded and said something Livilla didn't listen to, then, with his arm around her waist, guided her towards the aperitifs – and towards Clavicord – as if it was his own idea.

By the time they arrived within reach of Clavicord he had crossed the room and was now engaged in conversation with Rimbrant, the two of them gazing out at the sunset over the empty ski-slopes below. Livilla did not manage to hear what they were saying, and was uncertain whether a look seemed to pass between them as she and her escort approached. Making sure she stayed in role, she giggled at something her companion may have said, then pulled him towards the window, brushing past Clavicord and bumping into him as she did so.

'Look at the sunset!' she gasped, 'It's so romantic, don't you think?' The chinless man gestured an embarrassed apology to Clavicord, who shrugged good-naturedly as if to say, 'Women!', and caught up with Livilla. He smiled as he saw how he could take advantage of this moment.

'Why not step outside?' he suggested, gesturing to the balcony with a predatory expression on his face. Livilla's eyes widened.

'Do you think we could?' she asked, breathlessly.

'I'm game if you are', came the reply, and the two of them went through the French windows onto the balcony. They walked until they had passed the window, then the opportunist pressed Livilla against the wall.

'Whaddya think, Honey?' he said.

'This is what I think', said Livilla, applying pressure with her left ring finger to a particular nerve on his neck, and forcing him into unconsciousness before he had the time to be surprised.

She lowered him down onto the balcony, then checked the contents of her right hand. Clavicord's wallet was there, and, inside it, the card-key that she needed. Quickly, she kicked off her expensive high-heeled shoes and began the perilous climb across the wall to the next balcony along. Landing on it as gently as a cat, she checked through a gap in the curtains before hauling herself through a little open window and into Clavicord's study.

Hurriedly, she scanned the room for obvious and less obvious traps, then made her way past the mahogany desk and captain's chair to a large devotional image of the Saviour-King covering most of the far wall. She took Clavicord's card key and swiped it through a groove in the bottom of the picture's frame, which to the untrained eye simply formed part of the décor.

With the gentlest of hydraulic hums the picture ascended, revealing an unmarked metal plate behind it. Livilla pressed the plate in several places, correctly triggering the combination that would open its concealed compartment and shut off its alarm. Slowly the metal hinged forwards, revealing a small brass and scarlet casket inside, decorated with effigies of wailing angels in flight. Livilla reached for the casket, which weighed considerably more than she expected, and placed it on the desk to open it. This was one of the things she and Christopheles were after.

Her pupils widened with horror and shock as she lifted the casket's lid, but before she could close the lid and try to recover brilliant lights shone into her eyes from all directions. She could just make out the silhouettes of Clavicord's private bodyguard pointing weapons towards her from all around the room. A door opened from the hallway, and Livilla saw the silhouettes of two more men as they walked in: the chinless man, who was holding up a pair of high-heeled shoes, and Clavicord himself.

'Sorry, my dear', whispered Clavicord ever so gently, 'You've been well and truly played.'

The stone gargoyle continued to pulse and quiver, as if it was being fed animation and life itself from the wall it jutted out from. Fleeting flashes of colour, moving like rays of lightning, appeared all over its grey body. The cracks in its weather-beaten surface began to ooze a foul-smelling oily substance, which its stone exterior greedily absorbed. Spasms of movement travelled from its scaly wings to all parts of its frame, its wrinkled chest, its scythe-sharp talons, its newly-beating heart. The light in its eyes deepened to a furnace red, and it opened its beak wide as if in frustration that it hadn't yet received enough life-force to escape the building that held it fast.

※

They were nearly at their target now. Two hundred feet up the building they hung on thick ropes, climbing and hauling themselves up towards the top of the southern-most turret, which was where Popov and Christopheles had determined their objective lay, hidden somewhere in the labyrinthian storage bays that filled up the tower. The air was too thin to breathe now without respirators, and the intense cold was beginning to seep through their Element gloves. Another twenty-five feet further and they would be on the turret's roof, where the access panels lay.

The counter-attack came swiftly and with murderous force. Four of the Lazenby Club's private security troopers suddenly appeared on the northernmost turret, leaving both hands free to fire their vengeance-guns. At the same time concealed exits opened to the east and west of Christopheles's and Popov's men, and bulky, automated defence systems emerged, firing lasers and scatter-guns at them. Meanwhile, more defence troops appeared on the nearest turret to the east roof, firing even more vengeance-guns in their turn. The Sanctification team seemed caught in a murderous cross-fire.

They were vastly outnumbered, but they had trained for this. Christopheles's and Popov's men were spread out enough to prevent them from being trapped altogether, and each team offered covering fire to the other. All of them wore armour woven of diamond-hard titanium filaments under their chameleon-clothing.. It wasn't impenetrable, but it was tough, and shots would have to be lucky or very strong to get through, or past. Some of the men cried out and dropped away from their ropes as the attack began, either already dead or about to die from their wounds or their fall, but most others reached for their weapons and fired back. A well-aimed grenade exploded on the turret roof, and a confusion of vengeance-guns and body parts fell past Popov's team, clipping one unfortunate on the way, and making him fall too, screaming as he did so. Sounds of gunfire echoed off the surrounding peaks as the Lazenby Club and Sanctification forces joined battle, advanced, took cover and died. Brunnus managed to leap onto one of the blocky automated defence machines and forced its guns round so it shot into another, destroying it, only to be destroyed in his turn as a third automated machine trained its weapons on this new source of danger.

But more defenders kept coming, some on the roof and some leaning out of well-placed openings in the walls. It was an unequal battle. Popov, the left side of his face blackened from a too-close laser shot, turned towards Christopheles, whose rope, as luck would have it, swung a little way off from the main battle.

'Go, Christopheles. I'll hold them off here', Popov sent, before dispatching a sniper who had been aiming at Christopheles, and joining his surviving men in a furious last attempt at survival, and one meant to distract from Christopheles' final chance of success.

'The Saviour-King be with you', cried Christopheles, as he watched Popov advance towards his certain death, and hurriedly continued his increasingly desperate climb towards the turret roof. He ducked as a final grenade took out the last soldiers on the tower roof, then hauled himself up onto it, sprinted as fast as he could for the access cover, and was in.

᪥

He found himself in a low access tunnel containing a walkway and gangway for storage vehicles such as fork-lift trucks to move along. He moved in the direction most likely, according to his wrist-compass, to bring him near the key storage rooms, occasionally ducking behind pipes and wiring-boards as the last of the Lazenby Club's security force made their past him to the roof-top he had just left. Two hundred yards in, and he realised that he could no longer hear any sounds of battle: either he was too far inside the structure to hear anything outside anymore, or Popov and his fire-team were all dead.

Now he was descending a short, metal, spiral staircase. The soft red lighting that had illuminated his path at intervals now gave way to a more constant yellow glow. The staircase ended in a square ante-room, with another staircase descending from it, gangways leading off from two opposite walls, and, directly in front of him, a set of metallic double doors.

This was it. He glanced around carefully, then crossed to the doors and gently tried the handle of one of them. It gave. Cautiously, he opened the door wide enough to slip through, and entered.

Directly opposite him was a long, low window through which the blackening evening sky could be seen, but Christopheles' attention was drawn elsewhere. By the wall to his right, near various assorted packing-cases, stood Clavicord, nonchalantly smoking an expensive cigar held in his right hand. His left hand, however, gestured lazily towards Livilla, who stood a few feet away from him.

Livilla was not the decorous, desirable woman she had been earlier. Her dress was torn and filthy, bruises and scratches covered her legs, arms and face, and her golden hair, normally so immaculate, was wild and unkempt. Most of all, Christopheles noticed her eyes, which were inflamed, over-wide and shining with tears that then ran down her mucus-dripping nose. She licked her lips without co-ordination, and saliva splattered down her chin. She rocked jerkily backwards and forwards, as if balance was a skill she had not yet mastered.

'Good evening, Sanctifier', drawled Clavicord, 'Good of you and your wife to drop by.'

'What have you done to her', asked Christopheles, shocked and taken off-guard.

'I'm sure she'll tell you herself in a moment. You do realise that you've failed, don't you?'

'By the authority of the sacred name of the Saviour-King', began Christopheles, relying on the familiar, powerful words to retain the initiative, 'I arrest you on suspicion of heresy, ownership and distribution of tainted and unwholesome goods, and knowing collusion with Malevolence.'

Clavicord laughed with genuine mirth.

'I admire your pluck, but you really have no idea, have you? Consider your situation! Your friend and troops are dead, your wife – well, you see how she is – and, because your mission was unsanctioned – oh yes it was – no one knows you are here. So do me a favour and cut out the derring-do. You have your survival, and that of your wife, to consider.'

Christopheles looked at Livilla, feeling his control and judgement going. His instinct was to shoot Clavicord and rescue his wife, but he did not doubt that any such attempt would be unsuccessful and probably suicidal. Instead, reluctantly, he lowered his gun. As if this was a signal, Livilla lurched awkwardly towards him, her red-raw eyes staring at him madly as her arms gestured without control.

'Chris...to...phe...lesss', she hissed, as tears, snot and saliva oozed down her gaunt face to drip on her dress, 'It's over...I saw it...I opened...the...c...casket...oh!'

'Livilla!'

Christopheles stepped towards her, but she pushed out her hands to warn him away, and shook her head wildly, hair swinging in all directions.

'What', he said, still trying, despite the odds, not to give up, 'what did you see?'

'No', she breathed, 'no...Christopheles, listen...it's over...you must give into it...you must...'

Livilla managed to reach Christopheles, who held her hands. With true astonishment he felt her palm something, with much effort, into his fingers. A small explosive charge.

Livilla looked up at him, tears now running freely from her scarlet, bruised eyes, and tried, piteously, to smile.

'You must...give in...Christopheles, please...for the sake of our unborn child...'

Instantly, Christopheles' heart went cold. Livilla had used the code-phrase which meant that all was lost, and that his only remaining duty was to escape with the information he had, even if it meant leaving her to die. He gripped her hands and nodded, looking deeply into her distraught eyes.

'I...understand', he said, and kissed her, then walked towards the window as if deep in thought. As he reached the glass he turned to Clavicord and nodded.

'I'm glad you see sense', Clavicord smiled, 'and congratulations, by the way-'

That was as far as he got, as Christopheles flicked the charge against the window, shielded his eyes as it exploded in a fierce white light sending shards of glass everywhere, and threw himself out into the freezing night sky.

Down, down, down he fell, past the towers on the top of the mountain, past the defunct weapons-constructs hanging out of the brickwork, past broken bodies lying in the snow. He sky-dived past the mansion, stretching his arms out and pressing the catch that released the emergency mini-glider wings built into the back of his armour, his breath painful, his heart broken, his anger greater than ever before.

At last the hideous gargoyle was able to rip itself from the wall. With a deafening, echoing shriek, it extended its wings to their full length and flew downwards, growing all the while until it dwarfed the wall that had nested it, its features becoming more sharply defined and intensely malicious. It sneered cruelly as it caught sight of the tiny human gliding down from the castle above, and felt the urge to feed. With a kaleidoscope of colours appearing now here, now there all over its body, it let out another gleeful and piercing cry as it swooped towards its morsel, deadly claws extended, tail whipping through the air, beak stretched open and ready to cut and slice its prey. The human could only have had time for one moment of sudden shock and fear at the sight of the ghastly apparition before it was split in two, dismembered and torn to bits, then feasted upon in a greedy, indiscriminate manner fit only for the worst creatures of nightmare.

CHAPTER ONE

Like everyone else who had known them, Shenaria Calvert was deeply shocked by Christopheles' and Livilla's deaths, especially after their enormously happy and joyful wedding, which she, alongside many others, had attended so recently. She remembered how Christopheles had pulled her to one side during the reception and earnestly told her of his secret plan to treat Livilla to a sumptuous honeymoon at the exclusive Lazenby Club. She remembered that it was not his generosity towards Livilla that had surprised her, but Christopheles' concern with making sure that she, Shenaria, knew about their forthcoming trip. It was not like Christopheles to confide such things to Shenaria anymore, and she remembered being somewhat puzzled by it, but had put it down a last confidence for old times' sake. The Lazenby Club had also seemed a strange destination for Christopheles to choose - she had thought both he and Livilla were much more down to earth than that – but she supposed that he'd wanted to treat Livilla to something very special and unusual for their honeymoon.

And now, thanks to a ridiculous skiing accident, both of them were dead. High Sanctifier Lord Crooker had sent his own Special Representative to the scene, who had sadly confirmed the identities of the broken, frozen bodies lying pathetically in the snow, and, together with Sergeant Byrrion of the local Vigilants, had confirmed that the breaking of the ski-lift had been a genuine accident and that no foul play was suspected. Even Mr Clavicord, the proprietor of the Lazenby Club, had made a rare appearance on televid, humbly apologising for the tragedy, promising to fire the maintenance crews who clearly had not done their jobs properly, and reminding the world that, until this regrettable incident, the Lazenby Club had had an unsurpassed record of safety to compliment its luxury and desirability.

Even though Shenaria had had a history with Christopheles that, much earlier in their lives, had been strained and unpleasant, they had co-operated as friendly colleagues in peace for many years, and Shenaria's main feeling was one of waste. Both Christopheles and Livilla had proved fine agents, and both should have looked forward to full careers: though even as she thought this Shenaria knew it was an illusion – ultimately most Sanctifiers looked forward only to either death in the Saviour-King's service or irreversible corruption of the soul – and Shenaria knew which one she prayed for.

It had fallen to her to go through Christopheles' case-load and determine which of his investigations could be closed, which minor cases could be delegated to Truth-Extractors and students-in-training, and which major concerns she would inherit herself. It was while engrossed in such sorting that Shenaria's curiosity was piqued by what seemed to have been a standard precautionary affair, concluded with the familiar words 'No Concern' by Christopheles a fortnight previously.

Recently, the eagerly awaited and shortly to open *Divine Devotions* exhibition had arrived at Antrobus II, having already visited most other inhabited worlds in the sector. While it came with an enormous reputation from scholars, ecclesiasts and the general public alike, it was still subject to standard regulations, which required all exhibitions of any sort originating off-world to be subjected to a basic Sanctificational scrutiny. This checked for any possible trace of heresy or corruption, whether through message expressed or material used. Christopheles had been forthright in his opinion that such a blanket and indiscriminate security measure was inefficient and a waste of time, so it was no surprise that his cursory visit to an exhibition dedicated to the image and glory of the Saviour-King himself had quickly resulted in a ruling of 'No Concern'.

Ever since she was a young girl at her elementary school, Shenaria had been fascinated by the power of image and symbol. She had seen, and often felt, how easily and deeply visual, linguistic and even musical iconography could evoke visions, convey truths, bind or separate communities, motivate actions, and, above all, persuade. As a student in the fine and graphic Arts she had enjoyed conversations about the extent to which Art consisted of skilful rendering, original and pertinent juxtapositions, meaningful content and even artists' self-promotion.

All this had passed the time enjoyably enough until, one day while visiting her favourite gallery, she had been found laid out on the floor, thrashing and wailing uncontrollably, blood dripping from her nostril. It had come to her, as if in a moment of Divine revelation, that the power of image and symbol to shape and control people's imagination was not simply a pleasing and intriguing aspect of life, but was the crucial factor in determining whether people chose to follow the Saviour-King or the many Enemies raising arms against him. Allegiance to a symbol and the view of the world it represented could be cause enough for someone to behave heroically in the Saviour-King's name, or give himself over, heart and soul, to the evil carried out by man but inspired by the deepest Malevolence that had always plagued mankind. A symbol or word could worm itself deep enough into a man's mind that he would destroy innocent people by the hundred, destabilize successful and civilised communities and desecrate the most holy of shrines and institutions. The seductiveness of a perfect, mesmerising symbol could control a man's judgement so that he would believe that, no matter how destructive his actions, they were utterly justified and even desirable. Worse still, people could experience and be swayed by words, images and icons at a subliminal level, not ever realising that their wills were being manipulated and controlled by a Malevolence wholly destructive and evil.

Shenaria nearly died from the shock of this sudden, appalling realisation, and spent three months fighting off nightmares and terrifying visions in a secluded ward in the city's central hospital. Once she had subdued these and was released back into the world she was a different person. She immediately applied to join the Vigilants as one of its civilian staff. She could use her knowledge of Art and Iconography, she argued, to guard against the dangers she had seen during her epiphany. She was accepted for fast-track training the same day.

Unbeknown to Shenaria, her unusual case had caught the attention of another, far less public Valhallan organisation. She had been observed throughout her recovery and as she began her new life as a Special Advisor to the Vigilants. Soon she was ordered to attend another interview in an unmarked location with an anonymous question master. She wasn't told of the purpose or possible consequences of this interview, which was probably just as well for her sense of well-being, but she satisfied the tall, intense man she answered to, and shortly found herself transferred to an altogether different branch of Valhallan service. That was over ten years ago.

Now, together with her carefully selected team, she operated out of a discreet suite of rooms situated in Upper Berkeley, a comfortable part-residential, part-office district of Imperial City. The sign on her door read 'Iconography Consultant', and very occasionally people would visit her with old family documents or artworks they wanted help transcribing or understanding, or antique jewellery with obscure calligraphies that they needed to decipher. Only the favoured or unfortunate few knew of her real work as a member of the secret, but ever-present Sanctification.

❧

High up in Antrobus II's night sky, something was happening. Three specks of light appeared, seemingly out of nowhere, and grew in size until they were revealed to be men in single-use space-suits normally used only for the emergency evacuation of above-atmosphere space-craft. The men hovered for a second as one of Antrobus II's large, unmanned, Militariat communications satellites came into view, then flew towards it, attaching themselves to its surface at precise intervals. At exactly midnight in that particular time-zone around the planet, as they had rehearsed, they unscrewed three panels on the satellite's spherical surface, removed something from each revealed opening, and inserted something into each which looked like nothing so much as a curled up metal caterpillar. They waited until each caterpillar had burrowed into the innards of the satellite and disappeared from view, then meticulously replaced the three panels before releasing their helmet catches, letting their suddenly dead bodies drift away into space.

❧

Her day's work completed, Shenaria left her private, simply furnished office, and walked along the hallway to the farthest door. The red light beside it was lit, so she halted and crossed to a smaller adjacent door. Entering, she made her way past the concealed mechanisms that serviced this part of the building, stepped up a short flight of stairs and found herself on a narrow observation gantry. Here, she could gaze through the rectangular toughened glass one-way window to the large arena beyond.

Matthias and Modesty were engaged in one of their regular training duels. Matthias was stripped down to his white vest and fatigues, his muscular, heavy frame sweating heavily, while Modesty, as always, wore a midnight-blue cat-suit which emphasized her athletic figure – the exposed parts of which showed no signs of perspiration at all. Both were circling each other, their bare feet making no sound on the smooth floor. Their concentration was intense as they manoeuvred around the arena, but Shenaria knew that neither of them would have been able to see or hear her anyway. She glanced down at the control panel just below the window to see that scenario twenty-seven had been activated. This meant that Modesty had taken on the role of defender, with Matthias her adversary. Matthias had to inflict as many wounds as he could, while Modesty's role was to avoid such wounds any way she could – whether by disarming Matthias completely, injuring him or simply staying out of his way. She tended to choose the latter strategy, knowing that this was more likely to frustrate him into making poor judgements as they fought. He, on the other hand, tended to anticipate this choice of hers and try to force her to use up her energy in evasive manoeuvres before attacking for real.

They had each been trying to gain the advantage for thirty-two minutes when Shenaria arrived, and neither had been successful. True to this particular training scenario, Modesty was completely unarmed, while Matthias could use any and all weapons he chose. Right now he was attempting to draw Modesty's attention to his right hand, which swirled a wooden staff dramatically, while waiting for the best moment to reach for a hidden nerve-dagger with his left. Modesty, he knew, would anticipate such a feint, which is why his main attack would not be made with either nerve-dagger or staff, but with a sudden kick to the solar plexus – if he got the chance. Modesty moved faster than he did, so it was a question of deceiving her rather than out-manoeuvring her.

Modesty was not one to be deceived easily. Her intense blue eyes gave no clue where she expected the next attack to come. Every now and then she would leap sideways, or backwards, or feint such a move, tempting Matthias to reveal his hand too early. Always, she stayed just out of his reach. Always, she was completely conscious of the exact position of each of her limbs, of which potential moves her balance was advantageous for. She was aware of every aspect of herself. She knew how the smallest movements of her fingers could signal her next action, or misdirect attention away from it. She knew how her scent, when she and Matthias got very close, could distract him and put him off. She knew, because she had been trained to know. She had been in several situations when just such an acute awareness had saved her life.

They circled each other, both enjoying the workout, both refusing to admit that the match was even. Matthias smiled, as if he had her in a hopeless position; Modesty's expression gave nothing away, not even her appreciation of his psychological tactic. Without warning, Matthias swiped his staff behind her left leg, aiming for the back of the knee, but Modesty somersaulted backwards over the weapon, landing behind the swing, and consolidated her landing into a scissors-kick into the back of Matthias' own knee – as if playfully returning his own strategy against him. He fell, but turned his fall into a surprisingly graceful and efficient twist, and reached out for her, his powerful hands just missing her lithe legs. This time it was Modesty who changed tactics, by launching a powerful kick towards Matthias' chin: her first proper attack of the duel. He arched his head by a fraction, letting her small foot brush the stubble on his chin as it passed, then extended the move into a backwards roll, and was up on his feet, facing her once again.

They resumed their steady circling. Suddenly, he dropped his staff and barged straight into her, knocking her onto her back, and leapt down on her, pinning her arms to the floor above her head. Still Modesty's face remained impassive: it was as if she had seen this move coming and prepared for it.

This was the moment of truth in their fight, and both knew it. Either Matthias' powerful arms would pin Modesty down long enough for it to be counted as a wound, or Modesty would knee him in the groin or somehow otherwise escape his grip and slide away from him, to still be free and unharmed when the timed session came to an end. It was at this moment, when both of them were on the cusp of victory or defeat, that Shenaria changed the combat scenario.

Abruptly, the floor opened up beneath them, forcing them to fall towards the spiked surface twelve feet below. In an instant they were team-mates rather than adversaries. Matthias slapped the floor on each side of the opening with both his hands, and braced his arms and back firmly, stopping his own fall. At the same time, Modesty's legs gripped around his own, as if they were circus acrobats, and she swung, head down, short black hair hovering half an inch above the wicked iron spikes pointing up at them. Deftly, she swung her whole body upwards, gripping Matthias' back to support herself, then swiftly glided through the opening in the floor. Pausing only to see Matthias climb out too, she turned to face whatever threats the Battle-Room had in store for them next.

She didn't have long to wait. Little irregularly-spaced grilles opened up in the wall opposite them, and an assortment of projectiles shot towards them, some circular with wickedly serrated edges, some tapered to a point like spears, some small and spherical, as if they contained something they would release on impact. Instantly, they assumed a back-to-back position. Modesty dodged fluidly, letting projectiles whisk through spaces where her body had just been, while Matthias grabbed a short spear out of the air, his fingers just below its deadly point. He whipped it around, deflecting discs, spears and spheres, two of which collided into each other releasing, from one, a hail of tiny darts and, from the other, a noxious green gas. They avoided both, then Modesty stepped into Matthias' cupped hands, and he threw her high into the air.

Modesty spun round twice, avoiding the red lines of lasers suddenly streaming through the air, and attached herself to the nearly-smooth surface of the wall by what seemed to be force of will alone. She was ten feet above the floor, and the top of her head was adjacent to the toughened glass that Shenaria looked through. As the first shots were fired towards her, pinging against Shenaria's bullet-proof window, Matthias tossed up his nerve-dagger to her, which she caught and plunged into the wall in Shenaria's direction.

The nerve-dagger penetrated the wall and went on until it entered the back of the control panel Shenaria had altered the scenario on. The panel hissed and ejected wisps of smoke, and all the lights in the observation gantry and Battle-Room went off.

An instant later red emergency lighting lit everything up, but when Shenaria looked into the Battle-Room no one was to be seen. She pressed her face nearer the toughened glass to search more carefully. As she did so she felt a strong, muscular hand push her head against the window while another twisted her arm behind her, and a very cold, delicate needle nuzzled dangerously against the side of her neck.

'You win', said Shenaria simply, waiting until the needle was withdrawn and the large hands released their rock-hard grips, then turned to see a completely calm Modesty attached to the wall like a spider, with perfectly positioned Punishment Needles pointing towards her from both hands, and an incensed Matthias facing her on the observation gantry with taut arms ready to lash out, and rage in his deep brown eyes.

All around the planet, as each time-zone neared midnight, the same event occurred. Groups of three appeared out of nowhere and landed with mathematical accuracy on Militariat communications satellites. As one, they inserted more of the eerie, metal caterpillars, and watched while they burrowed through the thick, protective crusts of their targets. As one, their last living actions were to release their helmet catches and invite instant, unstoppable death. It was as if they – or someone they feared even more than death – wanted to be certain that they could never reveal the secrets that now escorted their stiff, frozen bodies into the dark, uncaring void.

Later, in the Relaxation Room, Matthias was still angry.

'Another second, and I would have beaten her. Thanks for nothing!'

Modesty smiled, and curled her legs up onto the sofa. 'The way I see it, you were saved at the last minute', she said, provoking him.

'Oh yeah? And you weren't?'

'The way I see it', interjected Shenaria, 'is that the two of you will have to take this back to the Battle-Room sometime. Meanwhile, let's have breakfast.'

As Shenaria spoke a dumb-waiter opened, revealing three full trays: a large, meat-based meal for Mathias, a plate of eggs, cheeses and avocado for her, and an exotic-looking collection of vegetation, plants and spices for Modesty. Their meals were regulated by Modesty, as Shenaria had recognised her expertise in personalised diets. Matthias and Modesty, as the main combatants of their operation, ate according to the needs of the mission, for speed, immediate energy or stamina as required, while Shenaria maintained an all-purpose diet, suitable (for short periods, at least) for supporting both long hours of investigative work and moments of sustained physical exertion.

They took their trays and settled at the chrome and glass table near the centre of the room. The sun was rising now, and Shenaria would soon lead the discussion of their action for the day ahead. Often they worked in a democratic fashion, with the most convincing argument or fruitful suggestion determining the course of events they would pursue, but both Modesty and Matthias recognised and respected the chain of command which operated if quick decisions were necessary – which was most of the time – Shenaria, then Matthias, then Modesty. Shenaria was the only fully authorised Sanctifier in the group, Matthias was her Truth-Extractor and Modesty, among other things, was her Assassin.

Now that food was entering his system, Matthias began to calm, and a small smile creased the corners of his eyes. 'Good play', he said, reaching for another forkful of steak, 'good timing'. He looked over to Modesty, graceful as always even when eating, and winked at her. 'We make a good team, Lady', he declared.

'You were slow', she replied, 'we could have put the system out half a minute before we did.'

'Now, now, children', smiled Shenaria before Matthias could rise to the bait, 'flirt in your own time. I'll ask you later – later, Matthias! – how you both crept up on me so fast: I'll need to watch that. Meanwhile, I would appreciate your thoughts about today's priorities.'

It was the signal to put the banter to one side and become the efficient team they were. Modesty closed her eyes, deep in thought, while Matthias finished his meal, took a large swig from his mug of Saviour-King Grey, and stood up, gazing at the spires and trees of Upper Berkeley through the window. Shenaria knew better than to disturb them, and instead brought out her ever-present notebook and the special, silver-plated stylus she always carried. No one but Shenaria could use this particular pen: it had been matched against her DNA and her brain-wave patterns, and she was aware of the devastating consequences if someone else tried. (She had commissioned the design of the stylus herself, after several instances when she could have really done with the aid of a computer, but the parameters of the mission at hand had prevented her from working at one.) She placed the notebook on the table and opened it just past yesterday's set of scribbles and decisions then pressed the topmost of two tiny buttons on the side of the stylus and sat back to watch as it wrote out today's message from the local solar system's Inner Chamber of the Sanctification.

From: The Office of High Sanctifier Lord Gallead Crooker

To: All authorised Sanctifiers, Antrobus Sector

Date: 06-07-22,005

Subject: Security Alert

Message:

Greetings, on behalf of the Saviour-King.

First, the good news. Thanks to the meticulous observations of Sergeant Byrrion, and the prompt conveying of his suspicions, we have been able to unmask and destroy a minor heretical sect attempting to set up operations in the outskirts of the Guildhall. Commendably efficient physical persuasion encouraged the survivors of our raid to reveal their aims, and give us some suggestion of the scale of their support network and resources: our grateful thanks to Lady Salfina Pureheart and her staff for their enthusiastic dedication to this matter.

Now, the problem: As we feared, the presence of the admirable *Divine Devotions* exhibition has proved to be something of a temptation to the enemies and opponents of the Saviour-King. It is clear from the final threats, curses and penitent statements of those captured before their executions that virtually all the malignant forces we battle against on Antrobus II have the exhibition in their sights. It would be a most powerful propaganda coup for the Enemy should this magnificent homage to the Saviour-King could be besmirched or destroyed.

Until further notice, our first priority will be to the security and purity of the exhibition and the faithful who will flock to it. The Vigilants will take responsibility for the safety of the public transport systems and other infrastructures supporting the exhibition. It will be *your* duty to secure the well-being of the exhibition itself. If one of the Enemy so much as farts at an effigy of the Saviour-King, you will answer to me personally.

You are authorised to carry out any and all security measures as you see fit. As always, it is better that the innocent die than the guilty succeed.

In the name of the Saviour-King,

Crooker

Shenaria closed her eyes for a second, then picked up her stylus and began writing something – in her own handwriting this time. A few moments late she closed her notebook and looked at Matthias.

'Over to you', she said.

This daily ritual was part of Matthias' training to become a full Sanctifier in his own right. Matthias had not had a scholarly upbringing, but Shenaria had recognised a potential in him that she was determined to realise, and had been granted Extraordinary Permission to train him herself. Each day, Shenaria would write down her response to the latest Sanctification communiqué, then invite Matthias to verbalise his own response, before they compared ideas. The aim was to develop Matthias' ability to think strategically and plan precise courses of action.

Matthias swept his plate away, and cupped his chin in his hands.

'It seems sensible enough at face value', he said, 'but there might be some questions we could ask.'

'Go on.'

'First of all, this exhibition has been touring the sector for a good number of years already. We need to determine whether there are any specific reasons to expect an attack on it now.'

'Good. What types of reasons?'

'I don't know … we're not dealing with rational people most of the time. Strange or rare astral conjunctions, patterns made by the planets as they circle the sun, anniversaries of significant historical events, whether any particular potential visitors are likely to be targeted – that type of thing.'

'All of which can be checked. Good. Anything else?'

Matthias thought for a moment.

'We need to check on the backgrounds of the Imperial Museum staff; especially those who will come into contact, or have some responsibility towards the exhibition.'

'I'd also check the invisible staff', Modesty interjected, 'Cleaners, café staff and the like.' Matthias looked at her as if to say *who asked you to butt in?*

'Again, good. Anything else?'

Matthias considered, then shook his head.

'Not that I can see right now. What about you, Princess?'

Shenaria nodded, and opened her notebook to what she had written.

'Yes, I can think of a few more questions. For now, given the security situation around this exhibition, and the fact that its potential targeting by servants of Malevolence could have been easily anticipated, I'd like to know why poor Christopheles was so quick to record a judgement of 'No Concern'. I'd like to know the extent of his investigation and whether or not he missed anything. I'd even like to know why the exhibition's initial scrutiny was given to him and not to me.'

Neither Matthias nor Modesty questioned her comments about another Sanctifier's work, or her right to make them. Neither thought her arrogant. They both knew that, when it came to matters involving images, effigies and symbols, Shenaria was the unsurpassed expert; the best there was in the whole sector.

'Here are the tasks for the day', she informed them. 'Modesty, you look into astral conjunctions, significant dates, and the like. Record any patterns that seem to emerge, whether to do with space or time or both. Get access to the museum's itinerary of forthcoming visits by the great and the good, and note any particular dates that might be tempting for the Enemy to target. Matthias, you find out about the museum's staff – all of them. I want to know about any who have ever had even a whisker of contact with heretical sects or Saviour-King repudiators. Bear in mind their position as museum staff: it might be worth checking the museum's catalogues for the presence of any suspicious artefacts, now or in the past. Check whether their families have any history of criminal or heretical activity. If there are any suspicious characters, pass their names on to Modesty in case she needs to deal with them. That's all for now.'

Modesty nodded once, then gracefully departed towards her own quarters.

'What will you do, Princess?' asked Matthias.

Shenaria stood.

'I think it's time I paid the *Divine Devotions* exhibition a visit of my own', she replied.

The three caterpillar-like mechanisms implanted in each satellite continued to burrow, exuding acids that ate away metals and plastics to allow them passage. They followed pre-determined routes, eating and ingesting the crucial components of each satellites communications relays. The semi-sentient caterpillars squirmed their way to the centre of each satellite, leaving tiny, slimy tunnels that corresponded exactly to warped, impossible three-dimensional patterns which nevertheless somehow existed.

Arriving at the exact centre of each satellite, the three caterpillars joined up with each other and began spinning ghastly cocoons around themselves. Then, their swollen, glistening wombs constructed, they slept, beginning their unnatural evolution.

CHAPTER TWO

Nine years ago…

Nine years ago High Sanctifier Lord Crooker had called Acolyte Calvert, as Shenaria had then been, into his private Sanctum in the secretive, unmarked reinforced steel construct known as the *Fortress Dedicata Profundis*, hidden and undeclared on the dark side of the dead Antrobus I's ice-moon. Called along with Shenaria was Christopheles Justinius, a young man whom Shenaria had not been able to stand.

Shenaria had taken to her initial Sanctification studies with a dedication and earnestness that had helped her deal with the vast amounts of information that she needed to become familiar with: Sanctificatorial protocols and procedures; critical case histories; the commonest lures of Malevolence that led to failure and corruption; specialist weapons training; and so on. Matthias could recall her talking about the routinely long hours she would put in, and how she was determined to succeed – whether or not she sustained any social relationships with her fellow students.

Christopheles, on the other hand, appeared to be an over-confident, flippant and uncommitted layabout who would rather spend his time engaged in sports or ogling women than working at his Sanctificatorial studies. Shenaria disliked him immensely, especially since he seemed to succeed in all things – combat tactics, strategy analysis, report writing, target practice – without a single sign of effort or dedication. He breezed in and out of his studies at the *Fortress Dedicata Profundis* as if unconcerned about missing five minutes of a military hero's talk here or the last chance to see a significant historical artefact there. It irked Shenaria that she, an obviously devoted servant of the Saviour-King, had to work so hard at her success, while Christopheles, who always looked as if he couldn't have cared less, achieved his constant success seemingly as easily as he breathed.

At this stage in her life, Shenaria had not yet learnt to dissemble, so her feelings about Christopheles were public and obvious – which meant that she was easy prey for his goading. He appeared to take particular pleasure in taunting her by talking loudly about the frivolous and social pleasures that would fill his evenings while Shenaria studied alone in her cell. She, on the other hand, tried to conduct herself as if she was above such concerns, but still found herself unleashing the most devastating sarcastic comments about him during seminars and military training drills. Their mutual animosity quickly became a tiresome irritation to their fellow acolytes, who were consequently all astonished when it emerged that Shenaria and Christopheles had woken up together after a sudden and explosive night of passion, and Shenaria had, for the first time ever, missed a training session.

Unfortunately for her, the lecture she had missed had been given by the great High Sanctifier Lord Crooker himself, who was not a man to suffer fools gladly. The following day, while the entire congregation of the *Fortress Dedicata Profundis* were assembled in the majestic Hall of Atonement for their morning devotions to the Saviour-King, he had called her to stand at the front of all her peers, tutors and servants. To Shenaria's deep shame, he asked her to explain publicly exactly what pursuits were more important than fulfilling her duties towards the Saviour-King, and made it absolutely clear that any repeat of her transgression would see her thrown out of Sanctificational training in disgrace.

As if this wasn't enough, it seemed that Christopheles had got off scott-free. Yet again, Shenaria felt that the odds were weighted against her, and that, for some reason, Christopheles carried the Saviour-King's blessing. She could not explain why she had ended up in Christopheles' arms that night (nor did she desire any repeat) and was dumbfounded when his taunting of her resumed, just as if nothing at all had passed between them. She determined to put an end to it, once and for all.

A week later, as the group of acolytes were about to practice interrogation techniques on a couple of recently captured low-level heretics, Shenaria burst through the door, waving an antique piece of parchment in Christopheles' direction.

'In front of these true witnesses', she began, 'and in accordance with the Ancient and Noble Decree of the Defence of Insulted Purity, as approved by the Saviour-King's own seal, I challenge you to a Duel of Incapacitation. The winner shall demand what forfeit he or she desires from the loser, which in your case, you dog's breakfast of a poor excuse for a man, will be your complete and utter removal from the *Fortress Dedicata Profundis*, the Sanctification as a whole, and any planet I set foot upon for the rest of my natural life. Do you have the balls to accept the challenge, you lousy, overblown piece of pestilential shit?'

Christopheles mouth gawped open with surprise, and his normally confident features turned pale. Everyone in the metallic ante-chamber stopped what they were doing and stared at the two of them. Books, scrolls and instruments of persuasion dropped to the floor around them. There was utter silence for a moment before Christopheles rediscovered his tongue.

'Wha...Wha...?' he attempted to say, 'The Duel of Incapacitation? But...but such a duel hasn't been fought for two thousand years, not since the Amaris Incident, when Sanctifier Josephus forced Sanctifier Velamis to remove both his own eyes! The incident was so shocking that the Duel was revoked as an Approved Procedure!'

Shenaria's eyes narrowed. 'So you have heard of a Library! Unfortunately, you haven't used it properly'. She waved the musty parchment under his nose. 'In a footnote to the Conclave of Hesperus, conducted in 16,324 by representatives of all nine Houses of the Sanctification, the Duel of Incapacitation was reinstated for use when 'material slights to the honour of the servants of the Saviour-King' have been declared. I so declare your behaviour towards me. Oh, and it wasn't your eyes I had in mind.'

Christopheles eyes widened. 'The Conclave of Hesperus? But Hesperus was destroyed while the Conclave was still in progress! No records of its discussions were ever found!'

Shenaria smiled, brutally. 'Not until three years ago, at any rate, when an archaeological dig on Hesperus' sister planet revealed an Info-capsule that had been fired there for safety by the delegates. Unfortunately, they all died before they could inform their superiors. Don't you ever read up-to-date journals?'

Christopheles swallowed hard. Shenaria gestured to one of the observation portholes looking out onto the desolate lunar landscape surrounding the Fortress, and smiled.

Now, shall we take this outside?' she said.

Twenty minutes later the two of them stood facing each other on the treacherous ice-covered surface of the moon, clothed in armoured self-sealing environmental suits that both slowed their movements and kept them alive, and waiting for the countdown to begin. They were accompanied by their chosen seconds, who had each opened a vacuum-sealed box and handed the two of them their weapons. Shenaria had challenged, so Christopheles had chosen which fighting implements they were to use. He had picked exquisitely balanced and elegant *shin-ru* rapiers: duelling epees that tapered to a lethal point, and could vibrate to accentuate their thrusting or slicing motions. It was clear to Shenaria that he wanted to take full advantage of his superior reach and height and try to deny her the opportunity to hit him at all.

Being a Duel of Incapacitation, neither opponent was allowed to kill the other instantly, though they could cause fatal injuries that would take effect after the duel had been concluded and the results mutually acknowledged. This would require a considerable degree of skill from them both.

They circled each other, both dexterously manipulating their blades in their right hands, as the countdown neared zero. According to the rules of engagement, neither could take a single step towards the other before the countdown concluded, but that didn't mean that they couldn't move. They observed each other carefully, watching for any habits of balance or patterns of movement that they could take advantage of, trying to give none away themselves.

This was what Shenaria was gambling on. Her acute sense of pattern did not only apply to static art, image and symbol, but to kinetic art, dance and movement too. She intended to fight defensively, both to lure Christopheles into overconfident mistakes (which she felt she had cause to expect) and to trump the pattern of his movements with a more intricate and bedevilling one of her own. She was sure that he would simply try to beat her through superior power: well, she had met men like that before.

The countdown reached zero. Almost instantly, Christopheles thrust directly towards her stomach, then wickedly sliced upwards with a move that would have opened her up from diaphragm to neck... had it connected. Shenaria had seen the thrust coming, and had let Christopheles waste some of his energy on it. As his *shin-ru* blade moved towards her, she twisted sideways and backwards, successfully avoiding it and threatening Christopheles with a hit on his underarm as he sliced his blade upwards.

They circled each other again. Christopheles was mildly impressed that Shenaria had avoided his first attack, but that did not stop him attacking again. He rushed towards her with a flurry of movements: thrusts, sideswipes, twists, feints and sharp changes of direction – all to no avail. Shenaria parried or avoided every would-be blow. She was laughing at him, he suddenly felt, and did not like the unusual feeling of shame and embarrassment that coursed through him as a result. It was as if she read his moves before he delivered them.

For her part, Shenaria realised that, for all her ability to second-guess Christopheles' moves, her stamina was not the equal of his, and she would begin to slow before he did. The uneven icy ground was not helping matters either, with both combatants forced to adjust their balance and footing more consciously and awkwardly than they would have had to in one of the *Fortress Dedicata Profundis'* combat and execution arenas. One slip from either, and the battle would be over, though Shenaria suspected that Christopheles' physical strength might allow him to brace himself against a sudden slither more easily than she would be able to. It became clear to her that she would have to sucker him in.

Christopheles tried a combination of twirls, thrusts and slashes that Shenaria barely avoided, and she surprised and maddened him by cutting past his blade at the crucial point and physically butting into him with her shoulder, making him almost lose his balance – not an illegal move, but certainly not one that masters of the art would consider gracious or artful. Fuming, Christopheles lunged towards her, and the point of his blade embedded itself into the most vulnerable part of the body in any duel – her sword arm. With a cry, she let go of her blade, dropping it out of her hand.

Christopheles paused, his anger and caution ebbing away as he realised that he had won, only to see, as if in slow-motion astonishment, Shenaria catch the falling blade in her left hand and thrust it towards his shoulder with a devastating upwards movement propelled by all her strength.

The decisive and winning blow made contact, but bounced off with the tell-tale electric sparking that revealed a personal force-field.

'No!' shrieked Shenaria, 'You CHEATED!'

'He did not', came the boom of a familiar, regal voice.

The two combatants turned as one, to see the decorated, brass chair being carried into view by four of the *Fortress'* lackeys, their faces hidden in their ice-suits. Seated upon the chair as if it were a throne was High Sanctifier Lord Crooker, his impressive frame, stern, scarred features and bronze regalia clearly visible through the environmental bubble that protected him.

'I will *not* have the Saviour-King's servants throwing their lives away on personal vendettas. Your lives are to be given in the Saviour-King's service – not in your own. You will die when your death brings the greatest benefit to the Valhallan Mission, and not a second before. Is that clear?'

Christopheles nodded and looked down, but Shenaria returned High Sanctifier Lord Crooker's gaze evenly and stood straight, even as she clutched her bleeding and stinging arm.

'I challenged Christopheles to a Duel of Incapacitation. This was in accordance with Sanctificatorial protocols and Valhallan law. I should be allowed my victory!'

'Your victory, Child, was in the capacity for thoroughness and attention to detail that allowed you to find the Hesperus paper and apply it to your own advantage. I am impressed, but I will not tolerate Sanctificatorial infighting, regardless of how richly it is deserved. Those devoted to Malvolence may brawl with each other, but we will have order here. The two of you will see to your wounds and attend me in my Sanctum in twenty minutes. That is all.'

The Sanctificatorial chair departed, leaving a quieter-than-usual Christopheles and a fuming, painfully injured Shenaria. She brushed off his offer of assistance and made her way back to the airlock with all the dignity her body had left in it.

Precisely twenty minutes later, the doors to High Sanctifier Lord Crooker's Sanctum were opened, and the cleaned-up and tended combatants were requested to enter. They stood side-by-side at the end of a dais and waited. Crooker, now attired in a scarlet velvet-sleeved cape over his regalia, entered at the far side of the room. He gestured for Shenaria to come forward, then consulted a small padd in his left hand.

'Strategy analysis – exemplary; weapons proficiency – excellent; knowledge of Valhallan Orthodoxy – second to none; attendance – one blemish. Yes, I have not forgotten. Tell me why you were prepared to throw all this away. You are granted permission to speak freely and without normal considerations of etiquette. Begin.'

'Sire, I am a dedicated servant of the Saviour-King. I study. I revere the sacred literature of the Valhallan Mission and respect the knowledge and wisdom of my Sanctificatorial tutors and weapons-masters. I have devoted myself and my life to the overthrow of Malevolence and the eventual final victory of the Saviour-King. And yet I have been ridiculed and abused by this man, who seems not to value the institution of the Sanctification, who acts disrespectfully towards learned texts and Valhallan servants. However you choose to punish me, Sire, I would dearly appreciate knowing this: why do you tolerate the presence of such a man in this noble organization?'

Lord Crooker acknowledged her speech impassively for a moment, then replied.

'Acolyte Calvert, consider the following scenario. Some powerful heretics and betrayers of the Saviour-King are hatching a dangerous plot: so dangerous, in fact, that the Valhallan Mission could be catastrophically damaged if the plot succeeds. Not enough is yet known about this plot for the Sanctification to act against it with sufficient confidence of success. What should the Sanctification do? Assume for the moment that we do not want to reveal our hand yet.'

Shenaria thought, then said, 'We should shadow those we suspect, and, if possible, infiltrate their meetings and organisations.'

'Very good, Acolyte. Now consider the same scenario from the Enemy's point of view. He anticipates that we will attempt to get close to him and penetrate his company. Now imagine that the Enemy is faced with two people attempting to make contact, either of whom might be a Sanctification agent in disguise: you and Christopheles. I ask you, which of the two of you would the Enemy suspect?'

Shenaria gasped as sudden understanding hit her.

'You are a good agent', continued Lord Crooker, 'indeed excellent in many ways. But you have one weakness. You wear your heart on your sleeve. Your affiliation to the Saviour-King is obvious – indeed, it defines you. You forget, in your zeal, that the Sanctification often operates in secret - just like the Inquisition of old. There are times, certainly, when we appear with the sound of trumpets to strike terror into the ungodly's hearts, and to show what devastating power we possess, but most of the time we let people's imaginations do their work for us. It is far better that the Enemy never know whether the Sanctification are present and always fear that they are. You are too obvious, Acolyte Calvert, and Sanctifier Christopheles was brought here to make you understand your weakness.'

'Sanctifier?' repeated Shenaria, stunned. Christopheles' posture changed; he stood straight and firm and looked directly at her: a different and more mature man than the flippant layabout he had seemed to be for so long.

'Yes, I am a Sanctifier', stated Christopheles. 'The purpose of the *Fortress Dedicata Profundis* is not so much to pass on general training and knowledge. That is only the minor part of what transpires. No, the major purpose of the *Fortress'* work is to identify Acolytes' blind spots and weaknesses, and see whether these can be overcome. I was tasked to deliberately goad you, to seduce you, and, above all, to sidetrack you. The Sanctification cannot afford to rely upon people who cannot keep their eye on the ball, or whose self-control is anything less than absolute.'

'Nor can we afford agents who make themselves obvious targets to the Enemy', added Lord Crooker.

Shenaria looked down at her feet, a confusion of anger, shame and realisation threatening to overwhelm her. 'Then I have failed', she said, simply.

'Acolyte Calvert, listen to me', ordered Lord Crooker. 'You have not failed. You identified a problem and dealt with it, using both your mind and body well. You showed a laudable intention to win at all costs. We have now brought another problem to your attention, and are confident that you will deal with it equally successfully. The *Fortress Dedicata Profundis* is here for people to learn. You have learnt. You are hereby granted the status and rank of Truth-Extractor, effective immediately. Congratulations, Truth-Extractor Calvert: we will make a fine Sanctifier of you yet.'

Shenaria looked up at the tall, imposing figure in front of her, and then across to where Christopheles stood.

'Sire', she said, 'Am I still allowed to proceed without normal considerations of etiquette?'

'You are', replied Lord Crooker. Shenaria crossed over to Christopheles and looked into his eyes with an expression of disgust.

'I accept my lesson as deserved', she stated, 'And I wish you to accept this as deserved too.'

A powerful, well-aimed knee connected with Christopheles' groin and he doubled over in sudden, excruciating pain. Shenaria returned to stand in front of Lord Crooker, and bowed before him.

'I will not let you down', she said.

And she never did.

CHAPTER THREE

At the Imperial Museum, ten miles east of Shenaria's suite of rooms, all was noise, confusion and rising irritation. The museum had been preparing to host the *Divine Devotions* exhibition for almost two years now, and the project had not been universally welcomed. Early on, some unlucky citizens had returned home to find that the entire expensive city block where they lived was going to be demolished in order for a brand-new wing of the museum to be built especially to house the exhibition. Unfortunately for them, they would have risked charges of heresy had they objected to this development, so the more intelligent of them kept their feelings to themselves. Nonetheless, as demolition and then construction work began on the new site, several low-level acts of sabotage had been committed, and the building crews attacked on occasion. However, once the Vigilants had made an example of one irate citizen (who had publicly attempted to circulate a petition demanding a re-think of the museum's plans) and a small gang of local trouble-makers had found themselves conscripted into military service (for trying to incapacitate a hydraulic digger), these acts of violence and vandalism had ceased.

Now, twenty-three months later, tempers had cooled to some extent, helped by the simple fact that the new Worship Wing of the museum was absolutely beautiful. Its ornate grey and pink Georgian marble walls were complimented by its superbly framed windows and the pillars and statues that gave the covered entrance such an evocative feel to it. Every line, curve, opening and decorative feature of the gorgeous, immense building seemed mathematically and aesthetically perfect, as if no other design could possibly have been arrived at (which, as later events were to show, was literally the truth). The formal gardens at the front of the building was constructed and planted in such a way that the colours and scents combined to evoke a sense of awe and perfection that provoked a welling-up of reverence and a feeling that to step through the giant doors, with their huge, graceful and astonishingly detailed depictions of angels and cherubs, would be almost to die with pleasure and fulfilment. Giant concrete murals of many of the Saviour-King's famous victories in battle faced outwards from every side of the building, forcing citizens to confront the littleness of their lives and achievements when compared to the Saviour-King's, making them feel properly humble and grateful to live by the grace of the Saviour-King and die at his behest. The building had been painstakingly designed from a special commission by Sejanius, an architect long renowned on his home planet of Sappharus and the surrounding sector, some light-years distant.

Even so, the mundane logistics of traffic control and freight-carrying were beginning to get the better of almost everybody's tempers. Impossibly long and wide vehicles approached the museum, only to get hemmed in by parked cars, which in turn had nowhere to go to get out of the way. A couple of bulky vehicles attempted to reverse towards the Worship Wing's delivery entrance at the same time, causing the drivers to argue about which of them had priority. A ramp laid across the steps leading up to the delivery entrance proved too narrow to accommodate the wheels of a huge gurney supporting a massive, prone statue of the Saviour-King. Other, similar incidents had been going on all week, as the bulk of the exhibits finally arrived.

As on the other days, when logjam and fisticuffs seemed unavoidable, a charismatic, well-tailored man stepped out from the Worship Wing and approached the various lifters, shifters and drivers in turn. A few softly-spoken words from him, and the problems, which up until that moment had seemed so intractable, seemed to simply melt away. Lorries that had been unable to manoeuvre around each other now performed the simplest of movements, and got past each other easily. Men straining to free a trolley wheel caught in a gutter pushed the trolley almost casually, and the wheel freed itself. Tempers calmed, hands were shaken in friendship, and the exhibits were delivered safely and without further incident.

Still, thought one of the truck-drivers as he wheeled his vehicle away, it was odd to see such a man, the envoy to the curator of such a reverent exhibition, be joined by three cavorting almost-naked women who wrapped their arms around him as he returned inside the building. His eyes must have been playing tricks, he decided.

✿

Closing the door behind him, the well-tailored man brushed off the attentions of his three clinging companions, mildly annoyed that they had risked such a public appearance. Instinctively, they took up a perfect, pouting group pose as they looked back at him, seduction in their eyes. The man regarded them dispassionately: the changes were subtle, but some could be picked out easily if one knew where to look. No longer were they just three young, good-looking pleasure-girls. Their nails were just that little bit longer and certainly sharper than they had been, the whites of their eyes were just that little bit too large to have occurred naturally, their breasts and thighs were firmer and tauter than they had any right to be. Less obviously, their necks could now turn so that they could look backwards, their arms and legs had become double-jointed and their shoulder-blades had begun to grow tiny little scales. Their saliva was becoming increasingly acidic. Their teeth were getting more and more pointed, and their voices were growing more musical: either huskier or more innocent-sounding, depending on their original styles of seductiveness. They exuded new scents which would not be registered consciously, but would nevertheless soon overpower any normal man in their immediate vicinity. The man doubted that the three girls, originally so pleased with their luck and increased salaries, were aware of the changes happening to them, and part of him wondered idly whether they would have approved or resisted had they known what they were transforming into.

He dismissed them with a word, and made his way through exhibit-filled corridors and halls to a door leading to the non-public areas of the Worship Wing. Soon he could hear voices: he could pick out Rimbrant's tiresome lecturing tones easily now, and admired the patience with which the other voices answered him. Patience did not come naturally to the well-tailored man, though he well understood the need to keep his usual personality in check. Adopting a more servile posture than he normally presented himself in; he knocked on the door and went through.

On the other side he saw Rimbrant hectoring two museum porters about the need for utmost care when carting statues and other precious exhibits. As always with Rimbrant, what started out as a word about taking proper care turned into a lecture on the background and artistic and historical virtues of the pieces being transported. The two porters, well used to this occurrence, stood still, letting Rimbrant's learned words fly straight over their heads, thinking about their forthcoming coffee breaks and how they weren't being paid enough to do this job. Eventually, Rimbrant finished his unnecessary potted history of the two statues lying on the porters' trolleys and the porters said *Yes, Sir* and left before he could resume. Rimbrant nodded to the well-tailored man, said a few exasperated words about the quality of the museum staff and went on his way.

The well-tailored man straightened up as he watched Rimbrant go, thinking to himself how much he'd enjoy feeding the man's old, decrepit body to the recently-released Gargoyle once all the work was complete. But for now Rimbrant was necessary – indeed essential – so his annoying fussiness was tolerated. The well-tailored man waited until Rimbrant was out of sight, then quickly opened what looked like a panel in the wall and entered the most secret part of the museum.

He soon found himself in large, dimly-lit chamber, the dimensions of which seemed to waver and shift unnervingly to his invisibly augmented eyes. The Gathering was just beginning. Figures that appeared just out of focus mulled around a large table shaped like an artist's easel. Discreet and almost unseen white-gloved servants silently delivered glasses and tit-bits. Sounds reached him as if they had travelled through a sea-shell. He estimated that more than forty people were in the room.

At the signal of a muted gong the Gathering sat and the room became quiet. A sudden grating and not entirely human-sounding voice resonated through the room – its speaker hidden, or at least not visible to the senses of the Gathered.

'Report', it demanded, simply.

An anxious young man stood up. Instantly a bright, sickly light shone on him from out of nowhere.

'The unfortunate Sanctifier Christopheles Incident has been concluded successfully', the young man said nervously. 'The Vigilants, and even the Sanctification itself, thanks to Lord Crooker's Special Representative's report, believe his death to be an accident. Christopheles himself believed his superiors had authorised his mission, but, as we well know, it was completely unsanctioned, and the Sanctification have found no reason to suspect foul play.'

'Good', said the voice, and the young man sat down again, visibly relieved as the foul light left him and cast itself upon the well-tailored man. The well-tailored man stood, feeling his own confidence drain away.

'Almost all the exhibits have arrived, without damage and without incident. The exhibition will open on the date we agreed.'

'*We* agreed?' asked the voice, calmly.

'The date you ordained', corrected the well-tailored man hurriedly, his heart fluttering with instant panic. Suddenly he couldn't breathe. It was if his throat was being throttled by two giant, remorseless hands. He gasped for breath, making a horrible gurgling sound, arms flailing, losing the rest of his dignity and control. The rest of the Gathering watched impassively for the two minutes that the punishment lasted.

'Careful, Mephistopheles', rebuked the voice, and the well-tailored man fell into his seat, defecating, sweating and panting for air, as the ghostly hands left him. Now the hideous light fell on a short, bespectacled man, who looked much more worried than he had done a few moments ago. He stood at once, nervously scratching his cheek before realising and stopping.

'Mr. Abbott?' requested the grating voice.

'Your Honour', replied Abbott, with a slight crack in his voice, unsure of which honorific to use.

'Let the *Enclave* note that we are pleased with your work. Very pleased, in fact.'

'Thank you, your Honour'. The short man coughed, then looked around the table – not that he could see the faces of the assembly. His nerves began to calm. 'The concept behind the neural caterpillar was a simple one, at least in theory', he continued, carried away with his own relief. 'The creature can store and manipulate any instructions and information one requires, including DNA data. It is completely undetectable while in its prone state, and will not set off any alarms regardless of what triggers them. Its secret is that it is semi-sentient, and can control its own evolution during its gestation period. It-'

'Thank you, Mr. Abbott: that will do. This is not a classroom. Gentlemen, please show your appreciation.'

The Gathering applauded Abbott, who nervously smiled back at where he assumed their faces to be. Just as he was about to sit down again, the voice resumed.

'Mr. Abbott. A simple round of applause is not enough to truly reward you for your efforts. I know we have already paid you for your services, but the *Enclave* would be pleased if you would accept this little gift. Mr. Maxillan, if you would.'

A chinless man got up and crossed the table to Abbott. He reached into his pocket and brought out a small object that he put on the table in front of him.

'With our compliments', Maxillan said slimily, before returning to his seat.

Abbott gazed at the gorgeous casket in front of him with wonder. It was beautiful. Brass and scarlet in colour, he could tell it was made of high-carat gold. It was decorated with meticulously crafted intricate reliefs of singing angels in flight. Without a doubt, it was the most desirable object that Abbott had ever seen.

'It's so beautiful...' he whispered, awe-struck, and caressed its surface ever so gently.

'Please', suggested the voice, 'open it.'

Abbott licked his lips and swallowed, then leant forwards towards the majestic container. He was so entranced by it that he did not notice the rest of the Gathering shield their eyes. He lifted the casket's lid.

His eyes widened suddenly and he had time to let out one startled scream of terror and shock - but it was already too late. His body palpitated wildly and his heart jumped in his chest in an immediate and deadly seizure. He stiffened, then slid to the floor, limbs still in spasm, mouth locked in a dreadful rictus, pupils wide and staring. The casket fell to the table with a clunk, its lid closing softly, seemingly of its own violition.

There was silence. Then three of the silent white-gloved servants approached the table. Two of them swept the corpse away with a broom, while the third carefully returned the horrible box to Maxillan.

'Mr. Winter and Mr. Kydd', continued the hidden voice, as if nothing had happened.

Two men, one slim and dapper, the other burly and ungainly, both nervous, rose from where they had been sitting together.

'Dispose of the body. Burn his laboratory. Erase all evidence of his existence. Afterwards, go to Sappharus, deal with Sejanius and bring his special box of papers and other particular materials to me. You will recognise it, gentlemen; it is a larger companion to the little casket that has just dealt with Mr Abbott, only this time made of mahogany. Be warned, though: it is much more deadly than the one you have just seen here.'

The men nodded, gulped, and left.

'That concludes our main business for today', said the voice, expressionlessly, 'except, of course, for the most important item. How is the woman?'

A balding, sharp-suited man rose, reluctantly. It was Clavicord.

'She has acclimatised to the treatment. Her body ingests what we feed her - despite her resistence', he answered. 'The incubation seems more successful than the parallel attempts being carried out on Sappharus.'

'As so it should', returned the voice, 'given our little casket and its treasures. Good. Unless someone has any further productive suggestions or pertinent observations, this meeting is over. You have one minutes' permission to offer any suchlike without being deemed impertinent.'

Clavicord coughed, perspiring heavily.

'You again', sighed the voice. 'Very well, speak.'

Clavicord bowed. 'Master, it is the Gargoyle. Waking it early to deal with the Sanctifier has begun to affect it. It wishes to escape and it seeks to feed. It may need sating sooner than we, er, was anticipated, if we wish to control it for what we have planned. Allowing it to feast on the Sanctifier seems to have awakened its appetite.'

'Sit', ordered the voice. Clavicord did so. There was silence for some minutes. No one dared so much as to cough.

'This may work to our advantage', declared the voice finally. 'Very well, we will bring forward our first demonstrations. As well as causing panic and misleading the Sanctification, these will serve to ensure that the Militariat are deployed as we desire. Clavicord, see to it later today.'

44

Clavicord nodded.

'Then that is all, Gentlemen. The Gathering is closed.'

As one the assemblage felt the owner of the voice leave their presence – though how they could not have said. A few of the Gathered engaged in automatic goodbyes, but most were happy to leave by the most direct route and as quickly as possible without further contact with their comrades. Mephistopheles, the now not-so-well-tailored man, went to repair his outfit and persona, while Clavicord hurried out to do his master's bidding. It was ten o'clock in the morning.

❧

In another part of the museum Rimbrant stood, looking with adoration at a large ornate pedestal. It was so finely detailed and well finished that most of the porters and other staff who had seen it and moved it had not realised that would only form the base of the most glorious and precious exhibit of all. It waited at the exact centre of the building, under the highest point of the ceiling, ready to support the forthcoming marvellous addition to the collection. (The exhibition was not a static thing, but, rather, one that was added to constantly, with Rimbrant having the cherished task of determining which exhibits would be shown on each planet that *Divine Devotions* visited. Sometimes this was determined by the particular planet's Valhallan history, as certain paintings, sculptures, writings and other works of art would resonate more with the citizenry than others; sometimes it was determined by the need to properly honour and frame newly-acquired exhibits.)

Rimbrant's breathing quickened as he contemplated the central pedestal and the majestic statue shortly to be placed upon it. Word of the *Divine Devotions* exhibition had reached as far as Earth, and even the Majestic Authorities of the fabled Temple of Valhalla itself appeared to have been pleased. In fact, they had sent something to add to the exhibition – for its stay on Antrobus II only – a giant, golden statue of the Saviour-King that the Saviour-King himself had commissioned, long before he ascended Mount Valhalla to make his awesome sacrifice on behalf of all mankind. The Saviour-King had been passing through Antrobus II's airspace when he had signed the commission, so the

Temple of Valhalla had thought it highly appropriate to lend the glorious statue for this venue of the exhibition.

Like all things so intimately connected to the Saviour-King himself, this statue was beyond value, and was being transported by an Honour Guard of *First Valhallans*: the most holy brethren of warriors and devotees that tended the sacred Temple of Valhalla itself. They consisted exclusively of descendants of the human family that the Saviour-King himself had been a part of before his ascension to Godhood, and, as such, could claim to have been favoured by the Divinity in some manner. Even now, the sleek Valhallan missionship *Commensurate Justice* was deep in space and travelling towards Antrobus II, its precious cargo overseen by the ever-watchful Captain Drusus and his faithful company of loyal and battle-proven First Valhallans.

The first attack took place just after noon. A passenger aircraft was making its final descent towards Imperial City's airport, when one of the passengers got the shock of his soon-to-be-ended life. Gazing lazily out of the window he jolted as he saw what seemed to be a gargoyle positioned on the port wing on the wing, horrible jaws opened and ready to bite off the wing of the plane. A closer inspection showed that it was still some way off; it had been a trick of perspective. This was hardly comforting, though, as that meant that the rapidly approaching harpy-shaped creature was huge indeed. The passenger yelled, as was soon joined by others as they, too, caught their first glimpse of the horror that made its way towards them. The harpy-like creature glowed in the midday sky like a maddened generator, and shrieked so loudly that eardrums popped and windows began to shatter.

Screaming, several of the passengers were sucked out of the new openings in the plane as it began its now uncontrollable descent. The dreadful stone-like creature tore limbs and heads off many of the humans as they fell, its claws rendering them and its maw slicing and swallowing them. Then it landed on the doomed plane, its ferocious claws sinking straight into the metal exterior. Passengers shrieked, panicked and passed out as the roof and overhead cabins were torn away, hurtling more hapless people into the air, and the giant, hideous head of the harpy thrust itself towards them and feasted. Some shots were fired towards the apparition by the remaining security personnel, but these simply bounced off and into unfortunates nearby. The harpy-like creature let out more hideous cries, and continued to feed greedily on the stricken passengers and crew as the broken plane plummeted to the earth below, only releasing the vehicle from its claws a hundred feet above the ground. It flew off, screeching piercingly, letting the descending chunks of metal and flesh crash into the buildings below, causing untold death and destruction as they did so.

Twenty minutes later, just outside Upper Berkeley, a monorail train travelling above the city's buildings and streets became the second victim of the apparition. Without warning a giant shadow passed over the windows of the train, instantly followed by a lurching collision. The first four carriages careened off the track, desperate attempts at braking useless, and fell straight onto the multi-shops below, while the fifth and sixth carriages hung halfway over the track. The huge, winged creature hovered in the sky, smashing windows and tearing off doors and roofs with its terrible claws to get to the foodstuffs within, ducking its misshapen head through the openings it made and pulling out human limbs and entrails with its cruel, pointed beak. People screamed and tried to jump and run away, but to no avail. Corpses and bits of corpses fell onto the smashed shops and land-cars below. The colours in the appalling beast's chest glistened more brightly the more it ate, and shots from hurriedly-arriving and terrified Vigilants did not even enrage the creature, let alone damage it or prevent it from eating its full. Finally – insultingly, even – it finished feasting and gazed round at those stupid or dutiful enough to still be in the vicinity, as if daring them to try something. Then it let out one more hideous shriek and flew off, contemptuously tipping carriages five and six completely off the monorail track and onto half the onlookers as it did so.

Matthias rushed into the suite of rooms, slamming open the door, only to find Modesty staring wide-eyed at the awful scenes now being repeated on the tele-vid. One terrified survivor of the monorail attack had termed the apparition 'The Angel of Death', and this name was now being used by all commentators. Matthias was breathing hard, having run the last mile and a half at full speed. As the Truth-Extractor of the group, Matthias considered it a matter of honour to look out for the safety of his companions, and the dreadful attacks on Imperial City had brought out all his protective instincts to their full.

'Have you seen?...' began Modesty, her impassive voice failing to mask her emotion. Matthias gulped for breath and shook his head violently.

'It's worse than you think', he told her, 'Shenaria was on that train.'

CHAPTER FOUR

Matthias and Modesty waited in the crowded and panic-stricken main reception area of the city's central hospital. They were not alone. Virtually half the city's population were there, desperately trying to find out the fates of their loved ones following the two appalling attacks. Some were conducting themselves with decorum and consideration for others, but the great majority were demanding attention and information through shouting, pushing and pulling unfortunate hospital staff around, and screaming. Already Matthias had had to go and crack open the head of a particularly annoying brute who insisted on taking out his anger and worry on a pale, shivering young woman who was trying to hold a baby in her emaciated arms while controlling a screaming infant at the same time. The woman – no more than a girl really – had smiled her thanks to him as the brute had gone off to repair his broken nose as best he could, and the infant had stopped being a nuisance instantly. Matthias had pointed to him and warned, 'Look after your mother, or I'll be back', and then gone back to the overcrowded line of plastic chairs where Modesty was sitting.

She was as graceful as ever, despite the evidence of carnage around her. Trolleys wheeled by, carrying destroyed humans, or remnants of humans. Some had breathing apparatus attached to them, some were covered in bloody sheets. Modesty was gently using her limited hypnotic powers to broadcast a subliminal suggestion to the waiting crowds that they should leave the gangways and corridors clear: her covert activity had already saved the lives of twelve people that afternoon, and given at least four others a fighting chance they wouldn't have otherwise had. She watched Matthias unload some of his anger and frustration at poorly-behaved people, knowing better than to criticise or interrupt him. She knew how attached he was to Shenaria, and how, as the group's only man, he considered their safety his personal responsibility. She watched the scene carefully, knowing that Shenaria would want her to be alert to any suspicious behaviour that might suggest that any of the crowd were connected to the attacks and were reporting back to their superiors about the levels of terror and damage the attacks had caused. So far she had not seen anything suspicious, but Modesty knew the value of diligence.

'Anything?' Matthias asked, as he approached.

She shook her head.

✿

High above the atmosphere, the neural caterpillars had changed. The glistening cocoons secreted around the Militariat satellites' pipework and electronic relays had expanded in size and grown in strength. Pipes and panels bent or broke around the cocoons as they developed. Acidic discharges from the cocoons' surfaces ate through protective plastic and metal cases covering the wiring to sensitive communications and sensory equipment. Tiny tendrils flicked out from the cocoon's surfaces and burrowed under the exposed and damaged casing until they found and wrapped themselves around the revealed wiring. Unnatural mewling sounds escaped from the cocoons, which began to thrash wildly for some seconds before settling again. The next stage of the caterpillars' evolution had begun.

✿

At last, some three hours after Matthias and Modesty had arrived at the hospital, a squeaky med-robot emerged from a corridor and beckoned them to follow. They were pleased to move, as the tele-vid screens had insisted on replaying the scenes of destruction over and over again, which was not very comforting to those waiting for news of their missing relatives and friends. Matthias and Modesty had paid close attention to the scenes; looking out for any signs of Shenaria on the screens, of course, but also studying the images of the 'Angel of Death' closely, and listening out for anything significant in the eye-witnesses' statements.

Now they followed the robot past little rooms and closed off parts of the corridor, all concealing horrible scenes of grief and anguish, or, much more rarely, happy and tear-filled reunions between those thought lost forever and their grateful loved ones. The smell of blood, death and antiseptic reminded Matthias forcibly of his military past, while Modesty's senses had never been exposed to such things in such intense quantities – except on the few occasions when she had been required to assassinate an entire household, and they had tended to be neater than the scene surrounding her now.

Eventually the med-robot brought them to a private room, and gestured them through the door. Inside they found Shenaria, alive, but unconscious, lying in a standard medical bed and covered by an insulation blanket. She was being fed by a drip, her face was scratched and mottled with bruises, and she had bandages covering her eyes.

Two hours after the attacks an emergency meeting of Antrobus II's High Council took place in a secure location. Among the many present were Tollius, Antrobus II's World Regent, Colonel Helbrad, the chief officer of the world's Militariat, Commissioner Bennett and Sergeant Byrrion of the Vigilants, High Sanctifier Lord Crooker's Special Representative, and Aurelius, the governor of Imperial City, where the attacks had taken place. It broke all security protocol, but since some members of the Council had already voiced their opinion that the *Divine Devotions* exhibition was either the target or the reason for the attacks, Rimbrant had been invited to sit in the meeting, and was present, along with his envoy, bound by strict oaths of confidentiality under pain of death.

The planet had been spared the realities of war and conflict for the last three hundred years. The military levies it had had to pay and the calling up of citizens for service in the interplanetary Valhallan Crusade had been Antrobus II's only experience of warfare in any living citizen's memory. Consequently, the attacks on Imperial City had been received with great shock, and the thought that these might only be the beginning of a more sustained campaign or attack did little to calm the delegates' nerves. Tollius had had trouble chairing the meeting when

51

it began, as only Helbrad, Byrrion and Lord Crooker's representative spoke and listened with any self-control and discipline, and it had only been Helbrad's reminder of the military might that the planet possessed that had calmed things down.

'The first thing to do', Helbrad was suggesting, 'is to identify all possible reasons for the attack. The second thing to do is to anticipate all possible next moves by the Enemy – whoever he happens to be. The third thing is to nullify these next moves, with lethal and pre-emptive force, preferably.'

'Surely', broke in Aurelius, 'we need to protect the citizenry and stop panic spreading. We don't want riots complicating matters, or providing the Enemy with a smokescreen. We also need to ensure that the citizenry remain confident in us, and that all those who helped out – the Vigilants', and he gave a little nod towards Bennett and Byrrion, 'and the medical services – know we value their efforts. We need to keep morale high, in case we face further attacks.'

'Completely agreed', replied Tollius, 'but such worthy concerns remain secondary at present.'

'How can we know the Enemy's next move?' asked Melching, a minor Employment Administrator. 'He could be planning anything! We can't use up all our military power chasing illusions! We need to know exactly where to strike. And I don't see how we can.'

'Thank you for your useful remark', returned Tollius, dryly. 'Does anyone have any suggestions?'

'We could go back to your idea – of identifying possible reasons for the attack – and work out the Enemy's potential targets from there', offered Byrrion.

'Alright', said Tollius, 'you all have two minutes to suggest such possible targets to me.'

The room quietened down, as the delegates, either singly, in pairs or trios, discussed and jotted down their ideas. Soon, everyone had finished, and pens had been put to rest. The Council looked towards Tollius. He motioned one of the Council's servants to dim the lights, then projected three columns onto the Briefing Wall: the first one headed 'Enemy's Targets', the next headed 'Why?' and the third titled 'Our Response'.

'Begin', he said.

'Let's start with the obvious', offered Aurelius. 'Either Imperial City's transport system was the first target, or Imperial City itself was.' He paused, while Tollius scrolled 'Imperial City / Transport system' onto first column of the screen. 'There are two possible reasons for this: firstly, the attack was meant to inhibit and compromise the transport system for several days, so we would need to project forwards and see what would be affected by this; and secondly, the attack was a test to determine whether the whole of the city could be assaulted.'

'There might be other reasons', offered Lord Crooker's representative, 'the attack might have been a demonstration, or a warning.'

'Let's come back to those in a moment', directed Tollius. 'Can anyone suggest any other targets that the Enemy might have in mind?

'We should consider the possibility that all Antrobus' major cities are under threat', stated Helbrad, 'and even the entire planet itself. This attack may have been carried out to test and observe our defences, or to soften us up before a fully-fledged invasion or uprising from within.'

A noisy consternation followed Helbrad's suggestion, until Tollius raised his hand for quiet to resume.

'Let us be clear about this', he said. 'Are you suggesting that the Enemy has a fleet of such creatures, ready to attack us? Or that the creature we experienced was just a figurehead for a more traditional attack?'

'I don't see how we can know for sure', replied Helbrad, to the disquiet of many, 'but it seems to me that such creatures might be able to terrorise and destroy, rather than control. I would bet on an invasion force such as the Militariat have trained to meet rather than a large-scale chamber of horrors.'

'Assuming that an invasion is planned', added Aurelius.

'Assuming that, yes', answered Helbrad. 'Of course, my responsibility as Officer-in-Chief of the Militariat makes me bound to consider such a possibility seriously. I would rather we were ready for an invasion that never came than were unprepared for one that did.'

'Aren't we jumping the gun a bit?' suggested Byrrion. 'Appalling as it was, we have only experienced one localised sequence of attacks; and this by some sort of creature rather than any army or group of any kind. Perhaps we need to concentrate on finding this creature and destroying it, rather than worrying about an invasion.'

'Perhaps we should go back a few steps', said Tollius. He turned to the Sanctification representative. 'Sir, forgive me for asking, but if your noble organisation had intelligence of any threat to our planet, it would tell us, wouldn't it?'

'It might', came the reply, 'if sharing such information did not compromise any investigation or mission of our own. In this case, however, I can tell you that we do not have any specific information about any army or fleet poised to attack Antrobus II. That does not, of course, mean that such a thing does not exist, it merely means that no such force has come to attention of the Sanctification. I assume your planet has its own First Warning system.'

'It most certainly does, Sir', said Helbrad, proudly, 'our Militariat satellites contain the most advanced and sophisticated detection systems available to the whole sector. They would inform us instantly of any suspicious activity taking place anywhere in our solar system, and even in the surrounding parts of the galaxy that border onto it. In addition, they are used in constant Militariat training in the use of planet-wide communications and co-ordinated manoeuvres. We may not have experienced military action for some time', continued Helbrad, 'but we are diligent in our preparation for it.'

'Then it seems', said Lord Crooker's representative, 'that you do not need to fear an invasion, at least in the immediate future.'

Some of the tension around the table ebbed away at this remark. People coughed and stretched, and Tollius signalled for fresh refreshments to be served around the table. As if by mutual agreement, the company took an informal, five-minute break from its deliberations. Rimbrant took advantage of this to turn to his envoy.

'I still don't see why I was requested to attend. These men can look after the safety of the city perfectly well. This is a waste of time!'

'Yes, Sir', replied his envoy Mephistopheles, 'but perhaps we ought to hear what they have to say. Their decisions may affect your noble exhibition in some way – even if only as far as adding extra security or altering the opening hours.'

'Sacrilege!' responded Rimbrant. 'No mere planetary council should prevent the Saviour-King's faithful paying homage to my glorious collection whenever the spiritual need arises! The glory of the Saviour-King should be above concerns as mundane as security issues!'

And I, thought Mephistopheles to himself, *should be above wishing I could wring your tiresome neck right now, but I will enjoy the moment when it comes*. 'I believe the meeting is coming to order once more', he contented himself with saying.

Tollius coughed, and the chatter in the room subsided. 'Well, Gentlemen', he said, 'if we rule out an invasion for the time being, what's left? A civil uprising? A coup by the military?'

'Sir!' exclaimed, Helbrad, shocked. Tollius smiled in his direction.

'Yes, I didn't think it was a serious possibility, Colonel', he said. 'Commissioner Bennett, what about a civil uprising?'

'Unlikely, Sir. We have been diligent in our pursuit of trouble-makers and criminal factions. Also, the attacks did not correspond to the known *modus operandi* of any group known to us.'

'Very well. So what does that leave? A one-off attack? A new threat? Do we believe all major cities to be in danger, or is the threat localised to Imperial City? Yes, Byrrion?'

'Sir, you know my opinion already. I believe that Professor Rimbrant's *Divine Devotions* exhibition is likely to be the catalyst for the attack – forgive me, Sir', Byrrion added in Rimbrant's direction. 'I believe that the presence of so august and venerable an exhibition is acting as an irresistible temptation to the enemies of the Saviour-King here and nearby. Saviour-King-repudiators, heretics and other malevolent sects will see an astonishing opportunity to strike a blow against the Saviour-King's name and image. I think that the attacks we saw earlier today were a dummy run for a larger-scale attack on the Imperial Museum, or the transportation routes that will service it once the exhibition is opened. It is my recommendation that the opening of the exhibition be delayed or cancelled until we have tracked down the creature that attacked us and identified its masters.'

Rimbrant rose, beside himself.

'It's an OUTRAGE!' he exclaimed. 'How dare this little minion propose such a thing? Do you not realise the honour that the presence of my exhibition lends your puny little planet? Cancel the opening? Then the Enemy will have already won, and Antrobus II will go down in History as the planet that was afraid to pay homage to the Saviour-King!'

Mephistopheles also rose, embarrassed and annoyed at his master.

'Sirs', he said, 'I apologise for the Professor's outburst, but you can see how passionate he is when it comes to the glorious exhibition. May I suggest another, more practical reason why *Divine Devotions* should not be cancelled? As some of you may know, the centrepiece of the exhibition is now on its way to us from Earth's sacred Temple of Valhalla itself, guarded by descendents of the Saviour-King's own earthly family. Antrobus II was chosen exclusively for this privilege, and you must see how it will look if the planet seems to slight such an honour. I assume that no one here would seriously like to be accused of Conspiracy to Foment Planet-Wide Heresy? You would be risking your lives at a minimum, and the entire Council's replacement too. I apologise for the interruption.'

Mephistopheles sat down, gesturing Rimbrant to do the same. Rimbrant, somewhat mollified, did so. There was silence around the table, then Aurelius spoke.

'Thank you, Sir,' he said. 'I, too, am of the opinion that the *Divine Devotions* exhibition lies at the heart of the matter, and that Imperial City has been singled out because of it. I believe that the attacks we just witnessed were carried out to put the faithful off travelling to the exhibition when it opens. I believe further attacks may be planned on the Imperial Museum itself. I do agree that we should certainly not cancel the exhibition, but it might still be wise to delay its opening until we have found out more about the attacker and tried to neutralise him.'

Rimbrant opened his mouth to speak, then thought better of it.

'Very well', said Tollius, 'the proposition is that we delay the opening of the exhibition for, what, a fortnight? Or until Governor Aurelius deems it safe to open. Sergeant Byrrion, you will treble the number of Vigilants on patrol in Imperial City, and arrest any and all suspicious characters. We need to retain the public's confidence. You will also assist Professor Rimbrant with his security: I want the Vigilants to be alert and obvious in and around the museum. We will not allow the Saviour-King's image to be besmirched. And we will track down that ... that 'Angel of Death', and destroy it utterly. Are we in agreement?'

Melching spoke up. 'What if we are completely wrong about this, and the attack has nothing to do with the exhibition? What if Imperial City was chosen this time just to divert us from the real target?'

Tollius considered the notion, then said, 'Colonel Helbrad, please call up your Militariat reservists and ensure that all observation points are manned and all personnel and equipment are fully prepared and ready for quick deployment anywhere on the planet, in case Melching is onto something. You are now on full military operational status. Commissioner Bennett, please ensure all Vigilants planet-wide are recalled from leave until the situation changes. Well, Gentlemen?'

There were nods and mutters of agreement from all around the table.

'The meeting is closed', said Tollius, 'Remain watchful and dutiful.'

Shortly afterwards, huge desert silos began to open, and a host of military vehicles were driven out into the late afternoon sun. Engines and fuel tanks were checked, missile tubes and cannons were loaded, tires were pumped and ball-bearings and connection points were lubricated and tested. With military precision, thousands of men loaded and checked small-arms weaponry, armour, clothing and personnel safety equipment. Camouflage nets were opened, examined, and, where necessary, repaired. Immensely-scaled combat drills and invasion scenarios were practiced on the desert sands that encased much of the planet's equator and southern hemisphere. Vulture fighter planes and other aircraft practiced attack runs and defensive manoeuvres. Results were reported back to Helbrad's office through the advanced satellite communications network surrounding the planet, as more and more Militariat reservists arrived to take their places in Antrobus II's efficient military machine. Meanwhile, Vigilants personnel arrived in force at regional armouries and fortresses across the world, and Urban Riot armoured personnel carriers were serviced and loaded with ammunition and missiles before emerging through the reinforced gates of the Vigilants' fortresses and onto the cities' streets.

The *Enclave* watched the planet prepare for war from their murky, hidden base, and a disembodied and somewhat grating voice sang happily to itself.

Back in the hospital Shenaria began to stir, twitching uncomfortably. Modesty leaned over from her seat by the bed and gripped Shenaria's hand. 'Relax', soothed Modesty, as Matthias came over from the window to stand beside her. Shenaria's features calmed, and her body settled, then she licked her lips and began to speak.

'Modesty…Matthias…'

'We're here, Princess', said Matthias. 'You okay?'

Shenaria nodded. 'My eyes…' she said.

'Don't open them', advised Modesty, 'they're bandaged.'

'You look terrible', added Matthias, 'but, by the Saviour-King, I'm glad to see you!'

Shenaria grinned, and turned her head towards Matthias' voice.

'You always say such nice things', she smiled, then sat up shakily. Modesty supported her. She waited until her head stopped ringing, then asked, 'How many survived?'

'Not enough', replied Matthias. 'We saw what happened on tele-vid. I thought you were a gonna.'

'I nearly was', said Shenaria. 'I was in the first carriage, and saw the hideous thing approach. When it knocked us off the tracks I thought that was it.'

'How did you survive?' asked Modesty.

'I smashed the window as the coach went over, and threw myself through it. I managed to grab the rail as the coach fell past. Those poor people. I hung there, watching the thing, then pulled myself up. It didn't see me at first. Then, when it went for me, I jumped down and managed to break my fall. But I guess that's when I passed out. I must have seemed just another corpse.'

'What happened to your eyes? asked Matthias.

'You can't…you can't look at it directly', said Shenaria, her voice wavering as she remembered the ghastly, drooling apparition advancing towards her. 'Its eyes are like suns. Its face…it had the most evil face I've ever seen', she finished. 'I never really believed that people could die from fright before', she added, 'but I believe it now. It was here to frighten us; I'm sure of that. It was meant to panic us into some kind of response.'

'It didn't frighten you', said Matthias. Shenaria grinned.

'Come on, Matthias; you know better than that. I was terrified. But being terrified has never stopped me doing the Saviour-King's work. And I think I might have done something useful.'

'What?' asked Matthias.

'I threw a tracer at it', replied Shenaria. 'I don't know if it hit, and there are a lot of other 'ifs' too, but if they're all alright, we may be able to track it down.'

'You never cease to amaze me', said Matthias, genuinely impressed.

'Now, you two', said Shenaria, 'fill me in about what's gone on.'

They did so. Modesty told her about the projected movements and patterns of Antrobus II's solar system – a minor sun-storm was on its way, though it looked like its effects would be minimal – and Matthias told her what he had found out about the Imperial Museum staff. This was not much so far, except that Rimbrant seemed to have his own personal staff too, and these would need to be checked as well. Most of Rimbrant's staff had originated on the world of Sappharus, which was where the *Divine Devotions* collection had first exhibited. It was also, coincidently, where the architect who had been commissioned to design the Imperial Museum's new Worship Wing, Sejanius, hailed from.

Shenaria didn't believe in coincidences.

'Sappharus will need visiting. Matthias, you investigate Rimbrant's personal staff; Modesty, you look into Sejanius. Try to get some copies of his previous designs, please: they may be significant.'

They sat with her for a while longer, until Shenaria told them off for wasting time.

'Time to go', she said, this won't wait'.

Much to Matthias' and Modesty's consternation, Shenaria removed the drip from her arm and lowered her legs to the ground, grimacing slightly.

'My clothes, please', she said, 'Matthias, if you wouldn't mind'.

Matthias looked away while Modesty helped Shenaria dress – though he was quite aware of her body in the room's mirror, and made sure that he observed the location of her injuries carefully. He would not let her down again.

'Are you sure this is a good idea?' asked Modesty, as the three of them made their through the sad and crowded hospital corridors towards the exit, Shenaria holding their arms for guidance and support.

'I am still a servant of the Saviour-King', replied Shenaria, 'and since I have been spared, unlike these unhappy folk, I will remain devoted to him. I never got as far as the *Divine Devotions* exhibition, so that is where I'll head.

'But your eyes', reminded Modesty.

'Well', said Shenaria, 'I guess Tru-D will just have to come with me. I'm sure they'll let guide dogs into the museum - even if they aren't entirely canine.'

Eighteen light-years away on the large and prosperous red planet Sappharus, just as the evening crimson sky darkened into black, two men approached a prestigious modern building that practically showed off its affluent and eye-catching architecture, and rang the brass, polished doorbell that was shaped like an angel. Some seconds passed, then the door was answered by an expensively-dressed but unshaven man in early middle-age. The man squinted through his designer spectacles at the two men leaning disrespectfully on the pillars surrounding the doorway, one slim, dapper and elegant, the other burly, ungainly and chewing, both back-lit by the planet's large, dramatic moon.

'Yes?'

'Mr. Sejanius?'

'Yes?'

'Good evening, Mr. Sejanius. I'm Mr. Winter, and this is Mr. Kydd.

CHAPTER FIVE

Matthias and Modesty touched down upon the surface of Sappharus just as the sun was beginning to set. They had conferred together in their private cabin throughout the journey, and had finished their preparations. Matthias had double-checked Modesty's equipment, and she had done the same for him. Matthias' belt buckle concealed his miniature, always carried, *H-Dini* tools and his nerve-dagger rested in a sheath under his sleeve. Modesty wore her familiar midnight-blue cat-suit with her sleek and delicately deadly Punishment Needles concealed in her wrist-bands, though her deadliest weapon remained her body itself. They separated as they left the air terminus, Matthias reminding Modesty to summon him if she got in to any trouble, and Modesty gently teasing Matthias by suggesting that he would need to call her first.

Modesty arrived at the first of the addresses they had tracked down during their inter-planetary flight. She found herself in a tree-lined boulevard in a well-heeled part of the planet's second city, Helix. In front of her stood a sky-scraper lit by a combination of the rising moon and harsh street lights, all flash and show, and no subtlety in its lines or materials at all. It was singularly garish to Modesty's taste; a modern architect's building. She circled the structure, observing the entrances, the cameras, the possible locations of any alarms. Finally, she stood between the doorway's two pillars, her eyes drawn to the unusual angel-shaped doorbell. Trained by Shenaria, she committed its design to her memory. For some reason it disturbed her slightly, but she couldn't put her finger on why. She was just about to ring the bell herself when she heard the noise.

It was faint, but definite, and Modesty listened closely, her head against the door. There it was again, and this time Modesty could make out a sequence of sounds being repeated: a thud, a grunt or groan, and a muttering of voices. She closed her eyes, trying to determine the location of the noises. Then she left the door, crept round to the west of the building, and began climbing the wall.

Past the first floor she went, then the second, then the third, then the fourth. Utilising a convenient ledge barely deep enough for her toes, she balanced herself around the sky-scaper until she was adjacent to one of the windows the sounds emanated from.

During her training as an assassin Modesty had mastered the art of *ninjutsu* – of being within a person's range of vision, yet remaining unseen; of blending with the surroundings so unobtrusively that she seemed part of them. Anyone who viewed her while she was in this state would simply not realise that they had seen her – and then it would be too late for them.

Silently, slowly, moving as if her body was fluid, not solid, she gradually became a part of the building. Her lithe frame matched the contours of the architecture surrounding her. One moment she was outside the window, the next she was part of the window frame itself. Nothing concealed her from the gaze of the men in the room except her own stillness and willpower – but that was enough.

She took in the scene that unfolded in front of her. To her left was a tall, thin weasel of a man, dressed in smart clothes that, to her educated eyes, were slightly too small for him. He stood, one hand resting on the back of a large, soft armchair to the front of him, one hand holding a lit cigarillo. His dyed-blonde, slicked-back hair showed his vanity. He spoke in what he obviously considered an educated, affected drawl, but Modesty could detect his actual poor sink-estate background easily.

Some feet away to the right stood another man, quite different in appearance. He was burly and thick-set, and ungainly in his movements. It was clear that he was the brute of the pair, with the other being the control; but both were simply low-level street thugs to Modesty. Right now he stood, adjusting a knuckle-duster with exaggerated detail, and smirking towards the man half-sitting, half-lying in the chair.

The man's clothes had been ripped and torn, and his face didn't look any better. A trickle of blood dripped steadily from a recently broken nose. Vicious cuts and bruises on his face bore testament to the knuckle-duster's work. The man grunted heavily as the short, thick-set man delivered a powerful blow to his stomach, and was sick over the arm of the expensively-upholstered chair.

'I said, lissen to Mr. Winter', whistled the thug through his teeth, 'we don' like wastin' time.'

'Now, now, Mr. Kydd', drawled the tall man, 'we don't want Mr. Sejanius to suffer unnecessarily, do we? Mr. Sejanius, I'll ask you again: where are your private documents? Identity papers, Confirmation of Birth: that sort of thing.'

Sejanius' head lolled with effort, then he turned to face Winter, with puke still on his chin.

'Money…' he said, with difficulty, 'lots of it. Take it. Take it all. Just…don't hit me again! I'll pay double, treble, what you're being paid now. Please…'

Winter pretended to consider the offer.

'Hmm. What do you think, Mr. Kydd? Shall we take the money and run?'

He leaned his face so close to Sejanius that the architect got the full benefit of his appalling halitosis.

'The trouble is, you see; then we'd be fugitives from the *Enclave*. And when the *Enclave* want you, they find you. Just like we've found you. So, sorry, Mr. Sejanius, it's tempting, but no deal. So, I'll ask you politely one more time: where are your papers? I'll count to ten, then Mr. Kydd will break the little finger on your left hand. Then the next finger. Then the next finger. Once Mr. Kydd runs out of fingers, he'll consider where to start next. Pulling out your nails, perhaps? He's got a sadistic imagination, haven't you Mr. Kydd? So: one; two, three…'

It was at this point that Modesty knew that, whatever was going on, she would kill these men, if only to release the universe from the torture of their laboured dialogue.

'Wait…' pleaded Sejanius, 'you've made a mistake. The *Enclave* were pleased with my work. I did exactly what they wanted. I did my best work for them. My masterpiece. Please…I've remained loyal. Let me speak to Mephistopheles. He'll tell you.'

Kydd pulled Sejanius forwards, then head-butted him back into the chair, causing another piteous squeal of agony.

'Now lissen, you turd! We're through messin' about! The *Enclave* want you dead! You can have it easy, or have it tough: 's up to you. Now, Mr. Winter here has asked for your papers. He won' want to ask you again. Where are they?'

Winter left the side of the chair and crossed over to the front of it, looking menacingly at Sejanius all the while. He was now between Modesty and Sejanius, with his back towards her. 'I do advise you to listen to Mr. Kydd, and respect what he says', he said gently.

Sejanius breathed hard, then gestured weakly with his one good hand.

'St...Study', he said. 'Box...Angel...'

He closed his eyes and lolled in his blood-stained chair. Winter nodded to Kydd.

'Awright', said Kydd, and left the room. Winter lifted Sejanius' chin in a cruel grip. Sejanius' eyes bulged as he seemed to see, impossibly, the window-frame uncoil itself behind Winter, and glide towards his back. He let out a muffled start.

'The *Enclave* thank you for your assistance', whispered Winter, snapping open a flick-knife, 'and grant you your just reward.' He thrust the knife forwards viciously, but, as he did so, he felt a frostbite-cold pinprick of intense agony pierce his shoulder to the bone. He cried out and dropped his weapon. Astonishingly, he felt the cold and the pain creep rapidly through his arm and back, and begin spreading to his neck and lower limbs. He felt himself being turned over, as the paralysis crept further around and into his body, and found himself looking into piercing blue eyes that were all the more alarming for their complete impassiveness.

Modesty propped Winter's frame up so it half-rested on Sejanius and half-rested on the base of the chair and made sure his rapidly degenerating eyes could see her. She searched through his clothes, removing a wallet, a vengeance-gun and two hidden knives, then turned to look at him.

'You are dying', she said, simply. 'Your paralysis will spread. You will lose all dignity. Soon you will have trouble breathing, and will die of asphyxiation. It will hurt – more than anything has hurt you before. Blink if you understand.'

Winter blinked. Sejanius looked at them both, unsure which to be most afraid of.

'I can stop this happening', Modesty continued. 'You will have one chance only to do exactly as I say and save your life. Blink if you understand.'

Again Winter blinked, with more difficulty this time.

'Good', said Modesty. 'Answer my questions immediately, truthfully and without hesitation, and I will save you. Do otherwise and I will make it worse.' She touched his chest with what looked like the tiniest of needles. Winter lurched forward involuntarily and opened his mouth in a rictus of agony. Modesty regarded him.

'Why are you here?'

'K…Kill Sejanius', slurred Winter, 'Retrieve box of papers.'

'What papers?'

'His identity…the plans…'

'Plans of what?'

'Don't…know, jus' all plans…'

'Who sent you?'

Winter closed his eyes, and did not answer. Modesty touched the Punishment Needle to his chest again. He gurgled, agonised.

'Who?'

'The *Enclave*. The Voice…'

'Whose voice?'

'L'v…L'v…' began Winter, then his body jerked backwards with the impact of the bullet that went right through him. Kydd had returned to the room. Modesty had heard the *click* of his vengeance-gun as the trigger was depressed, and had curved her back and neck ever so slightly, but just enough for Kydd's shot to miss her. Instantly she was on her feet, facing the door, but Kydd's feet could be heard as they ran away as fast as they could. She sprang to the corridor, in time to see him crash into the far wall at the corner of the stairwell in his haste, and drop a wooden box as he did so. Her acute ears heard him descend through the building. She crossed to the window to see him dash into the street below, climb hurriedly into a land-car, and desperately drive away.

She returned to Winter. He was dead. She realised that the shot had passed through him and penetrated Sejanius too. She rolled Winter's corpse off the chair and began to see what she could do for Sejanius.

'No…too late…' he said, feebly brushing her hand away as it tried to loosen his shirt around the spreading blood. 'Th..thank you anyway…'

'Mr. Sejanius', said Modesty, 'You are dying. Do you need to absolve yourself before the Saviour-King?'

Even dying, he was startled by her words. 'Who…' he said, 'Who are you?'

'Sanctification', replied Modesty, and the man shuddered as he closed his eyes.

'Of course…' he gasped, almost as if expecting her answer. 'I should have known you'd get me in the end…Yes…I have betrayed the Saviour-King, and I most earnestly repent…I don't want…to suffer eternal damnation…'

'Tell me', demanded Modesty, 'and perhaps your soul can still be saved.'

He nodded, weakly. 'Alright…The commission…perfect…so perfect…almost divine…My ancestor's work…I unearthed it…I used it…'

'What was your ancestor's work?'

Sejanius was gulping for air now, his throat making hideous wheezing noises. His hands flailed with no apparent purpose except to hold onto life. Suddenly, his body jerked upwards and forwards, tense and rigid, then collapsed onto Modesty's shoulder as the life left it. As it did so, his mouth breathed one last word into her ear. It sounded like 'tampal'.

Modesty lowered his corpse back into the chair where it had sat, and stood up. She scanned the room for any other sources of danger, then walked into the corridor and retrieved the heavy mahogany box that Kydd had dropped.

It was cuboid in shape, about two feet long and eight inches high. Black metal corners and studs reinforced it, and two black metal catches held the lid down. The wood was worked with some skill, and an intricate relief of an angel decorated the box's roof. It was locked.

Modesty put the box down, then crossed back to Sejanius and methodically searched his body. Around his neck she found a gold metal chain with two small black keys hanging from it. She unclasped the chain and tried the keys in the two locks. They fitted. She sat down and, carefully, opened the box.

❧

Matthias' first trip had been to the city's Hall of Records, where he had diligently collected data on Rimbrants' personal staff. It transpired that the great majority of them had previously studied under Rimbrant in Sappahrus' renowned *Collegia Baccalaureate*. None of these worthies had so much as a parking ticket or illegitimate pregnancy to blemish their records, and Matthias grimaced in distaste as he read one faultless and dull resume after another. But, just when he thought that the *Collegia Baccalaureate* could really do with one of Mistress Delicata's sector-famous orgies to liven it up, he came across an interesting detail.

He had leafed through the *Collegia's* old yearbooks almost as an afterthought, when his eye had noticed something. An entry about a student, Verulam, who would later become one of Rimbrant's staff, quoted a few lines from Verulam himself. Verulam had joked about the good times he had shared with his fellow 'Dems', and wished them good luck for the future. Checking more carefully, Matthias found that one or two more yearbook entries relating to names on his list referred to 'Dems'. No official description or record of what these Dems were could be found in the documents Matthias had to hand, but some deft computer hacking soon gave him access to confidential *Collegia* documents, where he tracked down the following memo:

From:	Misericord, Principal of the *Collegia Baccalaureate*
To:	All tutors, sages and security personnel
Date:	13-11-21,992
Subject:	The Dimension Society

Dear Colleagues,

We note with extreme distaste that the founders of the above fraternity society were last week found guilty of associating with known heretics and disseminating incendiary and corrupt materials, and rejoice in their swift executions.

From this moment on, the Dimension Society is abolished. All materials and resources granted to this fraternity group are withdrawn. Any student citing allegiance to the Dimension Society will be expelled from the *Collegia* and reported to the authorities immediately. The names of all previously known members will be passed on to the Vigilants to support their investigations.

Be warned! Any colleagues who refuse to comply with this instruction will be dealt with in the same manner. We will *not* allow our revered institute of learning to be used by any sympathisers of the corrupt or heretic.

From this moment, no mention of the Dimension Society in any *Collegia* records or discussions will be tolerated. They are *Persona Non Grata* and will not be acknowledged. That is all.

Misericord

Matthias printed the document out and searched further, but no extra information about the Dimension Society could be found. He noted that this society had been abolished long before any of the people he was trying to trace had attended the *Collegia*. He decided to keep an open mind about whether Verulam's 'Dems' were connected to the Dimension Society in some obscure way, or whether they were unimportant and something else entirely.

Some hours later, tired and irritable after so much paper-pushing and screen-work, Matthias left the Hall of Records and stretched his legs under the moon-lit sky. The only person he had not found any information on was Rimbrant's special envoy, Mephistopheles, and, for the moment, he was weary of looking. He wondered how Modesty was doing, and considered radioing her to check, but the thought of the teasing he would have to endure for this soon made him change his mind. He decided to change the focus of his investigation, and began to make his way towards the Grand Cathedral, which was where the

Divine Devotions collection had first exhibited four years ago.

Twenty minutes later he arrived outside the cathedral, which covered the entire surface of the hill situated in the centre of Helix. Even in the intense blackness of the night the cathedral was impressive. Its buttresses, arched doorways and windows and graven figures looked down upon all the inhabitants of the city, as if to remind them that the vision of the Saviour-King was always upon them. The immense structure dominated the horizon from all corners of the city, and Matthias had simply followed his eyes to reach it. Now he stood under the arches, gothic spires and unpleasant gargoyles that wrapped the surface of the cathedral, highlighted most dramatically under the silver moon. Commemorative and devotional inscriptions were carved into every stone, and Matthias ran his fingers along some of them, his spiritual side finding a moment of expression. He closed his eyes and silently prayed to the Saviour-King for a moment, then straightened up and reverently opened one of the huge cathedral doors.

As soon as he stepped inside, he knew that something was wrong. It was not so much anything he saw or heard, but that the feeling was wrong. Normally, when Matthias went into a Valhallan cathedral a sense of peace and belonging would descend upon him as soon as he entered – regardless of the time of day or what was happening in his life. That feeling was absent now, and worse, it had been replaced by a feeling of queasiness and rejection.

He waited until his eyes adjusted to the near-darkness, ensuring that his body was in cover from any foe whose eyes would already be used to the low light. Then he peered around the large stone pillar and looked towards the main altar and stained-glass windows at the far end of the cathedral. His eyes took in the shadowy shapes of the devotional carvings, the gorgeous silverwork, the rows of benches for the faithful and penitent to give their thanks for the blessings of the Saviour-King, the winged pulpit in the shape of a large golden Pyramid (the symbol of the Saviour-King's ascent of Mount Valhalla), the majestic organ, whose pipes twisted around each other in a metaphor of vast human crowds finding a common direction and purpose in worship of the Saviour-King, the huge, uneven stone slabs that constituted the floor – many of which acted as tombstones and memorial plaques for Helix's dead Valhallan heroes and ecclesiastical leaders. All seemed as it should be, except for Matthias' strange and unwelcome feelings of unease and resistance.

Without warning, an excruciating pounding started in Matthias' head, and he sunk to the floor in the main aisle, his hands over his face, groaning. He rubbed his temples, trying to relieve himself of the pain and, squeezed his eyes open and closed, trying to get them to focus. Even in his discomfort he was aware of how vulnerable he was, kneeling there on the stone floor, and attempted to raise himself up. He grabbed the back of one of the long benches, and managed to drag himself along it. He lay down, hidden from sight, and, with a great effort of will, quietened his breathing.

The pounding was not just in Matthias' head. Now it could be heard more definitely and clearly, as it emanated from the fluted speakers concealed in the metal angels and gargoyles that dotted the walls and pillars of the great cathedral. It sounded like bass drums, low organ notes and deep male chants mixed together as one. It was soon joined by a treble concoction of sounds – female voices, tambourines, harps, bells. The sounds were sickening, literally, and Matthias struggled to not give in to the impulse to vomit.

Then the air itself changed, misting and thickening. Matthias had one real start of alarm when the stench hit him; it reminded him forcibly of the poison gas deployed against his old unit during the campaign on Magda, and he was without his protective gas-mask here. His eyes began to water, stinging, and his mouth dried. He was still lying prone, face-down on the bench. His arm reached down and brought up a thick, beautifully embroidered hassock, and he buried his head in it, using the material as an improvised filter to breathe through.

Thankfully, the dreadful stench seemed to dissipate, or at least move away, and Matthias blinked away the last painful tears and took some deep mouthfuls of the, he hoped, more breathable air. The strange feelings that he had experienced on entering the cathedral were still present, but now they seemed centred, like a compass needle, on something exterior to him. This in itself reassured Matthias: one of his greatest fears was corruption or desertion of the soul, and to not feel sanctified when walking into a cathedral had seemed to him like a portent of the withdrawal of the Saviour-King's blessing. Now the peculiar sensations seemed at least to have a definite focus, which itself seemed to pass where Matthias lay hidden and proceed towards the main altar.

He gambled a look, squinting through small gaps and knot-holes in the bench. He saw, some feet in front of him, the backs of hooded, caped figures. These were comprised of all sizes, and Matthias deduced that men, women and children too were all present.

They shuffled along, facing away from Matthias and towards the altar, so he didn't see any of their faces. It suddenly occurred to him that he could see at all, and that the almost complete blackness of earlier had been replaced with a sickly, bilious-green light. He risked peering over the back of the bench in front to get a more informative view.

Now, the chanting had intensified, and the foul congregation had started clapping their hands slowly and rhythmically. In front of them, several steps away from the altar a figure stood that seemed ten feet tall. He gazed at the majestic scenes from the Saviour-King's rise and sacrifice that were portrayed in the huge stained glass windows at the back of the cathedral. He stretched out one unnaturally long and pointed arm towards them.

'Willing servants and devotees', the figure declaimed, 'Gaze at these revered pictures. Gaze at them well. The truth is about to be revealed.'

Matthias watched as the figure's cape and cowl were removed by three female devotees. The extended man stood there, naked, but looking as if all his skin had been removed. Revolted, Matthias made the sign of the Pyramid to himself.

'Matildia, Francisi, Jessila, come here', commanded the figure.

Three figures moved forwards and removed their cloaks, revealing themselves to be young women in advanced stages of pregnancy. They, too, were naked. As if they had practiced for this moment, they glided to the main altar and leant back on it, so their heads, arms and breasts lay on the top of the altar, with the rest of their frames exposed at its front.

Matthias could see what was about to happen, and grimaced. His every instinct was to prevent the unnatural sacrifice of the three women, but he knew such an attempt would very likely fail, and simply add another sacrifice to the ceremony. But he couldn't sit back and do nothing! He thought, hard, considering all the elements of the scene surrounding him, as Shenaria had taught him to do. An idea came to him. A long-shot. His one chance was that the freakishly tall figure would embark upon a liturgy of some kind before killing the women. A few minutes were all he would need, but there was no guarantee that he would get them.

Thankfully (thought Matthias to himself, ruefully), the extended man began chanting and declaiming, with the congregation joining in with systematic replies and gestures. The language that was used began to change from Valhallan into something that did not even seem human, and back again. The gathering swayed and chanted, clapped and groaned, as the three young women writhed as if in ecstasy. The leader of ceremonies unsheathed and brandished a wickedly long and curved sabre, and the crowd fell absolutely silent. The only sounds were the horrible pounding that still emanated from the concealed speakers and the sighs and gasps coming from the three trembling victims. The extended man stretched out his arm and pointed once again to the cathedral's stained glass windows.

Incredibly, the millennia-old images crafted into the cathedral's windows seemed to waver and change. Colours began to melt over each other. Shapes blended and merged. Strips of lead piping that separated segments of the windows from each other began to twist. Even the depictions of the Saviour-King began to lose their definition.

Matthias, appalled, had had enough. The extended man, now jabbering in a language that Matthias couldn't understand, raised his sword, and at the same time Matthias acted.

At once, a shocking, overwhelmingly loud and ear-splitting blast of feedback screeched through the cathedral's speakers, breaking ear-drums, making people thrash around in sudden shock and agony, and collide with each other. People fell over as their cloaks got caught in the flailing limbs, and screamed at the noise and the confusion. Several of the gathering convulsed with strokes or heart attacks. The three women whimpered and fell off the altar, covering their ears. The extended man screamed out, stretched both his arms out into the air, and burst. Some ruptured speakers fell away from the walls and pillars, bringing down pieces of metal and concrete on the assemblage below. Side-windows of the cathedral shattered. Some people panicked, and began to run for the exit. Others simply curled up and howled.

Matthias emerged from small alcove, the two thick hassocks held over each of his ears for protection now being allowed to fall to the floor. He moved, alert for threats and ready for combat. He watched as the gathering fell into confusion and either collapsed or fled. No one seemed a danger to him.

He made his way up a side-aisle that led to the Lady Chapel, and then to the main altar. The extended man was now an exploded man, and pieces of his revolting body covered the floor and adjacent furniture. The three women he had tried to save lay still, and he was unsure if they were dead or not. One of the gathering, furious and tearful, rushed towards Matthias, dagger in hand, but soon fell back, clutching a fatal wound to the stomach. Other members of the crowd, seeing this, fled. Matthias considered capturing one of them, but then one of the young women stirred, and he knelt beside her.

Her face was deadly pale, and her breathing forced and difficult. Her eyes fluttered, then she slipped back into unconsciousness. Matthias supported her gently, then reached out for an abandoned cloak and covered her with it.

He stood up and gazed at the stained-glass windows. They were exactly the same as they had always been. He rubbed his eyes, and looked again. They were as permanent and solid as he would have expected. He rubbed his eyes again, putting the hallucination down to the effects of the gas he had been breathing.

As he was rubbing his eyes the second time, a heavy blow hit him on the back of the head, and he keeled over, landing next to the pregnant woman he had helped.

The other two women stood behind him, trembling, still naked. One brandished the chunk of broken pillar she had knocked Matthias out with. The other looked at her with pupil-less eyes.

'Take him to the Dems', she said.

CHAPTER SIX

Back in Imperial City, security was the utmost priority. The gates of the city's seven Vigilants fortresses had opened, and all – save the reserve force – of the Vigilants' *Defender* APCs had deployed onto the city's streets. Checkpoints had been set up at all primary traffic intersection points. Snipers covered the immediate area surrounding the Imperial Museum from adjacent rooftops. Vigilants patrolled the streets on foot and bike, and rode all trains both over and underground. Citizens entering into what Sergeant Byrrion had termed 'the danger zone' risked being questioned, searched and having their possessions removed without warning. Observation points manned by Militariat personnel were set up around the perimeter of the city, so that the first sighting of any creature like the one that carried out the attacks of the previous day could be followed by immediate military action.

Already that morning there had been several attempts at further attacks. It was as if yesterday's destruction and the appearance of the 'Angel of Death' had been taken as signals for action by the various crazies, malignants and heretics that infested the city. An armoured land-car had attempted to ram and set fire to the museum, only to have been destroyed by a well-aimed volley of mortar shots. A man wearing a defiled priest's vestments and spouting hateful gibberish had attempted to set off several powerful grenades as he walked up towards the Worship Wing's formal gardens: a well-aimed sniper shot had evaporated his head before he could do so. Three copycat attempts had been made to derail carriages on the city's monorail system, the people attempting this had been riddled with bullets from well-placed Defenders. Unfortunately, a genuine team of railway workers just beginning to carry out maintenance work at a junction point were also gunned down: it emerged later that their supervisor had forgotten to inform the Vigilants about the planned repairs. Sergeant Byrrion was sorry about their deaths but unrepentant about his overall strategy: as well as keeping the city and museum safe, his chief duty was to prevent further attacks or uprisings, and, as far as he was concerned, fear of harsh reprisal was his best weapon.

As if the tension in the city wasn't high enough as a result of the previous day's attacks, Byrrion knew that in a matter of days a huge, majestic craft would descend from space and open to reveal a group of the legendary First Valhallans. No living person on Antrobus II had ever seen one of these fabled descendants of the earthly family of the Saviour-King. Byrrion had no idea how the presence of figures straight out of Valhallan mythology would affect the populace, but he thought it best to be prepared for the worst. Their presence might reassure or stimulate a burst of loyalty and patriotism from the crowds, or it might unleash fears of attack and drive them into unnecessary panic. In addition, the very presence of the First Valhallans on Antrobus II might be enough to drive the heretic and treacherous into ever-more audacious and wanton acts of violence and destruction.

Inside the museum the tension was hardly less. Rimbrant shuddered every time the vibrations of a passing Defender APC could be felt through the building, and cast anxious looks towards his precious exhibits, as if to check that they had not been harmed. Museum and exhibition staff, all of whom had suffered poor journeys to the building only to have been searched roughly as they arrived, were not in the best of moods. Mephistopheles found that his power to calm people down was stretched to its limit, but he persisted even though the effort was tiring. It was imperative that the exhibition opened as planned, so he did everything he could to make things run smoothly. His own patience was wearing thin, however, particularly with Rimbrant, whose highly-strung manner grew more unpalatable by the hour. Rimbrant bristled with annoyance at the presence of Vigilants personnel, and seemed to take it as a personal insult that his glorious collection should be subjected to their invasion. He had already lectured one poor officer on the destruction that would occur should the officer deign to fire his weapon within the building, and how the officer and Vigilants as a whole would be sued for any damages that might occur. The officer had not yet learnt what all Rimbrant's staff knew well – not to answer

Rimbrant back – and had patiently commented that his duty was to the security of the exhibition, and that he would only fire his weapon as a last resort. This simply prompted Rimbrant into a further torrent of complaint, until the officer was reduced to seriously considering what story he could tell to convincingly explain why he had had to shoot him.

It was into this atmosphere of tension and ill-temper that the city council's Citizens' Well-Being representative arrived, and demanded to speak with Rimbrant. On receiving the message from one of his staff, Rimbrant was beside himself with fury: his exhibition had been targeted by heretics, delayed by the planetary high council and besmirched by armed Vigilants personnel. Now it was to be answerable to a low-level regulation-loving paper-pusher. It was beyond belief, and he said as much. He instructed the unfortunate lackey to conduct the Citizen's Well-Being official to his private office, where he could give him a clear and explicit piece of his mind.

As he entered his office, he was surprised to see a short, raven-haired, perfectly-proportioned woman wearing dark eye-filters and accompanied by a golden collie-shaped cyber-hound. It seemed that the official either was blind or had severe vision impairments. The woman stood patiently by an austere wooden chair in the respectably-sized room, while her cyber-hound panted. It growled warningly and bared its titanium teeth as Rimbrant walked in.

'Easy, Tru-D', said Shenaria.

No word had come yet from either Matthias or Modesty on Sappharus as Shenaria had prepared for her morning's work, though she had not really expected to hear from them so soon. She had removed the bandages covering her eyes, and, with the aid of one of her staff, Miri, had bathed and tested her eyesight. Her vision was not completely gone: she was aware of colours and shadows, but shapes had no definition. For a moment she wondered whether she had lost proper sight forever, and considered how such a change might affect her work, then shrugged these questions away as unprofitable and self-centred. Miri put her clothes and equipment out for her according to her specific instructions, then left her for a while.

When Miri returned she had brought Tru-D with her. Tru-D was a cyber-hound that Shenaria had had constructed partly using DNA extracted from the remains of a dog she had had and loved throughout her childhood and teenage years. The dog had been devoted to her as long as it had lived, and Shenaria had considered its faithfulness to her as a model of that which should be given to the Saviour-King by his subjects. Once it had died, Shenaria had returned its loyalty to her by giving it a new life in a different form. The cyber-hound now licking Shenaria's hand was not her original dog, but it was of her, and Shenaria considered its existence as the repayment of a debt. Tru-D had also been continually adapted to further Shenaria's work as a Sanctifier, and it had qualities and abilities that were not obvious at first hand: the cyber-hound now at Shenaria's side had recently had its fourth upgrade. Now Shenaria stood in Rimbrant's office, only partly masquerading as the vision-impaired person with a guide-dog that she appeared to be.

'What idiocy will they think of next?' said Rimbrant, rudely, 'A blind person to check the museum for health and safety!'

'Professor Rimbrant, I presume?' said Shenaria, offering her hand, which Rimbrant ignored. 'I'm Melodia Praxis, from the City Office for Citizens' Well-being and Security. I trust you were told of my impending visit.'

'I certainly was not, young lady, until this very minute. Do you not think this could have waited? The city is already making such a fuss about nothing! I have to suffer security personnel everywhere I go. I don't see what good a blind woman could add to the situation! I shall complain to the council about their unwarranted interference and nosiness. 'Citizen's well-being' indeed!'

Tru-D growled, and Shenaria patted her gently, calming her.

'Professor Rimbrant, I understand that your exhibition has a reputation for the enlightenment of all Valhallan subjects, and that it has the power to strengthen faith and devotion to the Saviour-King. Is that correct?'

Rimbrant's chest puffed out in pride. 'It certainly is, young lady', he said, 'and that makes it all the more impertinent of your council to attempt to oversee it in this manner.'

'Professor Rimbrant', continued Shenaria calmly, 'is it then the truth that such enlightenment and strengthening is only available to sighted servants of the Saviour-King? Are you saying that those who are inflicted by blindness, or even those who have lost their sight in military service on behalf of the Saviour-King, have no welcome at your exhibition? That this collection is only for the already favoured? That faithful devotees of the Saviour-King, if they are injured or afflicted in some manner, may be told that they have no place here?'

Rimbrant paused, suddenly cautious and aware of where the conversation might lead. 'No, not at all', he said, more calmly this time. 'All the devout and faithful are welcome here, regardless of their, er, situation.'

Shenaria moved towards him and put out her hand. 'Professor, I would like to be able to report back how welcoming and helpful the exhibition is to all the Saviour-King's faithful. If a blind person such as I can appreciate the exhibition, and can manoeuvre around it in safety and comfort, then truly your great work is accessible for all, and you would deserve to be offered one of the city's highest honours. I must tell you that, as one of the Saviour-King's true subjects, I have been waiting with great eagerness to see this wonderful collection. I have read much about it, and marvel at your dedication. Professor Rimbrant, I would certainly appreciate it if you could guide me round.'

Shenaria had read Rimbrant correctly. He responded to her flattery like the vain man he was.

'It will be my pleasure', he said, and offered his arm for her to hold.

'Please don't worry about my dog', she added sweetly, 'she only attacks people when she thinks I'm in danger.'

Together they passed out of Rimbrant's office and back to the main entrance hall, Shenaria clutching Rimbrant's arm, Rimbrant explaining about the collection and Tru-D sniffing and turning her head to catch sight of everything. Rimbrant explained that he wanted her to get the full benefit of the exhibition, and so they would travel through the building in a certain order. The order, he said, was quite significant, and proceeded to explain how the exhibits were arranged in chronological, spatial and theological order. Visitors, he said, would move through the collection in a way that matched the first Valhallan explorations into space, the first colonisations, as well as in order of important historical and theological events. Consequently, the exhibition would lead people past some of the very first effigies and tributes to the Saviour-King ever made, even before the *Great Calamity* befell the Earth, and the Saviour-King ascended up Mount Valhalla to his final sacrifice and ultimately into Godhood. Then the exhibition would focus upon some of the first recognitions of the revealed Divinity of the Saviour-King, before sweeping visitors past later, more stylised and conventional representations. Afterwards would follow those dedications to the Saviour-King made by peoples and planets that had no direct history or experience of previous Valhallan culture: these tended to vary considerably, with the Saviour-King being depicted variously in the form of bird, spirit, golem, sun, or angel. Finally, explained Rimbrant, the exhibition would lead back, as if in a DNA helix, to where it began: to Earth and the Saviour-King as he was depicted and worshipped now.

Even with her vision impaired, Shenaria was conscious of distinct feelings coursing through her as she and Rimbrant made their way through the exhibition. She was very conscious of the directions they took and the patterns their movement traced. Without asking for Rimbrant's permission she occasionally ran her hands over some of the sculptures and reliefs, and would often ask him to describe in detail some paintings, etchings, glass-work or other dedications. Rimbrant, always a man ready to give a lecture, never tired of discussing the items on show, their artists and genesis, how they were received, how their planets of origin looked after and displayed them, the particular symbolism attached to certain of their attributes. Never had he found such an attentive audience, and he found himself reluctantly reconsidering the quality of Imperial City council staff.

Finally, after some hours, they reached the centre of the Worship Wing, and what was to be the pinnacle of the exhibition. Rimbrant guided Shenaria to a bench that oversaw an immensely well crafted and beautiful pedestal. Rimbrant explained about the statue that was right then on its way from the Temple of Valhalla itself. Shenaria sat, by this time genuinely overcome with humility and faith, but also completely aware of how the exhibition had promoted such heady feelings, even though she had hardly been able to see most of it. She told Rimbrant that she needed to rest for a moment, and asked if he leave her in quiet contemplation for a while. Rimbrant, pleased at her proper reaction to the exhibition, left her. She sat in a position of dedication and reverence, her head bowed towards where the giant effigy of the Saviour-King would be placed.

She continued sitting in the same position for a moment after Rimbrant had left, quietly praying to the Saviour-King, then sat up, not quite the dependent invalid she had so convincingly portrayed.

'Okay, Tru-D', she whispered, 'time to go to work.'

Elsewhere, a meeting was in progress, or, rather, a summoning. In a dark, shadowy room, people who could barely be seen sat anxiously around a large table, still shaped like an artist's easel, but now with splotches of hideous colours appearing upon it. No one present dared touch these evolving pools of colour, and the white-gloved servants deftly avoided placing any drinks or refreshments upon them. The Gathering were silent, waiting for the sickly light to appear and shine upon one of them. All hoped that the light would pass them by and leave them, concealed and safe, in the shadows. At least one knew that this was a forlorn hope.

As one, the Gathering became aware of an unnatural presence, as one would suddenly become aware of nausea or vertigo. Several people shuddered involuntarily. The dreaded light suddenly appeared, its source unclear, and shone directly on one of those present.

'Report', ordered a harsh echoing voice whose speaker could not be seen.

Clavicord stood, and wiped his forehead. 'The attacks by the Gargoyle have had the desired effects. First, the creature itself is well-fed, and is likely to sleep until needed again. Second, the attacks have caused the Planetary High Council to determine to defend the *Divine Devotions* exhibition, and devote many resources to its defence. Third, the Council have completely mobilised the Militariat, and called up all reservists.'

'So they will defend the exhibition', said the voice, greatly amused. 'How perfectly delightful! This is very good. You may sit, Clavicord'.

Clavicord sat, hurriedly. The light shone over another man, who stood.

'High Sanctifer Lord Crooker's Special Representative helped convince the Council that an invasion was not likely at the present time', he said.

'Thank you, Melching', said the voice, and Melching sat as the light moved away from him. 'I do love the Sanctification', continued the voice, 'and the way all Valhallan agencies defer to it. Well, it seems our meeting is almost at an end: most efficient, gentlemen. There only remains one further inquiry. Mr. Kydd.'

The sickly light fell on Kydd, who stood, trying not to tremble.

'I notice the absence of our Mr. Winter', declared the voice.

'He, er, he didn't make it. We got Sejanius, though. I shot 'im myself. 'E won't talk.'

'I see', said the voice, 'and Sejanius' papers?'

Mr. Kydd's face went white. He felt his bladder empty, and gripped the table edge for balance.

'Mr. Winter fouled up', he said. 'He 'ad the box – I got it for 'im myself! I shot Sejanius an' left, as we'd planned, expectin' Mr. Winter to follow me with the box. But he mus' have got clobbered by Sejanius before 'e died. He let 'is guard down. Or he betrayed us an' kep' the box for 'imself. I couldn't wait, as the shot was drawin' trouble. It's Mr. Winter you want, Boss. 'E's got the papers.'

There was silence, except for the drip-drip of urine falling from Kydd's trouser leg. The silence continued for a long time.

Finally, the voice spoke again. 'Thank you, Mr. Kydd. Mephistopheles?'

Mephistopheles rose, noting that the light still shone upon Mr. Kydd. He nodded towards the voice.

'Mephistopheles, you will track down Mr. Winter for us, and reacquire Sejanius' papers. In the meantime, please ensure that Mr. Kydd gets his due reward for his service last night for us. Mr. Kydd, if you would be so kind as to wait here, while your reward is brought in.

'Yes, Boss.'

The light went off. 'Thank you, Gentlemen. Mr Clavicord, I assume that all is still well with the woman?'

Clavicord nodded, and, eerily, the whole company felt the disembodied voice smile.

'Very good', it slithered, 'The *Enclave* will meet again just before the Day of Transformation. That is all.'

Once more the gathering felt a presence leave them, like a sudden relief from toothache, and once more they left. Kydd sat down at the table, careless that his arms leant in the pools of colour. Mephistopheles smiled at him, and he grinned back.

'S'okay', he said, weak with relief. 'I don't need no reward.'

'Oh, but you do', cooed Mephistopheles. 'I think it'll be quite to your taste. Enjoy!'

Mephistopheles left the room, leaving Kydd alone in it, still seated at the table. He looked round, wondering what his reward would be. He was pleased with himself, knowing that Winter, who couldn't talk, had taken the blame.

The door opened silently. In glided three absolutely stunning young women, lust and desire obvious in their expressions. They posed provocatively in the doorway, blonde, brunette and redhead, lascivious expressions on their faces. The brunette smiled at him, finger in mouth, while the redhead licked her lips. They began, slowly and teasingly, to make their way towards him.

'Well, this is lookin' up', said Kydd, an idiotic grin beginning to spread over his face. He made a forlorn attempt to straighten his tie and look presentable, hoping that the smell of his earlier disgrace would remain undetected. The three women swayed in front of him, tantalising him with their breasts, hips, legs. They opened and closed their mouths, looking at him with large eyes framed by impossibly long eyelashes. Every part of their barely clothed bodies seemed to shine and glimmer. They reached out to him, gently caressing his chest, his arms, his back. The blonde squeezed his thigh; the brunette breathed into his ear.

'Keep goin', ladies', smiled Kydd, then snapped, 'Ow!' as the brunette scratched his back. 'Mind the nails, Honey!' he yelled, then cried out again as the redhead scratched his thigh with all four fingers of her left hand. His eyes bulged as he saw the material of his trousers tear away as if it was nothing, and four quickly-flowing rivers of blood begin to cover his leg. The redhead bent down and sucked the leaking blood, looking up at him with large, innocent eyes. 'What is this?' exclaimed Kydd, and tried to rise, but the three women pushed him down. One, the blonde twisted her head all the way round as she bent towards his face, and he recoiled in alarm. Then he screamed, as piranha-sharp

83

teeth bit into his shoulders, arms and face. He began to yell again, only to have his tongue ripped away by an insistent mouth. The nails of three hands sunk deeply into his flesh, causing him to convulse and thrash his arms around. He tried to smash the women away, but they kept biting, tearing and piercing him all over his body. Blood spurted from a thousand tiny punctures, and cruel, deep gashes. His throat and skin began to burn from the acid that salivated out of the women. The strength of the women was immense, and he felt bones break as they squeezed and rubbed up against him. Before a vicious nail burst his eye he saw the redhead's face close up: it was a dreadful parody of a woman. Its pupils were shaped like those of a cat, its impossibly perfect cheekbones quivered as things seemed to fluctuate and move under the surface of the skin, its tongue and teeth were pointed. It oozed lust and desire in impossible quantities. With a last, Herculean effort, Kydd attempted to roll over and crush the women, but to no avail. Kicking out without control, screaming hideously, he lurched to the floor, with the three creatures that once were women intent on finishing their feast.

Soon it was over, and the three creatures, fondling and caressing each other as they wiped blood and remnants of Kydd's flesh from their mouths, their nails melting back into normal length, their scales receding into their backs, shoulders and upper arms. As Mephistopheles re-entered the room, accompanied by two servants equipped with broom and mop, they passed for seductive young women once again.

'Thank you, Ladies', said Mephistopheles, and fondled them casually as they left the room, noting with pleasure that all vestige of their former humanity was gone.

As part of the planet's military preparations, a maintenance team was tasked to check the operational status of the Militariat's communications satellites. In a camouflaged reinforced steel and concrete observation post at the inhospitable northern pole of the planet Ferrimor and his crew started to scan for any glitches or malfunctions.

'Why us?' complained Harris, 'why is it us sent to the arse-end of the planet in the bitter cold?'

'Shaddup, Harris, you bum', said Mitchell, screwing up his eyes as he attempted to steady the signal his computer was trying to receive.

'Yeah, shaddup, Harris', joined in Krumb, unscrewing the back of a faulty computer, 'you was drafted the same as the rest of us, an' we're all in the same boat.

'Way I see it', added Temple, 'is that we get sent here this time, we get sent somewhere nice an' sunny next time. So quit complaining.'

'Alright, that'll do', said Ferrimor. 'The sooner we check the signals an' report back, the sooner we can all go home to our wives. Or to someone else's.'

That brought a general chuckle and a few guffaws. The maintenance team got on with each other well enough, and they all knew that, cold as they all were, they could have been sent somewhere worse – like the bottom of the ocean, for instance, or out into space for real. With the exchange of a few more good-natured pleasantries and grumbles, they settled down to their work.

It was Krumb who first spotted it. 'Hey, Harris, you got this?' he called.

Harris peered at his machine, pressed a button to adjust it a few times, and peered again. 'What *is* that?' he said.

Ferrimor came over to look. 'Now what's the commotion?' he said, before stopping in his tracks as he saw the image on the screen. He gazed at it for a second more, then turned to Temple, knocking over a mug of coffee as he did so.

'Temple! Mayday! Mayday signal *NOW!*'

Temple, stunned, engaged his machine to send the signal, but never completed it. A blinding flash of white light filled the room at the same time that the thrown-in grenades exploded with an almighty boom. As the dust cleared, revealing broken bodies and computers, the tread of boots marching in unison could be heard. Dressed in white and grey chameleon-clothing, the fire-team entered the building. The new arrivals acted silently and efficiently as they checked the bodies and bayoneted any they thought might by still alive.

The leader of the fire-team paused by Temple's corpse and leant on it, trying to hear the faint sounds that emanated from Temple's still-operating computer.

'Hello?' came the tinny voice. 'Hello? Ferrimor? Maintenance Team Beta? Did you just try to contact us? Hello? Are you all right?'

The leader of the fire-team opened Temple's hand and removed his transmitter. 'This is Maintenance Team Beta. Ferrimor speaking. All clear here. Repeat: all clear here. All Militariat communications satellites fully functional.'

'Good news, Maintenance Team Beta', came the reply. 'Glad to hear it. See you at base later.'

'Over and out', said the fire-team leader, before disconnecting the radio. He peered at the image now showing on all working computer screens, and smiled ruefully.

'That was a close enough thing', he said. 'Radio the *Enclave* that we are successful. Then burn this place to the ground.'

CHAPTER SEVEN

Matthias awoke to find himself strapped to a large, stone slab in a dark, musty cavern. His forearms, chest and ankles were secured to the freezing cold and damp slab by wide strips of a thick, rough material that cut into his flesh painfully. The back of his head ached horribly, and his whole body felt scratched and pummelled. There was something else about his situation that was giving rise to feelings of nausea, but it took him a few moments to work out what it was.

The stone slab was suspended from above, and was swaying gently. Matthias was bound to its underside.

He tried to open his eyes and looked down, as his vision regained its focus. The scene that presented itself to him was deeply unsettling. He was, by his estimation, suspended at least fifteen feet off the ground: if the stone monolith were to be released he would be crushed to death in the fall. He could make out several indistinct cloaked figures standing below him, though their faces and builds lacked definition.

Matthias could tell he was severely dehydrated, and knew that his captors needed to do very little more for his discomfort to evolve into severe torture other than leave him where he hung. He breathed carefully, trying to diagnose any evidence of broken bones or other impediments to his condition. He found none, and thanked the Saviour-King for this mercy. He was still alive, so he reckoned that his captors wanted to drag information out of him before they put him to death.

Eventually, a figure moved towards the centre of the space below and looked up at Matthias. Suddenly, it threw a knife at Matthias. The razor-sharp knife impaled Matthias' left leg just below the knee and made him cry out in pain. Then the cloaked figure spoke, his voice sounding like a persistent grating of teeth.

'Your life draws to a close', said the figure, hatefully. 'You interfered with the Prayer for Transformation. You prevented the evolution of the Not-Yet-Born. You deserve nothing but terror and pain. These you will receive, unless you speak. You will tell us why you did these things.'

'You've made a mistake', said Matthias, as best he could through his parched throat. 'I did none of these things. I was a bystander. I tried to stop the person you want. I was there to observe, not to interfere or destroy.'

Another figure moved forwards to join the first.

'An observer?' said the second figure, incredulously. 'Then you will tell us, who were you observing for?'

'M...Mephistopheles', replied Matthias, taking one of the biggest gambles of his life.

There was consternation below. The figures that Matthias could see murmured and gesticulated to each other. Finally, a man who had not yet spoken called to others out of Matthias' eyesight.

'Bring him down!' ordered the man.

With a squeaking noise that set Matthias' teeth on edge, the slab began to descend. Matthias braced himself as the monolith edged lower and lower to the sharp and rocky ground below, unsure whether his captors meant to crush him against the cavern floor. At the last minute, many chapped and filthy hands reached out to the stone slab, and turned it over. Matthias groaned as the stone block thudded into the ground, feeling every sensation through his back. He lay there, sore and hurting everywhere. As he looked, hunched and damaged looking faces bent over him from all directions, all peering out from the same mildewed, grey cloaks. To Matthias' mind they resembled unrefined whisky addicts in the final stages of their addiction.

Then a cleaner, more powerful face looked down at him, suspicion in its eyes. It looked Matthias up and down, then spoke. His voice identified him as the figure who had first addressed Matthias.

'Name?'

Matthias' first gamble had paid off so far – at least temporarily, Matthias knew – so he continued with the same strategy.

'V...Verulam...'

At this the man stood up straight, and murmured something to one of the other cloaked figures, who nodded. The two of them conferred, then the powerful face bent down towards Matthias again until it was two inches from his own face.

'Prove it, Verulam. Convince us that you're who you say you are, or it will go badly for you.' He prised apart Matthias' right eyelids with his metal fingers. 'No one needs two eyes to survive. Convince us, Verulam, or I will remove this eye from your head.'

Matthias, role-playing the exact level of panic and terror that he judged the real Verulam would have had in such circumstances, told the watching figures of his studies at the *Collegia Baccalaureate*, of his teacher, the great Rimbrant, and of a thousand other incidental details that Matthias had committed to memory about Rimbrant's staff. He mentioned Mephistopheles only in passing, knowing that his lack of information about the man made this the weakest part of his cover.

'Please…' he finished, 'I'm not your enemy. I wasn't the one who destroyed your ceremony. I tried to stop him! I tried to fight him, but he was too much for me.'

'You were seen', said another man, 'coming out of one of the cathedral's alcoves with protection over your ears. How do you explain that if you weren't the one who sabotaged the speakers?'

'I saw what he was trying to do!' said Matthias. 'When I couldn't stop him, I tried to protect myself as best I could! It wasn't me! You've got the wrong man!'

'Very well, Verulam', hissed the figure with the metal hand, 'who was it? Who sabotaged our ceremony?'

Matthias described in great accuracy one of the men he had seen fleeing the cathedral.

The two men conferred once more, for what seemed a long time. Matthias wondered if they had bought his story, or whether his ignorance had meant that he had made easily-detectable mistakes. Eventually, Metal-hand turned back to him and gripped his chin harshly.

'We will go now and consider your story. You had better hope that we find it truthful. You have no idea what agony we can and will inflict if you have lied. Cherish these moments, Verulam; they might be your last.'

The two men left, followed by all the other figures. A huge door closed, and Matthias was left bound to the stone block in utter darkness.

He waited until he could no longer detect anyone's presence, then began to flex and relax his considerable muscles, attempting to cause the straps binding him to give a little. Patiently, ignoring cuts and tears in his skin, ignoring the stinging of the material as it sank into the underside of his wrists, he continued to flex and relax, flex and relax, working the material bit by bit. He had no idea how long he would be left, but instead of rushing he slowed his breathing and made the rest of his body quite still, so all his energy was spent methodically on tensing and releasing the muscles that pushed against his binds. Both his arms were dreadfully chaffed now, and inches of skin had rubbed itself away. He was in great pain, but still he continued. Eventually, he felt the strap holding his left arm down give a little, and redoubled his efforts there. One moment his arm was bound, the next he had pulled his stinging and aching arm free. He stifled a cry, and squinted, involuntary teardrops forming as he flexed his arm back into life. Then, once again, he calmed the rest of his body and concentrated on the task at hand, this time stretching his left arm further and further, extending his fingertips as far as they would go, and reaching for the handle of the knife that still protruded from his left leg.

Unbeknown to Rimbrant while he had guided Shenaria around the museum, Tru-D had been hard at work. As the three of them had progressed, Tru-D's special eye-pieces and other augmented senses had scanned every room and every art-work, carefully observing, smelling and measuring the various works of art. As she did so, the images collected through Tru-D's spectroscopic and x-ray vision and other bionic senses were recorded onto a high-performance hard-drive within her brain. Shenaria had previously known of Malevolent and heretical images being painted or sculpted over, and intended to check for any such occurrence here. The exact dimensions of the rooms they had passed through were recorded by Tru-D's invisible laser measurement technology, and Shenaria intended to compare these to the published plans of the building once she had returned to her base.

Once Shenaria had been left alone by the giant pedestal, she had nodded to Tru-D, who had bounded out of the room. Shenaria's vision was slowly beginning to heal, though shapes and details were still hazy, and a hidden mini-screen on the inside of her eye-filters allowed Shenaria to look out of Tru-D's eyes. Shenaria gently coaxed her to travel in certain directions and to focus on particular artworks that she had noted, always keeping Tru-D hidden from any guards, curators or maintenance crews. At regular intervals, Shenaria had Tru-D stop and scrape at specific exhibits with her sensor-pads: samples of the materials used to make the exhibits were stored under Tru-D's claws for later chemical and physical analysis.

Shenaria had travelled through the public quarters of the museum with Rimbrant, and now intended to investigate its more private and secretive parts as much as possible, while still keeping her Sanctificatorial status undeclared. She directed Tru-D away from the route that she had followed with Rimbrant, observing the details of the building through Tru-D's eyepieces as much as her own damaged eyes would let her.

As Tru-D neared one particular wall, her ears raised up in alarm, and she sniffed cautiously, reeling backwards as she responded to the strange scents that only her sensitive olfactory senses could detect. She looked up at the panelled wall where the queasy smells emanated from and yelped. Shenaria, concerned, called Tru-D back to her, then patted her and calmed her down. She ran her fingers around Tru-D's head, checking for any obvious damage to her sensory equipment, then stood up.

'Thank you, Tru-D', she said, 'time to go', and Tru-D, playing the part of a guide dog to perfection, walked Shenaria back to the main entrance of the museum. Shenaria stopped to let one of the receptionists know of the favourable report that the exhibition could expect from the 'Citizens' Well-Being' department, passed on her thanks to Rimbrant, and left.

Unknown to Shenaria, Tru-D's journey around the museum had been partly captured on camera, and, even as Shenaria made her way through the formal gardens at the front of the building, a copy of the disc was making its way to a dangerous man.

❧

Matthias had managed to reach the knife, and, grimacing, had pulled it out of his leg. He resisted the impulse to black out with the pain, knowing that he would most likely drop the knife, and pressed the flesh of his palm against its sharp blade to shock himself into retaining consciousness. The moment of danger passed, and he secured his grip on the knife before reaching over and cutting into the strap that held down his right arm. He hacked through, creating a long, red score on his bicep, then flexed his newly-freed arm, bringing it back to life. Matthias transferred the knife to his right hand and carefully sliced through the material binding his chest. Then he sat up, released his legs and swivelled them off the wet stone to the gravely floor below. He was free.

He stood up and arched his back, flexing his fingers and toes at the same time, ignoring the sensation of pins and needles as his circulation began to recover. Then he looked round, trying to get a proper idea of his surroundings. His hand went to his belt buckle, and he released a miniature, but very powerful torch, which he switched on. He held it at arms length in his left hand, knowing that he now showed up, and that any sudden shot aimed at him would most likely be aimed just to the right of the torch, where a person usually was if he carried such a thing.

Matthias saw the chamber properly now: it was carved into what seemed to be a natural cavern of rock. The wetness that glistened off many stone and flint surfaces suggested to Matthias that he was near the sea rather than being high up in mountainous territory. It occurred to Matthias that, if that was so, then there might be an exit to the water somewhere, which might be his way out. Not that Matthias intended to leave just yet: he wanted to know all he could about his captors and the scene he had interrupted in the cathedral. It seemed too much of a coincidence to him that the same building should have been used for the first showing of the *Divine Devotions* exhibition and the strange, heretical ceremony, and he knew Shenaria's opinion of such coincidences. He had already found out that his captors recognised the name of Mephistopheles: another link.

He treaded cautiously around the chamber, but found nothing of significance. Looking up, he saw that the stone slab he had been imprisoned on was attached to huge, rusty chains that descended from a small opening in the rock-face near the top of the cavern. He had a choice: either he could exit through the stone door that the hooded figures had departed through – assuming that it wasn't fastened or guarded on the other side – or he could climb the chains and make his way into the mechanisms hidden behind the rocky wall, and see whether he could penetrate the complex that way. Matthias made his choice.

Shortly afterwards Matthias' captors re-entered the cavern, only to find an empty chamber. Looking round, one of the cloaked figures pointed out bloodstains at periodic intervals on the lower chains. These had been made by the long cut in Matthias' palm. The figures looked up at the rusty metal links to the opening in the rock-face high above, retracing Matthias' escape route in their heads. The figure who had acted as the leader hit the stone block with in his metal hand in frustration, shattering a segment of it and creating sharp splinters of stone that fell to the ground. He said something to the others in a terse voice, and the group hurriedly left the chamber, intent on tracking down their prey.

A few moments later an unremarkable pile of rocks and stones in a corner of the cavern began to twitch, then move more purposefully, sending pebbles, rocks and stones flying. A dusty figure sat up, emerged from underneath the makeshift cairn, and brushed itself down. Matthias wiped the last of the grit from his eyes, then made his way cautiously through the now empty cavern and out through the still-open stone door.

In a luxurious room situated in the private quarters of the Lazenby Club, Clavicord was sharing a glass of whisky with two other men, when a knock was heard at the door, and an unflatteringly-dressed, rather dumpy woman entered.

'What?' demanded Clavicord of his wife, irritably.

'I'm sorry to interrupt, Enderby', said the woman submissively, 'but this just arrived for you by courier. It's marked 'urgent', so I thought you might like to see it.'

Clavicord snatched the package out of his wife's hand. 'You can go now', he said, rudely.

The woman looked at him ineffectually, a pained expression on her frumpy features, then went. Clavicord harrumphed, then sat in an expensive calf-hide chair and opened the package. He slid out the disc and read the message attached to it.

'Excuse me', he said to his companions, 'this'll just take a minute.'

Clavicord put the disc in a state-of-the-art player, and watched the grainy black and white footage of Rimbrant accompanying a seemingly blind woman through the Imperial Museum's Worship Wing, then of her guide cyber-hound nosing around the building. Clavicord was most struck by the way the dog responded near a particular wall that he was familiar with.

'Come and look at this', he said to his companions, then replayed the disc as they came over. 'This dog...what do you make of its actions?'

'They seem very methodical', said one of the men.

'It's just a dog, sniffing around', said the other, 'nothing to worry about.'

'Maybe so', replied Clavicord, 'but let's check.' He looked again at the message that had accompanied the disc, then turned to the chinless man who had just spoken.

'Maxillan, I want you to find out all you can about this, er, Melodia Praxis, and her dog. Discreetly, if you please. Let's not act until we're sure whether she's genuine or not. We don't want to raise suspicion again. Go now, please.'

'Yes, Sir', replied Maxillan, and went to collect his expensive coat.

'Oh, and Maxillan?' added Clavicord, just as the chinless man was about to leave. 'If she is genuine, then fine. But if you have the slightest suspicion of her, the very slightest, then she is to be killed. Is that clear?'

'Yes, Sir.'

'And if you do kill her', finished Clavicord, 'destroy the dog too. No more loose ends. We don't want another Christopheles.'

'I've never liked dogs', replied Maxillan. 'It'll be my pleasure.'

Matthias found himself in an uneven and slimy tunnel hewed out from the rock. It got more and more slippery as it dipped downwards. Matthias was moving slower than he normally would because of the wound in his leg, but he drew upon mental disciplines he'd learnt from Modesty to keep the pain at bay.

The passageway was lit at intervals by wall-mounted torches. Matthias considered taking one, then thought better of the idea. There was enough light to see by. His own torch was back in his belt-buckle.

He rounded a corner, then quickly jumped back before the two cloaked figures could see him. He crouched down to the ground, then peered around the corner again, using the rocks on the uneven ground as cover. The two figures were standing at each side of another stone door. Ostensibly they were guards, but Matthias' Valhallan Mission background immediately showed him that they had little military training. They stood awkwardly, their facing was not efficient to cover all approaches, and they were talking to each other. Matthias's old sergeant would have had them shot, but Matthias himself was glad for their sloppiness. He went for one of the oldest tricks in the book.

As the guards conversed, a sudden *ping* came from around the corner of the corridor. The guards stopped talking and looked in the direction of the noise. Then came another *ping*. One of the guards unholstered a vengeance-gun, and moved towards the corner to investigate the sound. Matthias was gratified to see that the other one didn't even cover him. The third *ping* was heard, and the guard followed the sound of Matthias' flicked pebbles and went round the corner, and out of his companion's eyesight.

A moment later the second guard saw his companion return and give the thumbs-up.

'Nothin', he said.

The second guard nodded, and reached in his pocket for a cigarette. This was to be his last action, as the disguised Matthias brought out his knife and cut his throat. He lowered the gurgling body, watching and listening out for any sign of more guards approaching, and took the dead man's vengeance-gun to add to the one the first guard had carried. Then he dragged the body to where he had hidden the first guard's.

Now, armed and camouflaged, Matthias peeped around the door. Seeing no one, he quickly opened the door and went through, closing it behind him.

Matthias found himself in a more furnished locale. Filled shelves covered one stone wall, while a granite-topped desk stood in the corner of the room, which was another carved-out chamber. Another stone door led out from a side-wall.

Matthias saw some telecommunications equipment on the desk, and made his way towards it. He picked up a pair of headphones and put them on, on the off-chance there was anything to hear, but to no avail. Putting the headphones down again, he scanned the desk for anything useful. He tried to open the desk drawer, but it was locked. Looking round to check for any interruption, Matthias pulled out one of his concealed *H-Dini* tools: a miniscule lock-pick. Soon he had opened the desk, but now he heard voices approaching. He quickly grabbed everything that was inside the desk drawer, stuffed it in his pocket, closed the drawer again, and stood, listening. The voices seemed to be coming from the passageway Matthias had entered by, so he quickly went through the other door, and leant against it, listening to the men's conversation as they entered the room he had just vacated.

He could hear two voices: the two he had heard while strapped to the stone slab. The metal-handed man spoke first.

'He's escaped us for the moment, but not for long. This Verulam is dangerous. We need to know what he was doing in the cathedral.'

'Why would one of our fellow Dems betray us?' asked the other. 'Do you think he's really working privately for Mephistopheles?'

'If so, we are lost', replied Metal-hand, 'but I doubt it. My guess is that he's trying to sell information about us for his own profit.'

'But then why would he sabotage the Prayer for Transformation? If he could have reported *that* to the Santification…'

There was the sound of a metal *slap* and a cry of pain.

'Don't ever, ever mention that disgusting organisation again', ordered Metal-hand. 'They've caused us enough grief over the years. At least now we are almost ready to strike back. We can report that the transformation was beginning to work, at any rate. Who knows how permanent it would have been had the sacrifice been completed? Still, it would be too dangerous for us to try again: the ecclesiastical authorities will put guards around the cathedral now. We will just have to report back what we have.'

'And if our report is not received favourably?' trembled the other voice.

'Then, my dear friend, you can say goodbye to your governmental position…and your life. Keep your nerve! I suggest we think about more profitable things, to try to ensure we remain in favour. Catching this Verulam would be a start.'

'What of our incubuses?' asked the other, 'what should we do with them?'

'Kill them', came the reply, 'and destroy the foetuses.'

Matthias heard the men move, and jerked back from the door, pressing himself into the rock-face in case the door was opened. It wasn't, but Matthias judged that he had better move. Creeping silently, he felt his way along the corridor he now was in, only using his torch once he had gone a considerable distance and around several bends.

Before him the passageway led to another opening – and nowhere else. Light and voices filtered out through the stone archway, and Matthias knew that the time for secrecy was leaving him. There was nothing else for it now, but to attempt an escape and get the information he had back to Shenaria.

He got as near to the archway as he could without being seen, and listened carefully. Three male voices, and one, tearful, female one. He tried to work out where the voices originated from. Once he was as confident about this as the situation allowed, he made his move. Before the cloaked figures beyond the archway had time to react, Matthias had flung himself into the room, rolling on the floor, then unfolding and sending shots flying from the vengeance-guns held in each hand. These made contact with the three men in the room, who collapsed. As one of them went down he attempted to raise his own weapon and fire back, only to find a knife suddenly jutting out of his throat. He gurgled and fell again - permanently this time.

Matthais breathed heavily, and covered the room with both pistols, but no other figures arrived. Then he turned his attention to the woman.

On a stone slab, the twin of the one Matthias had been imprisoned upon, lay a pregnant woman, gagged and bound by her wrists and ankles. It was the same woman that Matthias had tried to look after in the cathedral, and she was panicking and twitching and trying to move her head away from Matthias. She was clearly terrified.

Matthias laid a finger across her lips, and one across his own, signalling silence.

'I'm not one of them', he said. 'If you value your freedom, your life and your baby, come with me'.

Back in her suite of apartments, with Miri's help, Shenaria fed Tru-D, and, as she ate, she and Miri connected Tru-D up to a particular computer. She sat back to wait while Tru-D's data transferred itself. She was beginning to get concerned, as there was still no message from Matthias or Modesty.

While she waited, she retrieved Christopheles' report about Rimbrant's exhibition, and prepared to compare it to the information she and Tru-D had just collected. Then she got out her special stylus and pressed its topmost button, after selecting *braille*. Today's message simply confirmed that current Sanctificatorial priorities still remained the same with regard to the defence of the *Divine Devotions* exhibition, and reported back about the High Council's meeting and the advice given to it by Lord Crooker's Special Representative. There was nothing else.

As Shenaria put her stylus away, she heard the door of her premises being opened. She motioned Miri into safety, then unholstered her vengeance-gun and carefully made her way towards the entrance hall.

It was Modesty, who lay, white-faced and exhausted, on the floor. Her breathing was forced and her habitual gracefulness was missing. By her lay a mahogany box decorated with a beautifully carved relief of an angel.

'Shenaria…' breathed Modesty with difficulty, 'you'd better take…a look…at this…'

CHAPTER EIGHT

The next day began with a huge, concerted security operation that was destined to last some time. Starting in the early hours, Defender Armoured People Carriers deployed to pre-arranged points within Imperial City and disgorged heavily-armed Vigilants dressed in full body armour. Any late-night revellers, wastrels, drunks and other unfortunates were given one chance only to remove themselves from the streets being secured before being arrested, or, if they showed any resistance, physically damaged. The Vigilants moved without mercy, clearing the main arterial Great West Way that connected the city to the space port beyond. Parked land-cars were removed by Defenders prepared with riot blades, and destroyed. In the streets immediately surrounding the Imperial Museum families were forcibly removed from their homes – for their own safety, as Sergeant Byrrion put it. Every city building that bordered the Great West Way was manned by Vigilants snipers, who could be seen at windows, in doorways, on rooftops. Trees and billboards that were deemed to interfere with their line of sight to the street were torn up and pulped. Brutal barbed-wire fencing was unrolled and erected along the roadway. Underneath the route trained explosive experts and specifically equipped constructs searched the sewers and underground transport networks for any suspicious or concealed packages, taking anything they considered dubious to be destroyed. Relatives and associates of known criminals who lived near the route were removed to cells in the seven Vigilants fortresses as a precautionary measure. The Vigilants worked on a shift system: six hours on before being relieved for six hours, then back on duty again.

At the space port itself, and on the reaches of the Great West Way that were outside the city's boundaries, security was handled by the

99

Militariat. Spearhead battle-tanks patrolled and cleared the forty-mile stretch of road. More Spearhead tanks and snipers mounted strategic positions: hilltops, junctions, bridges. The staff that usually manned the space port were replaced by Militariat personnel individually chosen by Colonel Helbrad, who was himself present in the space port's gigantic main control room, along with Aurelius, Tollius and their personal bodyguards. All normal space travel had been suspended, and the whole area had been declared a no-flight zone and was completely off limits. Militariat troopers surrounded the space port's perimeter with orders to shoot any – and Helbrad meant any – unidentified personnel or vehicles of any description. Helbrad didn't believe in taking chances.

All Militariat activity was being monitored by and co-ordinated through the communications satellites that orbited the planet. At every Militariat base around the globe communications officers checked the state and movement of the weaponry, vehicle resources and Militariat personnel, accessing data updated and relayed by the satellites. Within ten seconds Helbrad could call up reliable data on the entire military force of Antrobus II: its strength, its manoeuvrability, its supply lines. If any attack did occur anywhere on the globe, Helbrad could both monitor its progress and see where the most profitable reserve forces and weaponry lay. He could oversee and direct pincer movements and other winning strategies from afar.

Today was no ordinary day – hence the frantic and highly-co-ordinated activity. This was the day that the ship *Commensurate Justice* was due to land on Antrobus II, along with its precious cargo and the legendary First Valhallans – the first that the planet had ever seen.

In the observation deck of the space port waited Lady Salfina Pureheart, and her private entourage, referred to as her 'Daughters' by those who knew her. They surrounded her closely as she gazed coolly through the toughened glass at the landing pad. Because of what they they had all been through together they regarded her with something approaching awe, and followed and protected her with a fierce and devout loyalty.

With her neat, tawny hair, now streaked with silver, her piercing green-blue eyes, her striking face and no-nonsense expression, Lady Salfina was not a woman to be dealt with lightly. Her immaculately polished and shapely jet-black corset showed off her impressive figure well, and she looked both remarkably attractive and exceedingly dangerous. This was nothing less than the truth: Lady Salfina was a veteran in the Saviour-King's service, and had now reached the honourable position of Arch-Deaconness. Throughout her long career she had lead from the front, and had built up a reputation for quick and inspirational decision-making and leadership. If Lady Salfina said something was so, then it took a very brave or truly foolish person to argue with her: she was not afraid of backing up her words with actions – and these had often been sudden and deadly. She currently had the honour of being in charge of Imperial City's famed and beautiful Grand Cathedral.

The 'Pureheart' of her name was an honorific; one that had been awarded to her following the incident during her previous duties. Lady Salfina had then held the rank of Deaconess, and was entrusted with running of the second cathedral in the capital city of Expasia on a planet in the adjacent solar system. One night, while she had been leading communion, a mass of the the city's Saviour-King repudicators and heretics had joined together and attempted to storm and destroy the building in a savage attack designed to bring terror and death. They had broken in, killing many of the congregation instantly, and threatening some of the all-female staff with rape and torture. They had clearly expected the rest of the congregation to cower before them, but Lady Salfina had risen up and led the rest of the junior nuns in a astonishingly fierce and deadly counter-attack, which had left most of the heretics dead and delivered the rest (in various states of injury) to the waiting arms of the Santification. These junior nuns had stayed with her when she took up her commission on Antrobus II, and it was they who made up her intensely loyal 'Daughters'.

Now Lady Salfina waited, patient and dignified, for the arrival of the *Commensurate Justice*. She wished both to add to the protection of the Valhallan ship's unique and priceless cargo, and to pay her respects to the Saviour-King through the glorious, golden statue that he himself had commissioned. She was also one of the few people currently on Antrobus II who had ever seen any First Valhallans before, and she looked forward to finding out more about Captain Drusus and his Honour Guard and sharing some stories with them. Her faithful Daughters also waited, excited and awestruck, and, she admitted wryly, *young*.

The 'all ready' signal was received by Helbrad, and he turned, smiling, to Tollius, who was doing his best to conceal his nerves and excitement.

'The space port, Great West Way and Imperial Museum are all secure, Sir', he said. 'Between us and Bennett's Vigilants, not even a pissed-off cockroach could approach the convoy without being seen and dealt with.'

'I hope you're right', said Tollius, 'Saviour-King knows I do. I know its just filling time now, but go through it again.'

'Speedhawk and Vulture fighter planes are scrambled and ready to the north', said Helbrad, also relieved to not have to wait in silence. 'First warning patrols and sweeps are taking place to the east of the city. Barricades have been set up to the south and west, with more Vulture fighter planes patrolling over a hundred mile radius of the city. In the city, Sergeant Byrrion has checked and secured all overground and underground routes, and swept for explosive devices. Armoured and visible Vigilants are patrolling the streets surrounding the Great West Way, and snipers are covering the route from all advantageous positions. All personnel involved in this operation have been outfitted with gas-masks, in case of biological attack. As I said, Sir, nothing and no one will be able to get through.'

'Alright', said Tollius, 'but, by the Saviour-King, I'll be pleased when this day's over, and the statue has been installed. Any more sightings of the Angel of Death?'

'None, Sir. It's whereabouts are a complete mystery. But we're ready for it this time. If it shows up today, it'll be blown out of the sky.'

'Good', replied Tollius.

The two of them relapsed into silence again. They had long used up their reserves of small talk, and now simply waited for the visitors and their cargo to arrive.

They didn't have long to wait. The Militariat satellites relayed images of the *Commensurate Justice* as it approached, and soon a Valhallan identity code was radioed through to those in the control room. Tollius radioed back his own code of authority, and Helbrad signalled his men to their final positions as the ship began its descent. Militariat troopers lined up to greet the new arrivals, and Tollius, Helbrad and

Aurelius brushed down their dress uniforms and made their way to the outstretched tarmac, to be joined by Lady Salfina Pureheart and her Daughters.

The noise of the ship's engines could be heard first, shrieking and whining, then humming more gently as, one by one, they were cut. Then the air around those waiting whipped into life as the descending craft caused something of a mini-tornado effect immediately below itself. Helbrad was pleased to see that none of his troopers moved a muscle or wavered in their positions, despite the gales. Then a massive shadow loomed over the entire space-field as the space-ship lowered towards it. With deceptive gentleness and grace, the huge, bulky and incredibly heavy craft landed, exhausting whooshes of smoke and steam as its airbrakes engaged.

The craft stood motionless for some minutes, its surface still red-hot from the descent through Antrobus II's atmosphere, but Helbrad was certain that much action was taking place inside it. Suddenly, with a smooth, fluid motion, a giant ladder eased down from the huge vehicle, its feet making strong contact with the ground. At the same time the first airlock opened.

As one, the personnel waiting looked towards the opening with great anticipation and excitement. Bodies tensed and heartbeats raced – except for those of Lady Salfina, who stood quite calmly, watching as the scene unfolded. This was the moment when legends would come to life.

As the congregation watched, a graceful yet huge figure appeared in the doorway of the craft. Massive, powerful and strong, there was not a weak line in his body or in the way he carried himself. His shoulders and torso were wide and his chest and arms looked as if they could have lifted mountains. He was clothed in a simple monk's white robe, underneath which was a body-hugging fine mesh armour of scarlet which reflected the glow of Antrobus II's sun. His epaulettes were decorated with Totems of Cleansing, devotional inscriptions, the signifier of his status and his name. His face, rather surprisingly, was composed of gentle and observant features, but the helmet that he carried in his hand and the sword by his side reminded the onlookers that he was garbed for war.

His deep voice spoke. 'I am Captain Honorius Drusus, of the *First*

Valhallans. I come on the Saviour-King's business. I ask permission to set foot on your most worthy planet, in the Saviour-King's name.'

Tollius moved forward, his frame puny in comparison with that of Drusus.

'I am Augustine Tollius, World Regent by the will and grace of the Saviour-King. In his name, I give you and your host permission to set foot on this, our unworthy planet, and offer you unrestricted welcome.'

The immediate formalities completed, Captain Drusus climbed down the ladder, and walked forward to shake Tollius' hand. Someone in the crowd let off a 'hooray!', and immediately almost everyone joined in, cheering and clapping. Helbrad forgave his troops this lapse of military discipline, as he found himself cheering too. It only seemed right for descendants of the Saviour-King's earthly family, up to this point only heard about in stories, to receive such a spontaneous and heart-felt greeting.

Drusus acknowledged the assembly's enthusiastic welcome with a gentle nod of his head, and the crowd subsided, falling back into their ranks. He looked towards the ladder as twenty other First Valhallans made their own way down and came to line up behind him in two rows of ten. They carried more powerful armaments - a sign, Colonel Helbrad thought grimly, of their understanding of the tempting targets that they and the majestic golden statue that they transported could make to heretics, terrorists and other followers of Malevolence.

Captain Drusus introduced all his men methodically, from Clarcillus and Benedict, who carried heavy fire-throwers, to Mercutio and Andreas, who were equipped with mortars. The Militariat troops marvelled at the First Valhallans' abilities to carry such heavy weapons seemingly without effort. Many, embarrassingly to themselves, felt queasy or afraid.

In turn, Tollius introduced Aurelius and Helbrad, whom Drusus looked at with the respect one fellow soldier gives another, and gestured to Lady Salfina, who came over to introduce herself.

'Captain', she said, 'I have had the honour of meeting with some First Valhallans before. I am pleased to be in such company again.'

'Arch-Deaconness', replied Drusus, 'I have heard of your good work on Expasia. I look forward to hearing more about it, should we have the leisure.'

A little smile crossed Lady Salfina's lips. 'We will', she said simply, then returned to her line.

Drusus turned to Tollius and Helbrad. 'It is ready', he said.

Helbrad clapped his hands. With an overpowering roar, out of a nearby hanger drove one of the planet's only two precious Death-Dealer tanks, the *Behemoth*. This was a monster of a tank, dwarfing all Militariat vehicles in sight. The barrels of its immense battle-cannons were wide enough to swallow several men. It took up the entire runway. The ground itself seemed to labour under its great weight. Its massive wheels and thick caterpillar tracks looked capable of crushing absolutely anything. It was one of the greatest signs of military might that Antrobus II could display, and the Militariat troops watching it approach the spacecraft felt as if they were invincible while under its shadow.

From another hangar appeared eight powerlifters, huge counterweights at their rears ready to compensate for the massive weight of their forthcoming cargo. The powerlifters walked to a pre-determined formation at the rear of the Death-Dealer, then the crew of the power-lifters and tank dismounted and stood to attention, waiting to be formally given the go-ahead.

Together, Helbrad and Drusus walked over to the men and inspected them. They were satisfied. Then, at a signal from Drusus, Micaeullus, the engineer, began his own investigation of the *Behemoth* and the power-lifters. Not a man moved for the half-an-hour that it took Micaeullus to check that the machines offered by the planet were of sufficient quality and repair to carry the precious cargo that had been brought to them. Eventually he pronounced himself satisfied, to the great relief of the Militariat's Maintenance Crew A, who had known that any different verdict would have meant the end for them.

The vehicle crews re-mounted, then, at Aurelius' initiation, the choir of Imperial City's grand cathedral began their beautiful, sturdy and inspiring hymns. They sang as the eight power-lifters marched towards a huge platform now being lowered from the Valhallan ship. Once the powerlifters were securely on the platform, it returned into the ship with them on it. After some moments of anticipation the platform began to descend again. As the power-lifters came into view it could be seen that they were carrying an enormous, prone statue, supported evenly by all eight of them. It was covered with thick, white protective drapes, but it still mesmerised all those watching. It was the golden statue of the Saviour-King – one that he himself had commissioned over two thousand years ago, and the whole assembly bowed their heads in awe.

The *Behemoth* revved up, and moved further along the runway. Behind it the twenty First Valhallans moved into formation. Then came the powerlifters, bearing their most precious cargo. Lady Salfina and her Daughters followed, along with other representatives of the ecclesiarchy who had been among those watching. An open-topped command land-car drove to the front of the line, and was mounted by Tollius, Aurelius, Helbrad and Captain Drusus. The rest of the Militariat troopers and personnel in attendance brought up the rear of the line, the infantry being led by a platoon of Spearhead tanks. The first of the celebratory Vulture fighter planes flew past, in strict formation. The procession to Imperial City was ready to begin.

As most of the city got ready to attend the procession, and were making their way to as near the barricaded Great West Way as they could get, and various licensed food-sellers, souvenir-hawkers, flag-sellers, military enlistment posts and others set up their stalls, an expensively-coated, rather chinless man entered the large City Administration building to the east of the museum. He passed through the marble-floored forum and rang the bell at the reception desk.

'Yes?' said the receptionist, rather surprised that anyone would choose today to visit the Administration offices. 'Can I help?'

'I'm looking for a Miss Melodia Praxis', replied the chinless man. 'I'm from the Imperial Museum. She visited us the other day, and I just wanted to make sure that everything was in order.'

'Just one moment', came the reply. 'Yes, if you go through that door there, take the elevator to the third floor, and turn left until you get to room three-forty-seven, then I'm sure Miss Praxis will be pleased to see you.'

'Thank you', returned the chinless man, then made for the elevator. As he stepped off onto the third floor he checked that his concealed pistol was operational, and flexed his fingers, looking forward to the pain he would inflict if this Melodia Praxis turned out to be in any way suspicious. He walked down the plain corridor and knocked on the unadorned door of room three-forty-seven.

'Come in', said a melodious female voice.

Maxillan entered, surreptitiously latching the door behind him as he did so. Before him he saw an early-middle-aged woman with dark hair sitting at a desk. She was running her hands down a spool of Braille that was being ejected by an adapted computer. She wore a dark eye-visor. In the corner of the room, on a cushion by a two bowls containing food and water, lay a golden collie-shaped dog, its metal augmentations and red eyepiece clearly visible. The dog, snoozing, lifted its ears and eyebrows and regarded the man who had entered.

'I'm Melodia Praxis', said the blind woman, reaching out to shake hands with the man. 'How can I help you?'

***

The city streets were buzzing now, and Sergeant Byrrion, who was overseeing the security operation from the grand entrance hall of the Imperial Museum, was not happy. He disliked crowds for their security risk at the best of times, and knew that it would be very easy for a group of malcontents or heretics to hide among the gathered populace and cause havoc at any moment. Consequently, he had ordered undercover officers and sniffer-hounds to immerse themselves in the masses. This was in addition to the constant marches of highly armed and visible Vigilants through the throng. Anyone acting suspiciously would be removed or killed, depending on the level of suspicion. Byrrion intended to take no chances.

His mood was not helped by the presence of Rimbrant, who, now that his big day had finally arrived, was being even more pompous and irritating than ever. Unfortunately, since it was Rimbrant's exhibition, and largely because of Rimbrant that the golden statue of the Saviour-King was coming to Antrobus II at all, Byrrion had no excuse to remove him. Instead, he had to listen to the miserable man. Rimbrant, he considered, was living in a dream world, where the whole mass of humanity would be so in awe of the Saviour-King's statue and so grateful to be living in a time when it would be revealed, that they would act nobly and reverently in glorious unison. For Rimbrant, security measures were an insult and a sign of the lack of faith of the authorities, and Byrrion was tired of arguing the point with him. Instead, he busied himself with studying the latest status reports, and checking with senior Vigilants personnel about the situation in their zones of the city. At last he received the report he had been waiting for, and turned to Rimbrant.

'Well, Professor', he said, 'the convoy has left the space port. It should enter the city gates in just under an hour.'

'The completion of my exhibition', said Rimbrant, in rapture.

'Thank you, Melodia', said Shenaria, as Miri applied ointment to her eyes. 'I owe you one. I'm glad there were no problems. Did you get a name?'

'Julius Maxillan', came the radioed reply. 'He said he was from the Imperial Museum.'

'Not a name I recognise', said Shenaria, 'but he won't stay unknown for long.'

'I took the liberty of getting Templar to tail him', added Melodia.

The real Melodia, who had been blind since birth, was one of the affiliated agents used by the Sanctification. Every branch of Valhallan service included people who, unknown to the authorities they ostensibly served, worked for the Sanctification, and Shenaria had recruited Melodia some years ago. She, and several other Administration officials, kept the Sanctification informed about everything that happened behind the scenes in the city council. Any awarding of contracts or letting of premises to suspicious organisations could be monitored. Any odd and unexplained voting patterns could be tracked, in case they revealed heretical allegiances. Shenaria had remembered Melodia shortly after returning from the hospital following the attack on the monorail, and had informed her of the subterfuge she had planned.

'Nice work', said Shenaria, 'keep me in touch'. She disconnected the link, then went to look in on Modesty.

Modesty was resting in one of the well-equipped med-beds in the large, antiseptic sanitisation room, covered in a metallic survival blanket. Totems of Cleansing and wards against damnation decorated the silver steel walls, and sacred texts lay open at appropriate prayers and liturgies on the toughened glass-topped tables. Two med-robots hovered over her, diagnostic instruments constantly in use. Modesty had flitted in and out of consciousness since collapsing on Shenaria's floor, and Shenaria's first action had been to try to secure her health. She hoped that Modesty's sanity was out of danger, and that she remained pure of soul. Shenaria knew, one day, that, should Matthias or Modesty ever succumb to the seductions and violations of Malevolence, then the task of dealing with them would fall to her. (This worked both ways: if it was Shenaria who became corrupted, then the task of removing her would fall to one of them.) She hoped fervently that this was not that day, and that Modesty would be able to fight off whatever demons and visions were affecting her. Until Modesty woke it was not possible to test her for corruption, so Shenaria waited and prayed for her faithful agent and assassin to recover.

She had not yet opened the box that Modesty had brought with her: instead she had enclosed it in a secure stasis-field and had it monitored by robot at all times. It could be dangerous. She wanted to see Modesty recover and ask her about it before she opened it herself: this would help her judge what precautions might be needed. She was also aware that, even with her now rapidly healing eyesight, her vision was still far removed from what it had been, and she didn't want to explore the contents of the box and miss something important, whether benign or deadly.

Modesty showed no signs of waking just yet. Shenaria crossed to the window and looked out over the city. She could see the preparations for the grand procession, and, while much of her wanted to attend it herself, she knew that her duties – to Modesty, to the Sanctification and to the Saviour-King – came first. She had kept tabs on the security preparations, and had talked with Byrrion about them. Her own plan was to meet with Captain Drusus that night – not that he knew.

Shenaria had finally heard from Matthias, whose own journey back to Antrobus II had been delayed by the temporary closing of the space port. He had said that he had a surprise for her, and some important information. She wondered what they were.

At last the impressive convoy reached the city gates. With great ceremony a formation of Speedhawk and Vulture fighter planes flew over the city as the vast gates were opened. The excited crowd waved and cheered wildly as the open-topped land car led the procession onto the city streets. Trembles and gasps of awe came from the throng as they beheld Captain Drusus and his First Valhallans. Retired veterans of Valhallan Mission units saluted as the First Valhallans passed, and children either cheered or cried in terror. Then came the massive Death-Dealer tank, provoking more gasps and cries, but these were nothing compared to the reception given to the proudly walking power-lifters and their precious cargo. As the shrouded golden statue of the Saviour-King passed them by, people sank to their knees in salutation and worship, moved beyond experience and expression. Some people wailed and tore their clothes in atonement, while others wept, or hugged their nearest and dearest to them, thanking the Saviour-King for the privilege of this sight. Several older or less-healthy citizens died of heart attacks and strokes as the profundity of the occasion became too much for them. Many hundreds of men, inspired to the depths of their souls, left their families and joined up to the military as soon as the procession had passed out of view.

The nearer the grand procession got to the city centre and the Imperial Museum, the more intense the crowd's reactions. There seemed to be a general swooning, wailing and crying. People gesticulated madly, all sense of themselves lost in the emanating glory of the Saviour-King. Even the line of snipers and hard-nosed Vigilants guarding the fencing were subject to its effects, and had to call on every morsel of military discipline they had not to simply join the exulting throng and lose themselves in it.

It was at this moment, when the ecstasy and rapture of the swaying and jostling crowd seemed to have reached fever-pitch, that the attack on the city began.

CHAPTER NINE

From the doorways of the decrepit buildings and ruins that made up the poor east side of the city, the first of them came. Hundreds of filthy and corrupt figures poured out of the abandoned zones and ghettos, to be joined by thousands more who oozed out of the polluted industrial wastelands long since left to rot by the city's industries. All were armed in some way, with clubs, vengeance-guns, knives, steel bars, fire-throwers and even industrial lasers. Shrieking and wailing, they lurched towards the city centre like locusts, smashing the doors and windows of every building they passed, slaughtering the terrified unfortunates inside and helping themselves to more improvised weaponry. Some citizens fought back valiantly, but were overpowered by the irresistible numbers of the attackers.

It was as if the rampaging horde had been unable to resist the draw of the golden statue of the Saviour-King, and, like lemmings, were doomed to launch themselves upon it. Their numbers rose steadily as they progressed, with opened manhole covers and avoided alleyways disgorging more and more, until the entire east perimeter of the city seemed swamped with berserk, salivating monsters.

Just to the west of this damned uprising, as the industrial sites gave way to more residential areas, others joined the tidal wave of malice and hatred that threatened the city. Out from tiny chapels and meeting halls poured those who had camouflaged their secret heresies under the guise of devotions and good works. Those who would never have admitted that they were corrupt were overtaken by their secret heretical tendencies and, shrieking hysterically, joined the mob. People wearing the vestments of priests, missionaries and Good Works volunteers could be seen within the uncontrollable wave of hate-filled people as it made its way towards the city centre, merciless in its random destruction of any and all who got in its way.

Sergeant Byrrion began receiving what he first thought were isolated calls for help from local Vigilant outposts situated in the east side, but then the volume of calls increased, and he realised that the situation was serious. His signal of utmost urgency was responded to immediately by all local Vigilants commanders. Ground patrols near the Great West Way intensified, and turned back any citizens trying to reach the grand procession, now ten miles from the Imperial Museum. Transport systems were halted where they stood, and the Vigilants travelling on the monorail and underground trains began to methodically search all the people now immobilised in the carriages. The three Vigilants fortresses to the east of the city opened their massive gates to release armoured and highly-armed Defenders that drove towards the reported disturbances, their sharp blades ripping through all obstacles in their way.

At the same time, to the north of the city, many of the Vulture fighter planes patrolling the area were targeted by anti-aircraft fire that seemed to emerge from concealed positions in woods and hills, and even some abandoned and redundant Militariat observation shelters. The volume of anti-aircraft missiles was thick, and many tens of Vultures were struck and downed before the situation became clear. The Speedhawks in the sky rapidly reversed their flight paths and tracked back over the air space where the Vultures had been hit, looking for targets themselves. The anti-aircraft fire seemed to come from an ever-increasing range of territory, and the pilots responded with varying degrees of confidence and success, this being their first taste of real combat rather than exercises.

But no matter how accurately the pilots seemed to fire their powerful missiles, the anti-aircraft fire grew more and more intensive. Two Speedhawks dropped, the pilot of one managing to bail out successfully, but the pilot of a third Speedhawk watched in horror as the bailed-out man landed and was immediately set upon by a group who emerged from the trees brandishing branches, stones and Crusader-swords with intense savagery. The third Speedhawk's pilot was so shocked by the horrible scene that he forgot to look in front of him, and lost his life as his plane collided with a Vulture plane that was desperately trying to manoeuvre out of the way, causing a vast fireball of metal and flame to engulf them both.

More and more savages emerged on the ground below, cheering and whooping, and setting up cannon and mortar fire-stations to attack the planes. The Vultures and Speedhawks targetted as many of the enemy as they could with their own guns, mortars and missiles but the number assailing them seemed to grow larger with every passing minute. There were hundreds of casualties now. It seemed that the entire territory north of the city was turning into one giant, and largely successful, anti-aircraft battery.

Meanwhile, to the south of the city, the marshlands began to reveal the heretics and malignants that they had concealed. Oozing foul slime and releasing noxious fumes, hundreds of concealed real and counterfeit Spearhead tanks emerged, intent on destroying the substantial barricades set up along the city's perimeter, accompanied by thousands of the damned, shouting their pestilential heresies into the air for all to hear. The Militariat troopers who first saw the dreadful line of tanks and heretics materialize like nightmare visions made real as they came out of the marshlands were panic-stricken and frightened beyond measure, and varied in their reactions. A few unfortunates remained paralysed from their shock and terror for too long, while others just lost control of their bladders. Some more resilient troopers – or simply those who realised that they would die if help was not forthcoming – radioed panicked and garbled messages to their sergeants and captains, who in turn passed the status reports and requests for aid to Helbrad's own staff.

Before any coherent response could be received, however, the attack had begun. The first of the enemy Spearheads rushed the enormous thick concrete and metal barricades, many of them falling victim to the anti-tank grenades placed in front of them, and the concealed pits that had been dug before the barricades' weakest points. Others fired their turret-mounted heavy guns at the blockade, causing screams as Militariat troopers died. Some shrieking missiles struck the barricades, causing intense flashes of light that blinded the nearest soldiers and booms so loud that eardrums were shattered. The barricades themselves cracked, but held, and Militariat troopers, as they regained their wits, returned fire, unleashing deadly volleys of missiles and flamed petrolium. Chemical weapons penetrated the nearest of the Spearhead tanks, causing one to explode and turn over on its neighbour. Grenades bounced off the Spearheads and exploded among the gibbering heretics, sending blood and body parts raining down over the attacking forces. The first line of Spearheads seemed to be stalled in its tracks, but the assault had only begun, and the newly-bloodied Militariat troopers holding the line could see no end to the vile, depraved and cheering forces that now redoubled their efforts against them.

In Shenaria's suite of rooms, the special stylus started emitting a DNA-coded signal only Shenaria could detect. Instantly she set the pen to *braille* and absorbed the urgent message it conveyed. Then she acted. She remembered well the lesson she had learnt from High Sanctifier Lord Crooker and Sanctifier Christopheles about the usual dangers of being obvious, but now it was time. Wearing her dark eye filters once more, she donned her normally ceremonial but still intricately equipped Sanctificatorial armour, which covered all of her save for her head. Dark green in colour, except for the dulled chainmail breastplate, it absorbed light and made her a more difficult target. It was made of a special light alloy that maximised both flexibility and protection. Together with the full-length jet-black cape Shenaria wore it made for an impressive sight, but it was more than just for show. Shenaria knew that, for now, the time for subtlety had gone. Looking as stern, powerful and merciless as she could be, Sanctifier Calvert began her journey to the Imperial Museum. No one tarried in her way.

As yet no one at the grand procession through the Great West Way knew anything about the attacks being carried out in and around the city, except for the company in the command land-car. With a nod from Tollius, Helbrad left him and Captain Drusus to continue to receive the crowd's adoration, while he himself slipped down below to co-ordinate the Militariat's responses and find out more. Tollius and Aurelius had agreed with Helbrad and Drusus that, unless there was an immediate danger to it, the procession should go ahead as planned, and the crowds would be kept in the dark about the events elsewhere. It seemed almost heretical to draw the crowds attention away from the giant effigy of the Saviour-King and suggest that they should disperse, and nor was Helbrad in the mood to award the enemy – whoever they were – such an easy propaganda victory.

Cupping his ears to drown out the adulating throng's cheers and shouts, Helbrad concentrated intently as he was radioed continually updated details of the assaults on the city. As he listened he gave quick, decisive orders: putting all desert bases onto the highest status of mobilisation; redoubling the transportation of munitions; calling in a second wave of Speedhawk and Vulture fighter planes and a flotilla of bombers from the southern hemisphere; directing called-up reservists to approach the city's fronts from the outside. He hoped to assault the massed Spearhead formation attacking the south of the city from the other side of the marshland it had sprung from. He hoped that the anti-aircraft batteries set up to the north of Imperial City could be overwhelmed and bombed out of existence. He hoped that Byrrion's Vigilants could hold the east of the city without extra aid, but readied four units of Militariat troopers to act as reserves should the Vigilants be forced to fall back. He sweated profusely, his responsibilities lying heavily on him. He would have felt better at least knowing who the enemy was, or having some ideas about their strength and numbers, but these remained unknown. He tasked the communications officers who monitored the Militariat satellites to see if some of their first-warning sensors could be turned inwards to Antrobus II itself, but he was cautious here: this seemed to be a home-grown attack, but Helbrad was not fool enough to rule out the possibility that it was the herald of something more.

As he listened to details about the growing number of reported casualties and the incessant encroachment of the enemy's grip around three sides of the city, Helbrad found himself wondering whether this was to be the end. Then he glanced behind him to where the immensely powerful *Behemoth* rolled, accompanied by the glorious, divinely-touched warrior-brethren of the First Valhallans, not to mention the golden statue itself, and was deeply ashamed of his moment of doubt.

Byrrion had received reports of the ever-nearing mobs and the destruction they caused with the same trepidation, but he was deeply determined that the city would be defended successfully. He had had all Defender crews and ground patrols equipped with hand-held fire-throwers, which he hoped would slow the advance of the hordes. All seven Vigilant fortresses had now disgorged every remaining Defender normally held in reserve, and these were forming mobile barricades along the arterial routes leading from the east into the centre of the city. Vigilants equipped with lethal grenades commandeered strategic buildings and high points on the rabble's likely routes. More of the deadly barbed-wire fencing was hurried erected around all sensitive areas – communication towers, financial institutions, reservoirs, food depots, artilleries – and around the entirety of the central zone of the city. These measures would, hopefully, serve to keep the savage attackers out, but they also served to seal in all the revellers, devotees and families who had come to see the grand procession; and Byrrion was not entirely happy with this.

On receiving the first reports of the assault, Byrrion had managed to get several Vigilants standing guard within the Imperial Museum to remove Rimbrant and his staff to safer places within the building. He remained in the grand entrance hall, able to concentrate without interruption for the first time that day. As Byrrion pondered his next move, he was startled to realise that he was not as alone as he had thought. With honed reflexes, he whipped out his vengeance-gun and moved his body into an effective defensive position against the wall.

'That won't be necessary', said a firm, powerful voice.

Byrrion looked, to see a taut, well-built figure emerge from the shadows. It was gowned in impressive deep-green armour. Its raven-haired head was framed by the collar of a midnight-black cloak. Even partially obscured by a dark eye-visor the woman's face was proud and determined, and Byrrion had the impression that the bearer of such a countenance would not have been fazed by anything in her entire life. A shiver of trepidation passed through him, though he realised that if the figure had wanted him dead then he would already be so. Nonetheless, he kept up his guard.

'Who are you?' he asked.

'Calvert, of the Saviour-King's Sanctification', came the reply, and a coded golden Pyramid was revealed. 'We have talked. You will update me on the situation *now*, and follow all orders I give you to the letter. You are a good man, but no deviation from these orders will be tolerated. I have been tasked to ensure the museum's safety, and I do not intend to fail in this task.'

Byrrion was tempted to ask *How did you get past security?* but thought better of it. Instead he said, simply, 'We're in trouble.'

Tens of thousands of berserk heretic deviants now poured through the east of the city, barely pausing to massacre all who were unfortunate enough to be in their path. All along the central north-to-south section of the city's forty-foot wide ring road, which the citizens of the city thought of as the natural barrier between decent society and the lower orders, a massive barrier of over two hundred Defenders stood, waiting for the onslaught that was inevitable. The crews of the vehicles and the Vigilants standing ready behind them could already hear the terrifying noises of the carnage being conducted as the barbaric multitude approached. The Vigilants clicked their sturdy protective helmets into place, checked Vengeance-guns, readied grenades and unlatched the safety catches on fire-throwers. The extra-armoured Defenders revved up, their riot blades ready both to act as shields and assault weapons.

The sounds of the horde got louder and louder, then came the first sight of fires being started and buildings exploding. Screams carried through the air as citizens fled for their lives, only to find their progress frustrated by the barricade of Defenders. Several Defenders reversed slightly, out of the drivers' sense of humanity, in order for those fleeing for their lives to have a chance to pass through into safety, but as soon as the enormous, uncontrollable sea of savages came into view, they moved back into position with military discipline, crushing many unfortunate people still trying to flee. More explosions were heard, and fires engulfed building after building, until the entire horizon to the east of the barricade seemed a sea of flame and destruction.

Then the first of the looming mob came into view, shouting, screaming and wailing. Some threw stone and rocks at the Defenders, while others fired acquired fire-throwers, pistols and guns towards the line. This caused mainly minor damage, but still some Vigilants fell, wounded or killed, and a few Defenders were immobilised or set on fire. Thousands of the ghastly mob, still out of range, simply screamed curses at the Vigilants, as if these would be enough to destroy them. More of the wailing, uncontrollable horde came into view, then more, and still more, until a huge mass of writhing, insane bodies pressed up against the Defenders.

They were met with withering volleys of fire of all description. Many of the attackers screamed and rolled about in agony as they were covered in burning petrolium. Others fell neatly and suddenly to the ground, great cauterised holes torn out of them by lasers. Heretics with less tidy wounds caused by vengeance-guns and grenades tore apart and dropped by the hundred.

But the press of bodies against the Defenders seemed heedless of these things. One Defender was rocked continuously, with two madmen taking the place of every one that was dropped by Vigilants fire. Massive and heavy as it was, it was still shaken and rocked, until finally it was rolled over, crushing several Vigilants and heretics adjacent to it, and letting screaming madmen through to hack, stab and flame the unfortunate officers holding the second line of defence. They were soon dealt with, but not without cost. Another Defender was rolled over in its turn, then another. As if this was a signal, the mass of Defenders moved forwards aggressively, shooting attackers with all their Vengeance-guns at point-blank range and crushing people mercilessly with their riot blades. Defender crewmembers threw grenades into the crowd, and flamed them unceasingly.

Any normal force would have at least contemplated retreating or regrouping, but not this one. The insane congregation simply threw themselves at the Defenders even more ardently, heedless of the risk of death or injury. The Vigilants stood their ground, but little by little they realised that they risked being overwhelmed and butchered.

Suddenly an order was signalled into every Defender and to every ground commander. The order was to retreat at full speed, immediately. Several of the Defender crews and standing Vigilants hesitated; even under such pressure, such an action went against the grain. The order was repeated, this time at full volume and in a female voice:

'Retreat! Retreat at full speed *NOW!* Clear the road! By order of the Santification.'

This was enough for the Defender crews. With a sudden and instant movement, the whole barricade of Defenders reversed at full pelt, laying down an intense, thick volley of suppressing fire and flame to prevent the horde following them. For a second the wide ring road remained empty, covered in wisps of burning petrolium, as the Defenders and Vigilants reached its other side.

Even the maddened crowd were momentarily surprised by the Vigilants' retreat. Then, seeing the wide road in front of them empty and inviting, they surged into it, yelling and screaming even more than before. The Vigilants gazed at them, terror-stricken and in fear of their lives. They had nowhere else to run to.

Just then the sound and vibration of immense explosives was heard. Defenders bounced up and down, and skidded into their neighbours. Vigilants fell into each other. Astonishingly, the whole central section of the street, all the way from its north end to its south, collapsed deep into the ground, taking virtually all the incensed and insane attackers with it to their doom. They fell into the enormous forty-foot wide pit in their thousands, crying out, screaming and dying. The Vigilants, safe on the other side of what used to be the road, looked on in utter astonishment and deep-felt relief.

Shenaria's acute sense of pattern had reminded her of the details of the city's layout, underground as well as overground, and this had given rise to her plan. Following Sanctifier Calvert's orders, Vigilants officers had commandeered the commuter trains below and ordered them to safety. Then explosive teams had rigged the entire section of the underground transport tunnels situated exactly below the ring-road with immensely powerful and aggressive explosives, and set them off as soon as the Defenders had moved back. The road had simply caved in and fallen into the tunnels below, crushing and killing most of the attacking horde, and completely cutting off the others.

The remnants of the horde could not reach the Vigilants, but the Defenders, with their ranged weapons had no such problems. The Vigilants, now sure of victory, filled the gigantic pit with bouts of flaming petrolium to finish off anyone still left alive in it, then shot and destroyed all the remaining deviants as they wailed and fled on the other side of the enormous crater.

One of the attacks on the city had been successfully repelled.

CHAPTER TEN

Byrrion received the news of the successful manoeuvre with astonishment and relief, and a wide grin broke across his face. He turned to the armoured figure standing by his side, who was now busy speaking into the radio.

'Thank you', he said, earnestly.

'It's not over yet', replied the Sanctifier grimly. 'Those Defenders are still needed. Make certain that no second wave comes from the east, then use the ring-road to get your forces round the city. Send half of them north, to join up with Commander Chaffron's Militariat squadron at the Saviour-King's Tower. Send the other half south, to reinforce Sergeant Harridan's barricades. Tell the Defenders still in the city centre to stop patrolling and get *here* as soon as possible.'

'Stop patrolling?' asked Byrrion, 'but…'

He stopped, as he saw the Sanctifier slowly turn her head towards him, fierce authority in her eyes.

'*Yes, Ma'am*', snapped Byrrion, hurriedly, and began to radio his orders.

The grand procession was now merely ten miles from the Imperial Museum, and the crowds that surrounded it were thicker than ever. Helbrad had ordered all communications systems not being used by the Militariat or Vigilants to be closed down. As a consequence, the celebrating masses watching the parade still had no idea of the danger to their city – and Helbrad wanted to keep it like that for as long as possible. He knew of the barbed-wire fencing barriers that Byrrion had

121

had placed around the city centre, and was keenly aware of the possible consequences should the crowds decide to panic. News of the attacks had now been passed along to the company of First Valhallans and to Lady Salfina and her Daughters, and they had taken action.

To great cheers from the awed and wildly excited onlookers, the twenty First Valhallans jumped and climbed onto the massive *Behemoth* as it rumbled along, and took up armed and defensive positions at equidistant places on top of its hull. They looked fantastic: their dynamic postures and unsheathed weaponry drawing cries and moans of awe and terror. Gleaming, deadly Crusader-swords swirled into life, heavy fire-throwers ejaculated bursts of flame and puffs of smoke, and mortars and heavy Vengeance-guns glinted in the sun as they were swivelled by the warrior-brethren. Meanwhile, Lady Salfina's Daughters unsheathed their guns, pistols and fire-throwers, and activated them. Lady Salfina herself drew *Excelsior*, her jewelled and dangerous longsword, and thrust it into the air. The crowd swooned and brayed, both overjoyed and petrified to see so much naked weaponry and military might. To them, the procession had simply embarked on a higher level of thrilling display, but the parading personnel themselves were aware that they were now at the highest level of alert, and scanned the air and ground around them, prepared for attack.

To the south of Imperial City, things were going from bad to worse. More and more depraved attackers emerged from the marshlands, gibbering hysterically, waving vengeance-guns, girders, maces, Crusader-swords – all manner of things. With them came the seemingly-unceasing flotilla of Spearhead tanks, now accompanied by all sorts of adapted land-cars. Some carried figures brandishing improvised and filthy hand-weapons, while others transported amateur and home-made fire-throwers and missile-launchers. The insane, determined, slime-covered battery threw themselves at the Militariat barricades, seemingly heedless of any damage or injury to themselves.

No matter the strength or accuracy of the shots fired at them, or the sea of blistering petrolium that covered them from head to toe, or the lasers and gunfire that cut straight through them, they kept coming. The real and imitation Spearheads butted and smashed into the barricades, often crumpling or exploding as they did so, or merely stopping in their tracks, only to be rammed by the vehicles behind, but nothing seemed to put the attacking force off. At one point, so many damaged, burnt and broken vehicles lay before the barricades that Sergeant Harridan thought that nothing sane would even attempt to get through or over them, but it appeared that the attacking horde were far, far from sane. Vehicles attempted to mount the crushed and flamed wrecks that lay on front of them, with various degrees of success. Harridan shouted at his Militariat troopers, and cajoled them to keep their nerve with every command-trick he knew, sometimes whipping them up into a frenzy of violence, sometimes screaming at their incompetence, sometimes threatening them brutally, sometimes sneering at their apparent lack of patriotism; anything, in fact, to prevent them from looking at the situation too closely and realising that they had little hope of victory – or even survival.

'The Saviour-King is with us!' he bellowed with all his strength, as he dispatched enemy after enemy with his vicious vengeance-gun and sword, praying more than he had ever prayed that it was indeed true.

Things were no better to the north of the city. The woods and forests seemed alive with anti-aircraft fire. It seemed that every tree concealed weapons intent on the destruction of the aircraft circling the area above. Commander Chaffron, overseeing operations from the Militariat airbase situated adjacent to the city's proud 'Saviour-King's Tower' communications complex, was desperately concerned. His chief worry was that the enemy would stop simply trying to destroy the fleet of Speedhawks and Vultures that filled the air and start launching deadly missiles into the city itself, presumably to either destroy the priceless golden status of the Saviour-King itself or soften the city up before a ground-based invasion could take place, or, even worse, both. He was perplexed about where such a force could have come from, and how it could have come by its apparently never-ending armoury, but knew that such questions would have to wait until after the attack was over – assuming, of course, that he and the city lived to see that day.

The firepower from the anti-aircraft batteries had been immense, and, even though many offensive positions had been completely destroyed, more had emerged, and the fleet of Speedhawks and Vultures was suffering. The difficulty of organising the successful and swift landing, re-fuelling and re-taking-off of the planes, while still keeping enough craft in the air to worry the enemy, was immense, and Chaffron was now on the alert for the one little mistake that he could so easily make that would be enough to wreck the entire defensive operation.

He had witnessed some of the most amazing flying he had ever seen, with planes circling and covering each other in an attempt to deny the enemy any targets, while trying to sight and destroy enemy positions themselves. Planes had manoeuvred impossibly close to each other, then suddenly separated, confusing heat-seeking missiles so that they exploded into hillsides and trees as much as possible. Some Vulture planes flew dangerously near to the ground, then veered upwards as they sighted anti-aircraft weapons stations, forcing the missiles following them to career into the weapons below. Unfortunately, such tactics were not always well-executed, or the flying itself just lacked the finesse required as the pilots, already suffering from the acute nerves brought about by their first ever real combat flying, got more and more exhausted. While many superb manoeuvres were carried out, several fighter planes collided unnecessarily, with the trees and hills below, or with each other, adding to the toll of death and destruction caused by the attackers below. Chaffron watched as the number of red blips in his computer screen grew in number, each one representing a lost plane. He could not see a good end to this battle, no matter how hard he tried.

The procession was now only two miles from the Imperial Museum, and the onlookers were filled to burst with intense patriotism, devotion and excitement. A convoy of Vigilants Defenders had recently surrounded the crowd, and now travelled along with it. Some of the more claustrophobic members of the crowd grew anxious at being sandwiched between the armoured personnel carriers of the Vigilants and the Militariat vehicles and infantry of the grand procession itself, but most of the celebrants simply accepted the Defenders' arrival as another stirring feature of the parade. If those in the crowd had looked properly they would have noticed how carefully the Defenders were positioning themselves and aiming their vengeance-guns, as if they intended to provide an unbreakable ring of thick armour and defensive firepower around the revellers and the statue in their midst.

Meanwhile, in the shell of the command land-car leading the procession, Helbrad was busy communicating on two radioes at once. He would talk and listen intently to a purposeful female voice on one, then break off and convey his orders on the other. He concentrated carefully on what the voice would ask or suggest. Helbrad was not used to having to share his authority, but such was the presence and forcefulness of the speaker, that he respected her leadership automatically. It helped that the actions that she ordered seemed strategically sound to him, and it helped even more that she was a Sanctifier – the one type of person that Helbrad feared.

'Colonel, what is the current status of the Great West Road – not the section you are on, but the section you have already travelled over, outside the city?' asked the voice.

'Just a moment…Still clear. We suffered no attack as we came through it. That's odd! You'd think the enemy would have struck at us then, before we benefited from the city's defences. Why would they let us get this far if they wanted to destroy the statue?'

'You ask good questions, Colonel', replied Sanctifier Calvert. 'Unfortunately, the answers to them will have to wait for now. Move your Spearhead tanks off the Great West Road to the northwest of the city.'

'The Spearhead tanks? But what if an attack does come down the Great West Road? We would be leaving an undefended, fast route for the enemy to take!'

The Sanctifier answered him, and a small smile flittered across his face.

'It's still a bit of a gamble', he said.

'All life is, Colonel', responded Shenaria, and proceeded to give him her next instructions.

'Commander Chaffron was incredulous when he heard the Sanctifier's orders.

'But, Ma'am', he stammered, 'we're already under heavy fire! We need all our Speedhawk fighter planes *here*!'

He listened to her next words with initial trepidation, then with the first glimmer of hope he'd experienced since the attack had started.

'In the Saviour-King's name!' he said, and started radioing his pilots with their new instructions.

❦

A new threat now began to emerge. The streets surrounding the barricades Sergeant Byrrion had thrown around the city centre were already full with citizens who had not been able to get closer to the grand procession, but now more and more people poured into them. The new arrivals emptied out of offices, eateries, shops and leisure facilities, from apartments. They seemed to be everyday workers who had finally managed to get out of their workplaces in time to add their voices to those welcoming the golden statue. At first it appeared that the celebrating crowd was simply growing in number as the grand procession neared its final destination, but it quickly became apparent that many of the newcomers were not friendly.

Without warning, they turned on their fellow citizens, and, yelling, began to attack them savagely, using anything they could lay their hands on as weapons. People began screaming and running. Some ran towards the central barricades, only to be crushed or trapped, while others were luckier and ran in the opposite direction. The attackers, having attempted to injure and terrify the crowd, now turned their attention to the Vigilants' barrier itself, and hurled themselves upon it, pushing and slashing, heedless of the damage the viciously barbed wire was doing to them. They ran at the barricade, rocked it and shook it, in ever-increasing numbers. The barriers began to give, slowly at first, then more easily, and small gaps between sections of barbed wire started to appear.

The celebrating crowd on the inside of the barrier began to scream and panic, and soon a wave of terror and fear began to percolate towards the grand procession itself, though at this moment it was still some way

126

away from it, and contained on the outside of the protective line of Defenders that encircled the main body of onlookers. Vigilant snipers on the rooftops of buildings bordering the Great West Way detected the commotion, but were unsure whether to leave their positions overlooking the processional route to go and deal with the disturbances now reaching their ears. Some snipers did so, and looked in alarm at the central barricade as it began to weaken and fall inwards at some points. One raised his long-barrelled vengeance-gun to fire at the new attackers, then hesitated, unsure of whether the sound of shots being fired would make the rapidly-spreading panic at the crowd's perimeter even worse.

Then the first missiles descended towards the city centre, as Commander Chaffron had feared they would. The squad of Vultures flying over the city centre intercepted them successfully, causing dramatic fireballs and explosions to appear in the sky, much to the delight of the central crowd, who thought they were witnessing a glorious firework display. More missiles were fired towards the city, and were intercepted, causing more colourful fireballs to appear and drawing great *oohs* and *aahs* from the onlookers. Then one of the missiles hit a Vulture, which ejaculated thick black smoke and spiralled downwards as the aghast throng looked on, finally disappearing somewhere to the west with a huge explosion. People screamed and children cried.

The action that followed was almost too fast for the multitude to keep up with, which was probably a good thing, as the very pace of events served to stall the wave of panic that threatened to erupt. An enormous hum of sound came from the sky above, and wave after wave of Speedhawk planes flew south over the crowd, seemingly very close over the assemblage's heads, causing small sonic booms in their wake. Then Militariat troopers were running along the front line of onlookers shouting *Protect your ears! Cover your ears! Protect your eyes! Look away!* Frightened, and responding to the authority in the troopers' voices, the people complied.

At the same time, the accelerating Speedhawks were radioed a set of co-ordinates, followed by the order *Clear this air-corridor now! All craft comply!* They immediately split to the left and right, so that two formations of aircraft flew in parallel, leaving a wide gap between them.

Then the massive Death-Dealer tank drew noisily to a halt. The

Behemoth's enormous main cannon resolutely tilted upwards, all military personnel covered their eyes and ears, and with a ground-shaking *boom*, the Death-Dealer fired.

To the south, Sergeant Harridan saw his doom approaching. The stout barricades were buckling now, and Harridan could see that they would not last for much longer. The screaming and wailing marsh-covered maniacs kept throwing themselves at the metal and concrete, and the combined weight and force of their Spearhead tanks and corrupted land-cars began to tell. Harridan radioed *Fall back!* to his troops, and the whole company, not now needing much incentive to carry out such an action, obeyed immediately.

Then he received a message through his earpiece, and gaped incredulously for a second, before recovering his wits and radioing *Take cover! Get down! Incoming!* His men, already operating off their nerves, dropped to the ground and covered their heads with alacrity.

The huge, fiery, rocket-powered Death-Dealer shells whistled through the air as they descended, then, with a blinding burst of orange light, exploded onto the first and second lines of Spearheads. Tanks and other vehicles flattened, melted, exploded and erupted into flames. Tires burst. Screaming figures, their faces and bodies blistered and blackened, ran around in agony, or collapsed, wailing to the ground.

The front lines of the attacking force had been immobilised, and could no longer move aggressively against the barricades. The following lines of vehicles were effectively stalled too, having nowhere to move to, being blocked in by the destroyed tanks to their fronts and the mass of vehicles to their rears. Then the whine of bomber engines could be heard, and two columns of Speedhawk heavy fighter-planes came into view. The Spearheads were easy prey now. The Speedhawks' massed missile and gun fire demolished the fighting capabilities of the stranded vehicles, and the stream of shells that fell upon them destroyed them for good. Straggling and half-melted survivors were finished off by the cheering Militariat troopers and the lines of Vigilant Defenders that had now arrived to add their firepower to the fray. The threat to the south had been neutralised.

To the north of the city, now that the Speedhawk planes had left, Commander Chaffron's remaining fleet of Vultures had changed their tactics. They had ceased trying to destroy the enemy anti-aircraft batteries for the moment, and were keeping further out of range, concentrating on intercepting any missiles fired towards the city centre. This tactic had effectively stalled the battle for the moment, as the anti-aircraft batteries were denied any immediate short-range targets, and were too heavy to be able to move towards the city at any pace. The casualties suffered by both sides had reduced for the moment, but that would soon change. To Chaffron's great delight, over a hundred Vigilant Defenders emerged from the ring road running by the Saviour-King's Tower, and began to tear their way into the woodland that concealed the enemy, their riot blades uprooting and destroying undergrowth on their route.

At the same time Chaffron began to receive reports of a massed force of Militariat Spearhead tanks lumbering up the western outskirts of the woods and forests. Their thick, reinforced reinforced steel hulls and sheer bulk went through the first lines of trees as if they were paper, and their heavy-duty cannons destroyed the denser thickets.

Between them, the Spearhead tanks and Defender APCs began to enfold the enemy in a pincer movement from north and west. At the same time, Chaffron ordered his Vulture fighter planes to re-engage the enemy emplacements with extreme force. The enemy had extremely powerful and effective weapons, but, even so, the slow-moving anti-aircraft crews could not aim them to the north, west and up into the sky at the same time. Some Spearhead tanks and Defenders were immobilised or destroyed, and several more Vultures were hit, but the enemy had no chance. Attacked from three directions by men intent on revenge for the damage and death caused, they soon crumpled, blown to bits by shells, mortar blasts, heavy gun fire and thousands of missiles. Militariat troopers armed with bayonets and vengeance-guns leapt from their Spearhead battle-tanks, and whooped through the woods, finishing off all enemy survivors. The danger from the north had been removed.

The grand procession was in sight of the Imperial Museum when the last attack came. The barricades set up around the city's central area finally gave, and hundreds of berserkers charged through, attacking and crushing the terrified crowd. Many were picked off by the roof-topped Vigilant snipers, now in no doubt about the wisdom of firing their weapons, and the rest found their way barred by the cordon of Defenders that surrounded the parade and the golden statue. Tank-mounted vengeance-guns fired into the crazed and unorganised mob as they attempted to charge the vehicles, and Vigilants within the vehicles fired their own guns through openings in the Defenders' armour-plated sides.

Even so, many hundreds of the horde managed to climb over or past the Defenders, and continued to advance towards the grand procession. As well as their improvised weaponry, several were equipped with more worrying arms: pistols, fire-throwers, knives and guns. They hurled themselves towards the parade, intent on its complete destruction.

The bulk of them didn't get very far. Militariat troopers formed disciplined lines and opened fire upon them, as did Lady Salfina's Daughters. Lady Salfina herself used her precious *Excelsior* to separate heads from torsos, weapon-toting hands from arms and lives from bodies. Half the First Valhallans stayed where they were, aggressively shooting attackers from the hull of the *Behemoth*, while the other half jumped down and brutally smashed their way straight through the enemy, slicing them into pieces with Crusader-swords, pounding them into pulp with enormous fists, and peppering them with shots from vengeance-guns.

At the museum itself, hundreds of the mob had rampaged through the formal gardens framing its entrance. They were met by Sanctifier Calvert, Sergeant Byrrion and many Vigilants who had been guarding the exhibition. Many of the horde targeted the female figure, assuming she was the weakest target. They were wrong, and they all died, as Shenaria wielded her deadly blade with great accuracy while simultaneously firing her vengeance-gun. Byrrion's own two guns accounted for many more, while the volume of fire from the furious Vigilants finished off the rest. Not one of the enemy had set foot in the Imperial Museum.

The normally civilised devotees, who had turned out in their thousands to welcome and honour the arrival of the golden statue of the Saviour-King, were so incensed, upset and maddened by the attackers that they now turned on all those still left, using nails, fists and teeth like barbarians, killing their fellow human beings with great gusto and savagery, and rejoicing in the blood they shed. Afterwards, many of the crowd would swear to their friends and families that the drapes covering the Saviour-King's golden statue had slipped for an instant, and rays of unspeakably gorgeous divine essence had enwrapped the faithful and inspired and empowered them to repel and destroy the last aggressors.

It was finished. The Militariat troopers kicked the bodies of the reprobates out of the way, ready for excommunication and unceremonious destruction later. Solemnly, the grand procession reformed. The great Death-Dealer tank powered up and the mighty powerlifters did likewise, hoisting the giant statue of the Saviour-King a few inches higher, to the cheers of all. The city's cathedral choir started a new wave of devotional hymns, which the recovering onlookers added their own voices to, feeling immeasurably blessed and uplifted. Captain Drusus, acknowledging the crowd's adoring waves, re-mounted the command land-car, together with Tollius and Aurelius. Helbrad, who emerged from the insides of the land-car, also received an enormous cheer as he took his place beside them. The command-car revved into life and, to wild screams from the relieved and excited spectators, led the parade through the final few hundred yards to the beautiful frontage of the Imperial Museum's Worship Wing. A Vigilant sergeant and a woman dressed in a full-length black cape and dark-green armour moved to the side and bowed, and, to enormous applause and cheers, the eight massive Powerlifters carried their most precious cargo under the tree-lined arches of the formal gardens, through the enormous double-doors and into the heart of the museum.

Both the grand procession and the assault on Imperial City were over.

131

CHAPTER ELEVEN

Over the next two weeks, along with the clean-up operation, an enormous investigation took place. Tollius and Aurelius, in common with all other members of Antrobus II's High Council, wanted to know who was behind the attacks, and what had prompted them. Wherever possible, the deceased attackers were identified from dental records or DNA scans. If they were, the entirety of their assets and properties were seized for the planet in the Saviour-King's name, and used to help finance the re-building of the city. The heretics' families, if they had any, had to renounce all allegiance to the dead men or face charges of treason and heresy themselves. Their life histories, affiliations and habits were scrutinised for any clue to explain their sudden, and, for most of them, quite inexplicable and out-of-character actions during the attacks. The heretics themselves were excommunicated and their souls were cursed for all eternity in a ceremony led by Lady Salfina. Their bodies were incinerated. Any honours they had earned during their lives were withdrawn.

Shenaria camped out in the giant Militariat Operations Centre, colloquially known as 'the Dome', for much of this time, suggesting avenues of enquiry, analysing data and discussing the planet's likely security status with Helbrad and Tollius. Only rarely did she venture out of the enormous circular building, mainly to examine various heretics' effects and interrogate their families and companions at first hand. She had had Miri bring her a minimum of personal effects from her suite of rooms, and had based herself in one of the Dome's guest apartments.

Shenaria was utterly exhausted, and her eyes, while allowing her half-vision now, got sore and tired easily. Still, she was not the only one working flat out, and she continued to make certain that she pulled her weight to her own satisfaction. Those around her in the vast, grey complex situated to the west of the spaceport marvelled at the dedication and energy of the woman, and this, combined with their natural fear around any member of the dreaded Sanctification, ensured that the quality of work done by all was very high indeed. Soon, some possible explanations began to suggest themselves, though, in Shenaria's mind, many questions remained.

Possibilities and lines of investigation were suggested and agreed in daily briefing meetings between Tollius, Aurelius, Helbrad, Salfina, Byrrion, Shenaria and Commissioner Bennett. Bennett had been so impressed by Sergeant Byrrion's resolve and actions during the attacks on Imperial City that he had promoted him to Captain. Lord Crooker's Special Representative was off-planet on other business, so Shenaria represented the Sanctification during these daily gatherings – not that anybody objected, since the successful defence of the city had been down to Shenaria in no small manner, and she was now something of a heroine in the Council's eyes. Captain Drusus was not present, as he oversaw the well-being of the golden statue, which now stood in its rightful place on the grand pedestal in the Imperial Museum.

One particular meeting took place twelve days after the 'Battle for the Saviour-King's Statue', as the attacks were becoming known as. It had been agreed that all findings reached by this stage would be shared with everyone, so the whole company could have a better idea of what progress had been made. Tollius, as the World Regent, chaired the meeting and spoke first.

'To re-cap', he began, 'we started our investigations with several agreed key questions, namely: Who were the attackers and where did they come from? Where did they get their vehicles and armaments? Were the attacks spontaneous or organised, and, if organised, by whom? What was the reason for the attacks? There are other important issues too, such as whether the Battle for the Saviour-King's Statue was related to the earlier attack on Imperial City, and, most pressingly, whether we have seen an end to aggressive action, or whether we can expect more. We also need to know whether the security services failed in their intelligence, and whether the use of Spearhead tanks and anti-aircraft weaponry against us could have been anticipated. Who would like to speak first? Yes, Byrrion?'

'Thank you', started Byrrion, standing. 'We have now identified the majority of the heretics whose remains weren't completely destroyed during the attacks, and have compared their backgrounds. It's odd: we were expecting them to have something tangible in common; shared membership of particular organisations, the frequenting of the same low-life establishments, employment by the same companies or individuals, things like that. But there's nothing; no common pattern at all. The attackers included known reprobates and criminals, the unemployed, wastrels, dealers in frowned-upon substances. But they also included the well-to-do, people at the top of their careers, people living affluent lives. They appear to have come from all social and economic classes, from the whole range of privileged or deprived, ignorant or educated backgrounds. There's nothing in common that would seem to have drawn these people together – except for their attack on the city. There isn't evidence to suggest they even knew each other before they joined forces against us. So…we know who they were, but I'm afraid we're completely lost as to what drew them together in such a manner. It seems beyond explanation.'

Byrrion sat down heavily, unhappy not to be able to offer more.

Commissioner Bennett stood. 'I'm afraid I concur with Captain Byrrion', he said. 'We've looked at the employment patterns of these people most carefully, and checked their record of attendance at devotional services and ceremonies. There's just no pattern. Some of them had histories that veered close to heretical behaviour, but others were the most devout and upright citizens you would wish to find. Any relationship shared between some individuals appears coincidental. Some ate in restaurants staffed by others, some bought their monorail tickets or holidays from each other. A few were family members, but not necessarily close to each other. Most were complete strangers. It's a real hodge-podge of a situation. It couldn't be more random. As Captain Byrrion says, it seems inexplicable that all these people suddenly woke up one day and decided to attack the city together.'

Bennett sat down too, conscious of the calm gaze of the female Sanctifier, and wondering how she would judge the investigative abilities of the Vigilants.

'I may have an explanation to suggest, Sir', said Lady Salfina quietly, 'but I'll wait until others have spoken.'

'Very well', murmured Tollius, 'we'll come back to this. What about the armoury raised against us? Has anyone anything to offer? What about the massed fleet of Spearhead tanks held off by Harridan to the south of the city?'

Helbrad coughed. 'We think we've found the answer to that', he said. 'Governor Aurelius and I mounted a joint investigation into the presence of so many Spearheads, and the oddity of many of them seemingly being counterfeits. First of all, I checked the Militariat military and storage bases planet-wide, but all their stock of Spearheads was still accounted for, and no vehicles had gone awol. Then Aurelius came up with his idea. Governor?'

Aurelius placed his cup of Saviour-King Grey carefully on the table.

'Thank you. While talking with the Colonel I remembered the *Industrium Accord*.' He turned towards Lady Salfina. 'For those of you from off-planet, this is the name of the ongoing arrangement that several of Antrobus II's most powerful dynasties have made with the factory moon *Industrium*, orbiting our sister planet, Beltean. It's one of Antrobus II's many trade agreements with off-world communities. The arrangement has been in operation for more than a hundred years now, with the full knowledge and permission of the High Council: indeed, I'm the one who now as to sign its renewal each year.'

He paused, uncomfortably aware that others around the table, particularly the Sanctifier, might view this declaration as a sign that he bore some responsibility for what had happened. No one commented, however, so he continued.

'How it works is this: every year *Industrium* sends a large complement of vehicles and munitions to territory in Antrobus II's southern hemisphere. This land is owned and run by the dynasties I mentioned, particularly the dynasty of the D'Authreau family. Almost every square mile of *Industrium* is taken up with manufacturing, and the rest is used for the storage of raw materials until they are required. The planet has no room for properly testing its products. Antrobus II, on the other hand, is covered by enormous areas of desert; land which is perfect for giving vehicles and munitions a proper examination and run-in. For a sizeable fee, the D'Authreau dynasty and others test out a whole range of tanks and missiles on behalf of *Industrium*, then return them to the factory moon to be shipped out to Valhallan Mission units.'

Helbrad took up the story.

'When Governor Aurelius informed me of this agreement, I went to investigate the House of D'Authreau and the others. Sure enough, the Spearhead tanks that were used in the attack had come from the fleet that D'Authreau's employees were testing.'

Tollius interrupted.

'But D'Authreau is one of our most respected citizens! Are you saying that Josephus D'Authreau is guilty of heresy?'

Now it was Commissioner Bennett who replied.

'No, but he's guilty of fraud, on a grand scale, and possibly of treason. We discovered that, while officially testing the vehicles, his factories were actually making cheap duplicates. We believe that he has operated an efficient scam for quite some time; sending the forgeries back to *Industrium* with undeserved certificates of good health, and secretly selling the genuine tanks and weaponry to unscrupulous Valhallan Crusade suppliers and possibly private militias at much cheaper prices.'

'Well, that explains the counterfeit Spearhead tanks', said Tollius, relieved to have one riddle solved.

'What makes you so sure that D'Authreau isn't guilty of heresy?' asked Shenaria quietly.

A hush descended around the table. People tensed imperceptibly, and Bennett considered his next words carefully.

'Your pardon, Sanctifier. I meant to say that D'Authreau is obviously guilty of fraud at this time. I will obviously leave all judgement of whether he has committed heresy to your organisation. However, I ought to report that the man was beside himself after the attack. He found it quite appalling that tanks that were in his care had been used in the Battle for the Saviour-King's Statue, and asked what he could do to make reparations. He seemed utterly, genuinely shocked. He confessed his fraudulent activities spontaneously and completely, and asked for the Saviour-King's pardon. When I left he was receiving medical attention. It may have been an act, but, if so, it was a profoundly convincing one.'

'Thank you, Commissioner', said Shenaria. 'I will require the names of all D'Authreau's customers, Valhallan Crusade or not.'

'Of course, Ma'am', replied Bennett. 'That's all I have to report', he finished, before sitting down hurriedly.

'We seem to be making progress', remarked Tollius, 'though I'm shocked about D'Authreau. What of the anti-aircraft weaponry that our brave pilots had to face? Was that also from D'Authreau s organisation?'

'It seems not', said Helbrad. 'The weapons used seem to have come from various private security forces belonging to individuals and companies situated to Imperial City's rich north. In most cases, the arms seem to have been stolen. The individuals who actually used the weapons against us were not necessarily members of these security forces, but, as Captain Byrrion reported earlier, consisted of random people from all walks of life. The existence of such weapons would have been common knowledge to those familiar with the individuals and companies to whom they belonged. They were all stolen shortly before the first attacks began.'

'The really odd thing', added Byrrion, 'is that one private security militia had no weapons stolen from it at all, and that no personnel attached to this security force or the company it served took any part in the attacks. It is as if it was exempt from whatever malignant force prompted the assault on the city. It seems to have been the only group of people not drawn into the battle in any way.'

'Odd', remarked Aurelius, 'though I suppose a company or security force can't be held guilty of any offence for *not* joining in the attacks. Perhaps their loyalty to the Saviour-King was simply of a higher calibre.'

Lady Salfina nodded, as if this made good sense to her.

'Who did this unaffected private militia work for?' asked Shenaria. Byrrion consulted his notes.

'Enderby Clavicord', he replied. 'He employed these soldiers, quite legitimately, to take care of the security of his very valuable business, the exclusive Lazenby Club.'

'I've been there', murmured Aurelius, 'very nice indeed. Worth a visit – if you've got a small fortune to spare.'

Shenaria sat back in her chair on hearing the name. First the accidental deaths of Christopheles and Livilla, and now this oddity. She made a mental note to find out more about Enderby Clavicord and the Lazenby Club.

Tollius coughed. 'Well, we appear to know who the attackers

were and where they got their armaments from. What we don't yet know is why the attacks took place. Lady Salfina? You said you had a suggestion?'

Lady Salfina rose, gracefully and impressively. She nodded to the company.

'I believe', she said, 'that we have seen a genuine miracle. Ask yourselves what name the attacks have become known by. 'The Battle for the Saviour-King's Statue'. I think that we have seen nothing less than a manifestation of the divine. Consider! Who is the ultimate truth, and source of truth? The Saviour-King. Whose power is greater than all others? The Saviour-King's. I believe that the very essence of the Saviour-King burst through his statue as it was carried from the space port to the Imperial Museum. His light shone through all the citizens of the city, and all of us. And it revealed us as we truly were. Those of us who were truly devout responded with overwhelming devotion, worship and loyalty. Those of us who were secretly against the Saviour-King in our hearts, even if we did not know it until that very moment, responded with an overwhelming urge to destroy him. It's like drawing poison from a wound: the presence of the Saviour-King through his statue drew people's real selves to the surface. The closer they were to the light, the more their darkness was revealed. That is why the attackers seemed so random in their identities, and that is why people who had nothing in common could suddenly act as one. They did have something in common: their rejection of the Saviour-King. As his irresistible light shone on them, they were bound to act in accordance with their true natures. All the heretics in your city had no choice but to act in the way they did, and now they are defeated.'

Lady Salfina stood in silent reverence for a moment, contemplating the miracle that had occurred. Then she opened her eyes and gazed at the company.

'As I said, a genuine miracle. The Saviour-King, in his grace, confirmed and revealed his presence to us. The Saviour-King himself was physically with us as we fought. We are among the most blessed.'

She sat down. No one spoke for a long time, as they considered what she had said. All of them were lost for words. Many had tears in their eyes. Shenaria sat back in her iron chair, deep in thought.

Eventually Tollius gathered himself. He cleared his throat.

'If…If what Lady Salfina says is true, and I have to say that I'm convinced, then it would seem that there was no organised threat to our city after all, but a spontaneous uprising, driven by…well, by divine intervention. If that is the case, then…'

Tollius paused, aware of the magnitude of what he had just admitted as a possibility. He tried again.

'If that is the case, then it would seem that the danger to us is gone. Do you concur?'

There were nods and murmurs of agreement. Tollius looked at them all.

'I'm going to adjourn this meeting', he said. 'I don't know about you, but I feel the need to pray.'

The easel-shaped table now pulsed with sudden sickly and malignant flickerings of colours that lurched towards those sitting around it as if they would jump out and drown them. Blood-red candles, sculpted to resemble figures being tortured, had been put on the table by the silent, now red-gloved servants; one by each member of the gathering. Looking carefully would reveal that the face of each effigy matched the face of the person it had been placed next to. Drops of red fell from the candles as they melted, not wax but hot blood. The drips seemed to merge into the diseased table and add to the revolting kaleidoscope of colour.

It was nearly the Day of Transformation. All those seated round the table looked forward to the time when all identities would change, and the very reality inhabited by Antrobus II would shift into something far darker than it was at present. Many realised that their own souls would cease in their present form and become something other, which at this moment could only be guessed at. Some relished the prospect; all feared it.

As before, a pallid glow fell on individuals in the shadowy room, and as before they rose to make their statements and answer questions put to them by a disembodied voice. The voice seemed to be becoming more slithery and slurry. It grated on the ears of the assembly. Somewhere in it could be detected the vestiges of a human sound, but only in its corruption.

The cold light fell upon Clavicord, who rose nervously.

'Speak', said the voice.

Clavicord trembled and attempted to gather himself. His first words came out in a squeak, and he blushed then started again. 'The city erupted into panic and violence as we had hoped, but not entirely as we had planned', he said. 'As you know we had the Gargoyle all ready to cause dread and confusion on a wide scale, in order to spark off agitation and bloodshed, but the scale of the violence that erupted was entirely unforeseen. It seemed to start of its own violition', he continued, 'and the Gargoyle was not needed after all.'

'No', oozed the voice. 'The violence did not start of its own violition.

'It was a precursor of the forthcoming Transformation and the emergence of our lord *L'vylaethazs*. The weaker souls in the city succumbed to the Malevolence in their hearts. *That* is what caused the conflagration.'

'Yes, Master', continued Clavicord, once he was sure that the voice had finished speaking. 'At any rate', the whole event was concluded successfully. The attacks on the city were utterly defeated. Happily for us, the Vigilants, Militariat personnel and even a Sanctifier were highly efficient in their defence of the golden statue, the museum and the city. The city now contains virtually no threat to the *Divine Devotions* exhibition.'

The voice sighed with delight.

'And so the authorities do our work for us', it said. 'Even the Sanctification had made the defence of the exhibition their highest priority. If only the poor fools knew! Our biggest fear was that the necessary uprising would have gone too far and put an end to the exhibition. Then all our long, long preparations would have been for nothing. Good, Clavicord. Is that all?'

'Yes, Master', replied Clavicord, and began to sit down.

'I think not', said the voice.

Clavicord stood bolt-upright, terrified and at a loss. Perspiration dripped into his eyes and off his nose. He waited for the voice to continue, nervously squeezing his fingers into his palms. Eventually the voice resumed.

'You carried out an investigation into one of Rimbrant's visitors. A certain Melodia Praxis, of the City Office for Citizens' Well-Being and Security. Were you not even going to inform me of this?'

Clavicord almost smiled, relieved.

'Oh, th…that!' he said. 'It was just a precautionary measure. I wanted to check no funny business was going on. I sent Maxillan to check her out, and she was genuine enough: she'd been employed at the City Administration complex for years. I didn't think you would want to be bothered with the details, since there was nothing of concern to report.'

'Oh no?' asked the voice.

As if in reply, an arched light was seen as a door was opened and closed, and two red-gloved servants brought something in. The whole gathering turned to look.

It used to be a man. Both its hands were missing, and what was left of its arms suggested that they had been mauled and chewed by huge sharp and jagged teeth. One eye hung out of its socket, and the other was bloodily absent. Its head and face were blackened and burnt. Its legs were bent unnaturally, as if they had developed extra knees. Two large, rough bite-marks had removed parts of its torso. Its jaw hung slackly from below one ear. It still wore remnants of the expensive beige leather coat its owner had recently bought. The servants held it up so close to Clavicord's back that its blistered skin touched the nape of his neck. He shuddered.

'So Melodia Praxis was safe, was she?' breathed the voice. 'In that case, tell me why your man Maxillan was followed when he left her office.'

Clavicord's mouth opened and closed with no sound. He tried to gather his wits.

'I didn't know! Maxillan reported no such thing!'

The arched doorway lit up again, and the two servants withdrew, taking the mutilated corpse with them. The voice sighed.

'No, he didn't, and because of that I am going to let you live, Clavicord. Maxillan, on the other hand, has paid the price for not passing on important information. That was him you just saw. The next time it will be you. Now sit down, and try not to annoy me again.'

Clavicord did so, with alacrity. The light swept across the table to land on Mephistopheles, who also stood nervously.

'Mephistopheles, I will leave it to you and your little girls to determine the identity of the man who followed Maxillan. Find out who he was and who he worked for. You will find him chained up in one of the storage rooms below.'

'Yes, Master.'

'Did you track down Mr. Winter?'

'Yes, Master, I did. I found him shot dead in Sejanius' apartment building, along with Sejanius himself, who was also dead. Unfortunately, the…the box was missing.'

Mephistopheles paused, waiting for a bout of excrutiating pain to be sent his way, but nothing happened. He continued, hurriedly.

'The bullet that killed the two of them came from Mr. Kydd's gun. I believe that Mr. Kydd killed the two of them and took the container for himself. I am at present trying to locate it.'

'The contents of the box will most likely kill anyone who opens it', said the voice, 'so its whereabouts may forever remain a mystery. You will have to look hard, Mephistopheles.'

'Master…' began Mephistopheles, 'There might be an additional possibility too. May I have your most gracious permission to suggest it?'

'Be warned', sneered the voice, 'if this 'possibility' is of little use to me, I will punish you for having the audacity to offer it. Do you still wish to make your suggestion?'

Mephistopheles licked his lips and nodded.

'Go ahead, then', said the voice.

'Well, Master, we don't know what has happened to the casket or how its contents have fared. It is at least possible that the item that we most need has been *damaged* in some way. Given that possibility, it might be wise to make use of Captain Drusus of the *First Valhallans* as a substitute.'

There was silence for a moment. The light surrounding Mephistopheles intensified. He began, despite himself, to tremble once again. Then the light suddenly left Mephistopheles and shone on everyone else in the room, causing people to gasp and try to protect their eyes.

'Learn from this!' said the voice. 'This is the kind of creative thinking I require from you! You will all emulate Mephistopheles in this manner! Do you understand?'

Everybody murmured in the affirmative, though most of them did not really understand what was going on. The glow moved gently back to Mephistopheles and delicately played on his surface.

'An excellent suggestion; thank you', continued the voice. 'I will leave the matter to your discretion. Let us move on. When do you plan on completing the preparations in the museum?'

'Tonight', replied Mephistopheles.

✾

Shenaria changed back into her civilian clothing and made her way out of the guest apartment in the Dome for the last time. The High Council had decided that the threat to the city had passed. Shenaria herself still had many unanswered questions, but she felt she would be more efficient pursuing them from her own suite of rooms. She bade farewell to Helbrad and Byrrion, of whom she had formed a very favourable impression, and began her journey home. She wanted to complete her investigations into the data retrieved by Tru-D, and to catch up with Matthias, who had called her several times during the past few days. They had not had a chance to compare notes thoroughly, and Shenaria wanted to know all the details about Matthias's adventures. Matthias, in turn, couldn't wait to hear Shenaria's stories about the First Valhallans, the amazing tactic she had used at the ring-road, and the final battle by the museum.

Shenaria had a sad journey back. The debris and misery caused by the attacks had been everywhere to see, and even though the populace felt joyous and proud of their victory, they still suffered grief at the loss of loved ones and the destruction of their familiar streets and buildings. All along her route Shenaria had witnessed women and children crying, and people shaking their heads and sitting down, exhausted from their efforts to clean up the debris and repair the damage. Shenaria herself remained full of anger at the attackers for the sorrow they had caused, and had been harsh in her treatment of the surviving ones, but this had not been as therapeutic as she had hoped.

She arrived back at her suite at around seven o'clock in the evening. Unusually, no light peeped out from under the front door, though there were no other signs of anything being amiss. Cautiously, Shenaria unholstered her vengeance-gun, and listened at the door. Nothing. Silently she unlocked the door, then swung it open, remaining in cover outside in the corridor. No shots came her way, so she risked a glance past the door-hinges. The entrance hall seemed empty.

Carefully, Shenaria made her way in, quietly closing the door behind her. Vengeance-gun raised, she went into every room in turn, from Matthias' quarters to the small, private chapel, to the relaxation room. There was no sign of any intrusion. Even Tru-D was asleep on her cushion. Resisting the temptation to relax, Shenaria continued to make her way around the whole apartment. All was well, until she got to the final rooms.

In the stasis-room the robot guard was lying in several pieces on the floor, and the stasis-field itself had been turned off. The box that had been retrieved from Sappharus had been removed and was missing. In the sanitisation room, Shenaria found Miri lying on the floor with her neck broken. The survival blanket was tossed to one side, and the med-bed was empty.

Modesty was gone.

CHAPTER TWELVE

Matthias and Shenaria walked through the busy sanitisation room to stand at one of the two beds now being tended to by med-robots. One med-robot was checking a saline drip, while another vigilantly scanned for vital life-signs.

Astonishingly, Miri had survived the attack. Shenaria had had her neck carefully supported and frozen, and Miri's body had been moved into a specially prepared med-bed. Now she lay before them, unconscious, unmoving, deathly pale. A nearby screen showed a representation of her heartbeat and movement of brainwaves. They were both slow and weak, but steady. Miri, like all Shenaria's employees, was tough.

'Let's hope she can remember what happened', said Shenaria. 'We need to know for sure.'

This was the first time Matthias had seen Miri since Modesty's disappearance the day before.

'I can't believe Modesty would do this to one of us!' exclaimed Matthias.

Shenaria turned to him.

'If she did, she must have been affected by something in that box', she said. 'Clearly she was agitated, and not herself.'

'How do you know?' asked Matthias.

'The Modesty we know would have made sure that Miri was dead', replied Shenaria, grimly. 'So, we have three possibilities. What are they, Matthias?'

Even in these circumstances Shenaria took the opportunity to develop Matthias's abilities. Matthias thought for a second.

'I can only see two, Princess. One: Modesty was influenced by the missing box in some way, and acted as a consequence of this. Two:

Some other person came here and removed both Modesty and the box, injuring Miri in the process. I can't think of any other possibility offhand.'

'Well', replied Shenaria, gloomily, 'there's always the possibility that the box *itself* did this. I hadn't yet found out what was inside it. A poor lack of judgement!'

'Come on, Shenaria, said Matthias, placing his almost-healed hand on her shoulder, 'You couldn't have foreseen this. And, as I've heard tell of it, you have been rather busy recently, what with the Battle for the Saviour-King's Statue and all. It's not your fault.'

Shenaria patted Matthias's hand away. 'You always say the nicest things', she said.

'Anyway', said Matthias, 'I know what really worries you'.

'What?' asked Shenaria, surprised.

'You're worried that Modesty has somehow been corrupted by this box and become a slave to Malevolence, and that as a consequence you will have to kill her.'

Shenaria nodded gently. 'Yes, Matthias, that is what most worries me.'

'Well, it seems to me', said Matthias, guiding her towards the door, 'that we're not going to find her here. Come on! I don't even know what this box looks like! Fill me in, Princess, and I'll track Modesty down for you. I'll rescue her from the influence of this box and destroy it. And then we'll be alright again.'

Shenaria nodded. 'Thank you, Matthias: you've snapped me out of it. You're right: I need to tell you all I know.'

They made their way to the relaxation room, and sat down around the chrome and glass table. Shenaria pulled out her special stylus and notebook. She clicked the lower of the two tiny buttons on it, sat back and half-closed her eyes. As Matthias watched, Shenaria fell into a deep trance. Her eyelids flickered, her mouth twitched and little spasms of movement erupted on her arms. Her hands gripped the edge of the table and clenched. Her lips opened.

'Box…' she breathed, frowning.

The stylus raised itself from the table and began sketching. Attuned to Shenaria's brainwaves as it was, it accessed all her memories about the box Modesty had retrieved: its appearance, its design. The stylus drew the box from every angle, then wrote down Shenaria's unconscious judgements about its weight and the measurements of its dimensions. Then, its artistry completed, it lay itself back down on the table; just an ordinary pen to the naked eye once more.

Shenaria groaned, and her eyes blinked and watered. Matthias, who had witnessed this procedure on other occasions, was ready. He slapped her on both cheeks and sat her up firmly. Then he pressed a glass of water to her lips.

Shenaria drank untidily for a moment, then breathed out long and hard and opened her eyes fully. She arched her back and stretched her arms, recovering physical sensation. Then, herself once more, she turned to Matthias.

'Let's see', shall we?' she said.

They both looked at the images that the stylus had drawn. These had captured every detail of the box, and now Matthias could gain an impression of its appearance. He studied it carefully, then suddenly started, and looked again more closely.

'Oh no', he whispered.

'What is it?' asked Shenaria.

Matthias pointed to the intricate relief of an angel carved into the roof of the box. Then his finger moved down to a word etched just below it in the tiniest of writing. The word was *L'vylaethazs*. It made Matthias's head ache to look at it, just as it had those many years ago.

'I've seen this word before', he said, passionately. 'It was in Brogan's office.'

'Modesty', whispered Shenaria, and closed her eyes, remembering.

Three years ago…

Three years ago, for one of her early missions as a newly-promoted Sanctifier, Lord Crooker had tasked Shenaria to investigate reports of heretical activity on Antrobus II's largest agricultural complex, *Granaria*. She had docked at Granaria's central trading port together with Matthias, whom she had employed on secondment for two years now, after requisitioning his service from the Valhallan Crusade during an earlier operation.

They were disguised as cereal buyers for a large multi-planetary foods conglomerate. Shenaria took the role of Matildia, a Trades-Commissioner, while Matthias became Avenus, a foodstuffs quality inspector. They had travelled second-class, as befitted the positions of such workers, and wore thick, woolly clothing that almost completely covered them. Matthias itched dreadfully: Shenaria seemed not to notice.

They had met Horatio, whose various companies held a virtual monopoly over all agricultural business carried out in Granaria. He was a smartly-presented middle-aged man, very proper in his manners, and had seemed genuinely welcoming. Shenaria could detect his obvious enthusiasm for his work, and his authentic pride in the high standard of grain his many workers harvested each year. He had looked her straight in the eye and answered all questions in what appeared to be complete honesty. Matthias, a good judge of men, had taken to him immediately, but Shenaria had advised caution.

'Don't forget', she had said, 'there is still the existence of heresy in this place, and we know that it is well-organised. Horatio, as the major employer, is well-placed to be behind it. We should expect it to be concealed well, and fronted by someone very plausible. Treat your first impressions with caution, Matthias.'

'I don't believe it's Horatio, so I'll make a bet with you' Matthias had replied. 'If Horatio is behind whatever heretical operation we uncover, then you can report me to my Sarge as an incompetent idiot, or dock my pay for a year, or exact whatever penalty you like. But if he's innocent, like I believe, then...'

'Yes?' smiled Shenaria, admiring his confidence and curious about what he would ask for.

'If he's innocent, and I'm right, then you employ me properly and for good. No more wondering if one day I'll go back to the Crusade. Not that I disrespect them', he added hurriedly, 'or I won't do my duty there if that's the Saviour-King's will, but...but I so enjoy working for you!'

'Alright, Matthias, it's a bet', said Shenaria, amused and pleased. 'If I'm right I'll exact a penalty, not that I'm going to tell you what it is, and if you're right you can work for me permanently.'

The two of them had been put up in one of Granaria's many

characterless trade hotels, and each day they went about their business. Shenaria would attend meetings with various representatives of the trade cartels, while Matthias would go out to fields of each type of cereal crop, and inspect its quality. Both would keep their eyes and ears open for suspicious activity of any type.

After a fortnight of this undercover work they were none the wiser. Neither had discovered any evidence or heretical opinion, behaviour or organisation. Shenaria, who had covertly recorded and listened to conversations and meetings of the powerful, and searched many supposedly locked drawers and safes, had found nothing of concern. Similarly Matthias had not witnessed any odd or dubious behaviour in the actions and routines of the field workers themselves. They were almost ready to report back that the original reports had been mistaken, when the situation changed dramatically.

Matthias, frustrated at the lack of progress, and bored by the perpetual days spent investigating crops in the fields, improvised a different, and less overt, course of action. In the dead of night he slipped out of the trade hotel and made his way to the nearest storage unit of the vast steel grain refinery, where the grain that he had inspected during the day was taken to once it had been harvested. Matthias had chosen this storage unit since it had been the one most referred to by the labourers he had rubbed shoulders with in the fields during the day.

He felt his way around the massive square structure in the pitch-dark night, looking and listening for anything out of place. A strong, heady yeast-type smell emanated from one end of the building, and Matthias, who had not come from an agricultural background himself, assumed that this was just a normal thing to expect.

A thin light shone from below one of the giant harvester entrances, and Matthias, surprised, made his way towards it. He peered through gaps between the huge doors and the thick steel walls. Inside, the storage unit was at work. Men equipped with huge pitchforks lifted the raw sheaths of grain from the giant grey harvesters and transferred them to massive conveyor belts, which carried them into some kind of threshing machine. Further back in the storage silo Matthias could just make out cut and trimmed grain pouring out into another indistinct container. This was as far as Matthias's vision allowed him to see, so, carefully as he could, he prepared to slip into the storage unit to take a closer look.

A strong hand grabbed him from behind, and another went over his mouth. Before Matthias could respond with the instinctive, devastating blow his body was poised to deliver, a voice whispered in his ear.

'At ease, Matthias. It's me', said Shenaria, and removed her hand from his mouth.

Matthias turned to look at her. He hadn't heard her arrive, nor had any sense of her approach.

'I'm glad it's you', he said earnestly, 'or I might be dead.'

'Learn from it', replied Shenaria, 'and explain what you're doing here without my knowledge or permission.'

Matthias did so, finishing, 'I just wanted to find *something*. This was the only place left I could think to look. I reckoned that if no one had anything to hide, then even if I was discovered there would be no harm done. And if something was being hidden…then I reckoned it was best to find it before we left, even if it led to danger. Anyway', continued Matthias, 'how did you know I'd be here?'

'I didn't', responded Shenaria, 'I just had the same idea as you. Now, quiet!'

She drew him into the shadows just in time for two men brandishing pitchforks to pass without seeing them. They disappeared into the storage unit, allowing the heavy doors to slowly swing shut. Just before the doors shut completely Shenaria and Matthias shot through and hid behind a large steel wheel of the nearest harvester. A second later another two men came through the doors, only instead of pitchforks this time they carried street-daggers. A further pair followed, also with street-daggers, then another, and another. Several more men entered, farmers and field-labourers from their rough, brushed clothing, all carrying hand weapons that ranged from pitchforks to hammers to home-forged short swords. They made their way to the far end of the storage silo, where the now-cut grain fell from the noisy agricultural machines into large wheeled containers.

As Matthias and Shenaria watched from their cover, the labourers all made way for a powerfully built man to walk through them. His muscular arms were bare and dirty, and were covered with long scratches and welts. This man carried a vengeance-gun and what looked like a flask of spirits. As he reached the centre of the crowd he put the flask to his filthy lips, bit the lid off and spat it into the onlookers, and sank the contents of the container in one long, greedy guzzle. Then men cheered as he drank, calling *Brogan! Brogan!* repeatedly.

Finishing his drink, Brogan belched loudly, wiped his mouth on one forearm and gestured with the other.

'Throw 'im 'ere, Boys', he said.

There was a shuffling in the crowd. Shenaria and Matthias could see a man bound with cord struggling against the five or six men who hauled him forwards and pushed him flat on the ground at Brogan's feet. His clothes were torn, and it was clear that he had been beaten up. One eye was swollen to twice its normal size, and dried blood covered his upper lip and chin. He tried to stand up and either launch himself at Brogan or run away, but he had the chance to do neither. Brogan aimed a brutal kick at his head, and the man went down again, breathing painfully and heavily.

'Brogan! Brogan!' yelled the mob once more.

Brogan circled the bleeding man, contemptuously.

'Well, well, so what do we have here, Boys?' jeered Brogan. 'A sack of shit?' He kicked the man, who doubled over and groaned. 'No, too noisy, I reckon. A strong man who thinks he knows better how things should be done?' He pulled the man's head up by its hair. 'No, too pathetic by half. A man who thinks he can betray the Union?' He looked directly into the man's one good eye. 'Yep, I reckon tha's just what we have. What say you, Boys?'

'Kill him!' yelled one man. 'Break his balls!' cried another. Brogan smiled, and spat.

'Y'know, the trouble with you boys', he said, 'is you're too generous-minded.' He aimed another kick at the helpless man, making him yelp. 'Whaddayou have to say about it, Bristow?'

'I didn't...' began Bristow, then broke off into a fit of coughing. He tried again. 'I didn't...betray the union. I was just...tryin' to get us a better deal...'

'Oh, was that it?' replied Brogan. 'Hear that, Boys? He was just tryin' to get us a better deal. Well, my sincere apologies, Bristow. Come here, an' I'll help you up.'

He reached out his hand to Bristow and began pulling him up, then drove a large fist into the bridge of his nose, breaking it. Bristow cried out and fell down, blood spurting from his damaged face. Brogan rolled Bristow over and placed one foot over his throat. Bristow writhed in pain and fear.

'Now listen, Bristow! You know how it works. The Union has the deal, an' I'm the one that arranges the deal. You have an idea how to improve things, you come to me. You don' try to take matters into your own hands. The people I work with wouldn't tolerate it, an' neither will I. I'm not lettin' some smart-alec on the make spoil the Union's little arrangement. I'm not riskin' anyone getting' suspicious about the grain. You got me?'

'But I was tryin' to make things better...for all of us', wheezed Bristow. 'I thought that if we could jus' charge a bit more for the grain...'

'Yeah, an' bring a whole load of Vigilants an' others down on our backs! I don' think so, Bristow. It's not broke, so we ain't gonna fix it. Alright, Boys.'

Brogan stood back. Six unkempt labourers moved forwards and hoisted Bristow up. They began to carry him, aloft in the air. The mob around them cheered.

'What are you going to do?' he asked, desperately. 'What are you-'

Then he saw what was happening and screamed.

'No! You can't! You can't!'

Matthias saw what was about to happen too, and got ready to intervene, but Shenaria stopped him with a gentle touch of her palm.'

'No', she said.

'But...' said Matthias, 'They'll...'

'I know', said Shenaria. 'No.'

Matthias crouched down in his hiding place once more, sick to his stomach, and, along with Shenaria, watched what happened through the spokes of the wheel. Bristow was screaming and struggling with all his remaining might now, but the six burly men were too strong. Emotionlessly, they carried Bristow up a ramp next to the large, noisy threshing machine and lifted him high above it.

'Brogan! Brogan!' shouted the gang of men, stamping their pitchforks into the ground. Brogan nodded. The six men tossed Bristow high into the air. He screamed, piteously. Then the scream stopped abruptly as his body met the vicious blades of the threshing machine, which started rocking and screeching. A moment later, pieces of gore and ichor spewed out of the machine along with blood-covered grain. The rocking increased, then subsided, and the threshing machine continued to work as if nothing had happened.

'The Saviour-King sees all', said Shenaria to herself, looking at Brogan with steel in her eyes.

Brogan himself looked sadly at the container full of body-parts, blood and grain. 'Well, we won't be sellin' this particular container', he said. 'What a waste!' Clean up this mess, Boys, then let's get out of here.'

An hour later the silo was as clean as it always had been, and Brogan and the mob of men had disappeared. Shenaria and Matthias emerged from their hiding place, stiff and suffering from cramp. Matthias gave vent to his frustration.

'I could have saved him!' he said, hitting his fist against the harvester.

'And what?' replied Shenaria, 'Given us away? We're not the Vigilants, Matthias, we're the Sanctification. We've learned that Brogan is running some sort of criminal operation, but we don't yet know whether it's heretical or not. If you'd rushed in you might have jeopardised this chance to find out. Keep our objective in mind at all times.'

'That's what my old drill sergeant used to say', said Matthias, 'but it still goes against the grain letting innocent people die.'

'That's what makes you a good person', smiled Shenaria, 'but, as High Sanctifier Lord Crooker is fond of saying, it is better that the innocent die than the guilty succeed. And how do you know Bristow was innocent?' she continued. 'You must see past your instincts and first impressions. Now, come on, let's not waste this chance.'

Together, they climbed past the harvester and made their way to the neatly arranged lines of wheeled containers at the rear of the storage silo. Each was full of cut and washed grain, ready to be weighed and packed before being sent for delivery to Granaria's many off-world customers. Matthias and Shenaria took different containers each and began to check them. Matthias wasn't certain what to look for, so he examined the grain for any anomalies with some of the tools he used to flesh out his cover as a foodstuffs quality inspector. Shenaria took a more direct approach, and put a small sample of the grain on her tongue.

She gasped, and hurriedly spat out the particle of grain, then shook violently and fell to the floor. Her head thrashed from side to side, and her body convulsed. With a desperate effort she reached inside her cloak and drew out a small vial. Her quivering hands unscrewed the lid, then she put it to her mouth. Her body stopped shaking and slumped to the ground, still rocked by little spasms.

Matthias was by her side in an instant, supporting her head and checking she still breathed. Her mouth opened and saliva dripped out. She managed to open her eyes and looked at him. Her frame began to calm.

'Easy, Princess', he whispered. 'You're alright now.'

A long moment passed, then Shenaria coughed twice and attempted to sit up. Matthias supported her carefully. Shenaria touched Matthias's hand.

'Thank you, Matthias' she said softly, 'I'm alright now'.

She stood up and drew herself to her full height. Then she turned to Matthias, fierce purpose in her eyes.

'The grain is tainted', she stated. 'Not just mixed with inferior foodstuffs or even poisoned. It has the taste of Malevolence about it. No doubt, once it's cooked, it would seem like normal grain, but it isn't. This is contaminated in the worst possible way. Anyone eating this regularly would find their whole body becoming attuned to Malevolence. Their resistance to evil would literally be eaten away. We have found our heresy, Matthias: this is it.'

Matthias blanched. 'But this grain is shipped to hundreds of worlds! Not to mention Valhallan Crusade flotillas and bases! Are you saying that all of these have been exposed to tainted grain?'

Shenaria looked at him.

'I am' she said, but no more. We are going to destroy it. Explosives, please, Matthias.'

Matthias nodded, and released several grenades from the concealed pockets in his jacket. They shared them out, then systematically went through the whole refinery, placing them where they would do the most damage. Then they opened the fuel tanks of all the harvesters, packing-constructs and other agricultural machinery they could find, allowing lubricating oils and thick, sickly petrolium to drip out. Highly inflammable fumes soon filled the air. Finally, Matthias set the timer that would detonate the grenades, and they made their way out through the large doors they had originally entered by.

As soon as they exited they were set upon by a huge gang of men. The first few didn't have a chance, as Matthias's nerve-dagger whipped accurately through the air, slicing windpipes and arms, and stabbing through vital organs. Shenaria's own short-sword and vengeance-gun accounted for many more of them, and they dropped with screams and gurgles. Shenaria and Matthias fought back-to-back as they had trained, and fought well, but the numbers of the mob seemed never-ending, and eventually they were overpowered. Matthias was dropped to the ground by a shot that grazed his temple, while Shenaria was felled by a dart aimed at her from the back of the crowd. The nearest of the gang-members moved in to finish them off, but was held back by a large, brawny man, who stank.

'No', said Brogan. 'Let's make a proper example of 'em.'

When Shenaria and Matthias woke, they found themselves lying surrounded by ill-smelling refuse in a filthy steel skip. Their arms were tied behind their backs in ungentle knots and both of them had been disarmed - or so their assailants thought. As they regained consciousness they could make out the group of men who had attacked them – the same group that they had seen earlier in the storage silo – all surrounding them, and all wearing sadistic smiles on their faces. The sky overhead was still too dark to see everything clearly, though the silhouette of the storage unit could be made out behind them.

One man stepped forward. It was Brogan. A half-smoked, cheap cigarette stuck out from his mouth, and a brutal cudgel hung from one burly hand. His other hand roughly encircled the waist of a waif-like girl who couldn't have been more than sixteen. She was painfully thin and her intense blue eyes looked too large in her emaciated face. His coarse grip on her had clearly caused bruises on her stomach, which,

Shenaria saw, were matched by other forced discolorations of her skin all over her almost completely exposed body.

'I don' know who you two are', he said through his yellowed and stained teeth, 'but I'm Brogan, head of the Farmers' Union in these parts. An' I object to my union's activities bein' spied upon. Ain' that right, Pixie?' he added, giving the girl a rough slap on her behind. 'So, who are you?' he added, staring down at them both.

Shenaria got to her feet awkwardly, then stood and looked up at him with all her dignity. The rim of the refuse container came up to her chest. Matthias did likewise and stood next to her, substantially taller. Unseen by all the men he gave her hand a particular squeeze - one that she recognised with approval. She gave an almost imperceptible nod, then turned all her attention back to Brogan.

'I am Sanctifier Shenaria Calvert. By the authority of the sacred name of the Saviour-King, Brogan, I arrest you on suspicion of heresy, ownership and distribution of tainted and unwholesome goods, and knowing collusion with Malevolence.'

Brogan laughed, and several men laughed with him, though Shenaria was gratified to see a good few turn pale. The girl Brogan gripped so roughly opened her blue eyes fully, and looked at Shenaria with new animation in her face.

'Oh yeah?' said Brogan, 'an' what's that mean, exactly?'

'It means that you are dead', replied Matthias.

All humour left Brogan's face. He let go of the girl and stepped towards the refuse container. Then he took out his half-finished cigarette and pressed it into Matthias's left cheek. Matthias didn't flinch at all.

'You've got it the wrong way round, scumbag', he said. 'Come on, Boys, let's show them that the dreaded Sanctification isn' so tough.'

He backed a step away, and three of his gang came forward and started pouring petrolium into the refuse container. Shenaria and Matthias could feel the foul-smelling liquid soak through their clothing. At a nod from Brogan the three men lit matches and dangled them near the container.

'Say bye-zee-bye, Sanctifier', sneered Brogan. 'Give the Saviour-King my regards – in person.' He signalled the three men to drop their matches.

Then everything happened virtually at once. Shenaria found that her bonds had been cut, and, together with Matthias, launched herself out of the skip, startling some of their captors, who flinched and yelled out inadvertently. Instead of attacking them, though, Shenaria and Matthias ducked down by the refuse container and shielded their eyes.

Then the thrown and dropped matches landed in the fuel-soaked rubbish. The petrolium caught with a loud *whump*, but even louder was the deafening explosion that came from the storage silo behind them.

The grenades that Matthias and Shenaria had prepared had detonated, taking most of the grain refinery with it. Many of the men present were caught in the enormous blast, and had faces burned away and limbs torn from their bodies by the shockwave. They flew into the air and fell to the ground, screaming. Shenaria and Matthias, still crouched on the opposite side of the steel refuse skip, were sheltered from the worst of it.

Brogan picked himself up and bellowed loudly. He forced his still-shaking body to march straight up to the skip and whipped out a deadly vengeance-gun, which he aimed at the two of them from point-blank range. An ugly grimace crossed his features, and his stubby finger began to tighten around the trigger.

He never got to fire his gun. To his immense amazement, he felt the cold steel of a thin, serrated blade slice through his throat. Wheezing and clutching his neck as if his hands could stem the flow of blood, he turned to see his attacker.

The waif-like girl stood, balanced on the rubble she had climbed up on to reach his neck. In her right hand was a tiny dagger, and she smiled, though her eyes remained cold. Then she walked right up to him, and, with great efficiency, gave his body a little push.

It was enough. Brogan fell into the now fiercely burning refuse container. His arms flailed helplessly, and terror shone through his eyes as his flesh began to melt. His final sight was that of Matthias's face joining the girl's to look at him.

'Told you so', said Matthias.

The rest of the mob were either dead, wounded or fled. Matthias rounded up the survivors and tied them up, while Shenaria tended to the girl, wiping dirt and blood from her face, and checking the condition of her bruises.

'What's your name?' Shenaria had asked.

'Modesty', the girl had replied.

It was not her real name. It turned out that Brogan and his mob had abducted the girl from her family nearly six years previously, and had all used her for their chores and pleasure ever since. They had named her 'Pixie', but the girl had privately given herself the name *Modesty* to help her retain her purity of character despite the indignities she faced on a daily basis. She showed Shenaria the tiny book of Scripture she kept concealed in her bracelet.

'Every night I prayed for the Saviour-King to come and rescue me', she said, 'and now, through you, he has.'

Shenaria and Matthias had the granary destroyed, and thoroughly searched the offices kept by Brogan and all other officials of the Farmers' Union, which was where they had seen the word *L'vylaethazs*, scrawled on an unfinished document. Shenaria had immediately had the entire complex of offices burnt and excommunicated, without explaining the detail of why to Matthias.

'All I can say', she had said, 'is that a major servant of Malevolence operated here. I will not corrupt your mind by speaking further.'

Before the offices were put to the torch, Shenaria had extracted a full list of the names of the members and supporters of the Farmers' Union, putting it safely away to follow up the next morning. When she awoke, both the list and Modesty were missing. Matthias and Shenaria searched for her, but with no luck. Matthias voiced the opinion that she had gone to search for her family, but Shenaria wasn't so sure.

That night, Modesty returned, and gave the list back to Shenaria, asking for her forgiveness. Every name on it had been crossed off. Upon investigation they found that every single person who had been named on the list had been killed.

'I have paid them back', said Modesty, bowing her head. 'I will accept any punishment you think I deserve.'

'It's not punishment I had in mind', Shenaria had replied, smiling. Matthias had whistled, impressed.

Arriving back on Antrobus II, Shenaria had Modesty's health

checked, cleaned her up and got her clothed properly. She took over a room in Shenaria's suite and was visited by a private tutor who taught her to read and write. Once Modesty's fitness, well-being and education were established, Shenaria had sent her away for advanced training at the secretive and elite *Fortress of Assassination*, which no one outside the Sanctification knew even existed.

Two and a half years later, Modesty had returned, now a highly skilled assassin, and offered her services to Shenaria, in thanks for her rescue. Shenaria had accepted her offer immediately.

But now she was missing.

'Princess', asked Matthias, 'do you think that this…this *word*', he said, pointing reluctantly, 'has affected her in some way? That she might be regressing into the teenage girl we rescued?'

'If that is all that's happening', replied Shenaria, 'I'll be very relieved. Make no mistake, Matthias, if this word and what it represents has caught her in its sway, then she'll be very, very dangerous indeed.'

CHAPTER THIRTEEN

Back at the Imperial Museum final preparations were being made for the grand opening of the *Divine Devotions* exhibition. The formal gardens that led to the Worship Wing had been re-planted following damage done to it during the last moments of the Battle for the Saviour-King's Statue, and gardeners checked the health and appearance of the colourful new blooms. Rooms and exhibits were dusted and swept, catalogues were checked, and merchandise prepared. Rimbrant was his usual fussy and pedantic self, but his outbursts of bad temper had been muted since the attack and near-destruction of the museum.

The staff themselves were also still in a state of recovery, and their efforts to continue to work as if everything was normal were frustrated every time one of them had to go to the central exhibition hall. Not only did the glorious golden statue of the Saviour-King stand there on its pedestal, still wrapped in its drapes until the formal opening of the exhibition, but three First Valhallans stood on guard around it at all times, dwarfing any others in the room. Staff entering the central hall would forget what they had come for and gaze with rapture at these towering scarlet figures who still seemed to have steeped straight out of the pages of myth. Some of the workers would tremble uncontrollably as they caught sight of the First Valhallans' sanctified vengeance-guns and Crusader-swords, weapons that had actually been used in battle for the sake of the Saviour-King. Then there was the statue itself. People would fall to the ground before it and quail or recite litanies or prayers. Others would lose all control and confess their sins, then have to be removed, weeping, by their fellows.

Despite the lack of dignity that these involuntary actions often caused, there was a surprising atmosphere of peace and contentment in the museum. The workers felt as if the Saviour-King himself was truly with them. Even Rimbrant himself was overcome by awe more than once, and forgot to finish his impromptu lectures or admonishments, much to the relief of almost everyone.

Mephistopheles watched the proceedings with great care. His chief interest lay in the display of power that he could sense pervading the very air of the museum. Everywhere he looked, people were affected by what they deemed was the presence of the Saviour-King, and their whole activity was shaped by it. This pleased Mephistopheles greatly, and he looked forward to the completion of the *Enclave's* plan, when he would be one of those to wield such power over the citizens of Antrobus II – and far beyond.

From his vantage point just inside the adjacent room, he gazed at Captain Drusus, imagining how weak the man would seem when stripped of his dress armour, weapons and, indeed, identity. Others saw a giant figure commanding his squad with enormous authority and confidence, but Mephistopheles saw just a pawn in the power-game that would shortly be played out. In truth, he pitied the man, knowing what was to happen to him. But the hour had not yet arrived. Mephistopheles turned away and continued to act out the part of Rimbrant's envoy, eagerly awaiting the time when he could put away such a detestable role and reveal his true self to the blissfully ignorant world.

He had not been able to track down the whereabouts of the box Mr. Kydd had stolen, and was angry with himself for having had Mr. Kydd destroyed before retrieving this information. He caught himself beginning to show his frustration, and quickly took himself out of sight of the museum workers to where he could let off steam.

He made his way down to the basement of the Worship Wing, to where the main storage rooms were situated. Pausing to make certain that no one could follow his movements, he quickly unlocked a door concealed in the wide corridor's decorative panelling, and let himself through.

On the wall before him, casting eerie shadows in the half-light, hung a man suspended by a large butcher's hook. Blood pooled on the floor two feet below him, where it dipped from the many injuries his body had sustained. His left forearm had been skinned, and its insides gleamed sickeningly. A large, mottled bruise completely covered his exposed stomach. His right kneecap was no longer attached properly. His head hung down, but jerked upwards with every move that the redheaded woman made.

Her features had continued in their transformation. All her limbs now seemed impossibly long. The curves of her body had been accentuated in a ghastly manner. Hints and echoes of breasts seemed to cover her entire chest and stomach. Her almost entirely exposed flesh seemed to shine and glisten more than any normal woman's would. Her hips seemed to convey insidious invitation. Her thick, musky scent pervaded the room. Her fingers ended in long, slender, razor-sharp nails, while her feet had become more animalistic. Spikes and scales protruded from her seductively arched back. Her eyes were impossible large, and still looked at him from under their huge, full eyelashes with a tauntingly innocent expression. She stroked the man's cheek and licked her lips, then continued with her feast.

Mephistopheles watched as she tore a chunk of flesh away from his right arm with the piranha-sharp spikes that now substituted for teeth, causing him to open his mouth and scream in anguish. Her brunette and blonde companions cavorted lasciviously in front her, fondling each other while awaiting their own turn.

'Enough', he said.

The blonde and brunette eyed him viciously, but stopped their gyrating. The redhead hissed, and glided down to the ground, leaving the tortured man to swing off the brutal hook. Mephistopheles approached him.

'Well?' he asked, mildly. 'Have you reconsidered? Are you ready to talk? Why did you follow Maxillan? Who do you work for?'

The man spluttered and coughed out blood and teeth. He attempted to raise his head.

'I...work for the City Administration. Security staff. A man visited Melodia Praxis, one of our staff, and acted suspiciously. Because of this I was sent to follow him. Normal protocol... No other reason... Standard practice...'

The man's voice tailed away. Mephistopheles considered him for a moment, then punched him hard in the kidneys. The man gasped and shuddered, and tears came to his eyes.

'Come here, children', beckoned Mephistopheles. The three once-were-women slithered over to him and formed a sensuous lascivious tableau. Then all four of them regarded the suffering wretch suspended in front of them.

'You've seen and felt what my girls can do', said Mephistopheles. 'Look at them! See how much they desire you! You should feel blessed. Have you ever seen such beauty? Most men have never experienced the like. But consider…do you realise how close pleasure is to pain? Have you never wondered how your nerves can tell the difference? These girls can. They can lead you to the most intense pleasure, but that's not their interest. No, their own delight comes in the creation of the most exquisite pain. They will weave your nerve endings to form a tapestry of the most hideous agony. I think you've realised that now. You've only experienced this one' he said, stroking the redhead's hair, 'but she is as an amateur when compared to these other two. So consider carefully. You will only get the one chance. Do you wish my girls to continue in their machinations, delicately stoking your nerves until you scream with agony beyond endurance? Or are you ready to tell me who you work for, and have the pain cease for all time? Well? Which will it be? Are you ready to talk?'

The man hung for a moment, silent and unmoving. Mephistopheles nodded, and the three creatures began to unravel from each other and advance upon their captive. Catching sight of them, the tortured man began to whimper.

'No…no more…' he breathed.

Mephistopheles gestured the women to stop. He gazed at the man, who was now weeping openly.

'Are you ready to talk?'

The man nodded. 'Yes…'

'Name?'

'Templar…'

'Alright. Now, without any lies or attempts at deception, Templar, tell me who you work for.'

Templar shivered, and broke. 'Sanctifier Shenaria Calvert', he replied.

166

Matthias crouched over the med-bed in the sanitisation room and conferred with one of the med-robots monitoring the patient. Miri was still unconscious but her life-signs were strengthening and becoming more stable. While there were still risks to her health, and a question of whether she would be paralysed, it seemed that she was no longer likely to die as a result of her injury.

Reassured, Matthias moved over to the other occupied med-bed, and looked at the sleeping woman. She had almost reached full term now, and her own life-signs fluctuated wildly. Matthias had come to visit her a great deal since rescuing her from the Dems, and now regarded her well-being as his personal responsibility.

She lay in the med-bed, connected to drips and sensors. Every so often her expression would contort and screw up, and her hands would move randomly, as if she was suffering from intense nightmares of some kind. Then her body would relax once more, and her face would lighten. Matthias took a cool flannel and gently wiped her brow with it.

Shenaria entered the room and came over to sit down next to him.

'Any change?' she asked.

Matthias shook his head, then reconsidered. 'Yes, there has been one', he said. 'When I first saw her, in the cathedral, her eyes seemed not to have any pupils. When I next saw her, when I rescued her from the Dems, they looked like normal eyes again. Sorry, Boss, I've only just thought of it.'

Shenaria considered. 'That's a good sign, Matthias, and might mean that you got to her in time. But if her pupils disappear again, you are to kill her immediately, and without hesitation.'

Matthias nodded. 'I hope it doesn't come to that', he said.

Shenaria called over one of the two med-robots in attendance. 'How long before her child is due?' she asked.

'Labour could begin at any time', responded the emotionless metal voice of the robot.

'Show me the latest scan', ordered Shenaria. The robot's chest-plate opened and a print-out emerged. Shenaria took it and regarded it for a moment before passing it on to Matthias.

'Do you notice any anomalies in the foetus?' she asked. Matthias looked at the image carefully.

'It's not really my field', he said, wryly, 'but nothing looks odd to me.'

'Obtain a new scan every half-hour', directed Shenaria, 'and inform me immediately if there are any changes.'

'What are we looking for?'

Shenaria rose.

'Think back, Matthias', she replied, 'to your experience in the Cathedral on Sappharus. What was the last thing you saw before your trick with the loudspeakers?'

Matthias also rose.

'But, I told you, Princess, it must have been an illusion. I thought I saw the images on the stained-glass windows begin to change somehow. When I checked they were all fine, as you'd expect. It must have been the effect of the air and the music. They caused me to hallucinate.'

'Perhaps', replied Shenaria, 'perhaps. But when you were captured by the Dems, what were you accused of doing? You told me in your report, remember?'

'The leader – the one with the metal hand – he said I had prevented the 'evolution of the Not-Yet-Born'. Well, good! I couldn't have stood by, Boss, and watched the defilement or slaughter of pregnant women.'

'I know, Matthias, and you did the right thing. But did the leader accuse you of anything else?'

Matthias thought carefully.

'Yes, he did. Apparently I interfered with the 'Prayer for Transformation', whatever that was.'

Shenaria nodded.

'Exactly, Matthias. So now I am looking out for any signs of transformation. If this woman or her baby seem to change in any way, I want to know. I need to establish exactly what was to have been transformed – and why. I doubt it was just stained-glass windows.'

'Why don't you call this Mephistopheles in?' asked Matthias. 'These Dems seemed to recognise his name.'

'True', responded Shenaria, 'but remember that the *Divine Devotions* exhibition was staged in Helix's cathedral. The Dems would have met Mephistopheles as a matter of course because he was Professor Rimbrant's envoy. They might have simply feared that Mephistopheles had discovered their activities. Or he might be involved himself, but if so, Matthias', and her eyes narrowed, 'I do not intend to reveal my cards to him just yet.'

Matthias smiled, then his attention was diverted by an urgent beeping that came from the med-bed. The med-robots instantly checked readings and medication. The woman's eyes opened, releasing an unhealthy-looking yellow discharge. Her nostrils dilated and hers pale lips quivered. Sweat appeared across her brow.

'Matthias...' she said.

Matthias knelt by her and cupped her tiny hand in his more powerful ones. 'I'm here, Jessila', he said, reassuringly, 'you're alright'.

Jessila gasped and tensed, then a low moan escaped from her throat.

'The woman's labour has begun', observed the expressionless voice of one of the med-robots. 'It seems to be progressing abnormally fast.'

Jessila gasped again, and gripped Matthias's hand.

'Don't let my baby die', she said.

Instantly, Shenaria gripped her other hand and looked at the palpitating woman straight in the eyes.

'Why should it die?' she asked. 'What do you fear, Jessila?'

The woman's blanched and squeezed her eyes shut. Then she opened them again and stared straight at Shenaria. Her grip on Shenaria's hand tightened. More yellow matter discharged itself from her nostrils and the corners of her mouth. Matthias wiped her head with the flannel once more.

'Something...' she breathed, 'something injected into me. Into my womb. Soon after my second visit. I resisted – I did! But too strong. Don't know what it was...might affect the baby. Not been right since...' Her voice tailed off. Shenaria stroked her cheek gently.

'Your second visit where? Where was this done to you? Where Matthias rescued you from?'

Jessila shook her head, then cried out through clenched teeth as her labour pains intensified. The two med-robots were now in position to help deliver the baby.

'No...' she said, struggling, 'not there. Here...this planet. Expensive...club...'

She broke off and screamed, her eyes closing once more. Her body thrashed about, causing the thin succour-sheet to half-fall towards the floor.

'The child is coming', said one of the robots.

Jessila screamed again, more piercingly. Her grip on Shenaria's and Matthias's hands grew so tight that her nails began to draw blood.

'Easy, Jessila', soothed Matthias. 'We're with you.'

A blood-covered head began to emerge from beneath the succour-sheet. Jessila screamed, loudly and hideously, then let her head fall back on the pillow. Her eyes opened.

There were no pupils in them.

Shenaria started. 'Matthias! Kill her! Kill her now!'

Matthias looked down at the woman he had rescued, flooded with emotions, his heart beating fiercely. He grimaced.

'Saviour-King, forgive me', he said, and plunged his nerve-dagger straight through her heart. The woman jerked upright and cried out, then fell back, calm now. She gazed at Matthias, and one of her fingers stroked his hand. A sigh escaped her lips and she fell still. Pupils reappeared in her eyes before all life left them forever.

Matthias gripped the tiny, dead hand in his palm.

'I'm sorry, Jessila', he said, and closed her eyes. Then he gently released her hand and walked to the window.

Shenaria stood and addressed the two med-robots.

'I want a full autopsy of this woman and her child done *now*', she said. Then she joined Matthias at the window and put her arm around him.

'This job really stinks sometimes', he said, tears in his eyes.

***

Darkness had fallen, and most of the museum workers had gone home for the day. Rimbrant's own personal staff had retired to their rented quarters. The Worship Wing was empty, but for the strategically scattered security staff and the three First Valhallans currently on watch in the majestic central hall.

Now, with the successful conclusion of the Battle for the Saviour-King's Statue, Captain Drusus had concurred with Byrrion's, Helbrad's and Aurelius's judgement that the risk to the security of the exhibition was now minimal. Nonetheless, he had ordered that there were never to be less than three of his squad guarding the golden statue of the Saviour-King at any time, though there were often more. Others kept watch for any sign of the strange creature that, as Drusus had been informed, had attacked the transport systems of the city in previous days.

Satisfied that he and his men were fulfilling their duties towards the well-being of the Saviour-King's statue, Drusus commenced his own security tour of the building. Much earlier in his career he had learnt that, no matter how efficient and reliable cameras and sensors could be, nothing could take the place of proper patrolling. Humans, and most particularly the divinely blessed humans that formed the First Valhallans, could use their instincts and follow hunches in a way denied to even the most sophisticated technology.

So Drusus marched through the building, one methodical step at a time. All seemed as it should be, until he reached a certain corridor on the second floor.

As he approached a corner of one of the less-used hallways, he thought he saw a glint of light appear from a doorway. He blinked and looked again, but no doorway was to be seen. He approached the wall, and regarded it carefully. It appeared to be a solid, panelled wall, no different to any other in the building in design or material. But he was certain that he had seen a door open.

This, he considered, was where humans had the edge over machines. He was quite certain that a surveyor-construct, should he bring one in, would scan the wall before it and conclude it was just that: a wall, with nothing out-of-the-ordinary about it. But Captain Drusus was no surveyor-construct, and he had learned to trust his instincts.

He moved back from the section of wall in question, never letting his eyes wander from it. As he did so, he reached out and switched off the corridor's lighting.

There. In the sudden complete darkness he saw, just for a moment, a tiny magenta glow surrounding a panel of the wall. It was so faint that any normal man could have easily considered that he had imagined it – and then it was gone. There was no sign of anything abnormal.

Captain Drusus trusted his senses. Carefully, he approached the wall a second time. He took off his scarlet helmet, and, leaving it on the floor, pressed his head against the panel that he had seen illuminated, and listened.

There. He could just make out the sound of liquid pouring. Then it stopped. An indistinct male voice could be heard, followed by several more feminine noises.

Drusus placed one of his giant hands against the wall panel and, with great precision, pressed. He heard a soft *crump* as the hidden locking mechanism broke. Then he pressed the panel again, and it opened inwards. He slipped through, knowing that there was no light shining through from the corridor to give away his presence.

He found himself in an indistinctly-lit chamber, the dimensions of which he could not make out. Deep, dark shadows seemed to fill the corners and edges of the room, making them impossible to be seen. Directly before him, illuminated by a faint magenta glow from above, was an immense table. It seemed to be constructed out of one huge piece of white marble. Part of Drusus's mind wondered how the floor could support its weight.

Seated at the odd easel-shaped table was a well-dressed man, surrounded by three extremely attractive women, draped around him in various positions of abandon. The purist in Captain Drusus objected to the sight instinctively, but he still found the women intensely captivating; a most unusual sensation for him, and one that gave him pause.

The well-dressed man laughed at something one of his companions said, then turned and seemed to catch sight of Drusus for the first time. He coughed, put down his glass and stood.

'Oh…Captain Drusus. Welcome, Sir. We didn't hear you enter. Please, do come and join us.'

Drusus moved towards the group, recognising Mephistopheles as he did so.

'Mr. Mephistopheles', he said, 'Ladies. Forgive me, I did not mean to interrupt your private…gathering.'

Mephistopheles smiled.

'Please think nothing of it. I can quite understand your puzzlement. I know that this room does not feature on the plans you were given, and I can see why you would wish to investigate it.'

As Mephistopheles spoke the three women purred, and gazed at Drusus with large, inviting eyes, throwing him oddly off his stride. He concentrated and regained his focus.

'No, Sir, it did not. It is my duty to investigate anything suspicious and keep the golden statue safe.'

'Quite so', replied Mephistopheles, 'and I must convey to you the enormous gratitude that my master Professor Rimbrant and I feel towards you and your noble men. We feel most privileged and extremely humble to be graced by your devout presence and watchfulness.'

Drusus nodded. 'We go where the Saviour-King decrees. You have no need to thank us.'

'Anyway', continued Mephistopheles, 'I ought to explain about this room. You have seen yourself how tirelessly Professor Rimbrant's and the museum's staff have worked in preparing this exhibition. I'm sure you can anticipate how hard their labours will be once the exhibition actually opens. The Professor and I thought it best it they were given a special place to retreat to, to relax and recuperate in private. The idea was to ensure that no members of the public could inadvertently disturb the staff's leisure time, so the entrance to the room was disguised. Unfortunately, there was a misunderstanding. The existence of this room was only to have been concealed on the exhibition plans given out to museum visitors, but our printer removed it from all the plans in error. That is why you weren't aware of the room's existence, Captain. I do apologise, and I'm sorry that it slipped my mind to tell you. There is nothing sinister afoot, Sir; I give you my word on it.'

'It is not a problem, Sir', replied Drusus, 'though I must insist on receiving full and correct plans as soon as possible. It is most important that my men and I have all the information we need to ensure the golden statue's well-being.'

'Of course, Captain', smiled Mephistopheles, 'you shall have them first thing in the morning. Now, since you are here, won't you take a moment to sit with us and tell us tales of your adventures as one of the Saviour-King's most favoured? Or at least sit and have a drink with us? I can assure you this vintage whisky is worth crossing solar systems for.'

Drusus paused. It was not his way to sit and drink, or pass his time in idleness. Yet he was skilled in diplomacy, among other things, and had no wish to insult the envoy of Professor Rimbrant in any way.

'Thank you, Sir', he said. 'I will sit with you for a few minutes before resuming my patrol.'

Drusus sat, only to be immediately surrounded by the three stunning women, all of whom gazed at him with lascivious expressions. The brunette glided her sinewy hand along his armoured thigh, while the redhead stroked his shoulder and licked her lips.

'Please forgive my companions', said Mephistopheles, warning them to desist with his eyes. They scowled and retreated a little. 'They are very excited to see a real First Valhallan in the flesh. I do hope you will excuse them.'

'Of course, Sir', replied Drusus, though in truth he was beginning to feel very uncomfortable. He couldn't put his finger on why; it was not as if he hadn't been exposed to beautiful women many times before.

Mephistopheles passed him a glass of whisky, toasted him, and talked amiably about trivia for a few moments. Then he stopped, as if a thought had suddenly come to him.

'You know, Captain', he said, 'since you are here, perhaps you could help with something.'

'I'd be happy too', replied Drusus, trying to ignore the heady, musky scent that seemed to emanate from the three women. 'What is it?'

'Well', continued Mephistopheles, 'it occurs to me it might actually be a security issue, so it is very useful that you're here to give your advice. Earlier today, I found a strange object that had been placed in Professor Rimbrant's private quarters. At first I thought it might have been an exhibit that the professor was studying, but there is no record of it in the catalogue. The professor himself has no knowledge of it. So I'm beginning to fear that it has been planted here by someone. It might have been a gift, I suppose, but I'm just beginning to wonder whether it might be dangerous in some way.'

Drusus rose, alert now.

'Where is it?' he asked, 'I need to check it is safe.'

Mephistopheles also rose. 'Well, Captain', he said, 'as it happens, it is right here. I brought it with me to think about while having my break.'

'Let me see', demanded Drusus.

Mephistopheles nodded, and gestured to the women. The blonde and brunette glided out of sight. Then they re-emerged from the shadows carrying a small, intricately carved casket. It was brass and scarlet in colour, and covered with beautifully detailed effigies of wailing angels in flight. They put it down on the table in front of Drusus, who regarded it carefully.

'I have no idea what it is', said Mephistopheles.

'I will find out', said Drusus, determinedly, and opened the casket's lid.

Shenaria caught up with Matthias as he emerged from the Battle-Room, sweating from his exertions.

'Anything?' he asked.

'Something', replied Shenaria, 'some information.'

They made their way to the Relaxation Room and Matthias prepared two cups of Saviour-King Grey while Shenaria organised some papers over the chrome and glass table. He brought them over, and the two of them took a mouthful before Shenaria passed one of the papers to Matthias for him to look at. He swallowed his tea and looked at it.

'What's this?' he asked.

'It's the original report by Christopheles about the *Divine Devotions* exhibition' replied Shenaria.

'The one where he says *no concern?*' asked Matthias, wryly. Shenaria nodded.

'Now look at this', she said, passing another sheet towards him.

Matthias began to look at it, then stopped.

'But this is a private letter to you.'

'I know, Matthias. It's alright, you can read it.'

Matthias did so, then looked at Shenaria. 'I don't understand', he said. 'It seems just to be a letter from Christopheles, a personal letter. Not Sanctification business at all.'

'That's right, Matthias. I was looking through Christopheles' report on the exhibition again, when I remembered this letter. Do you notice anything?'

Matthias looked more carefully.

'The writing style…' he began.

'Yes, Matthias. And the ink. And the font. And the paper. The report and the letter were written by different authors on different machines.'

'I don't understand', said Matthias.

'I checked with the Fortress Dedicata', replied Shenaria. 'I found out several things. The person who asked Christopheles, rather than me, to investigate the *Divine Devotions* exhibition initially, was Lord Crooker's Special Representative. The report Christopheles wrote was also submitted to Lord Crooker's Special Representative.'

'Well, okay', said Matthias. 'That's not suspicious in itself.'

'Not yet', responded Shenaria, 'but then I managed to get hold of this.'

She passed a third piece of paper to Matthias, who read it carefully.

'This is an internal memo about something else entirely', he observed. 'How is it connected?'

'You're right, Matthias, the content of the memo is unimportant. But compare it to Christopheles' report. Look carefully.'

Matthias did so. Then he sat back and whistled.

'It's from the same machine', he said, 'and it's in the same style. Whoever wrote this memo also wrote Christopheles' report, or, at least, re-wrote it.'

'Exactly', replied Shenaria, pleased with him. 'And the person who wrote that memo was also Lord Crooker's Special Representative. So, we have two possibilities: either Lord's Crooker's representative copied out Christopheles' report for distribution, adding his own stylistic flourishes, or...'

'Or he ditched Christopheles' report and substituted this one instead', finished Matthias.

'Exactly!' said Shenaria.

'What's his explanation?' asked Matthias after a moment's thought.

'That I don't yet know' responded Shenaria, but I have insisted on finding out. In fact, I am expecting him to call...'

A chiming sound interrupted her. She grinned, and crossed to a nearby computer.

'At least he's a good time-keeper', she said.

She touched the keyboard, and the screen flickered into life. Shenaria watched as the image of a man she had only ever seen at a distance in real life came into view.

'Special Representative', she said, courteously, 'thank you for responding so quickly.'

'Sanctifier Shenaria Calvert', replied Popov from the screen, 'I'm so very pleased to make your acquaintance at last.'

CHAPTER FOURTEEN

As Drusus began to open the casket he appeared to glimpse a whole galaxy, compressed and contained in an uneasy spiral full of dark, pulsing colours – as if the matter swallowed by a black hole in space had been captured and solidified. As his hands continued their movement the captured galaxy seemed to explode. Drusus screamed as tiny particles of dark matter pierced him like radio waves. The after-image of the spiral shape etched itself on his retinas, burning and torturing him. The intensity and uncleanliness of the unnatural sight was too much for his mind to accommodate.

His body, shocked into paralysis, fell forward heavily, smashing the edge of the thick table and sending shards of marble in every direction. He rolled onto the floor, breaths coming only with difficulty, blood beginning to accumulate around his nostrils and ears. His eyes stared ahead of him, rigid and unblinking.

'Hurts, doesn't it?' sneered Mephistopheles, leering at him.

Drusus's mind began to overload with dark images that seemed to press upon him almost physically. The spiral shape carved into his eyes seemed to suck all his thoughts towards it. It was as if all his memories, all his principles, lost their own character and adopted new contours. Even his identity seemed to bow itself out of kilter. It was as if an equivalent spiral, or helix, rather, had appeared at the centre of his soul, and all that his whole self was beginning to mould itself around it. His mind screamed, though only a weak gurgle made its way out of his dribbling lips.

Worse still, he recognised some quality this helix-shape had. Even as it began to dominate his soul in the foulest and most insidious ways possible, he was stunned to realise that there was an echo of something almost holy about it.

'Wha...' he managed, barely. Mephistopheles leant down beside him, and cooed.

'Shocking, isn't it? You find yourself defiled, violated. But you recognise something, don't you? Something you revere. Something you worship.'

Drusus now lay completely motionless, stretched out on the floor. He couldn't even move his eyelids, but watched helplessly as Mephistopheles gestured to the three women, who laughed maliciously and moved out of his vision. The table, so white and plain when he had entered the room, now started to pulse with thick, unnatural colours that matched the ones playing across his mind.

'You are strong', whispered Mephistopheles, beginning to unfasten Drusus's dress armour. 'Only a First Valhallan like you, or perhaps a High Sanctifier, could have witnessed that sight without already being dead. I'm glad of it, because we need you alive for a little while longer.'

He tore off Drusus's cloak and attempted to release his chest-plate. It wouldn't give. With a grunt, he beckoned to the women, who returned. Now Drusus started to see them for the foul and hideous creatures they really were. All their feminine attributes were exaggerated, but underneath these lay the presence of something vile, malignant and unnatural which now began to show through their glistening skin. As they relinquished their concealment, Drusus could finally determine their true nature.

They had become demonic. They were Enchantresses.

Mephistopheles kissed them one by one, then said something to the redhead, something that Drusus couldn't make out over the pounding in his ears. He still lay completely paralysed, motionless and helpless. Mephistopheles returned to him.

'My apologies, Captain. Where are my manners? We were discussing your predicament and what may have caused it, I believe. Now, where were we? Yes, you're quite right; you had noticed the presence of something almost holy, hadn't you. I bet you're dying to know what it is. In fact, that is literally true: you *are* dying to know what it is.'

The redhead came back into Drusus's field of vision, a vicious circular saw in her unnaturally long and pointed fingers. Mephistopheles smiled.

'Well…I'll give you a clue', he whispered. 'I'm sure you've heard it said that none may look upon the face of the God-Saviour-King and live.'

Blood began to flow out of Drusus's tear ducts. His saliva turned an unhealthy shade of puce, and his skin began to lose all colour and moisture. He was helpless to react or defend himself as Mephistopheles changed his position on the floor as if he was a baby. With his dwindling self of will and identity he tried to make out what Mephistopheles meant, but understanding eluded him.

'We need something from you, Captain', said Mephistopheles. 'Something to make our work perfect. You'll pardon us, I hope, but we need to take it now in case it becomes affected like the rest of you.'

Mephistopheles nodded, and the other two Enchantresses reappeared, also equipped with circular saws. With all the changes to their faces and bodies they were still the most seductive women Drusus had ever seen.

'Your Divine Imprint, Captain; your DNA', finished Mephistopheles.

At last Captain Drusus had the first glimmerings of understanding. He began to see what the double-helix shape etched into his soul attempted to imitate. He knew what his genetic inheritance was, and saw, with profound shock, how this might be used to turn such an imitation into reality. With a final, heroic effort, he attempted to refute the changes imposed upon him. He managed to turn his head.

'No…' he breathed.

Mephistopheles's eyes widened with surprise, then he grinned evilly.

'Captain, I take my hat off to you. Such strength and determination! You really are the most astounding specimen of humanity I have ever come across. Not pure humanity, of course. Indeed, it is exactly your rare blessings that make you interesting to my master.'

'Who?…' managed Drusus, weakly.

Mephistopheles smiled and shook his head.

'Sorry, Captain', he said, 'that information will remain with me for the moment. Now it is time for you to say goodbye.'

Mephistopheles's face lost all affability, and he stepped back out of Drusus's vision. The three ghastly Enchantresses leant forward and leered over him, rubbing parts of their unnatural, seductive bodies up against him. Then they turned on their brutal circular saws.

The last, agonising sensation Captain Drusus felt was of the merciless blades hewing through his flesh. The woman-things laughed sadistically as they ploughed through his body and ended his life. Then the brunette plunged her foul hand into the gaping wound she had inflicted, and tugged at something. A *snap* was heard, and her blood-covered hand emerged, dripping with gore, holding a squashy still-pulsing object covered with blood and bits of vein. She licked her lips and hissed with pleasure.

Mephistopheles took a pair of sanitised gloves and a medical container from the pocket of his immaculate jacket, and, with infinite care, picked up the heart that contained Captain Drusus's Divine Imprint and sealed it away.

'Thank you, Ladies', he smiled, 'Excellent. Dispose of the corpse in whatever manner you think you would enjoy. Then get rid of this armour. Find Drusus's helmet and pass it on to Clavicord: it would look good in his trophy hall. Then meet me in the central hall. We have one more job to do tonight.'

Clavicord wandered through the luxurious crystal room and gazed out of the window into the night sky and towards the ski-slopes below. Then he sat down in his favourite chair with a sigh. The Lazenby Club was closed to guests for the time being, officially for re-decoration. He looked over with contempt to where his wife, Calista, was busying herself fussing with ornaments. He thumped the arm of his chair.

'Drink', he demanded.

Calista stopped what she was doing and went straight to the ornate, antique drinks cabinet. She poured him his favourite expensive tipple and brought it over to him. He took it without thanking her, and she returned to her ornaments without a word. Clavicord wondered exactly when it had been that she had lost her backbone. Still, she had her uses, he thought, and she kept out of the way when important matters were being decided.

A bell chimed somewhere in the building. Without a word, as if it was all that was expected of her, Calista left the room to greet the new arrival. A few moments later she showed him into the room. She took his coat and got him a drink.

'Get out', said Clavicord, rudely, and his downtrodden wife left the room without a sound.

Clavicord rose from his chair and moved to greet the man. He shook his hand, observing, as he always did, the new arrival's charismatic presence and exudation of power. He was a handsome, confident man.

'How did it go?' he asked his visitor.

'She suspects', replied Popov. 'She is canny, that one. I should have noted her as a potential danger, especially after her impressive performance at the Battle of the Saviour-King's Statue.'

'A battle we needed to be won', Clavicord reminded him. 'It was just as well she was alive for it.'

'Agreed', replied Popov, sitting down languidly on one of the room's antique sofas and taking a mouthful of vintage brandy. 'Now, however, things have changed. She has worked out that I wrote Christopheles' report.'

'According to Mephistopheles, she was also the one who sent this Templar to follow Maxillan', added Clavicord. 'I don't like it. We've already dealt with two Sanctifiers: questions might be asked if we have to deal with a third. How did you leave things with her?'

'I admitted writing Christopheles' report', answered Popov, to Clavicord's surprise, 'but only in the sense that I re-wrote a report he submitted to me. I told her a cock-and-bull story about how Christopheles was being considered for a higher office, and how I was overseeing all his work. I told her that I had re-written his report in order to model how it ought to be done by a representative of such an office. It was part of his training towards promotion.'

'Good story', exclaimed Clavicord, impressed. 'Did she believe you?'

'It's hard to say', responded Popov, after a moment of reflection. 'As I said, she's a very intelligent woman. A good adversary', he added, with a wry smile, 'not as easily led as Christopheles.'

'Then what do you think we should do?' asked Clavicord.

Popov finished his drink, put his glass down on an exquisite antique table, and rose to his feet.

'Normally', he said, 'I would advise caution and continue as normal while keeping her under surveillance. After all, she might well believe someone with my status and authority. However, I think the stakes are too high this time. We cannot afford anything to go wrong at this crucial stage. No, I think that what we should do is destroy her utterly and completely; her, and all those who consort with her.'

Clavicord walked towards the window and looked out at the barely-visible ice-topped mountains that surrounded them, as if deep in thought. Then he turned and smiled.

'I'm so pleased you've said that', he smiled. 'My own thoughts exactly. More-so, I think the time for subtlety has passed.'

He beckoned Popov to the window, and gestured towards the south of the building.

'Yes', he continued, draining the last of his own drink, 'with the Day of Transformation about to begin, the moment for subtlety has gone. We didn't need the Gargoyle to bring the planet to military readiness after all, but perhaps its moment has finally come. I think it is time for the Gargoyle to feast again.'

Even draped, and surrounded by almost complete darkness, the giant golden statue of the Saviour-King seemed to exude a glow of intense holiness that drew the eye – and, indeed, the soul – towards it. Mercutio, Philmanus and Fabian, the three First Valhallans currently standing guard around the statue in the majestic central hall, still found themselves affected by its presence, even though they had spent months travelling with the statue aboard the *Commensurate Justice*. Now, as they stood in strategic positions around the hall, still as statues themselves, they found their attention being drawn towards the imposing effigy and away from doorways and windows where sources of danger could emerge from. At least, this was the explanation Mercutio gave himself when suddenly the empty chamber became an occupied one.

None of them had sensed the figures approach, which in itself startled the First Valhallans and gave them pause. They raised their weapons reflexively, and shone lights on the new arrivals, ready to cut them down should the merest hint of a threat become apparent.

Sergeant Fabian was the first to recognise the intruders, or at least one of them, and signalled the others accordingly. Mercutio lowered his long-sword and Philmanus his vengeance-gun. Fabian himself kept his own vengeance-gun trained on the new arrivals simply to make a point about how near they had come to death for approaching without warning.

'Mr. Mephistopheles', he said, 'Ladies. What is your business here?'

'Always on duty, Sergeant', replied Mephistopheles. 'Good: I approve. I am glad to see that the Saviour-King's finest live up to their reputation.'

'Your business, Sir?' repeated Fabian, patiently.

Mephistopheles smiled.

'Why…the same as yours. You are tasked with the security of the most precious golden statue. I am tasked with overall responsibility for the well-being of the entire exhibition. I would be derelict in my duty if I did not check for myself that you were not derelict in yours.'

'Sir!' replied Fabian, offended.

Mephistopheles spread his arms in a gesture of peace-making.

'Please, Sergeant, let's not have any unnecessary misunderstanding. I did not doubt for one moment that you and your fine men would be resolute in your guardianship. Nonetheless, I work for a professor who, let us say, is a bit…intense about his exhibition, and I had promised him that I would see for myself.' He shrugged. 'After the Battle for the Saviour-King's Statue, you cannot entirely blame Professor Rimbrant to be rather protective about his collection. It did take him decades to accumulate it.'

Sergeant Fabian lowered his weapon.

'I understand, Sir, and can assure you that the First Valhallans, who have already looked after the golden statue faithfully for months, will continue to do so. The statue, and Professor Rimbrant's exhibition, are both quite safe.'

Fabian nodded towards his men, who resumed their positions on guard. Mephistopheles' female companions gasped and swooned. Mephistopheles smiled.

'Oh, forgive me, Sergeant, I didn't introduce my colleagues. Please meet Felicity, Venus and Helena. Girls, go and say hello.'

The three women separated and glided across the ornate central hall until each one faced a different space marine. The soldiers looked at the captivating and inviting figures, unsure of what to make of them. They looked innocent enough, in fact the blonde woman, Venus, seemed little more than a girl. Mercutio, Philmanus and Fabian did not realise that their actions and reactions seemed to be slowing down as they gazed at the women, whose heady, musky pheromones were being responded to below the level of consciousness. The women smiled and gazed invitingly at the Valhallans with impossibly large eyes, mesmerizing them little by little.

Then the women began to undulate and sway. Slowly, enchantingly, provocatively, they shimmered and turned, captivating and hypnotising the men. As they did so they began to change. Their hair grew more luxurious and full-bodied. Their skin shone and glistened, even though there was almost no light in the chamber. Their breasts seemed to push against the increasingly insubstantial clothing they wore. Their limbs extended, fingers becoming claw and pincer-like. Scales and razor-sharp spines materialized on and through their shoulders and backs. Their tongues lengthened and grew more pointed.

As they continued in their enticing and will-sapping dancing, Mephistopheles walked around the men, completely unnoticed by them. He withdrew Phimanus's vengeance-gun from his hand and pointed it at his head – no reaction. He reached up and slapped Sergeant Fabian's face – again, no reaction. He shouted *The Saviour-King is dead* at the top of his voice – no reaction. Finally, he stopped, pleased.

'Thank you, Ladies', he said.

The Enchantresses stopped their dancing, though every move they made remained seductive and inviting. Mephistopheles circled the three of them, going to each one of them in turn. He kissed each one full on the lips, and put something that was too small to see in each creature's claws. Then he stepped back.

'If you please', he said.

The three Enchantresses floated upwards off the floor and gravitated towards the golden statue of the Saviour-King. They circled it, flying around it in disturbing double-helix patterns for some moments. Then they glided to land at precise intervals on the statue itself, one over the heart, one on the centre of the back and one on the middle of the forehead.

The statue seemed to resist their presence, as, for a moment, the Enchantresses' grace left them and they stumbled, almost falling. But they regained their poise and returned to their pre-arranged positions. Mephistopheles walked around the massive pedestal below, checking their positions, then went to sit on the bench where Shenaria had sat only recently. He nodded his approval.

The three ghastly Enchantresses ripped tiny holes through the drapes that covered the statue, allowing a wonderful radiance to shine through, which they avoided, hissing with displeasure. Then they placed their nails over the incisions they had made, grimacing with the pain of being so close to such holiness. They held their hands in place for a few minutes, long enough for the tiny neural caterpillars Mephistopheles had given them to begin burrowing almost invisibly into the statue itself. Then, at a signal from Mephistopheles, they glided back down to the floor to stand before the three seemingly paralysed and unaware First Valhallans. As they did so, they began to resume their former forms, becoming once again, as far as the eye could detect, at least, three voluptuous, gorgeous women.

The First Valhallans blinked, regaining physical sensation. All had the impression of a passage of time, yet nothing seemed to have happened. Their bodies seemed to suffer the final seconds of a bout of pins-and-needles, but this was gone almost instantly. They drew themselves to full attention, puzzled and alert, only to see things as they were before. They were standing on guard being addressed by Mephistopheles, Professor Rimbrant's envoy, who was introducing his companions.

'Felicity, Venus and Helena', he was saying, 'are so pleased to meet you. Girls, say hello.'

'Hello', the three women said, demurely, with wide eyes, apparently in awe of the soldiers. The First Valhallans, almost despite themselves, nodded back.

'Thank you again, Sergeant', said Mephistopheles, 'I can reassure our Professor Rimbrant that all is well. Goodnight to you and your men.'

'Goodnight, Sir', replied Sergeant Fabian, 'I'm pleased to be able to reassure you.'

Mephistopheles scooped up his companions and they were gone. The three First Valhallans looked at each other, as if to check that everything was alright, then resumed their diligent guard duty, putting the midnight visit down as an oddity rather than anything to be concerned about.

High above their heads the three neural caterpillars continued to burrow into the aeons-old golden statue of the Saviour-King, beginning to prepare it for the transformation to come.

Matthias sat alone at the chrome and glass table. He lifted the mug to his lips and took a swig of coffee, not for the first time that night, then returned to the papers spread out in front of him. Shenaria had presented him with all the information they had gathered so far and tasked him to put it together in a meaningful manner. He had no doubt that Shenaria herself had already identified patterns in the data and decided upon certain courses of action, but he appreciated the challenge. Shenaria had left him for a few minutes in order to bathe her still-sore eyes and to see if the med-robots had finished their autopsies of Jessila and her child. Neither of them had even considered retiring for the night, and now it was as pitch-black outside as it always got in the small hours of the morning.

Miri had begun to recover, though she was still unconscious. Her life signs had strengthened considerably over the past few hours. Matthias had been pleased to hear this: he had a high opinion of Miri, and knew that she was much more than the simple maid-servant she appeared to be.

He yawned, and attempted to regain focus. So far he had compared the data collected by Tru-D to the published plans of the Imperial Museum's Worship Wing, and found some discrepancies. It was very cleverly done, but, if he was right, the museum contained several rooms and corridors that had been concealed from the general public, the Vigilants and even from Captain Drusus's First Valhallans. He had marked these down to be investigated. Matthias had also gone over the content of Christopheles' report on the *Divine Devotions* exhibition carefully. Now that he knew that it had been re-written by Popov, he had looked for obvious changes of writing style that might give clues as to which parts of it were original and which had been replaced by something else.

He was now attempting to relate his experience on Sappharus to the events that had followed, but had had to pause in this while he waited for the autopsies to be completed. They might give some clue as to what the interrupted *Prayer for Transformation* had really been about.

Shenaria re-entered the Relaxation Room. Matthias turned to greet her, only to be surprised by her appearance. She was wearing her dark green armour, chainmail chestplate and jet-black cape. Her dark eye filters hung loosely around her neck. There were moments when Shenaria truly looked like the Sanctifier that she was, and this was one of them. Even Matthias, who had seen her garbed like this many times, still had to catch his breath at her impressive and powerful appearance. He stood, respectfully.

'Our next move', said Shenaria, answering the question in his eyes, 'will be decisive and for all to see. The time for subterfuge has passed. I have simply got myself ready.'

Mathias patted his concealed nerve-dagger. 'I'm always ready, Boss' he grinned.

The two of them sat down and looked at all the information spread out before them. Shenaria cast an eye over Matthias's scribbled notes.

'Any thoughts?' she asked.

Matthias explained his discovery about the concealed areas in the Worship Wing, and Shenaria nodded.

'I thought as much', she said. 'Tru-D's reaction to a part of the building suggested that something wasn't right. Good. Any other thoughts, particularly about Christopheles and his report?'

Matthias shook his head. 'It's very difficult, Boss. Without knowing what Christopheles wrote originally, it's hard to say what's been revised. Do you believe Popov's story? That he re-wrote the report as part of Christopheles' training?'

'It's quite plausible', responded Shenaria. 'I expect you remember all the times I've gone over your own paperwork for you.'

Matthias grimaced, and Shenaria smiled.

'So it does happen', she said, 'and it's quite proper when it does.

However', she continued, 'I happen to believe his story is a pile of horse-turd from beginning to end, and that something has been purposely concealed from the Sanctification.'

Matthias nodded. 'I'm so pleased that's your opinion too', he said.

'Alright: think backwards', suggested Shenaria. 'Let's assume, for the moment that Christopheles did not write *no concern*; rather, that he did find something that worried him. He was an astute man, Matthias.'

'I wish I'd met him', said Matthias. 'I'd have liked to hear his version of your fight. I have a sneaky suspicion that he was winning really!' he teased.

Shenaria smiled. 'You always say the nicest things', she said. 'Now: back to business. If we assume that Christopheles was concerned after all, then what was the logical thing for him to have done?'

'Investigate', replied Matthias immediately.

'Quite', continued Shenaria. 'He would have investigated. Only, shortly after he wrote his report, he was dead.'

Matthias gasped.

'But we know he and Livilla died in an accident!' he exclaimed. 'It was checked out!'

'Was it?' asked Shenaria. 'Did you happen to see who it was who confirmed how Christopheles and Livilla died?'

Matthias shook his head, and sifted through the piles of paper until he found the confirmation of death report. He read through it, then sat up in shock.

'By all that's holy!' he cried.

'Yes', agreed Shenaria, 'it was Popov who wrote that report too.'

'But that means…' started Matthias.

'Yes, Matthias', continued Shenaria, 'that means that we don't know what really became of Christopheles. Or of Livilla. Only that there was a cover-up of the truth.'

'Bastard!' exclaimed Matthias.

'There's more', said Shenaria. 'Where were Christopheles' and Livilla's bodies – assuming that those were their bodies – found?'

Matthias checked the report again. 'At the Lazenby Club', he said, 'north, in the mountains.'

'Yes, the Lazenby Club. A coincidence, is it not, that the security forces of the Lazenby Club were the only ones *not* to get involved in the Battle for the Saviour-King's Statue? Not to mention that poor Jessila had something done to her at an 'expensive club' too.'

'I know you and coincidences', said Matthias. Shenaria nodded.

'Precisely', she said. 'So, what we know now is this: Popov was, and is, a traitor and heretic. He suppressed Christopheles' report on purpose and was involved in his and Livilla's deaths – or disappearances, at least. The Lazenby Club, and therefore Enderby Clavicord, its owner and proprietor, are also players in this game. Something wrong with the *Divine Devotions* exhibition has been covered up: and it isn't likely just the undeclared layout of the building. So what do we do?'

'Just before you decide that', said Matthias, 'is there anything you've learnt from the autopsies that might help us?'

Shenaria stood. 'Yes, Matthias, there is. I know it is small consolation, but you were quite right to kill Jessila and cause the death of her baby. They were becoming demonic. The baby…well, lets just say that the baby could have killed us all very quickly had it been allowed to live much longer. It was not wholly human.'

Matthias closed his eyes for a moment. 'I had hoped I'd rescued them in time', he said.

'I know', said Shenaria, 'but at least their deaths were not in vain. They have helped us get closer to identifying the threat to Antrobus II. We can anticipate that the transformation, or transformations, being prepared will also be demonic in nature. And I am very, very worried about the possible scale of events.'

'Why is that?' asked Matthias.

'Firstly', answered Shenaria, 'your vision of the stained-glass windows changing. Secondly, something Lady Salfina Pureheart said while I was in the Dome.'

They sat in silence for a while, both tired, but both infused with a sense of urgency. Then Matthias got up, poured himself another coffee and brought one for Shenaria too.

'And what of Modesty in all this?' he asked anxiously. 'Any clues?'

Shenaria shook her head sadly.

'None, Matthias, I'm afraid. Miri is not in a fit state to tell us what happened, and there's no other lead. There's no way of working out where…'

Her voice tailed off, and she stared into space, eyes wide open.

'Princess?' asked Matthias. 'Are you alright?'

Shenaria stood, slamming her mug down, spilling caffeine over some of the papers.

'Curse me for an incompetent novice and a fool!' she cried.

Matthias also rose. 'What…what is it?' he asked.

Shenaria turned to him, her eyes alive with fire and fury directed at herself. She breathed heavily, and regained control. Then she spoke in a measured, quiet voice.

'Matthias, go into Modesty's quarters and bring me something intimate of hers. Anything: I don't care what.'

Matthias obeyed straight away. He left the room, only to return almost immediately. In his hand was the bracelet that the girl Modesty had concealed her precious book of scripture in.

'Here, he said. 'I've only rarely seen her without this on. Will it do?'

Shenaria nodded. 'Very much so, Matthias, thank you', she said. 'Sometimes I can't see what's under my own nose. 'Nose' being the important word.'

She walked to the doorway.

'Tru-D!' she called, 'Tru-D! Here, Girl!'

A moment later, the golden cyber-hound padded through the door and licked Shenaria's hand. Shenaria knelt down next to it and stroked its back, then held Modesty's bracelet to its nostrils. Tru-D sniffed the bracelet all over.

'Alright, Tru-D', she ordered, 'That's who you're after. Fetch!'

The monstrous gargoyle hurtled determinedly towards its target. It had been chained to the mountain-side for too long, and was furious and full of hate. Its hideous, immense wings bore it through the air at an uncanny speed, batting away birds without care. It grotesque claws longed to pierce and rip human flesh, its mouth dripped acidic saliva in anticipation. Sickly colours cascaded over its body as it flew over the perimeter of Imperial City, its presence alerting Militariat and Vigilant duty personnel, who raised alarms immediately. Its pin-prick eyes glowed with flame, and its cruel, pointed beak let out a litany of terrifying shrieks. It rushed towards its prey, full of malice, hunger and evil. It desired only to cause intense suffering and death. It seemed even faster and larger than before. Two Militariat Vulture fighter planes that attempted to intercept it were caught in the fiery gaze of its eyes and blew up in gigantic fireballs. Missiles that exploded on its surface seemed only to increase its fury. It shrieked again, and dived towards its helpless target, glowing with iridescent fire, screaming with menace, followed by impotent military aircraft.

Five minutes after Matthias had gone to get Modesty's bracelet, the gigantic, appalling, gruesome harpy smashed straight through the wall of Shenaria's apartment, bursting apart masonry, rupturing fuel lines, exposing electric cables. The intensely hot fires in its eyes set everything alight, and the noxious fumes it exhaled combined with the fire, electricity and the leaking volatile fuels to explode with massive force. The entire residential block seemed to detonate, lift up from the ground, bulge outwards, shatter and collapse heavily to the ground, utterly demolished. Windows of all the surrounding buildings blew out, many of their walls collapsed and more fires started. Several Militariat planes flying above were caught in the immense shock waves, lost control and crashed to the ground. Rubble, twisted metal, broken glass, debris and human bodies littered the ground, crushed, ripped apart and burnt; all that was left of the entire apartment building, all consumed by a gigantic, incredibly hot furnace that consumed everything in sight. There were no survivors.

CHAPTER FIFTEEN

A week later the Grand Opening of the *Divine Devotions* exhibition finally arrived. Celebratory banners draped from all the windows in the city. The streets themselves shone as if they had been swept and washed clean for the occasion – which was exactly what had happened.

The worst of the damage caused during the Battle for the Saviour-King's Statue had been cleared up – or at least made safe – and the bizarre stone corpse of the hideous harpy-like gargoyle that had perished during its final attack on the city had been ritually destroyed by immersion in the most vicious acid. In the city's enormous, ancient, gothic cathedral, Lady Salfina Pureheart had presided over a mass wake held for all those who had suffered and died during the attacks; a service that was broadcast live throughout Antrobus II. Not a vehicle moved, not a person spoke, during the long, reverent, sad and solemn ceremony. The entire planet halted its business to pay its respects.

After the introductory intonations of allegiance and chanted confessions to the Saviour-King, Aurelius had prayed for the souls of the inhabitants of Imperial City who had perished, Byrrion and Bennett for those of the Vigilants lost in action, and Helbrad for the members of the Militariat who had sacrificed themselves for the city, the planet and the Saviour-King. Together with Tollius, and even the great High Sanctifier Lord Crooker, who had made a rare trip to the planet especially for this poignant occasion, Lady Salfina had led a special prayer in memory of the brave Sanctifier Calvert, who, it was considered by all, had been responsible for the successful conclusion of the Battle for the Saviour-King's Statue and the survival of Imperial City, and who, together with her entire staff, had been killed by the foul Angel of Death in its last action.

Insufficient remains had been left for a proper burial or cremation to take place, so Lady Salfina ceremoniously burned icons of Sanctifier Calvert's duties and status: Totems of Cleansing, Sanctificational insignia and rings of office, and a burial cloth finely woven with nine sacred symbols, each representing a founding house of the Valhallan civilisation. Finally, her own voice breaking as she did so, Lady Salfina lifted a single, perfect Sanctificatorial Pyramid to her lips, kissed and blessed it, and threw it onto the now flaming pyre. People, the majority of who had never seen Sanctifier Calvert and who had only heard of her in these past few days, wept openly on seeing this gesture, unable to restrain their grief at the loss of their so-recent heroine. Even High Sanctifier Lord Crooker's normally stern face was widely believed to have shed a tear that day, though, of course, no one dared make sufficient eye contact with such a man to know for sure.

After such a mournful culmination of all the loss and damage Imperial City had endured, the citizenry itched for any excuse to be festive and joyous once again. The Grand Opening of the *Divine Devotions* exhibition a few days later proved to be the catalyst for just such a celebration. If the earlier crowd, the one that had attended the original procession which brought the Golden Statue of the Saviour-King to the city, had been thought large, then the new crowd that packed the streets for the Grand Opening dwarfed it by more than twice its size. Men, women and children filled every available square inch of space in the city centre – and far beyond – all waving, cheering and crying with awe, excitement and relief. People even went so far as to climb onto the Defenders periodically placed around the Imperial Museum, and the Vigilants, swept along with exuberance of the crowd, let them, and even helped some of them up. No one expected any danger this time: the threat had been defeated by the planet's wonderful Militariat, the noble Vigilants and the sadly missed, heroic Sanctifier Calvert. Even the Angel of Death that had terrorised the city so badly in the days before the battle was no more. No, the time for misery and death had passed. This was a time for joy.

At the appointed hour the gates to the meticulously planted formal gardens that led to the majestic grey and pink Worship Wing were opened by two of Lady Salfina's stern and beautiful Daughters. An enormous cheer filled the air, drowning out even the gigantic cathedral choir's hymns for some minutes. People craned forwards and stretched up onto their toes to try to see what was going on.

To great cheers the city's dignitaries emerged from the gardens' three tree-lined avenues and joined each other at the now-opened gates. They were dressed in their most splendid and formal attire, and looked very impressive indeed. First came Tollius, wearing all the crests and embellishments that marked him out as World Regent. He was joined by Aurelius, who was equivalently dressed. Then came Colonel Helbrad, wearing the medals he had earned during engagements as a Sergeant of the Valhallan Crusade many years ago. He received a huge ovation from the masses, whose respect for his leadership of the planet's Militariat had never been higher. Captain Byrrion, if anything, was cheered even more loudly and enthusiastically as he emerged, being something of a local hero. His new uniform still looked fresh off the peg, however, and Byrrion, who had not yet got used to his promotion, felt rather self-conscious in it.

Then came Lady Salfina Pureheart, unyielding and stunning in equal measure. She was eye-catchingly beautiful in her shining Arch-Deaconness gown, but the aura of danger she exuded gave the awe-struck crowd pause, and they were muted in their response to her. She looked coolly at the multitude, and there was not a man, woman or child who did not feel the power of her steely gaze, and who did not give thanks that they did not have to answer to her. Her ecclesiastical identity and trappings reminded the throng of the focus of the exhibition, and, just for a moment, the crowd quietened and became thoughtful and reverent. Lady Salfina smiled inwardly; she fervently believed that fear of the divine Saviour-King was necessary for the salvation of the soul, and was pleased when she could be a vehicle to convey such a feeling.

The moment passed as soon as Sergeant Fabian and his body of First Valhallans arrived, marching in perfect union and discipline. This was only the second time that the citizenry had laid eyes on any First Valhallans in living memory, and the effect was still profound. People hollered and yelled, excited and awe-struck in equal measure. Many just gazed at the First Valhallans, open-mouthed and dumb-founded. Men saw how puny they were when compared to the Saviour-King's divinely-touched elite, while women looked at the huge and perfect warrior-brethren with a multitude of feelings ranging from desire and wonder to the need to be protected. Children craned their heads to look upwards, and marvelled at the sight of them. The First Valhallans themselves seemed – as, indeed they were to some extent – beyond humanity in their responses. They marched and stood where their duty required them to march and stand, and did not otherwise recognise or engage with the crowd, except, of course, for their remaining alert to any potential threat that it might pose.

At the most subtle of signals from Sergeant Fabian, the First Valhallans formed two lines; an honour guard once again. Through the middle of these lines walked Professor Rimbrant, supported and guided by his envoy. He was not dressed differently for the occasion, but instead wore his familiar cloak and looked like the fusty academic that he was. His envoy, a much more carefully and sophisticatedly tailored man, walked him respectfully to the front of the dignitaries. Many of the crowd knew who he was from tele-vid, but an equal number did not, and there was an audible sigh of disappointment at the anti-climactic appearance of this frail, old scholar, who reminded those lucky enough to be educated of the kind of person they had hoped never to have to meet again.

Rimbrant adjusted his pince-nez, coughed, and began to speak, inaudibly. His envoy immediately interrupted and guided the professor's attention to a microphone. Rimbrant brushed his envoy away, irked, and began again. This time his voice could be heard.

'My friends', he began, 'faithful and dedicated servants of the Saviour-King, one and all. I welcome you to my humble attempt to spread the glory of the Saviour-King across the universe. Those who truly worship the Saviour-King, for you I have laboured. The *Divine Devotions* exhibition is at your service.'

He bowed. The gathered crowd, who had expected a much longer speech and steeled themselves against it, were taken by surprise at his brevity. The two Daughters who had opened the gates now joined Rimbrant, carrying a three-foot high facsimile of the Golden Statue of the Saviour-King, covered in a plain white drape. They placed this on the ground before Rimbrant. Rimbrant bowed again, and ceremoniously removed the facsimile's drape. The now-revealed tiny golden statue was still enough to draw a gasp of awe, as people remembered the procession and battle that the original had been caught up in, and the feelings that it had evoked as it had made its way towards the museum.

198

'The *Divine Devotions* exhibition is now open', declared Rimbrant. 'Thank you all.'

Everybody cheered, and the massive, extensively-trained cathedral choir started up again with a rich and glorious version of *The Saviour-King is My Comforter and Rest*. Bit by bit the whole multitude joined in, and as Rimbrant and his envoy, Tollius, Aurelius, Helbrad, Byrrion, Salfina and Fabian made their way back through the lines of First Valhallans and formal gardens towards the Imperial Museum itself, it seemed as if the entire city was singing in worship.

Back in the Grand Cathedral, in a corner of an access corridor high above the areas of worship where the recent mournful ceremony had taken place, lay the ornately-decorated wooden box that Modesty had retrieved from Sappharus, seemingly dropped on the dirty wooden floor either through hurry or shock. The box was thick and strong, but had still weathered some damage. Two of the black metal corners had bent with the impact and caused the mahogany surface of the box to split and crack in several places. On the lid, the intricate angel relief had suffered some damage to one of its wings. One of the metal hinges of the box had twisted, with the result that the lid of the box no longer sat true. A thin, sickly pale green light shone through the gap between the lid and the main shell of the box. A spider, lowering itself down from the ceiling, happened to pass into this light. It immediately shrivelled up and dropped to the floor, petrified and dead. Something in the box had been activated.

Modesty herself lay unmoving in a derelict alleyway someway distant from the Grand Cathedral and the riches of the city. The irresisitible compulsion that had caused her to attack Miri, take the box and move it to its present location had faded away, along with her consciousness, her short-term memory, and almost her life. She was in a dreadful way. Her unmoving body was pale, her face was sunken and drained. She sprawled out over the sharp, uneven ground where she had collapsed. Barely a breath escaped her throat. Her dreams, if she had them, were beset by demons.

An unkempt man dressed in rags drew near. 'Whass this?' he murmured to himself through thick, alcohol-laden lips.

He knelt over the unmoving body.

'Well, well', he drawled, his spittle flicking on her. Then he grunted dirtily and reached for her cat-suit, trying without success to find its fastenings.

A sudden deafening bark startled him, and he turned his face, only to be knocked to the ground by a golden dog that leapt on him. Its steel jaw tore a chunk out of his arm and he cried out and pulled away. The dog snarled at him viciously, baring its teeth and bracing itself to jump at him once more. He yelled again, then fled, swearing and cradling his injured arm as he went.

Tru-D went over to Modesty's still body, sniffed it and tenderly licked it, the cyber-hound's augmented saliva passing over powerful anti-biotics, purifiers and stimulants as she did so. Then she squatted down to guard the unconscious woman, and, unknowing of the funeral that had recently taken place, sent a signal to Shenaria.

With the *Divine Devotions* exhibition now officially open, there was an order and proper procedure for everything. Consequently, the huge multitude of citizens patiently queued up to be admitted while the dignitaries of the city had their own private viewing of the collection. Tollius, Helbrad, Aurelius, Byrrion and Salfina went first, personally escorted by both Professor Rimbrant and Sergeant Fabian. Following them was a second wave of important people, the other members of the planet's High Council, successful men of industry, diplomats, decorated veterans of the Saviour-King's service and various other key figures of the planet's economy and culture, including Clavicord.

These first privileged visitors followed Rimbrant through the set route through the exhibits as he talked them through the evolution of the image and representation of the Saviour-King as the Valhallan Crusade had stretched across the galaxy over the years. He showed them beautiful and moving sculptures, paintings, effigies and other artefacts that tried as much as any created materials could to encapsulate and evoke the divine nature and presence of the Saviour-King. The guests saw for themselves how the Saviour-King had been conceptualised and worshipped over the aeons, and how these conceptualisations had varied between planets close to Earth and those utterly removed from it. They saw how the Saviour-King had been imagined by cultures that had been colonised early, and had actually experienced the presence of the Saviour-King himself before his ascension into Godhood, and by cultures to whom the Saviour-King was a God they learned about and experienced through mystery rather than tangible presence. All of them were moved, and all of them had their eyes opened further, even Lady Salfina, who had studied the theology of the Saviour-King at great length during her ecclesiastical training.

By the time the dignitaries arrived at the great central chamber of the Worship Wing they were already full of emotion and overwhelmed by the concentration of images and effigies that they had seen. Tollius even had to excuse himself for a few minutes to get some water, and Byrrion felt his heart would burst. Now, immense in its presence in front of them, was the revered and precious Golden Statue of the Saviour-King, of which so much blood had been shed. It was still in its drapes, and three First Valhallans remained on duty around it. The second wave of dignitaries came to join them, and the whole company, with the exception of Lady Salfina and Sergeant Fabian, who remained standing, sat on the carefully-arranged benches situated all around the giant pedestal at the base of the statue.

Rimbrant walked to address them dwarfed by the statue behind him. Even he seemed overcome with emotion, and his envoy had to support him for a moment.

'Sergeant Fabian, if you please', he said. Fabian joined Rimbrant, also dwarfing him, but looking amazingly small himself against the gigantic statue that commanded the entire room.

'We have reached the moment', said Rimbrant, his voice full of emotion, 'that I have waited and prayed for since I began collecting towards this exhibition. Ladies and Gentlemen, you have seen how mere mortals have portrayed and conceptualised the Saviour-King since the dawn of the Valhallan Crusade. The sights you have seen are impressive and moving, but I do believe that they will all pale against the statue about to be revealed. This is a representation of the Saviour-King as commissioned by the Saviour-King himself. It is a clue as to how the blessed Saviour-King *looks to his own eyes*. I have not seen it yet, and I do believe that even Sergeant Fabian and his valiant men have never seen it uncovered.'

Fabian nodded, and Rimbrant continued.

'What we are about to see, my good friends', continued Rimbrant, 'is something that very few mortal men have ever seen. You', he gestured with open arms towards everyone, 'were good enough to fight, and some of you lay down your lives, for this statue. Now you, and I, will be blessed in return by the Saviour-King's benevolence. It is time to unveil the Golden Statue of the Saviour-King.'

Rimbrant shook for a moment, and his envoy led him back to his seat next to Aurelius, where he sat, breathing heavily, closing his eyes for a moment. Then he turned to look at the statue again.

'Sergeant Fabian, if you please', he said. Fabian nodded once more and addressed the absolutely silent gathering.

'Captain Drusus, whom I serve faithfully in the Saviour-King's service, myself and all my men were tasked by the highest authorities to bring this precious statue here. Even so, it seems that Captain Drusus has been commissioned for another task on behalf of the Sanctification, according to High Sanctifier Lord Crooker's Special Representative, and we must all go where our duty lies. Consequently, the great privilege of unveiling the Golden Statue of the Saviour-King falls to me.' He paused, then continued simply, 'I am honoured'.

Fabian stepped to one side and signalled to the three First Valhallans, who each pulled a cord hanging from the austere drapes. There was a moment when nothing seemed to happen, then the drapes swiftly fell away from statue, revealing its glory to the mesmerised assembly.

It was utterly magnificent. The shades of gold that it was formed in seemed utterly right to convey the Saviour-King's purity and divinity. Its body was perfectly proportioned and muscular, giving the impression of litheness and suppleness even through the cold materials it was formed from. Its hands seemed to capture the essence of every type of action that hands of a god could perform: smite the enemy; comfort and enfold the faithful; raise up the devout; embrace suffering humanity; offer mercy. Its head carried absolute authority and its eyes infinite compassion. Every person present felt as if the Saviour-King himself was individually looking deep into their soul through eyes that would see everything. Lady Salfina's features shuddered in rapture, while Helbrad openly wept without shame. Apart from the sounds of involuntary crying and sniffing there was utter silence, as anything human voices and language could say in response to the statue seemed completely inadequate and presumptuous. All present were completely overcome.

Mephistopheles nearly died, and, later, had to be carried away for medical attention, while Clavicord choked and went beetroot-red as the secrets of his soul were completely laid bare. For the first time since he had involved himself with the *Enclave* he began to have doubts.

'What a shame', remarked Lady Salfina to Captain Byrrion once they had emerged from the museum, 'that Shenaria never got to see the Golden Statue for herself. She would have been the first to appreciate it fully.'

'She certainly deserved to see it', replied Byrrion, sadly. 'It is much to do with her that you, I and this whole city have such an opportunity at all. She was an impressive woman and servant of the Saviour-King, and it's a crime that she's no longer with us.'

'Don't forget', said Salfina softly, 'she's right with the Saviour-King himself now. She won't need a statue for her faith or comfort, no matter how brilliant.'

'I know', replied Byrrion, 'but I still miss her.'

'Me too', sighed Salfina.

After the dignitaries had completed their visit and left the building, the general populace were allowed to commence with their own visits. Each party of visitors was led along the same route by one of Rimbrant's staff, and each party was overwhelmed in turn as they came to view the magnificent and divinely-inspired Golden Statue of the Saviour-King. The museum staff quickly realised that they had under-estimated the strength and depth of people's responses to the exhibition and its concentrated evocation of the Saviour-King, and organised extra first-aid facilities, contemplative beds for overcome visitors to recover upon, and carefully-placed water fountains and containers of tissues, so visitors could prevent themselves from becoming dehydrated and dry their eyes. They also had the good sense to considerably increase the size of their souvenir stands to cater for those who could not leave without taking some kind of icon of their visit with them.

The Ecclesiarchy, informed by Lady Salfina, and with Rimbrant's willing consent, sent priests and missionaries into the museum to minister to the citizenry, offer comfort, take spontaneous confessions and extend their mission. Aurelius authorised the funding and provision of extra transport services, including the now repaired monorail. The exhibition was rapidly becoming a great event in the history of Imperial City, and even of Antrobus II as a whole, as people from across the entire planet made pilgrimages to see the Golden Statue of the Saviour-King for themselves. Rimbrant looked on from his office, and often mingled with the visitors in the great central chamber, gratified, happier and more fulfilled than he had ever been.

He was not the only one. Somewhere, undeclared, hidden, powerful, the owner of an eerie, compelling voice watched as the entire world came under the sway of the *Divine Devotions* exhibition, and cooed sickeningly to itself. Everything was going to the *Enclave's* plan, even better, in fact, than had originally been anticipated.

✾

High above the planet, the revolting neural caterpillars that had been inserted into the Militariat communications satellites finally completed their unnatural evolution, and emerged, slurping and mewing, from their slimy, contorted cocoons, now perverted further into something even more ghastly. The repulsive new creatures waited patiently. They waited for the *Enclave* to feed them with direction and instruction. They waited for their foul comrades to complete their own hideous evolution within the very heart of the Golden Statue of the Saviour-King down on the planet below.

They waited to bring corruption, despair and death to the whole world.

CHAPTER SIXTEEN

Elsewhere in the solar system the dead planet of Antrobus I continued in its familiar route around the sun. Above it orbited the ice-moon that housed the secretive *Fortress Dedicata Profundis*. No Sanctificatorial training had taken place here since the Battle for the Saviour-King's Statue and the cold, reinforced reinforced steel base now lay empty, except for a skeleton staff - mostly maintenance crew and guards - and the ever-present prisoners. Life-support systems operated only at their lowest settings, and most of the kitchens, leisure facilities and libraries were dark and closed.

One particular set of chambers lay sealed off and draped with the sternest warnings not to enter. It could only be reached by a single high-security corridor and entered through a thick titanium door that was secured by both physical and psychic locks that were heavily trapped. The low-level red light that illuminated the corridor at this midnight hour also served as a sensor designed to detect any intruder and automatically energise harsh security measures should one be discovered.

All private Sanctificatorial apartments within the *Fortress Dedicata Profundis* were secured with the same care, though only this one was sealed off in such a manner. It was the suite of rooms that had been inhabited by Sanctifiers Christopheles and Livilla since their marriage, and both caution and a sense of propriety had led to its being protected and preserved in such a manner. Inside, it was exactly the same as it had been since Livilla and Christopheles had left on their doomed and unsanctioned mission. Nothing had been touched. No visitors had been allowed to enter. Lord Crooker had ordered that it should remain completely undisturbed for the present, and so it did; a still memory of two brave and devoted people that could be traced through the objects, minutiae and space that had made up their lives.

One of these objects was Christopheles' personal computer, which sat on the polished maple desk he had been fond of and used for a long time, since Shenaria had given it to him as a token of reconciliation some years after their fight on the surface of the ice-moon. Softly, and without any noise or warning, the screen of the computer flickered into life. Names of files cascaded across the screen faster than the eye could follow. A blinking yellow Pyramid icon appeared, indicating that someone was attempting to access and copy these files. The first firewall was broken, causing a loud and piercing siren to start up. The computer fought back, trying to send out traceable worms and viruses to whoever the intruder was, but these were destroyed and the files being stolen remained complete and uncorrupted. A second firewall was smashed through, and now the apartment was filled with epilepsy-inducing flashing lights. Concealed pockets of acid opened up within Christopheles' computer, as it attempted to destroy its own hard-drive before sensitive files were breached. The corridor outside the apartment filled with heavily-armed guards, who waited while the locks to Christopheles' chambers disengaged, then shot past the slowly opening door into the apartment.

No one was in sight, so the guards instantly turned their weaponry on the computer. A burst from a chemical gun evaporated the hard-drive and melted most of the other components. An exploding shell destroyed the conductor that fed power to the computer, then an intensely-hot blast of fiery petrolium from a fire-thrower finished off both the computer and the desk. Two guards, who had been standing by with extinguishers, covered the burning desk with foam, putting out the fire and preventing it from spreading. The leader of the group plunged his heavily-insulated hands into the foam and brought out the sad remains of the attacked computer. Some of the acid it had secreted ate through a portion of his glove, causing him to swear.

'Did we make it?' asked one of the guards holding an extinguisher.

The leader of the group peered at the remains in his hand, and nodded. 'I hope so', he replied grimly, 'or it's curtains for us. Check the apartment, then seal it from the outside.'

Like the well-trained team they were, the men went through the apartment methodically. No intruders, or any other signs of intrusion, were found, leaving the soldiers with no clue as to who had tried to hack into Christopheles' computer. Their search complete, they turned off the flashing lights and plunged the chambers back into darkness. Then they left, waited until the locks had re-engaged, and re-sealed the rooms from the outside. Most of them returned to their quarters. The leader went to report the attempted break-in and take the consequences. Four soldiers stayed put and adopted guard positions outside the door to Christopheles' and Livilla's apartment, and prepared to remain there until further orders were received.

Ten minutes after the guards had left a panel in the ceiling opened up. A well-built figure forward-rolled out until he hung from his strong fingertips, his feet dangling several feet above the floor. His companion also emerged from the ceiling and climbed down the first figure, before jumping deftly to the ground, landing softly and without noise. The first figure also descended quietly, and the two of them silently and warily checked the chambers for any guards still present. None were, so they convened in a corner well away from the entrance, so that they could switch on a gentle torch without fear of any light peeping out under the door to the corridor beyond.

'Just as I hoped', said the second figure who had descended, 'they left guards outside the apartment, but not inside. Sloppy.'

'Lucky for us, though', replied the first figure. 'Did we get it?'

The second figure checked a piece of equipment that could hardly be seen by the soft light of the pencil-thin torch, and nodded.

'I think so', came the reply. 'I'll know soon. Keep watch, and alert me if any Sanctification guards seem to be coming back. We can't afford to be interrupted now.'

'We could have done with our assassin', grumbled the first figure. 'She'd have kept them busy!'

'Yes, I know', replied the other, 'but she's not healed enough for this kind of thing just yet. Besides, she's got her own small task to do.'

Three miles to the west of the Imperial Museum the regular midnight mass held at the city's imposing, gothic cathedral had drawn to a close. This service was mainly attended by those wealthy citizens who lived nearby and who could afford bodyguards (while the cathedral was situated in a luxurious and leafy part of Imperial City, it was never advisable to walk alone during the dead of night), civil and military personnel who had just come off or were just about to go on duty, and some of Lady Salfina's Daughters and other staff.

Sister Magdalene, one of the Daughters on duty during these hours, had made her devotions to the Saviour-King during the service, and was now heading for her humble cell high above the majestic and imposing Lady Chapel. As she walked through the tall, narrow passageways leading to her simple quarters, she thought about the truly great *Divine Devotions* exhibition that had opened a week earlier, and how it had captivated the entire world. Never had Sister Magdalene witnessed such genuine and deep outpourings of belief and devotion than among congregations of people who had visited the magnificent installation before attending cathedral services. She even knew of several folk who had given up their careers in order to spend as many hours as they could under the gaze of the holy Golden Statue of the Saviour-King. Sister Magdalene felt blessed beyond words to be alive and present at the very time that this sacred collection should visit her planet, and marvelled that such a thing should have come to pass.

Filled with such thoughts, she did not give as much attention as normal to her walk, and rounded a corner in the gloomy passageway without noticing the eerie pale green light that emanated from beyond it. But it was too late. As she came into full view of the strange mahogany box lying broken on the floor, the illumination that shone out of it enveloped her and trapped her fast, as if a dense, suffocating spider's web had attached itself viciously to every pore of her body at one and the same time. Sister Beatrice gasped and opened her eyes fully in shock, then fell heavily to the damp stone floor, unmoving and still as death. The shimmering light played around her body in an almost liquid manner, and seemed thicker and more deliberate than any mere light could be. It seemed to sense Sister Magdalene's inward grace and holiness, and reacted to this in two different ways simultaneously: it both slid off her, as if a skin of oil prevented it from getting further, and penetrated her, almost brutally, as if any such barrier was not to be tolerated. Her immobile forehead began to turn a sickly shade of olive, and her breathing became irregular and difficult.

Sister Magdalene would have died from this assault, but for a fortuitous and powerful intervention. A lithe, supple golden-eyed

208

woman suddenly appeared from the shadows. She glided purposefully towards Sister Magdalene's comatose body, but stopped with a shock as she caught sight of the horrible mahogany casket. For some reason it seemed familiar to her, though she could not place why, and it filled her with an unexplained feeling of dread.

The golden-eyed woman shuddered and averted her face from the box and the sickly light that emanated from it. Quickly, she lifted up Sister Magdalene's unconscious body as if it weighed nothing, and carried the loyal servant to her cell, unseen by all who passed near her. Once there the golden-eyed woman made Sister Magdalene comfortable on her pallet, then injected her with something and recited a litany of healing and purity. Sister Magdalene's breathing became more regular and easy.

The golden-eyed woman quoted certain chapters from Holy Scripture that she had learnt by heart many, many years ago. Slowly and definitely the colour on Sister Magdalene's forehead returned to normal, and her comatose slipping-into-death transformed into a deep sleep, if not one that was entirely free from nightmares. The golden-eyed woman remained impassive upon seeing this, though inwardly she was pleased that the Daughter's life had been saved. Finally, in completion of the errand she had been tasked with, she slipped a hand-written note into the unconscious white-haired woman's cold palm. The she disappeared back into the shadows as silently as she had come.

When Sister Magdalene awoke, cold, stiff, suffering from cramp and exposure, she remembered nothing about her encounter with the strange, deadly mahogany box. She did not recall the effigy of an angel that decorated its heavy lid, nor did she remember the cold, green light that had shone from it. She had no idea of how close to death she had come, or of the appearance or identity of the golden-eyed woman who had saved her. Her body simply hurt and her fingers were so numb that it took her a while to realise that anything was held between them at all. But as soon as she discovered and read the note that had been placed there she was running and stumbling down the passageway without dignity or grace, shouting for Lady Salfina with all the urgency that her dehydrated frame could muster.

The tiny neural caterpillars that had burrowed deeply into the heart of the Golden Statue finally completed their accelerated evolution. The foul cocoons that had held them were torn open from within, and the daemonic creatures that emerged slithered towards the same point, their unnatural senses directing their otherwise blind tunnelling. They met, and joined in a horrible union, and began secreting physical and psychic poisons into the Golden Statue's torso. Visitors to the exhibition looked up at the noble statue in rapture, completely unaware of the corruption being prepared within. A sickening, chittering noise, far beyond the range of human hearing, began within the Golden Statue, and was instantly taken up by all the hideous creatures infecting the Militariat communications satellites orbiting many miles above, a chorus no less nauseating, monstrous and defiling for being utterly unheard.

The stern figure sitting in Christopheles' quarters finished retrieving the data stolen from the now-destroyed computer, and looked at the print-outs with narrowed eyes.

'Look at this', she said.

The other, who had remained on guard until this moment, came over and read the documents that the Sanctificatorial guards and defences had tried so hard to destroy.

'Bastard', he said simply. The first figure nodded.

'I'm afraid so. Christopheles and Livilla were manipulated hook, line and sinker. They even thought their mission was sanctified and approved by Lord Crooker himself. Look what they were after at the Lazenby Club.'

The standing man read further.

'Now it all makes sense', he said. 'That traitor Popov! Did nobody suspect him?'

'Only Sanctifier Calvert', replied the seated figure ruefully, 'and possibly too late. Her funeral took place last week.'

They watched as Lady Salfina and her retinue of Daughtersleft the imposing cathedral in the early hours of the morning, seemingly in a great hurry. They did not know of her destination, not did it interest them. All they had waited for was the moment she and her company removed themselves from the majestic basilica. That moment had now arrived.

The first wave surrounded the relatively deserted cathedral, pressing themselves against the rain-soaked grey stone walls. They waited, checking that their presence had not registered with any inhabitants left inside. Then they signalled the second wave over.

This new group were equipped with weapons more powerful than the first wave's knives and daggers. Most carried silenced vengeance-guns and pistols, though a chosen few held knives or swords. The Dems had reported the earlier interruption of their foul ceremony in the cathedral in Sappharus's capital city Helix, and the *Enclave* were not willing to take any chances this time.

The bulky, camoflaged man who led the attack made two quick gestures with his fingers. These were replicated by other men carefully placed at certain points around the vast building. All ground floor entrances to the cathedral were opened swiftly and simultaneously, and a number of the first wave went through. Some minutes passed in utter silence, then some of the attackers re-emerged, their bladed weapons covered with globules of fresh blood.

The rest of the men poured through, filling the main chapel, then spreading out to control the side-chapels, chambers of devotion, ante-rooms full of books of scripture, ceremonial candles, plates and ecclesiastical cassocks. The main areas of worship secured, the second wave launched themselves up winding stone and metal staircases to the rooms of contemplation, libraries and teaching areas, then even further up to the residential cells. Everyone they met was dispatched brutally and instantly, whether man, woman or child. Maintenance crews, ceremonial assistants and all their family members were murdered in their sleep or wherever they were met. The intruders hurried through the edifice, their aim to secure the entire building before any alarms could be raised. They gave no thought to the majestic architecture, the profoundly moving engraved inscriptions, the gorgeous artwork, the antique furniture, the artefacts whose materials alone were worth a fortune. They ignored everything except their brutal task, which they completed thoroughly and successfully before returning to the main chapel below.

None of them had paid any attention to an unusual mahogany box left abandoned in one of the corridors. It lay unnoticed and unmolested, just another piece of immaterial debris.

The doors to the cathedral were opened once again to let four robed and hooded figures enter, then securely bolted from the inside. The four figures stood while the entire Gathering made its way to the rows of stone pews and sat. A horrible parody of devotional music began to sound from the arched loudspeakers placed at strategic intervals on the massive fluted pillars. The debased congregation took up the tune, chanting, thumping their fists on their thighs. Their harsh voices became louder and louder, and their movements more violent. Without exception their faces seemed to become more angular and wretched, and their blank-eyed scowling and chanting became almost hypnotic in nature. A strong and disturbing smell reminiscent of ammonia and mace filled the chapel.

Three of the four figures unclasped their hoods to reveal their faces and identities: Clavicord, Mephistopheles, Popov. The other remained concealed. This figure walked slowly up the centre aisle, followed by the other three. Behind them, three seductive, swaying creatures – Mephistopheles' Enchantresses – joined the procession. The watching congregation moaned, danced, swirled, waving their arms about without direction or purpose, rolling their eyes, salivating disgustingly. All were captivated by the figures that moved between them; all were reduced to creatures of lust, hunger and madness. Their free will evaporated with their full consent and collusion, and they shook and jerked in their seats, puppets to their masters' desires.

The concealed figure reached the dais and turned to face the flailing congregation. It stretched its arms out, and Popov, Mephistopheles and Clavicord took up their positions before the ancient altar that had received so many prayers and sacrifices in its long, noble history. Mephistopheles' face shone with an intense rapture, and his eyes closed as the grating cacophony swept over him. Popov stood tall and proud, as if this was the day when all truth would be revealed and he would take his rightful place by the side of his real master. Only Clavicord looked pale and lost, as if the enormity of what was about to take place was too much for him. His face looked uncharacteristically pasty, and he fought the temptation to wipe beads of sweat off his eyebrows and nose, letting them collect and drip instead.

The concealed figure clapped its hands slowly three times, and even through its hood and mask its eyes could be felt by the flock. They ceased their gyrations and sunk, empty and will-less, into their pews. The leader spoke with a disturbingly slithery and sinuous voice that seemed to have a sickly aftertaste rather than echo. The last time this voice had been heard had been during an assembly around a blotchily-coloured table in a concealed chamber somewhere within the Imperial Museum. This was the first time that the Leader of the *Enclave* had been knowingly witnessed in the flesh by any of the Gathering, and they groaned and shuddered to realise that this was who was before them now.

The Leader smiled, and somehow all knew that the foul figure had done so, even though it remained draped and shadowed. It smiled maliciously and vindictively. The first row of the congregation shrank back involuntarily, in terror.

'The Day of Transformation has come at last', said the leader, deceptively gently. 'We have prepared for it for, oh, these many years, and now it is here. Was there ever so much joy in the world?'

The vacant onlookers did not reply. The music leapt and became a harsh pounding that caused people to retch, shake uncontrollably and even, in some cases, die. The stench of ammonia thickened and became literally poisonous. Members of the congregation gurgled and gasped for breath, their eyes watering sickly fluids, their noses dribbling pus and blood. The soldiers who had secured the basilica lost all military posture and discipline, and wailed and moaned as they collapsed and fell. The three Enchantresses cavorted madly around the pulpit, as if it was an object made solely for their debased pleasure. Mephistopheles moaned in ecstasy, and Popov's eyes rolled backwards in a horrible manner. Clavicord whimpered, mewed, and wet himself. Only the Leader seemed strong and unaffected. It drew itself up to full height, and continued to draw itself up until it levitated several feet off the ground. It glided past the cathedral's vast, beautiful and moving stained glass windows, each of which evoked a scene from the Saviour-

King's crusade, ascent and sacrifice, then returned to hover above the altar. The Leader addressed the dying congregation.

'Willing servants and devotees', it declaimed, 'Gaze at these wrongfully revered pictures. Gaze at them well. The truth is about to be revealed, and invited into the world.'

The floating figure continued to speak, but not in Valhallan. The words and sounds that emanated from its lips did not resemble anything humans should have been able to produce. Horrible, tearing, piercing, frightening sounds juddered together as if battling for supremacy. The mouths of the slowly and painfully dying gathering opened to match the vile and ghastly sounds now filling the cathedral.

The very architecture itself seemed to object. Stone pillars appeared to buckle and struggle against their defilement. Huge, monstrously heavy slabs of marble flooring cracked and tried to break free from their millennia-old positions. Walls and archways squeezed and stretched, like a huge pair of lungs gasping for its final breaths. Empty pews flew into the air and collided with each other, splintering, falling and crushing those below. Books of Holy Scripture launched themselves into the air, pages tearing themselves out, as if the violation of the holy place could be resisted by the visual appearance of the hand-written sacred words. Some of these landed on members of the congregation, who screamed as they were burnt by the touch of such consecrated texts.

The Leader extended its hands out even further, and finished its unnatural evocation. It pointed to the wonderful stained glass windows, and let out a final, immensely deep sigh.

The sacred images, etched so lovingly into the massive windows so many thousands of years ago, began to shimmer and lose their clarity. Colours ran and overlapped. Shapes appeared to go out of focus. Cracks and pops were heard as thick strands of lead piping burst and altered in their direction. The superbly painted scenes from the Saviour-King's life and mission bulged, collapsed, blended and merged. The faces of the saintly characters depicted in the windows seemed to open their eyes and mouths in horror as the Transformation overtook them, evaporating their true identities, subverting and changing their role in the scenes, changing their nature to something debased and demonic.

The images of the Saviour-King himself were the last to be affected, as if these contained a stronger power and resolution. They seemed to offer resistance to the Transformation being imposed upon them.

The Leader did not appear unduly concerned. It flew higher and leered at the transfixed congregation, the malice in its expression absolutely clear even underneath its now melting mask. It spoke again.

'The truth is imminent, my good friends. The truth will set you free. The truth is worth dying for. The truth *will* be died for.'

The three Enchantresses, lost in ecstasy, shook and swayed, their claws moving as if they were reeling something in towards them. And so they were. They were fishing for people's very souls. Row by row, these precious objects were harshly sundered from the seated, shrivelled up, vacant-eyed and now dead bodies that had housed them, and pulled into the engorged Enchantresses' mouths. The Leader watched as the entire gathering were systematically turned into empty corpses; men, women, children, politicians, soldiers, tradesmen, clergy, all.

Popov, Clavicord, Mephistopheles and the three Enchantresses were all who were left below. The Enchantresses fell, overfull from their feast. The three men quivered and shook, and all needed to steady themselves to prevent themselves falling or blacking out.

Mephistopheles recovered himself first. 'The Sacrifice is complete', he managed to say.

The Leader smiled, and gestured to the stained-glass windows. 'Ah', it breathed.

All images of the Saviour-King had vanished from the glass, leaving a vacuum, a vacuum that was even now filling with images of something else, something other, something to run from in terror, something truly debased. The essence of evil.

L'vylaethazs.

CHAPTER SEVENTEEN

Normally the square was busy and full of noise, rushing people and activity, but now, in the dead hours of the night it was eerily quiet in comparison. The only sounds came from the wind as it vibrated through awnings and piles of refuse and the persistent rain. The stalls had long been packed away for the night, and the market was utterly deserted, except for a lone dog, sniffing hopefully at discarded food wrappers.

Covered by at least four of her faithful Daughters, Lady Salfina advanced purposefully down one of the empty windswept avenues to the location jotted down on the note Sister Magdalene had urgently passed onto her. Her eyes searched for any sign of danger or betrayal, but found none. They found no sign of anything, but Lady Salfina knew the value of patience, and waited.

No one emerged from the shadows, no one signalled from any concealed hideaway. She stood, straight-backed and resolute, scanning the abandoned streets for any change. A soft signal whispered in her ear.

'Status, Lady?'

'Safe. Hold fast', she replied.

She had only concentrated on the signal for a second, but something in the square had changed in the meantime. Salfina tensed, as she tried to place what it was, then smiled, as she realised that it was only the dog. It had turned its attention to some debris fluttering around the wheel of one of the more nearby stalls. Salfina relaxed once more, then paused. She had the impression that the dog looked at her quite deliberately before resuming its explorations. Invisibly, she readied and aimed the pistol hidden in her long black coat: she had met weapons-constructs of all shapes and wrapped in all manner of disguises, and had no wish to die as a result of carelessness.

This time there was no mistake. The dog looked directly at her, panted and wagged its tail. The she rolled over, as if she wanted to be tickled.

Salfina grinned to herself. If this was a trap, then it was a peculiarly endearing one. She decided to take the bait, but not before sending a signal that would ensure the destruction of the dog if it made a single suspicious move. Then she moved out of cover and towards the creature.

It remained prone, large eyes watching Salfina as she approached, tail flopping lazily. Lady Salfina knelt down beside it and automatically stroked its golden fur.

'Well, now, you're intelligent', she said, 'and not entirely natural either. I see. Who sent you, I wonder?'

As if in answer, the golden cyber-hound's collar opened up and dropped a small item onto the ground. For a single, awful moment Lady Salfina thought that it was a tiny grenade and that her end had come, but the cyber-hound continued to enjoy her cuddle, and Salfina remained alive and unharmed. She picked up the decorous object and studied it.

It was a miniature, beautifully crafted, Sanctificatorial Pyramid.

***

The effects of the nauseous Ceremony of Transformation were not confined to the vast basilica. Invisible shock-waves of unnatural substance and energy flew out in all directions, looking for their prey. People sleeping in nearby residences gasped and flailed around, suffering the most invidious nightmares and disturbing visions, as the unseen miasma of violation passed through them. Several literally died of fright. Others woke instantly, convinced that the world had ended. Many lurched awake, to find that they had soiled themselves, or murdered their partners while they slept. The feelings of queasiness and rejection that Matthias had suffered in the cathedral on Sappharus were experienced by everyone in the demonic force's path, only ten-times-fold. The most devout and faithful of people woke suddenly, appalled and distraught, to find the Saviour-King gone – and the space he left unfillable.

The almost-conscious waves of malice erupted from the defiled cathedral in wider and wider circles, penetrating dwelling-places, offices, galleries, factories, every type of structure. No material, no matter how strong, could stand in the way of the nauseating energies that struck it. Everything, whether organic or inorganic, was immersed in the irresistible wash of corruption and violation, and began to corrode inwardly. Structures buckled and lost their strength within, and so did people. Normally strong-willed folk, and those who prided themselves on their high levels of resolve and sense of direction, crumbled inside, lost and vulnerable to the waves of evil, malevolence and tyranny that washed through them. Even the smell of the city changed, becoming putrid and unwholesome; the scent of life exchanged for the stench of death.

The fetid energies continued to pulse out of Imperial City's cathedral for miles around, affecting each and every object and being caught in their wake. They penetrated through the very soul of the city. Not a single building, structure, man, woman or child escaped their influence.

Not even the Imperial Museum, and the *Divine Devotions* exhibition: the *Enclave's* key target and the catalyst for what was to follow.

As the sickening forces flooded through the museum, they seemed to sense the special significance and sacred nature of the location. If a human eye could have seen them, then it would have witnessed how the revolting waves suddenly jerked, deviated from their previously straight trajectories, and coiled themselves around the museum, or at least the Worship Wing that housed Rimbrant's magnificent collection. They wrapped themselves tighter and tighter around the building, like venomous snakes around their helpless prey, squeezing and suffocating it. Then they vanished into the building itself, only to be replaced by more and more force-waves of corruption that strangled the museum in their turn. Any human eye that could have witnessed this would have seen these ghastly energies pulse and glow with nauseating pustules of colour, similar to those that had earlier infected the table the *Enclave* had sat at during their treacherous preparations.

Inside the exhibition all was dark. The day's visitors and bulk of staff had left long ago, and the only figures still within the glorious Worship Wing, so carefully designed by Sejanius, were Mercutio, Andreas

219

and Benedict, the three First Valhallans on duty that night. The vast accumulation of holy images and effigies of the Saviour-King stood, proud in their declaration of loyalty, purity and devotion. The Golden Statue of the Saviour-King itself seemed to shine waves of benevolence down on the First Valhallans standing guard so loyally below.

Then the invisible rancid mist of malice began to seep through the bricks and marble of the building, slowly at first, then with more and more force. Intangible energies of corruption attached themselves to all the exhibits they met, leaching into them brutally and overpoweringly.

The three First Valhallans suddenly jolted and lurched as their sense of smell detected the waves of corruption penetrating the building, but they could not identify their source. They raised their weapons and scanned the apparently empty chamber, but saw nothing except each other. One by one they screamed, as they felt their inner selves being defiled and their very identities being eaten away. With increasing desperation they tried to invoke holy names, recite protective litanies, and call on the Saviour-King to protect them, only to find, to their immense astonishment and horror, that the words would not come.

Andreas broke first and fired his vengeance-gun at Mercutio, raving at the corruption he could sense growing within his fellow First Valhallan. Mercutio, equally aghast at the darkness he felt growing around Andreas's soul, fired back. They both fell, both dying, both certain that the other was the Enemy and the source of the growing defilement.

Benedict, his own soul growing black, watched his two companions destroy each other, and in a last, desperate attempt to survive the spreading violation, hurled himself onto the pedestal that supported the Golden Statue. Crying out in despair, he flung his arms around one of the statue's calves and hugged it; a mute, last-ditch attempt to recognise and call for the Saviour-King's blessing and be shielded from the waves of damnation that threatened to infect and destroy everything.

The front of his armour, where it made contact with the statue, melted into nothing, scalding his arms, chest and face beyond repair. The skin of his hands, and several fingers, were completely burnt off. Benedict screamed and fell heavily onto the marble floor far below, breaking his back as he did so. In his last moments of consciousness he looked up at the golden effigy towering above him, his tear-filled eyes searching for any sign of divine acknowledgement or salvation from the god he had served so loyally for so long.

Appalling, there was no such thing. The monstrous Golden Statue looked down at him from an uncrossable distance with what seemed like utter contempt, and even sadistic pleasure at Benedict's pain and despair. Benedict gazed with overwhelming horror at the satanic effigy that loomed over him, wondering how he had ever worshipped and adored such a demonic and hate-filled god, and felt his faith to be utterly betrayed. He died, not of his enormous injuries, but of a shattered heart and a spirit profoundly and completely broken.

The waves of despoilment had made their way deep into the Golden Statue. The pure, inner essence of the marvellous sculpture had already been attacked and violated by the noxious neural caterpillars, and so the way had been paved for the newly-released demonic energies to enter and take hold. The statue's inner resistance was not completely destroyed, but was brutally overcome and swept aside. Corruption gnawed at the heart of the statue and the final phase of the ghastly Transformation wrought by the *Enclave* began.

The spiritual centre of the Golden Statue collapsed and was immediately replaced by a contaminated and spiteful alternative. The outside of the massive effigy appeared exactly as it always had, but its inside had utterly transformed. An onlooker would have seen precisely the same frame, the same stature, the same hands, the same face, but these had been altered deep within, and the aura the sacred sculpture gave off had changed beyond recognition. Eyes that had once gazed out with love and compassion now looked down with hatred and derision. Hands that had embraced faithful mankind in fellowship and understanding now accused and tortured. A god that had raised up the devout and needy now destroyed the weak without mercy. The shades of gold that had represented purity and divinity so exactly now signified nothing except absolute domination and tyranny. The sense of overwhelming goodness that had emanated out of the statue, blessing all whose eyes fell upon it, was replaced by a crushing sensation of evil, bleakness and despair which would destroy all hope and sense of meaning forever.

It was the same for all the images and effigies of the Saviour-King throughout the entire exhibition. All transformed from objects of purity, dedication and wonder, to ones of hatred, wickedness and oppression – though nothing seemed to have changed on the outside. The whole exhibition ceased being a holy collection of sacred works created to worship the Saviour-King, and became a foul compression of nauseating idols dedicated to a far darker power – though they all looked exactly the same. The concentration of evil in the exhibition was thick and overpowering, and far beyond any human mind's capacity to absorb or resist.

That was not all. The superb Worship Wing, that had been so carefully commissioned by the *Enclave* and so meticulously designed and built by Sejanius, was not just a marvel of function and aesthetics perfectly blended together. Sejanius had based his designs on discoveries he had made about the heretical work of one of his ancestors – discoveries that had been hidden well for over two thousand years. The Worship Wing was not just a beautiful container for the *Divine Devotions* exhibition, it was a conduit. The malignance that manifested itself through all the corrupted and despoiled effigies of the Saviour-King was nurtured, coalesced and magnified by the building itself, as if the whole edifice was some kind of sickening musical instrument – though *instrument of torture* might have been a better description. The thick Malevolence that infested the chambers was tuned, amplified and, finally, broadcast to the city beyond.

❦

The Ceremony of Transformation was over. The last washes of diabolical energy pulsed out of the cathedral and flew over the city, dissipating as they went. Mephistopheles, Clavicord and Popov sank shakily into the nearest seats, while the still-engorged Enchantresses remained wrapped around each other, comatose, on the stone floor. The pathetic corpses of the *Enclave's* faithful remained in the same positions they had been in when death overtook them, sitting and kneeling at their pews, hands pressed together in foul prayer or spread in the air in gestures of ecstasy. The Leader looked at the dead congregation, satisfied that all had gone to plan, and floated back down to the ground. The images on the stained-glass windows slowly began to return to normal, but even though they recovered their original sacred appearances their essences no longer had anything holy about them at all.

Even as they prepared to leave, none of the *Enclave* left alive in the basilica knew that, high above their heads, lay the box of Sejanius that they had wanted so much but failed to retrieve. It, too, had been affected by the Transformation. Inside it lay innocuous-looking papers and artefacts that, only now, once the nauseating energies had washed over them, had begun to peel back thousands of years of concealment and reveal themselves for what they truly were.

Salfina followed the cyber-hound as it led her out of the market-square and onto a main road, deserted at this time of night. An unremarkable commuter land-car drove past her and stopped a few feet ahead. A supple, athletic woman dressed in a blue-black cat-suit stepped gracefully out of the vehicle and opened the boot, and the cyber-hound jumped inside. The woman then closed the boot and opened the passenger door as Salfina approached. Now that she was closer, Salfina could see that the woman had golden eyes that shone with an unnatural brilliance.

'Please, enter', requested the stunning-looking woman politely.

'Who are you?' asked Salfina, 'And why should I trust you?'

'My name is Modesty', replied the driver, 'and the Pyramid you conceal in your left hand should tell you why to trust me. Welcome, Lady Salfina. Thank you for responding to the note I left for you. Now, please, before we are observed.'

'This had better be good', answered Lady Salfina coldly, before climbing aboard the back seat. She had barely sat down before Modesty sped the vehicle away.

'Your questions will be answered very shortly', she said through the weapons-proof reinforced steel barrier.

As the land-car sped off in the moonlight, the rest of Lady Salfina's Daughters accelerated their Defender and stealthily followed it from some distance away. They did not need to see the land-car that they trailed; the concealed trackers that Lady Salfina wore were enough.

Later that night Militariat bases around the globe began receiving messages of high alert. The urgent messages seemed genuine enough, as they had been received through the Militariat's exclusive communication satellites, contained the proper code-words, and were quite consistent with each other. Messages apparently from Helbrad and other high-ranking officials told of intelligence reports that suggested that the planet had been surreptitiously invaded for months, and that now the hidden enemy were gearing up their forces to strike. In turn, Helbrad and virtually all the regional commanders received messages purportedly from survivors of strategic outposts that reported how they had been attacked and destroyed without warning by overwhelming forces. A mixture of spurious and genuine orders and messages were sent to and fro, as suddenly anxious men tried to respond to the planet-wide misinformation that emanated from the communications satellites.

The hideous, swollen creatures that had grown within the satellites followed the commands of the *Enclave*. They accessed all military codes and protocols. They sucked up and spat out top secret information. They generated messages from generals and commanders that were indistinguishable from the real thing. They received genuine communications from panicking soldiers and passed them on subtly or completely altered. All messages passed through the creatures' slithery membranes. No soldier talked to another without the message shifting into what the *Enclave* wanted it to be. Troops calling comrades who had apparently asked for help received the evidence they asked for. Completely fictitious dangers were corroborated – it seemed – by trustworthy officers. Instruments designed to measure the impact of explosions or quality of air after poisonous emissions had been suspected duly confirmed that bombs had fallen or gas attacks had been launched – even though, in reality, none had.

Antrobus II was convinced that it was under sustained and heavy attack, and set out to defeat all invaders. Military bases which had remained fully operational since the attacks of the Angel of Death, now disgorged troops, tanks and aircraft by the thousand. All advanced towards the nearest cities, convinced that an Enemy Within had taken control of them. The loyal Militariat wanted their cities back.

As the *Enclave*, and the Demonic master it served, had planned, the planet, with all gusto and urgency, prepared to go to war on itself.

As the civilians of Imperial City awoke, it was as if they had emerged from a shared nightmare of terror and despair. With relief, men and women looked around to see that everything was as it always had been. With relief, they turned to their own personal icons of the Saviour-King and prayed for another day. With relief, they attended morning services as usual, before setting off to work and putting the foul night visions behind them.

In their minds they remained as they had always been, loyal to the Saviour-King. But it was not the same in their hearts and souls. While the good citizens believed that they served the Saviour-King, they now served the power that had so appallingly desecrated and violated the Saviour-King's image. They served the essence of evil.

L'vylaethazs.

The *Divine Devotions* exhibition was the fulcrum for this change. All the many thousands who had passed through its doors had been mesmerised by the images they had seen, and moved and astounded by the sheer concentration of holiness in the museum. People had left the collection with their faith re-invigorated and with a profound feeling that they had come as near to touching divinity as they ever would.

Now the same people remained equally dedicated, devoted and sure of the Saviour-King's power, but, unbeknown to them, it was not the Saviour-King their hearts and souls revered, but the darkness that now exuded from every sacred effigy in Imperial City. Where before the Golden Statue had forced people's true natures to come to the surface, now it smothered and suppressed them, and overlaid them with its own. The citizens of Imperial City became worshippers of Malevolence without even realising. They did not know that it was no longer the Saviour-King who looked at them out of the eyes of the effigies and icons all around them.

One person did know. He realised the truth as he took his daily morning walk through the hall of his collection. He screamed, as the sudden realisation hit him.

All around, every image, every icon, every effigy of the Saviour-King that he had lovingly collected and tended to for his entire adult life laughed at him. They laughed at his attempt to publicly venerate an impotent god. They laughed at his vanity, for thinking that he had in some way done his god's work for him, when, in fact, he had played directly into the hands of a much more malicious power.

Rimbrant fell to the floor, eyes bulging with horror, choking and defeated. His paralysed frame lay where it had fallen, helpless to even express his utter despair. The last conscious thought he had before blackness overtook him was of the words of the Saviour-King's Prayer. Then he lay still.

The effects of the Transformation went through the entirety of Imperial City, and far beyond. People who had made pilgrimages to the *Divine Devotions* exhibition from other cities and continents were the first to be affected. The icons and souvenirs they had bought no longer represented the Saviour-King. Slowly and insidiously, almost all sacred images on the planet began to lose their wholesomeness and take on the foul, putrid nature that threatened to envelop the entire world.

Every city on Antrobus II was approached by all the massed infantry and tank squadrons that local Militariat bases could muster. The Vigilants patrolling the city walls were astounded to see them draw near, but recognised their friendly uniforms and tank patterns, and relaxed, even opening city gates to let them in. Duty Captains dismounted from their command vehicles and look-out posts and went to greet the new arrivals. The Militariat had been held in high regard since the Battle for the Saviour-King's Statue, and not a one of the smiling, hand-extending Vigilants thought it necessary to approach their planet's heroic troops with any caution.

The Militariat on the other hand, thought very differently. Their eyes narrowed as they gazed upon the duplicitous men who had thought to take their cities from them, and, even, now, advanced towards them with smiles on their faces, still hiding behind the façade of friendship. The men of the Militariat had no truck with betrayal, and clicked their weapons' safety-catches off as the smiling Vigilants officers approached.

The land-car stopped outside a round building that Lady Salfina had become very used to during the preceding weeks. Modesty opened the passenger door for her, and together they made their way towards a discreet side-door into the circular structure known as the Dome.

It was pitch-black inside, and Salfina had only walked a few steps when she realised that her escort had disappeared from her side. Alert now, she attempted to draw her vengeance-gun surreptitiously, only to find herself immobilised from behind by two strong arms and hands that brooked no resistance. The thinnest of knives was held to her throat.

'Who do you work for?' spoke a purposeful voice directly into her ear.

'The Saviour-King', she replied, unhesitatingly.

The muscular arms relaxed, and the knife withdrew. Bright lights suddenly illuminated the ante-room.

'At ease, Matthias, she's one of us', came a steely voice.

Lady Salfina blinked and looked around the room. She saw Modesty standing some distance away, along with the cyber-hound and a servant-woman wearing a neck-brace. All watched her intently. The well-built man who had held the knife to her neck broke into a smile and nodded warmly in Modesty's direction - though, mindful of his standing orders, he still did not show any reaction to the recent change in the appearance of the assassin's eyes.

'Good to see you, Lady', was all he said to Lady Salfina. Then he addressed someone behind her. 'All clear, Princess.'

Salfina turned to see a raven-haired woman dressed in impressive dark green armour, framed by a jet-black cape. Her presence was enormous.

'Thank you, Modesty, Matthias', said the woman.

Lady Salfina stepped towards her and bowed.

'At your service, Sanctifier', she said.

'This way, Lady Salfina', replied Shenaria determinedly, 'We haven't got much time.'

CHAPTER EIGHTEEN

The first clash took place in the city of Porthos in the Insobar Peninsula, eight thousand miles to the west of Imperial City, and part of a completely different continent. The Militariat had approached this particular city by sea, travelling stealthily by submarine and battleship. Crowds promenading along the beaches and waterfronts had been surprised to see the great iron crafts suddenly emerge from the choppy grey waters, but had reacted with excitement and joy on seeing these manifestations of the planet's heroic military force. The local Vigilant commander, Lieutenant Calvadore, had ordered flags to be raised, and he and his closest staff had marched to the port entrance in their dress uniforms, intending to honour the new arrivals with proper decorum and ceremony.

The battleship captain, Marchius, had other ideas. As the flotilla drew near to the port, cannons and other heavy weaponry emerged through portholes and took aim at the enthusiastic, jostling crowds of Vigilants and civilians.

Most people watching thought that this was just an exciting display of military might, and cheered for the approaching mariners who, unknown to them, were planning to massacre them all. A few citizens instinctively realised that something was wrong, grabbed their children and ran away as fast as they could.

They were the lucky ones. Captain Marchius looked at the line of traitors who lined the waterfront, and marvelled at their audacity to, even now, keep up their pretence of loyalty. He had read the reports of how the people of Porthos, led by the treacherous Vigilants, had brutally blown up an entire local Militariat training complex and mercilessly and cold-bloodedly killed all survivors of the blast. He resolved to be equally unforgiving in his turn. Those who tried to take control of

Antrobus II would answer to the Militariat, he determined, and grimly prepared for his first real taste of combat. It was a shame that it had to be against fellow Antrobians, but that was their doing, not his.

The giant cannons erupted without warning, the immense noise rupturing many people's eardrums. Huge shells smashed into the structures lining the waterfront, splintering and collapsing them. Fires started and people screamed. The astonished Vigilants looked on, open-mouthed with horror and disbelief, until Lieutenant Calvadore's sharp orders snapped them into action. They fired volleys of grenades across the flotilla, and sprayed all decks and surfaces they could see with petrolium, setting fire to masts, flags and sailors with equal ferocity. The first ship of the flotilla crashed into the port, breaking a huge chuck of the concrete edifice away, and throwing hundreds of people into the now fiery waters below. Vigilant Defenders fired round upon round of high explosives onto the ships, and were fired on in their turn. Water and land-based vehicles blew up and caught fire, spreading death and destruction in their wake. The Militariat and the Vigilants chose the same moment to launch close combat attacks, and met each other with their sabres, vengeance guns, knives and teeth. Furious, vicious fights took place, with few lasting more than two seconds. Mutilated and brutally injured men fell to their deaths, completely unaware of how they had been manipulated. Each force was convinced that the opposing group were traitors. Each individual combatant regarded himself as loyal to Antrobus II and to the Saviour-King. None had any idea that all the death and misery caused was on behalf of an entity far more malevolent than any they had ever imagined.

Variations of the same story took place all around the globe. In Quest's End, an unfortunately-named city near the equator, the Vigilants officers patrolling the city wall were simply crushed against it as the Militariat drove their mighty Spearhead tanks straight through the barrier. They continued until they reached the city's main square, which then became the setting for a prolonged and angry fire-fight. There were few survivors on either side. Near Kingcester, one of the main northern cities of Antrobus II, the Vigilants struck first, having heard about deadly Militariat actions in the nearby industrial city of Borrington. An approaching Militariat attack force was ambushed from two fronts and destroyed without mercy, as the Vigilants extracted what they considered to be revenge. At Paranie, a tropical city that normally dealt with nothing more taxing than holiday-makers having their wallets stolen, hundreds of Militariat Defenders emerged from the surrounding jungle to set fire to the entire city quite systematically. The desert city of Abu Marda was bombed to submission by Speedhawk and Vulture fighter planes flying overhead, but not before at least half of these had fallen to Vigilants' fire.

It did not take long until completely genuine messages reporting attacks and asking for help joined the fictitious ones put out through the Militariat communications satellites, making a bad situation much worse. Authentic noises of alarm and well-meant identifications of the enemy added to the panic and confusion wrought by the *Enclave* and the foul creatures that their neural caterpillars had become. The armed forces of the planet jerked about in anger and desperation, and reacted before they thought. All were convinced that an invasion or uprising had taken place. All were convinced that the other was the enemy.

All did the work of the real enemy – without once being aware of it.

Commissioner Bennett contacted Colonel Helbrad in a worthy attempt to sort things out face to face, but Helbrad's anger was such that he refused to have anything to do with a man he now regarded as the most insidious of traitors. Captain Byrrion, similarly, marched on Commander Chaffron's Militariat headquarters in Imperial City, confident that he and Chaffron could work together, as they had done during the Battle for the Saviour-King's Statue. He was shot down and injured as he approached, an action which prompted the disgusted Vigilants' prolonged attempt to level the building to the ground. World Regent Tollius, and all surviving members of the Planetary High Council that could be traced, were driven at full pelt to their secret underground nuclear shelters, unsure if they were still in charge in any meaningful manner, or if they simply had to wait for the end of what appeared to be a sudden, deadly and completely unexplained civil war.

High up in their mountain-top base, key members of the *Enclave* watched with glee as the planet of Antrobus II fell into Malevolence and despair. They watched as the world was attacked from all fronts. The cities of the planet neared collapse as they tried to contain the military conflicts breaking out everywhere. The people of the planet, pulverised by abrupt and appalling civil war, fell sick with despair and anguish. Desperately, as one, they put all their remaining faith and hope into the hands of the Saviour-King.

Only it was not the Saviour-King any more. Unknowingly, unwillingly, despairingly, the people of Antrobus II commended their futures and their souls to the most malevolent evil of all.

L'vylaethazs.

On the ice-cold moon orbiting the dead planet of Antrobus I, High Sanctifier Lord Crooker watched and waited, a grimmer than usual expression on his scarred face. The plush velvets that decorated his newly-re-opened chambers gave nothing away of the steely atmosphere and sense of urgency within.

Lord Crooker strode through the operations room, dynamic and frightening in his bronze armour. Servants remained absolutely alert for any orders he might give or questions he might ask. He was not a man to keep waiting, or to display normal human insecurity to, and the recent break-in that had taken place in Christopheles's quarters had not improved his mood. Nor had the death of Sanctifier Calvert or the persistent lack of response from his special representative, Popov.

Lord Crooker made his way past his usual Chair of Command, situated in the exact centre of the operations room, to the Sanctificatorial spy screens that dominated the large wall to the front of the chamber. Without rudeness or arrogance he pushed an observer aside and studied the screen in front of him. It was one of many that displayed scenes from the apparent madness that had suddenly overtaken the Vigilants and Militariat of Antrobus II.

'Comments?' he invited.

A brave observer responded, much to the relief of the others, all of whom knew that any perceived failing on their part could lead to the harshest of punishments.

'The Vigilants and the Militariat each seem to believe that the other is the enemy. Both consider the other to have acted treacherously and acted first. Both regard themselves as acting in defence of the planet', he said.

'Who are they taking their orders from?' demanded Crooker.

'That's the odd thing', piped up another observer. 'Both organisations are following their chains of command, as appropriate. There is no indication of any group or individual orchestrating the violence below. It is as if both organisations are responding to genuine reports of attack.'

'Any heretics under surveillance among those giving orders?' Crooker asked.

'None', came the reply. 'No heretical activity has been reported on Antrobus II since the Battle for the Saviour-King's Statue.'

'And what, exactly,' thundered Lord Crooker, pointing to the chaos displayed on the screens, 'would you call *this*?'

The operations room fell silent. No one dared to speak. Lord Crooker stared round at his underlings, incensed, then returned to his Chair of Command and closed his eyes.

'We will determine the cause of this situation', he declared, after a while. 'We will decide whether or not the planet is suffering merely a physical malaise, as seems most unlikely, or a spiritual one. If spiritual, we will consider whether the planet can be healed. If so, we will heal it, regardless of the measures we may have to take. If not, we will destroy it, rather than allow heresy or apostasy to spread.'

He closed his eyes once more, and was still. Some minutes later a discreet, anxious cough in his ear roused him again. He turned, to see a white-faced observer bow before him.

'If you please, Lord', stuttered the observer, 'you might wish to see this.'

Lord Crooker rose to his full height, dwarfing everyone else in the room. He faced the nervous observer.

'This had better be worth seeing, Marcius', he said.

'Yes, Lord', replied Marcius as they crossed back to the screens. He pointed to one in particular – one that was not centred on Antrobus II.

It showed a small space shuttle entering orbit around the ice-moon. The space shuttle changed trajectory until it hovered directly over the *Fortress Dedicata Profundis*. Then it began to descend, and entered the atmosphere. Identification requests and demands were broadcast towards the spacecraft from suddenly appearing giant loudspeakers.

Concealed anti-aircraft batteries began to emerge from the surface of the moon and take aim at the descending craft.

Crooker hit a button, so communications could be heard.

'...Repeat, request identification. We *will* open fire if no identification is received. You have twenty seconds', broadcast a harsh, metallic voice.

No reply.

'We are about to open fire', declared the metallic voice, with a new sense of urgency. 'State your call sign *now*.'

No reply.

'All stations, wait ten seconds, then blast that ship out of the sky', came the order through the loudspeakers in the operations room.

Then one of the observers gasped and held up a just-disgorged piece of paper.

'A message!' he exclaimed, astonished. 'It's got through all our firewalls!'

'Read it', ordered Lord Crooker.

The observer did so. *I still think Christopheles cheated* he read. Instantly Lord Crooker hit the intercom.

'Belay that order!' he shouted. 'Don't harm that ship!'

The anti-aircraft weapons folded and disappeared beneath the surface of the ice-moon once more. The space shuttle finished its descent in peace, landing directly opposite the main entrance to the *Fortress Dedicata Profundis*. A force-field was switched off and Lord Crooker strode through the fortress's gates, protected by an environmental bubble once again, but unaccompanied this time.

The airlock to the space shuttle opened, and a space-suited figure emerged. It climbed down a ladder that slid out of the rocket. Then it turned to face Lord Crooker.

'I said I wouldn't let you down', radioed Shenaria through her helmet.

The mahogany box shuddered and creaked as the tempestuous energies released by the nauseating Ceremony of Transformation ceased washing through it. It lay on the corridor floor, unmoving and unimportant to the naked eye.

It was anything but. Inside it some previously innocuous-looking artefacts and papers continued to waver and change. Layers of disguise implanted into them thousands of years previously began to disintegrate and peel away, as if an acid could choose particular layers of skin to eat through and leave others unaffected. With gentle hisses the supernatural concealments that had convinced almost everybody for so long bubbled away into nothingness, revealing truths that someone had gone to enormous lengths to hide all those many years ago.

The Leader of the *Enclave* had retired to some dark and undeclared destination, leaving Popov, Mephistopheles and Clavicord alone in the luxurious crystal room of Clavicord's club. The three Enchantresses had also taken themselves off, and Mephistopheles, at least, had thought better than to ask them how they had intended to spend their time.

He had been the first to recover properly from the Ceremony, and was now looking forward to the various culminations of their plan. He knew that, if all continued to proceed as smoothly as it had done so far, he could expect rewards of a richness and substance that was far, far beyond what most ordinary mortals could ever hope to receive.

Popov was also pleased that the end was in sight. He had waited to throw the hated costume of Sanctifier to the Saviour-King aside and be completely true to his infernal, corrupt nature. He had treated the need to show allegiance to the Saviour-King as a challenge and game of wits, and considered that he had outsmarted Lord Crooker and all the petty minds of the Sanctification, who were foolish enough to not know the enemy when they looked straight at it.

Only Clavicord seemed not to have recovered fully from the Ceremony, and sat in his customary chair completely lacking the charisma and presence he usually exuded. His frame seemed to suffer from sudden occasional palpitations, and his skin was covered with an unhealthy-looking sheen of perspiration. He had not even had the energy to be as habitually rude as always to his wife, Calista, when she had served them all their drinks.

Now he gazed out the window at the ski-slopes below, looking for all the world as if he expected the chaos and despair they had visited upon the rest of the world to rise up through the snowy crags and envelope his home too.

'Oh, snap out of it, Enderby', said Popov. 'We knew what we were getting into. Everything's gone our way! Sanctifier Calvert is dead, and the Ceremony has been successful. The Statue has been infected, and the planet has turned upon itself. What more do you want? A certificate of merit?'

'Let him be', drawled Mephistopheles, cruelly. 'If he's not up to the Transformation, who cares? This world will shortly be in the power of *L'vylaethazs* for all time, and we will be among his favoured. If Clavicord doesn't make it, well, we don't need him any more. He's done his bit, and that's enough.'

Clavicord rallied to some extent on hearing these remarks. He sat up straight for the first time since they had returned to the club.

'You forget, Gentlemen, that without my influence, and without my finances, not a single aspect of the *Enclave's* plan would have come to fruition. Who paid for the transportation of the *Divine Devotions* exhibition in the first place? Me. Who dealt with three Sanctifiers, including the most dangerous one, Calvert? Me. Who, even now, is nurturing the final aspect of our preparations? Me. So don't insult me, and don't dismiss me. *L'vylaethazs* might well favour me above all of you, and if he does, I won't forget what you've said tonight.'

Mephistopheles glared back with scarlet eyes. 'Really?' he replied. 'And I suppose the Golden Statue got infected all by itself? And Captain Drusus voluntarily gave over his Divine Imprint?' He sat back in his chair. 'Don't give yourself airs, Clavicord. This plan needed all three of us.' *Whether or not it still does* he thought to himself.

Popov raised his glass. 'Here's to the *Enclave*, a model of co-operation and mutual support!' he said, ironically, before downing his whisky. 'So what's next?'

As if in answer, the light from the chandeliers dimmed suddenly, dropping the room into complete blackness. The three men choked, as if their windpipes had been seized abruptly. Popov dropped his glass, which splintered on the floor. Clavicord jerked in his chair, and Mephistopheles thumped backwards into the wall, his perfumed head denting the expensive plaster.

'What's next', oozed an eerie, thick, disembodied voice, 'is that you remember your place and that you work for *me*.'

The pressure on the men's throats eased, and they gasped for breath and soothed their necks with palpitating fingers. Beads of sweat appeared on each one's forehead as they attempted to recover themselves.

'Soon the whole planet will have descended into irreparable Malevolence', slithered the voice. '*L'vylaethazs* will have complete dominion over the people of this world. We need only wait a short while before the final step. You will control yourselves in the meantime. *L'vylaethazs* requires those who are strong and steadfast, not those who bicker and get above themselves. Signs of weakness will *not* be tolerated. Do you understand?'

Fearfully, the three men nodded.

'Good', said the voice, and vanished.

Lord Crooker followed Shenaria through the airlock and into the space shuttle. He was greeted by a dignified woman wearing a neck-brace, who bowed and took his cloak. Another woman, wearing sigils that marked her out as an Arch-Deaconness, saluted as he entered. A well-built man and his supple-looking partner rose from their game of Domination, and stood to attention.

Crooker nodded in their direction. 'As you were', he said.

The man and woman sat down and resumed their game. Crooker strode towards them and looked down at their board for a few moments.

'Better luck next time', he said, before returning to Shenaria, who had waited by a small table for him. They were both joined by Lady Salfina, and sat down together.

Matthias glanced at the small group as they began their deliberations, then looked back at the board in front of him.

'Which one of us did he address?' he asked the golden-eyed woman sitting opposite him.

'You'll find out', replied Modesty, her face giving nothing away.

Miri had offered Lord Crooker some refreshments, but he had waved them aside. He turned to Shenaria, questions in his eyes.

'I apologise for meeting you like this', said Shenaria, 'but it was important that none of your men would be privy to our conversation. Miri has switched on a damper: no one will be able to eavesdrop on us from outside the ship. You are the only person to even know the identity of your visitor.'

'My men are all trustworthy', replied Crooker, but Shenaria shook her head.

'They probably believe so themselves, but some may work for Popov', she explained.

Some minutes passed while Shenaria filled Lord Crooker in about the situation. He let her speak, only asking questions when he needed to clarify certain details. He had always trusted Shenaria's integrity and loyalty, and resisted the impulse to tell her that she must be mistaken, even when her story seemed improbable or outlandish. Lady Salfina's presence and occasional remarks also helped to convince him of the truth of Shenaria's tale, or at least prevent him from dismissing it out of hand. Once Shenaria had finished speaking he sat back in his chair and considered the situation.

'Why did you come here?' he asked, finally.

Shenaria smiled. 'Because I know you, Sire. I know that you would not idly stand by and watch Antrobus II sink into Malevolence and heresy. And I know you would willingly destroy the whole planet if it meant that the taint of heresy would be prevented from spreading further.'

'And so I would', replied Lord Crooker, 'And so I should.'

Shenaria nodded and leant forwards, staring into his auburn eyes.

'Antrobus II is my home', she stated firmly. 'Its citizens do not know what has happened to them, and do not deserve what has happened to them. They do *not* deserve to die because heresy has been imposed upon them. I have come to you to ask a boon. Give me, give *us*', she said, gesturing to include the entire company, 'twenty-four hours to eradicate this foul taint of heresy before you condemn the entire planet to death.'

Lord Crooker matched her gaze.

'And if you fail?' he enquired, coldly.

'If we fail', responded Shenaria, 'if you do not hear of our success within that time, and the planet remains despoiled and in darkness, then we would be better off pure and dead than alive and damned. You would have my blessing to destroy us all.'

Down on the planet itself the situation escalated further and further out of control. The fighting and mutual distrust and hatred was no longer confined to the forces of the Vigilants and the Militariat. Many individual citizens, responding to the malevolent messages in their heads, turned upon one another, convinced of each other's heresies and betrayals. Others wept and prayed, desperate for some sign of the Saviour-King's support and blessing, desperate for some hope, no matter how small.

They did not find it. Where once their minds had resonated with all the many aspects of the Saviour-King that signified love, mercy, brotherhood and salvation, now they were filled with dreadful visions of domination of the weak, torture of the sinful and absolute power and contempt for humanity. Their very souls began to give way, and their resistance to the Malevolence that radiated through them began to crumble.

The space-shuttle that Shenaria had commandeered from Imperial City's space-port had left the *Fortress Dedicata Profundis* and now headed back towards Antrobus II on its final journey. Miri made certain that its course was set correctly, then joined the others around a functional steel conference table.

They all looked prepared to Miri's eyes. Shenaria wore her green Sanctificatorial armour and jet-black cloak, and her sabre hung by her side. Matthias had his *H-Dini* tools and nerve-dagger ready in his belt. Modesty's punishment needles had been sharpened and re-poisoned. and Lady Salfina had cleaned and re-loaded all her weaponry.

'You never said how you escaped the Angel of Death', Salfina was saying to Shenaria.

'Tracer', butted in Matthias. 'Luckily for us, Shenaria had managed to put a tracer on the Angel of Death when she first encountered it. We had a warning of its approach.'

'Thank you, Matthias', smiled Shenaria. 'Remind me to call upon you the next time I lose my own voice.'

'Sorry, Princess', replied Matthias, flushing, and changed the subject quickly. 'So, what's our plan? There's not enough of us to intervene in every fire-fight on the planet.'

'Quite true', answered Shenaria, 'so we go to the source.'

'The exhibition', said Modesty, quietly.

'Yes, the exhibition', responded Shenaria, a little bitterly. 'The one we were tasked to protect. I realised what was happening once I thought about what Lady Salfina had said in the Dome. Salfina, if you wouldn't mind?'

Lady Salfina took up the explanation.

'You remember the Battle for the Saviour-King's Statue? I had the strongest conviction that the attacks had not been pre-meditated, but had been results of people's true natures coming to the surface. The Golden Statue had been the catalyst for this phenomenon. The divine presence of the Saviour-King had manifested itself through the statue.'

'I don't follow', said Matthias. Modesty looked at him. 'And neither do you', he continued, 'so don't look at me like that.'

'You're so easy to goad', said Modesty.

'Consider the ceremony you interrupted', said Shenaria. 'A ceremony of transformation. What exactly got transformed?'

'Stained-glass windows', replied Matthias.

'Think further, Matthias. What was on those windows?'

'Pictures. Stories. Images of the Saviour – battle, murder and sudden death!'

'Yes, Matthias', finished Shenaria, 'it was the Saviour-King that was being transformed – or at least our local versions of him.'

'So consider', continued Lady Salfina, 'We know the Golden Statue deeply and irresistibly affected people's inner selves. What if the statue itself has been corrupted? What if a Malevolent force now rests within the Golden Statue, and, indeed, the rest of the effigies concentrated in the Imperial Museum? And what if the Statue still has the power to affect people's natures like it did during the Battle named after it?'

'Perhaps that would be enough to set man against man', said Shenaria, 'and explain our civil war.'

'But on such a scale?' objected Matthias. 'That would need a lot of power!'

'I agree', replied Shenaria, 'and the source of such power needs to be found.'

The group sat in silence for a while.

'So we go to the exhibition', said Modesty quietly. 'But if we destroy it, then surely the enemy has won anyway? It would be a great propaganda victory for them if we were forced to destroy such a marvellous and sacred collection. They would laugh if we had to perform such a desecration ourselves, especially after all the efforts spent in the exhibition's defence.'

'You're right', stated Shenaria, 'except for one thing. No one said anything about destroying the exhibition.'

Modesty and Matthias looked at her, uncomprehending. Shenaria stared back at them, deep resolve in her expression.

'We go to perform an exorcism', she said.

CHAPTER NINETEEN

As the space-shuttle neared Antrobus II Shenaria prepared her little company to meet their deaths. She had not said as much to Lord Crooker, but she considered their chances of success to be small – not that this absolved her of the duty to try.

She had given them all purification tablets to dissolve in their mouths. These were not designed to purify water, or indeed any physical substance, but to purify the spirit. Each consisted of different coloured consecrated salts that had been compressed into tiny tablets. Like sticks of rock they contained words that ran through them, only these words were the sacred words of scripture. Psalms, prayers and divine testaments were absorbed by the group. Lady Salfina had warned Shenaria that the very air of the Antrobus II might well carry the infection that seemed to have gripped the planet's peoples, and Shenaria wanted her group's resistance to be as strong as it possibly could be.

At Shenaria's request Lady Salfina had led them all in a service of communion, and they all dedicated whatever was left of their lives to the Saviour-King, and prayed to be delivered from corruption and evil. Despite Shenaria's outward determination and show of optimism, none of them mistook the scale of the odds against them, and all took some moments for their private prayers and commendations.

After the service Shenaria talked with everyone aboard the shuttle individually and privately, including Lady Salfina's Daughters, who had joined them for the mission. She knew that each one of them was willing to risk her life by coming on this journey, and she wished to show every one of them her respect and gratitude. She passed through the ship, acknowledging and speaking with all, before returning to her tiny, private cubicle to meet with each of her own personal staff, particularly Miri, Modesty and Matthias, and their chief ally, Lady Salfina.

Once Modesty had left Shenaria's tiny, private cubicle, it was Matthias's turn. He waved at Modesty's departing back cheerily, before gazing at her solemnly and steeping through the curtain.

Shenaria smiled at him as he entered, and gestured for him to sit. He complied, stroking Tru-D automatically as he did so.

'What did Lord Crooker say when he found out we were the ones who broke into Christopheles' rooms?' he asked.

'I didn't tell him', replied Shenaria.

'Princess!'

Shenaria smiled, then her expression hardened. 'The next time a traitor like Popov infests the Sanctification, I want to be able to move against him as soon as possible. I do not intend to alert Lord Crooker - or anyone who works for him - of weaknesses in his security if he can't see them for himself.'

She leaned forward.

'Okay, Matthias', she said, 'I've been watching you. Out with it.'

'What do you mean?' he replied. Shenaria grinned.

'I know when you've got something on your mind', she answered. 'You can talk here. In fact, I insist. We are *not* going to go into battle with issues left unresolved.'

Matthias struggled with himself for a few moments, then relented.

'Alright', he said, reluctantly, 'It's Modesty.'

Shenaria breathed a sigh of deeply-felt relief.

'Thank you, Matthias. Now I know that your dedication to the Saviour-King, and to me, is stronger than your loyalty to your close friend. I know how fond of Modesty you are.'

'You are too', Matthias countered, and Shenaria nodded.

'Yes I am, but you know of what I fear.'

Matthias started. 'Are we at that point?' he asked, truly worried.

'Before I answer that', responded Shenaria, 'tell me what you've noticed about her. Besides the obvious, that is.'

Matthias nodded, and collected his thoughts.

'After Tru-D had tracked her down, and you went to find her, you warned me that she'd changed', he began. 'You asked me not to respond to any changes I saw in any way. And I haven't.'

'Good', said Shenaria, 'And?'

'I haven't once mentioned her eyes', continued Matthias, 'but the thing is, neither has she. She hasn't explained what happened to them, and she hasn't teased me about not enquiring about them myself. She hasn't referred to them in any way. I've seen her looking in the mirror while preparing for action, and she hasn't reacted to her new reflection at all. It's as if...'

'Yes', mused Shenaria, 'It's as if she *isn't aware that anything has changed.*'

Matthias looked at her. 'That's exactly it', he said. 'To me that's more worrying than anything.'

'Me too', agreed Shenaria.

They sat in silence for a moment, deep in thought.

'I know what caused the change', offered Shenaria, 'or at least, I know the event. What I don't know yet is what's behind it.'

Matthias finally voiced his fear. 'Boss, when Jessila went into labour, and her eyes changed, you had me kill her.'

Shenaria nodded. 'I did. And in the nick of time.'

Matthias sighed heavily, and came out with it. 'Do you want me to kill Modesty too? Is she also a danger to us?

Shenaria took his hand and cupped it between both of hers. She shook her head.

'No, Matthias. Or, at least, not yet. Oh, if Modesty's eyes had lost their pupils, like Jessilas's did, then I would have had no hesitation in ordering you to kill her – if I hadn't already killed her myself. That would have been proof that something demonic had happened to her. But the change in Modesty is different. It's reminded me of something, and I can't quite put my finger on what yet. Until I can, and until I know for sure whether Modesty's transformation is for good or ill, then we will leave her untouched.'

'What if you don't put your finger on it until it's too late? None of the other transformations that have happened seem to have been for anyone's good', responded Matthias, glumly.

Shenaria smiled grimly, and released his hand. She stood, impressive as always in her Sanctificatorial armour.

'I have some faith in her', she said. 'Remember what Modesty has already faced in her life, and the inner strength she has shown in surviving it. Remember how, for years, she used Holy Scripture to see her through. I want to ask you a favour, Matthias. If Modesty acts in any way that you think suspicious or treacherous to us, I want you to hesitate before you act. Give her the benefit of the doubt, at least once. Will you do that?'

Matthias was dumbfounded. It took him a moment to find his voice.

'Princess, I…I've never heard you give such an order before. Are you sure you're alright?'

Shenaria broke into peals of laughter, causing Matthias's mouth to gawp open in further astonishment. She recovered herself, chuckling and smiling.

'Matthias, you are a gem', she stated with genuine affection. 'My home planet's gone to pot, forces of darkness have taken over everything, we're on a mission that is very likely to lead to our deaths, and you ask me if I'm alright! Well, I am now! To fight with you at my side: how could I not be alright? Now, come on, time to get ready. Just keep the favour I asked you.'

'I will, Princess', said Matthias. 'For you, Modesty and the Saviour-King's sake, I will.'

Four Militariat combat aircraft circled the space shuttle as it descended through Antrobus II's wind-swept atmosphere. Their crews were wide-eyed with panic by this stage and trigger-happy as a result. Shenaria knew that getting back to the planet in one piece would be a feat in itself.

'Unidentified spacecraft, state your identity, or be shot down', the leader of the squadron ordered over the tannoy, as the planes zoomed past. 'You have ten seconds.'

'We are Sisters of Benediction', came the instant reply. 'We have travelled from the Great Cathedral of Helix on planet Sappharus. We have come on a pilgrimage to visit the *Divine Devotions* exhibition now gracing your planet. We have permission granted to us by the great and majestic Lady Salfina Pureheart herself.'

One by one the aircraft flew by, slowing down to peer through the shuttle's windows. The pilots saw lines of women dressed in nuns' garments, holding books of scripture and rosary beads. The women were being led in a service of devotion by a tall, imposing figure dressed in ceremonial ecclesiarchal gown.

'Welcome, Sisters; you may land', signalled the head pilot, before leading his squadron away.

The group waited until the planes had flown out of sight, then divested themselves of their white coverings, revealing metal armour underneath.

'All clear', called Lady Salfina, and Shenaria and the others emerged from their hiding places.

'Thank you, Lady Salfina: thank you, all. 'The great and majestic Lady Salfina Pureheart', eh?'

'If you've got it, flaunt it', replied Salfina, po-faced. Shenaria grinned.

You may land us now, Miri', she said.

They separated as planned once the shuttle had docked at the space-port. Shenaria, Matthis, Modesty and Salfina boarded the unobtrusive land-car that Modesty had driven previously, and set off for the centre of Imperial City. Lady Salfina's Daughters began to move stealthily northwards to their arranged destination, to meet up with the others later, assuming they all survived that long.

Shenaria looked sadly at her home city as they passed through the deserted evening streets. Vehicles lay abandoned where they had crashed or been shot at. Scorch marks, smashed glass and other signs of damage showed where low-level fire-fights had taken place. Rubbish, debris and even several corpses lay uncollected, randomly draped over roads and pavements. Street lights operated only intermittently. It was even worse than the aftermath of the Battle for the Saviour-King's Statue, as then, at least, there had been an atmosphere of hope and recovery. Now there was no such thing, only an all-pervading air of despair. Shenaria was pleased she had insisted on everyone taking purification tablets, but wondered how long they would hold up for.

She got out of the land-car as they neared the grand cathedral.

Matthias had requested to come with her to offer protection, but she had instructed him to go with the others.

She crossed the wide tree-lined avenue that sat alongside the cathedral, her eyes alert for any suspicious movements. The wind sang through the branches unhealthily, raising the hairs on the nape of her neck. She made her way to the imposing, arched double-doors that fronted the cathedral, then paused.

They were not quite closed.

Vengeance-gun in hand, she leant against one of the doors, making it open silently and slowly, then slipped through as soon as the opening was big enough. She took cover behind the nearest pillar, listening out for any sign that her entrance had been noticed.

The first thing to hit her was the stench. It was appalling, and Shenaria had to control herself not to gasp out loud. She covered her nose with her glove and blinked her watering eyes clear. Partially recovered, she turned her head ever so slowly, scanning for danger, odd shadows, anything. There was no obvious threat, so she began to cautiously walk up the centre aisle.

Then she saw the corpses. They had remained in their seats, and were now beginning to decay and putrify. Little maggots crawled along and burrowed through the bodies' grey, exposed skin. Some corpses were distended with unwholesome gases, while others had already begun to inwardly collapse. Shenaria was aghast and appalled.

'By the Divine Saviour-King', she hissed through gritted teeth, 'What has happened in this place?'

She continued to make her way past the scene of mass death and towards the giant altar. She climbed onto the dais, noting the odd, horribly sweet smell that emanated from it. She saw the darker spot of ground where Clavicord had wet himself. She observed the burst-apart paving slabs and scattered pages of scripture, and sighed.

'So it was here', she said to herself, before turning to look at the stained-glass windows. Involuntarily, she gasped and lurched backwards, losing her balance and falling.

The beautifully-coloured and presented figures that faced her no longer conveyed anything divine. The aura of evil that emanated from them was almost too much to bear. There was a central figure in almost every panel, a figure that purported to be the Saviour-King, but was anything but. This figure stared at Shenaria coldly, maliciously and with complete contempt.

Shenaria groaned, and got onto her hands and knees. She closed her eyes and raised her head. She crawled shakily towards the nearest stained-glass window, then opened her eyes.

'I know you', she said, her voice harsh and only emerging with difficulty. 'I have met you. And I have beaten you, *L'vylaethazs*.'

The central figure in the stained-glass window seemed to turn its head to look down at her, amused. The corners of its mouth seemed to smile.

'In Granaria, remember?' stuttered Shenaria. 'I burnt Brogan's office to the ground and destroyed your plans.'

With a wrenching noise a whole pew lifted itself off the ground, dislodging all the corpses that had rested on it, and flew towards Shenaria with sickening speed. It crashed into the marble wall beside her head, covering her with splinters. Shenaria smiled.

'You don't frighten me', she said, and opened her eyes.

The figure in the window hesitated, astonished that anyone had enough courage to look it in the eye. Shenaria spat at it.

Her spittle burned into the window like acid.

'You don't frighten me', repeated Shenaria, and, shakily, got to her feet before walking away from the window. 'You are dead', she said, without even looking back. 'Your power only comes from those who believe in you and fear you, and *I don't*.'

She continued to walk away from the window and towards the stairs. Chunks of masonary cracked away from their moorings and flew just past her, more pews erupted and sped her way, missing her by a fraction. Gargoyles fell from the walls above to land at her feet: nothing touched her.

Shenaria reached the stairs and ascended past the main area of worship to the next landing, and then the one beyond. Then she sank into a corner, shivering with exertion and strain.

'I've passed my test of faith', she whispered. 'Thank you, Saviour-King, thank you.'

Matthias, Modesty and Salfina dismounted from the land-car just out of sight of the Imperial Museum, and left Miri in it, ready to drive at a moment's notice. Matthias had memorised Tru-D's data about the building and led them to a service-entrance away from the main entrance.

The Worship Wing no longer looked as impressive as it had done. The sculptures surrounding it were pock-marked with damage from small-arms fire, and the banners proclaiming the *Divine Devotions* exhibition were tattered and uncared for. The formal gardens that led to the main gates of the museum were more overgrown and weed-ridden than they had been. Uncleared leaves smothered some of the delicate flowers that had been planted at great expense. It seemed that the citizens of Imperial City had had too many other concerns to maintain the appearance of the museum properly.

Matthias led them into the building and closed the door behind them. The museum appeared dark and deserted, but Matthias was in no mood to take chances. They crept through empty corridors, passing now-dusty exhibits and effigies of the Saviour-King – or, at least, things that resembled the Saviour-King on the outside. Matthias leant his shoulder against a small statue as they approached a doorway, only to lurch backwards in pain as his jacket and skin burnt away where it had rested. The air itself felt dense and tainted, and the group proceeded with caution. Lady Salfina mouthed a constant litany of faith and protection to herself.

They neared the central hall, and Matthias signalled Modesty over. He spoke quietly into her ear.

'Okay, Lady. Time to put your *ninjutsu* training to good use. Good luck.'

Modesty blended into the shadows instantly, and was no longer to be seen.

'Where did she go?' whispered Salfina.

'Knowing Modesty, she's probably still here, checking we're doing our jobs properly', replied Matthias, wryly. 'She's going to scout out the main chamber for us. We'll wait here until she gives us the all-clear.'

In utter silence the two of them took cover behind statues and pedestals, positioned their weapons in readiness, and waited.

Shenaria followed the directions Modesty had given her. She climbed stairs and passed through narrow corridors, saddened by the evidence of slaughter all around her. She determined to make those responsible for it face the justice of the Sanctification. She mouthed a blessing for the souls of the fallen as she continued on her way.

She came across the box as she rounded a final corner.

'There you are', she said.

She approached the mahogany box carefully, mindful of what had happened to her assassin. She circled it, looking at its decorations once again. The damaged effigy of an angel seemed to gaze out at her with guile-less eyes.

'No you don't', said Shenaria. 'You're not getting away this time.'

She put her hand into a pocket sewn into her cloak and brought out the eye-filters she had worn while her eyes had been healing. She put them on. Then she sat down next to the box and prepared to open it. She said a last prayer to the Saviour-King and, with some effort, lifted the box's lid.

A putrid green light shone out of the casket and turned her face the colour of bile. She fought back the urge to retch, and peered inside. She saw several objects in front of her, but all seemed out of focus, as if a transluscent membrane of some kind was between her and them.

She lowered one closed hand gently, until it just touched the opaque, unnatural barrier. Then she opened her fingers, letting the Totem of Cleansing she had concealed make contact with it.

The supernatural film burst and shrivelled away at the Totem of Cleansing's touch, releasing an even stronger light into Shenaria's face. She gasped and sweated, finding it suddenly difficult to breathe. The light intensified, forcing Shenaria to squint, even behind her protective goggles. With determination she thrust her hand deep into the casket and felt for one particular object that she could only half make out.

She felt her hand close around it, and pulled back her arm hurriedly. She slammed the lid of the box shut once more. Then she slumped for a few minutes, utterly exhausted from her endeavours, breathing heavily. Her eyes lolled, and her body shivered.

She did not know it then, but her eyes had been affected too, only not in the same way as Modesty's. Ironically, it had been the very injuries her eyes had sustained earlier that had prevented her from dying when she looked into the box. Shenaria herself thought her eye-filters had protected her, but she was wrong.

She recovered somewhat, and sat upright. The tingling sensation in her fist reminded her of the object she had retrieved. She opened up her hand and looked at the item it held.

It was both her worst fear and her greatest hope.

'Saviour-King, preserve me', she breathed, overcome.

Twenty minutes after Modesty had disappeared there was still no sign of her.

'Something's wrong', decided Matthias, and signalled Salfina to join him.

They made their way through the final hallway towards the central chamber where the Golden Statue stood. Around them were strewn bodies, toppled-over icons and discarded souvenirs. The stench of evil grew stronger as they approached.

As they entered the central room itself the very air seemed to press aggressively against them. The Golden Statue towered over its pedestal, seeming to follow their movements with its eyes. Matthias recognised the sensations of queasiness and rejection that he had experienced in the cathedral on Sappharus, but knew that they were imposed rather than genuine. He shrugged them aside. Lady Salfina made little mewing sounds as the same sensations made themselves felt, but Matthias gripped her hand for a moment.

'Don't believe it', he said firmly. Salfina gulped, and smiled at him grimly.

'Thank you', she said.

They split up. Salfina paused to kneel by a figure lying still on the marble floor. It was Rimbrant. She mouthed a prayer on his behalf, in genuine sadness, then placed a Totem of Cleansing into his right hand.

'For the Saviour-King's faithful servant', she whispered.

Meanwhile, Matthias explored the other half of the chamber. He was shocked to discover the corpses of Mercutio and Andreas, their injuries revealing how they had killed each other. Then he came across the charred and broken body of Benedict.

Deeply saddened and angered at the disrespectful deaths of the First Valhallans, Matthias drew himself up to signal a warning to Lady Salfina, only to find he was too late. With horror he saw a dark figure move towards her at an astonishing speed. Lady Salfina saw it too, only not in time to defend herself. The figure touched Lady Salfina with great precision, and vanished. Salfina, shocked beyond words, raised a weakening hand to her injured chest, then toppled over and was still.

'No!' shouted Matthias, and rushed towards her, all caution gone. He knelt before her body in time to see her breathing cease and her eyes lose their light. He cradled her little hand for a moment, then turned, ready to kill whoever had been responsible for this outrage.

That was when he felt the cold pierce his own chest.

Waves of numbness spread out from the wound, and it was all Matthias could do to move his head and look his attacker in the face.

Modesty stood before him, pulling a Punishment Needle out of his chest, and watching him collapse onto the floor.

He gazed at her as all feeling in his body ebbed away. Saliva dribbled from his mouth as he tried to voice a final word.

'Traitor...' he managed to breathe.

His last sight was of Modesty looking at him with a profound expression of sorrow upon her normally emotionless face.

CHAPTER TWENTY

A few minutes later Mephistopheles entered the central chamber, surrounded by his three cavorting Enchantresses. He clambered over bodies and debris until he stood at the base of the Golden Statue's pedestal. He sniffed the putrid air.

'The alarm was triggered', he said. 'Someone's been here. Spread out and find him. And if any of these bodies show any sign of life', he added cruelly, 'end it for good.'

The three unnatural women hissed and slithered over the corpses scattered around the marble floor, looing and scenting for intruders. They rolled bodies over unceremoniously, including those of Matthias and Salfina, and flew around the room making hideous and sickening mewing noises. Mephistopheles himself took out a hefty torch and shone its powerful beam into all corners of the chamber, finding nothing. The four of them spent some time diligently searching and checking for signs of life, then convened back by the vast pedestal.

'Nothing', spat Mephistopheles. 'This is not pleasing. You will search further.'

The Enchantresses twisted around each other in a semi-erotic parody, then glided away from each other, each making her way to a different area of the museum. Mephistopheles watched them go, then turned to face the Golden Statue.

'Nearly done', he smirked, 'Nearly over. Your reign is almost upon us. I should pity any fool who's tried to enter here.'

He began to chant, an eerie, haunting chant. The slitherings that came out of his mouth did not sound human, but more like the chittering of locusts. Little echoes of these noxious noises seemed to emanate from some of the despoiled icons and effigies in the room, then more, then, finally, all. The air grew thicker, and the room darkened with a miasma of corruption.

As Mephistopheles continued in his foul worship of the giant effigy in front of him, he did not notice a tiny change elsewhere in the chamber.

It had come between one moment and the next. Suddenly, and instantaneously, Matthias realised that full consciousness and sensation had returned to him. He lay as still as possible, hoping that he had not inadvertenty advertised his continued life to the enemy. He was not a master of *ninjutsu* like Modesty, but nor was he a complete novice, and he continued to lie perfectly immobile, completely undetected by Mephistopheles. His pupils scanned the room as much as they could without any eye movement, and he was gratified and relieved to realise that Lady Salfina also still breathed.

He did not know if Modesty had simply failed to kill him and Salfina, the way she had not succeeded in dispatching Miri, or if she had deliberately saved their lives. He wondered whether she was lost to Malevolence, and whether her skill as an assassin was lessened because of a demonic influence, or perhaps some remaining inner integrity had prevented her possessed body from murdering them. On the other hand, he wondered if Modesty remained true, and had detected Mephistopheles' and the Enchantresses' approach and, with great precision, made certain that he and Salfina had appeared dead to them. He wished with all his heart that he did know.

Then it occurred to him that if Modesty was an enemy, then she could still be present, though hidden from him through her *ninjutsu* skills. He grimaced inwardly.

One thing at a time he told himself. *Get rid of the enemy you can see before you worry about a possible enemy you can't.*

The red-haired Enchantress re-entered the chamber, and Matthias remembered to stay immobile. She floated to just in front of his forehead, and leered at Mephistopheles seductively.

Now's as good as ever thought Matthias, and made his move.

As the Enchantress silkily cavorted in front of him, she did not notice the shadow grow around her. At the last moment she turned, only to feel Matthias' nerve-dagger brutally penetrate her heart.

Matthias had hoped that the kill would be swift and silent, but it was neither. The Enchantress threw back her head in a ghastly expression of rapture, and moaned out loud. Then, much to Matthias' astonishment, she pressed herself onto the blade and fell on top of him, pushing them both to the floor and pinning him to the ground. She writhed about in a mixture of fury and ecstacy, and Matthias felt an unpleasant warm liquid seep into his clothing. He tried to push her body away, but she gripped fast, and sank her sharp teeth into his shoulder.

Mephistopheles' head snapped round, and his red eyes stared at the dying Enchantress and the muscular man trapped beneath her.

'Felicity!' he yelled, and flew towards them, rage in his scarlet eyes.

He landed by the woman and placed his hand on her neck, shuddering as he felt the last of her life leave her. Then he faced the helpless and ensnared man beneath her. All control left his face, which turned even more malignant than usual.

You *dare*?!' he hissed.

A brutal knife was suddenly in his hand, and he stood over Matthias, nostrils flaring.

'For this, you die', he snarled, and thrust the cold steel forwards.

But Matthias wasn't there.

The tip of a nerve-dagger burst out from the front of Mephistopheles' immaculately-tailored suit. Thin rivulets of blood dripped down the expensive linen and onto the floor. Mephistopheles turned his head, astonished to see Matthias standing behind him. His mouth filled with blood, and he smiled.

'Nice trick, for a human', he sneered, and pushed Matthias away.

Matthias shot fifteen feet backwards, collided with a metal statuette, twisted, fell to the floor and yelled loudly. His arm had broken. Mephistopheles looked at him, grunted, then pulled Matthias' nerve-dagger out of his back. He held it up and licked his own blood off it.

'Yours, I believe', he hissed, and threw the dagger towards Matthias with venomous force.

A gloved hand appeared from nowhere and caught the dagger, immediately throwing it in another direction entirely. An attacking Enchantress whipped round in mid-air as she was struck, and fell down to the ground, impaling herself further onto the deadly blade, moaning orgasmically as she writhed in pleasure and pain.

'Venus!' gasped Mephistopheles, as the blonde once-was-woman died.

Lady Salfina advanced upon him with accusing eyes.

'Salfina', don't!' warned Matthias from where he lay.

Mephistopheles laughed dangerously, and propelled himself forward, as if he would pummel Salfina to the ground. She side-stepped him, stabbing him with a short blade as she did so. He turned to face her again and laughed maliciously.

'Well, well! An Arch-Deaconness! A true follower of the Saviour-King! How vile this must all seem to you! How unholy! It will be my pleasure', he leered, 'to make you share in this degradation! You will suffer beyond your-'

He stopped, suddenly alert. His breathing became ragged and difficult. His body resonated with a piercing pain, the like of which he had never experienced. He looked at Lady Salfina, abruptly forced to reassess her.

'What have you done?' he cried with harsh astonishment, feeling the sensation in his limbs leave him.

Lady Salfina held up her tiny silver knife, and stared coldly at Mephistopheles' rapidly failing body.

'Consecrated blade', she said, 'Used in rituals of purification. I thought it might come in useful.'

Mephistopheles said nothing, but toppled over and lay still. Salfina bent over him and whispered into his ear.

'By the authority vested in me', she said softly, 'I excommunicate you from the Saviour-King's blessing and the Saviour-King's sight. You will spend all eternity in foul damnation. All your worst fears will be realised. Every pain you consider unendurable you will have to endure. There will be no end, and no mercy. This I give to you as a proper reward for your depravity and evil. Now go beyond the curtain of death, and never return to the light again.'

She stabbed both his eyes. His body shuddered, and relaxed, and he descended to hell, to remain there forever.

The final Enchantress shrieked and dived into Salfina's back, pushing her over and ripping her cloak. It twisted round in the air and attacked her again, scratching her face and knocking her head against the marble floor, dazing her. Then it flew high up into the air, screamed piercingly, and rushed down towards her for its final attack.

The vengeance-gun shell blew her apart. Blood, flesh and gore splattered all around.

Matthias groaned in pain from where he sat, and dropped the weapon from his damaged arm. The he rose shakily to his feet and went over to Salfina.

She still breathed, though the skin of her face was torn open and stung badly. He knelt beside her, noting her injured leg, and helped her sit up.

'Thank you, Matthias', she said. 'Now, let's do what we came for.'

They got to their feet unsteadily and supported each other as they walked towards the base of the Golden Statue. They looked up at it. It seemed truly overpowering and invulnerable, and the closer they got to it the more a thick cloying stench of evil threatened to overcome them. They both felt its hypnotic draw, and knew that their faith and willpower were the only things standing between them and eternal malevolence.

'Whatever you're going to do, do it fast', advised Matthias. 'We can't hold out forever.'

'Faith, Matthias', chided Lady Salfina, and set to work.

She opened some pouches on her belt and took out little candles, a holy Pyramid, a bottle of holy water and a tiny, highly cherished, leather book of scripture. She sprinkled drops of the water at the base of the giant pedestal, murmuring incantations and prayers to herself. She moved her finger in the symbol of the mountain in the dust on the floor, then arranged the candles and Pyramid carefully. Then she opened the little book of holy words and began to recite the Litany of Exorcism.

Though they were far away from the air outside it seemed as if a gale blew up. A dense, unpleasant wind brushed through the chamber, creating tiny dust-storms and causing statues and effigies to whistle and creak as it blew through them. It grew stronger, whipping into Matthias' and Salfina's hair, eyes and cheeks, causing Salfina's torn face to sting even more painfully. The tiny book's pages rippled and threatened to be torn away.

Salfina persisted with her rite, adding litanies of purification and restoration to her chant. The wind grew stronger and wailed around them, and it was all they could do to stay in one place. The despoiled Golden Statue loomed over them, and Matthias was certain that its massive fist was tensing and and preparing to smite them into dust. It looked down at them with complete and utter hatred and contempt, and Matthias felt his heart skip a beat.

Salfina reached the end of her recitations, and stopped.

'Did it work?' called Matthias. Salfina stared upwards at the evil figure above them.

'We wait', she replied.

The winds grew even stronger for a moment, then calmed and quietened. All that could be heard was the sound of Salfina's and Matthias' breathing. Everything was still. Matthias began to relax.

'Right', he said, 'let's get back and -'

The gales returned, redoubled in force. The two of them were thrown to the ground. Candles uplifted and blew out. The tiny book of scripture was torn from Salfina's hand. A deep, echoing laugh filled the chamber.

They looked up. Ever so slowly the Golden Statue began to move. Its mouth tightened. Its eyes narrowed and pierced them with its intense gaze. It began to raise its giant clenched fist.

'Almighty Saviour-King, preserve us!' prayed Salfina.

Then there was another figure amongst them. She strode between the two of them, the wind whipping through her cloak and raven hair, and met the Golden's Statue's gaze, eye for eye.

'Saviour-King grant me a true eye and a strong arm!' she shouted, and threw something at the Golden Statue with all the angry force in her body.

The vial hit the statue at the exact centre of its forehead, and smashed. A viscose, deep red liquid poured down the statue's face, into its eyes and mouth and down over its shoulders and chest. The statue froze once more, then seemed to expand as if it was about to burst. All its limbs tensed and shook, and the pedestal it stood on vibrated with the effort to contain it. Its mouth opened in an awful rictus of pain and disbelief.

Then it was as it has always been. The rivulets of red liquid running down it were absorbed into its golden surface and disappeared from view.

Instantly there was a lightening. The whole atmosphere within the chamber changed profoundly. No longer was there a miasma of hatred and corruption infecting the museum. Waves of holiness and blessing inhabited the place once more.

Shenaria looked up at the Golden Statue. It was her Saviour-King again. She sank to her knees in exhaustion and relief.

Matthias helped her up.

'What was that?' he asked.

Shenaria turned to him.

'It was the Saviour-King's own blood', she replied.

The three of them stood, feeling waves of benevolence and healing emanate from the restored statue. They bowed their heads towards it. Then they moved through the chamber, automatically righting statuettes and effigies of the Saviour-King as they did so.

A hand reached out and touched Shenaria's ankle. She bent down to see Rimbrant's prone body. He was breathing weakly, and uncontrollable tears were streaming from his eyes.

'Th...thank you', he whispered, and died.

Shenaria got up, saddened and weary, and went to inspect Mephistopheles's corpse.

'I hope you sent him to hell', she said.

'I did', replied Salfina, simply.

Matthias went to retrieve his nerve-dagger from the dead Enchantress and rejoined his companions.

'I guess this means we're successful?' he asked.

Shenaria looked at him grimly. 'It's not over yet', she said.

This time there was no attempt at stealth. Lady Salfina's entire retinue of Daughters made their way up the mountain-side, mercilessly dispatching all resistance that came their way. Automated defence systems that emerged from concealed openings were blown apart with powerful grenades. Perimeter guards attempting to defend the complex were ambushed in carefully set-up crossfires. Men firing from platforms and roofs above the climbing attackers were fired upon in turn by more Daughters who emerged around them. Fighting was vicious, but the outcome was never in doubt. The defenders were outnumbered and outclassed. Those who surrendered were disarmed and bound; those who didn't were killed.

Meanwhile, Shenaria and her little group inched towards the

Lazenby Club, travelling in its own funicular. They had dealt with its driver and guards before any alarm could be sent, and now approached their prey slowly and deliberately, hidden from sight.

Matthias sat on the edge of a luxurious chair, oblivious to the magnificent view that passed outside the windows. He cradled his bandaged arm absently.

'So…it really was the blood of the Saviour-King himself?' he asked for the fifth time, unable to fully take it in.

Shenaria nodded. 'Yes, and it saved us all. The touch of the Saviour-King himself on the Golden Statue eradicated all traces of Malevolence and corruption within, and restored it to its proper state. Without it we, and the whole world, would have perished.'

Matthias whistled. 'How were you able to look at it?' he asked.

Shenaria knew what he was getting at. It had long been a point of dogma that no one could look upon the Saviour-King in any manner and live. She shook her head.

'I don't really know', she replied. 'Perhaps because my eyes had been injured by the Angel of Death and I didn't really see it properly, or perhaps because it came from the Saviour-King before his ascension into godhood, or perhaps…'

Her voice trailed off. She tried again.

'Or perhaps because I had permission. Perhaps we were the vehicle for the Saviour-King's work to be done.'

They contemplated this possibility for a few moments.

'Let's not get too big for our own boots', remarked Salfina, wryly. 'The work's not finished yet.'

'Thank you, Lady', responded Shenaria, and smiled.

Matthias was not done yet. 'And what of Modesty?' he asked, deep emotion breaking through. 'Did looking in the box send her mad? Why did she disappear again during our fight in the cathedral? Is she…is she still one of us?'

Shenaria had been told of what transpired in the museum, and took his hand.

'I wish I truly knew, Matthias', she said softly, 'but, for what it's worth, I still believe in her, wherever she is. Remember that Modesty has helped us. Before she collapsed she told me that the *Enclave* were after Sejanius' box, and now I believe I know why. I think I know what the Lazenby Club did to Jessila and the others, and what they were trying to achieve.'

She did not have time to explain, as, with a soft bump, the funicular arrived at its destination. They were out instantly, moving swiftly into cover, watching for any sign of attack. None came, so they approached the ornate entrance to the exclusive resort.

Shenaria thought of the betrayal of her friend Christopheles, and was filled with an intense anger. Even Matthias shrank back from her a little, seeing her in this mood. As she sometimes did, she looked like the Sanctifier that she was, strong, resolute, powerful, utterly ruthless and determined. Matthias was pleased they were on the same side.

They entered the reception area. All was quiet. It looked like the premises were deserted, though the sounds of gunfire reaching them from the outside demonstrated that this was not the case. They moved swiftly and silently, opening doors and checking the rooms beyond. There was no sign of life. Shenaria sent Tru-D ahead to sniff out the territory. The cyber-hound returned just as stealthily as she had left, her expression signalling that all was clear. Shenaria had brought Tru-D just in case Modesty was somewhere on the premises. Tru-D had tracked down Modesty once, and Shenaria hoped she could do it again.

They entered the curved hallway that would lead to Clavicord's study. Salfina rounded the corner first, and gasped. The others hurried to join her.

Hanging on a wall full of trophies of various kinds was the helmet of Captain Drusus, with his poor, decomposing head still inside.

'Bastards!' exclaimed Matthias. Then he started as he saw Shenaria's face go completely white.

'This makes things worse', she whispered, 'much worse'.

Then things got worse in a different way. Heavily-armoured guards burst from adjacent doorways and covered them from all directions. Matthias attempted to raise his gun, but his injured arm slowed him down, and the weapon was knocked out of his hand. A knife was placed across Lady Salfina's neck. Tru-D attempted to bite one of the guards, and was knocked down, yelping. Three guns pressed into Shenaria's flesh.

'Enough', said a voice.

Out of the study emerged two men, Clavicord and Popov. Clavicord looked at the powerful Sanctifier, and shrank before her steely gaze. Popov, on the other hand, walked straight up to her and smiled.

She spat in his face. 'Traitor', she hissed.

Popov laughed, and wiped away her spittle.

'You play a good game, Calvert', he said, unceremoniously, 'and you have set us back a little. But no matter. We will still succeed. The damage has already been done to the planet, and now we shall take full advantage of it, and claim it for our own. Oh', he added, as if as an afterthought, 'your Saviour-King will still be defeated. Show her, Clavicord.'

The other man wiped his face nervously, then, mindful of his appearance before his guards, recovered himself.

'Take them to the woman', he said.

The group were marched some way, until they reached a dismal area used for punishment and imprisonment. Damp stone cells led off from the main walkway. Guards opened the door to one of the cells, and the group were pushed through. Four soldiers covered them, ensuring that they didn't try anything. Then Popov walked into the room.

'I know you, Calvert', he said, 'You're just dying to know what we've got up our sleeves, aren't you? Go on, admit it to me. Make my day.'

'I am the Sanctification', replied Shenaria coolly. 'I know your plans, and I know your heart. You are condemned.'

Popov laughed. 'Of course you do', he sneered. 'And I'll just bet you've anticipated *this*.'

He clicked his fingers. Two of the guards left, returning a few seconds later from an adjoining cubicle. They pushed a wheelchair into the cell.

A pale, emaciated, heavily pregnant figure was strapped down in the chair. Her skin had rubbed away where cruel restraints had chaffed against it. Her face had an unearthly pallor to it, and her eyes were sunken and tearful. Her fair hair was matted and looked like it had not been washed in a decade. Her dry and cracked lips murmured tiny little noises of pain. Her torn clothes were stinking and filthy. She was been fed by drips that led to her arm, stomach and nose.

Even in her tortured state, Shenaria recognised her, and her heart fell.

It was Livilla.

They were pushed into one of the prison compartments, then the thick door was locked and they were left alone.

'Everybody alright?' asked Shenaria. Everyone nodded.

They brushed themselves down and considered their situation. Their weapons had been removed. All they had were the contents of their clothes, but this did not leave them helpless. Matthias' eyes narrowed as he checked his hidden *H-Dini* tools, and Salfina pressed her hand against her tiny book of scripture, knowing that this was all she needed. Even Shenaria had a surprise or two left to her.

'What happened to her?' asked Lady Salfina.

Shenaria grimaced. 'Matthias and I came across something similar before', she said. 'Three women, one of whom at least had been impregnated with something in this building.'

'With what?' enquired Salfina.

'I think', responded Shenaria carefully, 'that it was synthetic DNA. And not just any DNA. I think there was an attempt to replicate the DNA of the Saviour-King himself.'

Salfina gasped, and Matthias went pale.

'Do you know what you are saying?' exclaimed Salfina. 'It is sacrilege!'

'It is', agreed Shenaria, 'and I'm afraid that it might well be even worse.'

She did not elaborate, but stood in silent contemplation for a while. Livilla had been a friend of hers.

'What now, Princess?' asked Matthias, to snap her out of it. It worked.

'Well, let's see', replied Shenaria, gratefully, 'If you were the Sanctifier here, what would you say we do?'

265

'I'd say that we break out, rescue and restore Livilla, kill Clavicord and Popov, and get out of here', he offered instantly.

'Correct', said Shenaria. 'So what are you waiting for?'

Matthias' face broke into a wide grin.

'Well, alright!' he said.

He crossed to the thick steel door. A minute later a *click* was heard. Matthias looked through the bars to check no one was in sight, then pulled the door open.

'I do love these tools', he said, replacing them in his belt.

The group made its way back to Livilla's cell, and Matthias put his lock-picking skills into play once more. The door opened readily enough, only this time an alarm was triggered.

Instantly Matthias and Salfina covered the doorway, flattening themselves against the corridor's wall and facing both the directions any possible assault could emerge from. Shenaria dashed into the cubicle.

'Livilla!' she cried, as she reached the wheelchair. Livilla looked up at her with grateful, moist eyes.

'We've come for you, and we're going', said Shenaria. She wheeled the chair round, and got to the doorway as the attack began.

Armoured men entered the corridor from both directions, firing wildly. Several shots hit the teams coming the other way, and some men stumbled and fell. Matthias picked up a vengeance-gun from a dying man that landed at his feet and began to shoot at the attackers. Salfina dived into the first wave of guards that met her, breaking necks and dislocating limbs expertly. She was soon armed too, and together she and Matthias blasted the attackers into defeat. Most lay dead, but some had run off, and the group knew it was only a matter of time before they returned in greater numbers.

'This way!' called Shenaria, trusting in Tru-D's nose to lead them out by the quickest route.

They rushed through corridors and hallways as fast as they could, though Salfina's injured leg slowed them up a little. From some distance they could hear the sound of breaking glass, and brightened at the knowledge that Lady Salfina's Daughters were beginning to break through into the complex from the outside. Shenaria led the group out, pushing the wheelchair as carefully as she could, given their speed.

The passageway they were in led her into a large, circular room with several exits.

'Which way, Tru-D?' said Shenaria.

But Tru-D was not there, and nor were the rest of her team. A thick, steel panel had lowered behind her, separating her from the others. It had descended so fast that Matthias had run straight into it, and been sent flying. Had he been a second earlier, he would have been split in two.

Shenaria saw that all the other exits were sealed in the same fashion. The chamber she was in reminded her of her own, now destroyed, Battle-Room, only hers had been rectangular in shape. This was definitely an arena of sorts, and old bloodstains could be detected on the walls and floor.

Livilla began rolling her head, and making warning sounds.

One of the steel panels lifted just long enough to let someone in, then slammed down again. It was Popov. In his hand he carried two *shin-ru* rapiers. He smiled wickedly at her.

'Nice try, Calvert', he said, 'But no use at all. Your team are surrounded, and it's only a matter of time until they are all dead. I'm so pleased you tried to escape, as it makes killing you all the sweeter. I knew you'd run this way.'

They circled each other warily, Shenaria still pushing the wheelchair all the while, protecting Livilla, and Popov manipulating the blades like the expert he was.

'Do you know?' he said, 'I had to suffer hearing Christopheles go on and on about your ice-moon fight together. It seems you really impressed him. I've always been intrigued by the trick you pulled, and wondered how you'd have done against me.'

He tossed her one of the swords. It skidded across the ground, putting her nerves on edge, and landed by her feet. She picked it up.

'Oh, you'll notice that your blade is hardly what I'd call sharp, and that its balance is all wrong. If you think I'm really going to give you a chance, then you're quite mistaken.'

'Coward', she spat. Popov smirked.

'Oh, come on!' he laughed, 'I'm not that stupid! I just fancy a little fun with you before you die. Who knows, I might explain everything to you if you perform well enough!'

'By the authority of the sacred name of the Saviour-King', said Shenaria in reply, 'I condemn you to death and eternal damnation for your crimes of treachery, heresy and betrayal. And by my friendship to Christopheles I invite you to die at my hand.'

Popov chuckled. 'In your dreams', he said.

They began to move round the arena, keeping their backs near the high circular wall that surrounded them. Popov swished his foil through the air, making it whistle. Shenaria kept hers utterly still, watching his footwork, observing the way he used his muscles and noting the range of his movements. Then she stepped forwards, and swung her blade towards his head.

He parried, but Shenaria had expected this, and changed the direction of her swing. Her sword sliced past the tip of his nose.

'Bravo', he said, 'Try this.'

He sliced his blade sideways at waist-height, threatening to slice her in two. Her hips swerved ever so slightly, and the wicked sword missed her by a fraction. She chopped down on his bicep as his arm passed, only to see her weapon bounce upwards.

'I shall send the repair bill to you', said Popov, looking at his damaged shirt, then attacked her in earnest. His sword moved in a blur of slices, stabs and thrusts, and his feet danced around the Sanctifier's with ease.

'Now, how did it go?' asked Popov, before answering, 'Oh, yes', and stepping close enough for Shenaria to get in under his blade. She duly complied, and Popov stabbed her right arm brutally, making her cry out and forcing her to drop her rapier.

Then he butted her sword out of the way so she couldn't catch it in her left hand.

'And that', he smirked, 'is how Christopheles-'

He gasped with shock and surprise as Shenaria slammed into him with her full weight, knocking him to the floor. She rolled off him quickly and stood, ready for any return attack.

There was none. Popov sat, opened-mouthed and stunned, gawping at the small, thin cylinder that protruded from his chest.

It was her stylus.

Popov looked up at Shenaria in mute appeal, then fell onto his side.

'For Christopheles, and for me, you bastard', seethed Shenaria into his ear, and pressed one of the two tiny buttons on her pen. Popov screamed, and his body agonised as a giant electric shock coursed through it. Shenaria watched as he died, then retrieved her pen, wiping it on his clothing.

'Bastard', she repeated, and spat at his corpse.

She stood, caught her breath, then cradled her injured arm and returned to Livilla, who had been anxiously following the fight.

'The pen is mightier than the sword', she said. 'Now we go'.

She pushed Livilla's wheelchair to the wall, and began to circle round it, looking for any switches. She found a small panel of controls, recognising their Sanctificatorial design from those that had been in her Battle-Room.

'That's lazy of you, Popov', she said, and pressed the correct switch.

The steel panels shot up to the ceiling, and Matthias, who had been patiently drilling through the metal, tumbled to the floor.

'You always did know how to make an entrance', smiled Shenaria, immeasurably pleased to see them all. They joined her in the centre of the arena, equally relieved to see her. Matthias looked at Popov's body with some satisfaction.

'Serve him right', he said.

'Don't move', came a voice.

Through the opening that Popov had entered by came Clavicord and two armed guards. He aimed a heavy-duty scatter-gun at them, and Shenaria knew that even a bad shot would be enough to kill them all.

'Easy, Matthias', she warned, preventing him from running to his death.

'That's better', said Clavicord. 'Thank you for returning Livilla to me.'

The guards moved forwards, took Livilla's chair, and carefully wheeled it to where Clavicord stood.

'I can't have you removing her', he continued, 'She is most important to me.'

'And I know why', said Shenaria harshly. 'I know what you've done, Clavicord. I know. There are no secrets from the Sanctification.'

Clavicord shivered involuntarily, then regained his composure.

'A bit too late, wouldn't you say?' he answered her, 'Now that you are going to die.'

'It's never too late, Clavicord', interrupted Lady Salfina. 'I saw you when you visited the Golden Statue. I saw how it affected you. Do you really want to be shut off from the Saviour-King's blessing forever?'

'Shut up', said Clavicord, more sharply than he had intended.

Shenaria observed this and took up the cue.

'We know what you've done, and what you plan', she said. 'We know how you stole Captain Drusus' Divine Imprint and mixed it into your synthetic DNA to give it authenticity and power.'

Clavicord gasped.

'We know', continued Shenaria, 'that you have impregnated poor Livilla here with your diabolical mixture. We know that you intend her to give birth to a replica of the Saviour-King, or, rather, an Anti-Saviour-King. A god whom you can control. Isn't that right, Clavicord?' she snapped.

Perspiration broke out on Clavicord's brow, and his control of the gun wavered.

'It's a wonderful plan', he said, thickly, 'wonderful. With your Saviour-King defeated by *L'vylaethazs*, and with the whole world in the grip of civil war and Malevolence, how could anyone stand against our Anti-Saviour-King? We could have anything we wanted. Power. Domination. Control. Over anything.'

He raised his gun and took careful aim at Shenaria.

'Are you certain?' she answered back. 'Do you know what you're turning away from? Are you sure *L'vylaethaz* will reward you the same way the real Saviour-King would? Are you sure you could control your artificial god? Are you sure you really want to turn away from the Saviour-King for all time?'

He steadied the gun. 'Not another word', he said, sweat pouring from his brow.

'It's not too late, Clavicord', continued Shenaria, determinedly. 'Renounce your plan, and the Saviour-King will receive you back. You do not have to spend all eternity in hell.'

Clavicord's knees buckled and his body shook. The gun shuddered in his hands, but still he held it aimed at Shenaria.

'Continue', said Shenaria, 'and you most certainly will.'

'No', mouthed Clavicord, shaking, and the shot echoed through the chamber.

It was not Shenaria who fell, but Clavicord. He stared backwards in astonishment at the Leader of the *Enclave* and the smoking weapon that had destroyed him. Then he fell to the floor, dead.

'Honestly, Enderby', slithered Calista, his wife, as she removed her hood, 'Must I always do everything myself?'

She looked at them all with intense hatred in her eyes. There was no mercy that any of them could see, and they all knew that this was the most dangerous enemy of all. Livilla moaned on seeing her, and Calista raised her weapon warningly.

'Shut up, Bitch', she said. Then she looked at Shenaria with complete malice.

'You've caused me too much trouble', she stated, and fired.

Then everything happened at once. Tru-D jumped up in front of Shenaria, and yelped piteously as the shell meant for Shenaria exploded in her chest. She fell to the ground, smoke emerging from the awful, gaping wound in her golden body, and lay still. At the same time Calista gurgled, and touched her hand to her throat, to feel it cut right through from ear to ear. Her head toppled hideously to one side, detaching itself from her neck, and she collapsed to the ground, as dead as her husband. The two guards followed suit.

Modesty emerged from the shadows beyond, lethal Punishment-Needles held in both hands, golden eyes shining.

'It's over', she said.

Shenaria knelt by the remains of her faithful dog, her body shaking uncontrollably.

'Oh, Tru-D', she said, and burst into tears.

EPILOGUE

The neural creatures within the Golden Statue had died with its restoration, and their death-screams had been transmitted to all their companion creatures infesting the Militariat communications satellites. They were all reduced to inertness and destroyed. Communications slowly returned to normal.

Tollius and the others emerged from their nuclear bunkers, and set about making things right. He, Aurelius, Helbrad and Bennett, put out a joint communication explaining matters and making it clear that no one was the enemy and that all aggressive action should cease. The planet resumed its peaceful course.

Captain Byrrion survived his injuries, and was visited often by Shenaria while he recovered. He told her that he hoped to fight alongside her again one day. She told him she hoped it wouldn't be necessary.

As her own headquarters had been destroyed, Shenaria requisitioned the Lazenby Club itself for her new base. She felt she had become too famous during recent events to operate precisely as she wished as a Sanctifier, so the secluded mountain-top building would help her fade into the background once more, and suited her purposes perfectly.

Sejanius' box was transported to Shenaria's new control-centre with extreme care, though the threat from it seemed to have gone. The contents of the box were purified and preserved, and Shenaria spent much time and energy studying them.

Lady Salfina bade her farewells, at least for the time being, and set off to oversee the repair and reconsecration of Imperial City's grand cathedral. She and her Daughters, she promised, would always be at Shenaria's service whenever they were required.

Livilla was sent home to the *Fortress Dedicata Profundis* and received special care. No one knew whether her child would be human or something else, so she was watched carefully. Lord Crooker had promised Shenaria to look after her and keep her from any danger – including any that might emerge from her presently-unborn child.

Matthias and Modesty resumed their normal banter and mutual training with a passion, though every now and then Matthias caught himself looking at her golden eyes and wondering.

I still don't know he thought.

He also had the impression that something had changed about Shenaria too, though he could not quite put his finger on it. It seemed, if anything, that she looked *more deeply* at things, though what gave him this feeling he could not say.

One morning Shenaria called Matthias and Modesty into the new briefing room, which was the same room that Livilla had infiltrated so long ago. She seemed quite animated.

'Look at this', she said, gesturing to a little leather book in her hand. 'This was in Sejanius' box. His ancestor was one of those who designed the Temple of Valhalla itself. Look what these scribblings suggest! We may have to investigate-'

Matthias closed the book firmly.

'Not today, Princess', he said, and nodded at Modesty.

'What are you doing?' asked Shenaria, surprised.

'Come with us', was all Matthias said.

They walked Shenaria down a corridor that she had rarely explored. They stopped by a large, plain door.

'Go inside', ordered Matthias.

Shenaria raised her eyebrow. 'I hope this isn't one of your pranks', she said, and went through the door.

Tubes, wires and scientific equipment filled the large room that she found herself in. She turned to the two of them.

'What is this place?' she enquired.

'Go further', was all Matthias replied, and Modesty startled her by breaking into a wide grin.

She walked further into the room, then gasped as she saw what it was. Matthias and Modesty caught up with her.

'It was our idea', he said, 'but Lord Crooker paid.'

'Just as well, given your salary', said Modesty to him, jokingly.

They both followed Shenaria's gaze, and saw what she did. Shenaria broke into a run towards it, crying out.

The golden cyber-hound wagged its tail on seeing Shenaria, and bounded towards her, tongue hanging out happily. Shenaria stroked it, smelling her collie's familiar scent.

'It wasn't easy convincing Lord Crooker to put up the money', lied Matthias, 'but once I talked to him he saw sense.'

'He listens to you, of course', said Modesty.

Shenaria let the cyber-hound lick her face, and laughed. She could feel where the repair work had been done, and knew how meticulously it had been carried out. She knew that the two of them had supervised every part of it.

'Happy birthday, Princess', said Matthias, 'from both of us.'

Shenaria tickled the dog behind its ears, happy beyond words.

'Hello, Trud-E', she said.

Follow the continuing adventures of Sanctifier Shenaria Calvert in *The Night of Decision* – coming soon!

ABOUT THE AUTHOR

Steven Popper is a university lecturer working in the fields of child development and teacher training - but that is just his job. In real life he is husband and father to the best wife and son on the planet, and a fan of thrilling futuristic adventure stories from 'Captain Scarlet' to 'Star Trek' to 'The Terminator'. 'The Day of Transformation' is his first attempt to write the kind of story that he enjoys so much, and has been written for his son, who one day will be old enough to tell him what he thinks of it.

In addition, Steven knows the real Shenaria Calvert, and is quite aware of the peril he faces if the story fails to convey the truth of the calamitous events that took place to her complete satisfaction.

Lightning Source UK Ltd.
Milton Keynes UK
16 May 2010

154237UK00001B/20/P

9 781449 067496